SCAM AT
MOUNT DIABLO

MIKE MACKAY

MMH PRESS

Published by MMH Press 2022
Copyright © 2022 Mike Mackay

National Library of Australia
Cataloguing-in-Publication data:

Scam at Mount Diablo/MMH Press

ISBN: 978-0-6456259-8-1
(paperback)

ISBN: 978-0-6456259-9-8
(ebook)

To Danise, my wife, the best and kindest doctor in the world, who has allowed me the time and space to write, and kept telling me to do this in my own voice and stop trying to be clever.

ACKNOWLEDGEMENTS

To my publisher, Karen McDermott, for her abiding faith in my work.

Danielle Line, the superb copy editor, who keeps the Scam series charging along and keeping me in check.

Tracey Regan, the wonderful proof editor who like a ninja spots things we all missed.

Dylan Ingram, the voice of consistency and getting this out to the world.

CHAPTER ONE

The CE warehouse stood at the dead-end of Innes Avenue, a cracked road lined with struggling grass. They'd added to the building over the years, and it needed repair, just like its neighbors. Someone had painted it blue, and it matched the sky at ten to seven on this spring morning. Perhaps the owners wanted it to look like a happy place in which to work. The email said to use the staff entrance at the back when the reception was unattended. It was on the edge of Bayview-Hunter's Point bordering on India Basin, parts of which had a bad reputation. Jack was fond of his 1999 truck, so he was happy to abide by the instruction and drove through the open steel gates onto the cement roughened with grit, which crunched under the Yukon's tires as he went around the back of the building, avoiding the potholes, and parked.

A rattling sound started when he reached for the switch to put up his window. Instinctively, he turned his head to the noise to see a forklift, sixty feet away, coming straight at him with the forks raised three feet off the ground. There was no driver, and it was moving like someone running, whereas when working, they should work at less than walking speed. Left unattended, with its momentum, it would hit the driver's side, and the forks would go into and possibly through the truck's door.

Jack reversed his truck with the accelerator pedal pushed to the floor, the tires smoking, leaving rubber marks on the concrete. He watched the forklift buck and sway over the rough surface. A wheel went into a pothole. It jumped ten degrees to the right, wobbling like jelly, past the truck into a stack of pallets, scattering them and stalling.

Jack heard a yelp as a small brindle-colored dog ran out. It had blood on its shoulder and hip. Jack parked and walked towards the dog, talking to it like a mother comforting a child. The dog snarled at Jack, showing its teeth and gums. It limped back under the mess of pallets. Jack got down on one knee. The dog struggled under the pallets to a cardboard box with flooring of a few rags and stretched around to lick the wounds it could reach. Jack scanned the yard. There was no one.

Jack's appointment was in less than ten minutes. He needed to go through the warehouse, so he wore his safety boots for protocol, jeans for comfort, and a long-sleeved white shirt to look professional. Yesterday he had a haircut, military style, high and tight, zero on the sides, number two on top. The early morning spring chill massaged his scalp. He went through the staff entrance and into the warehouse to see the pallet racking five levels high, full of electronic consumer goods. Jack's email told him to go to a door, and he could see it, a hundred and fifty feet away.

He walked until he heard a scraping noise above him and stopped to look up. A cardboard box was inching out at the top level. Jack stepped back and watched a one-foot cubed cardboard box land at his feet and smash open on impact, revealing a white two-slice toaster that most probably would no longer work. Jack picked up the toaster and stepped over the packaging, listening and keeping his eyes on the shelves above him.

Four men came into the row in front of him. They were wearing high-visibility industrial clothing. Yellow shirt with a silver reflective band and the CE logo across the chest, navy-blue denim pants with a silver reflective band above the knee, and industrial boots. Three came up to his shoulder, but about ten pounds heavier. Indistinguishable in their uniforms, shaved heads, and beards. The fourth one was three inches taller, shaved head, clean-shaven, twenty pounds heavier than his own six-foot, one-eighty pounds. Jack stopped walking when they were eight feet away.

One triplet took a half step forward. "In case you haven't figured it out, stupid, you're not welcome here."

Jack assessed the sequence in which they would come at him and thought of Kenny, who would advise he upset their order of attack. "The forklift and the falling toaster, that was you guys?"

"We'd hoped you'd take a hint and go. Now it looks like we'll have to stuff you back in your truck with bruises and blood as a souvenir."

"I'm sorry I didn't pick up on your subtlety, but you must understand I have an appointment with Martin Geller in five minutes, and I don't like being late. I think it's impolite. Don't you?"

"You're not going to a meeting with Martin Geller or anyone here at CE," said the big guy. "Get him."

It was like releasing attack dogs as the big guy raised his hands, turning them into fists. The one on the left kicked at his groin. Jack sidestepped the kick, knocking it into the speaker's path, who was now making his move. Jack hit him straight in the face with the toaster, back-handed it into the face of the third one, and then back to the first one. He passed them and flipped the toaster to the big guy, who caught it instinctively with both hands like a football as Jack stabbed a kick at his groin, sending him to the ground with a groaning noise and a hammer fist to the back of his head.

Jack kept walking to the door at the end of the row, tugging on his shirt to ensure it was on straight as he stepped into the foyer. No one was there, but the directions given to him were straightforward. He walked down the concrete passageway behind the reception desk for fifty feet, passing three closed white doors on each side until he came to a set of open double mahogany-grey wooden doors. Jack's dealings with Martin had only been via email.

He looked inside. Two men sat at a twenty-foot-long dark brown wooden table with five black low-backed executive chairs on each side. A boardroom with the smell of furniture polish and old leather.

"Martin Geller?" said Jack.

A man in pleated navy-blue trousers, a custom-made white shirt, no tie, no jacket, and a sensible haircut across his black hair stood and extended his hand. "Martin Geller. Nice to make your acquaintance, Jack, and please call me Martin."

He came up to Jack's shoulder, was of average build, and exuding an energy not uncommon among entrepreneurs, gestured towards the other man.

"May I introduce Peter Wasserman, our CFO."

Peter used his arms on the side of the chair to push himself to a standing position. He was an inch taller than Jack, but his stooped posture made him two inches shorter. His floppy black trousers and white shirt, half a size too large, indicated clothes were the least important part of his day, or they had fitted him in the past. Wispy gray strands of hair did not cover a scalp with small liver spots.

"Call me Peter," he said as they shook hands.

The firm grip from the arthritic hand bent like a claw from someone who looked like he needed a good night's sleep surprised Jack.

Stella had told Jack that Martin had turned fifty a month previously but still held a military bearing. Peter, Stella did not know, but Jack figured he was older by twenty-plus years and had a shuffling gait like he was wearing ankle cuffs.

Stella had volunteered his services because Martin Geller was an old friend of her dead husband from when they were in the Marines together. Jack knew the story of her husband, Bobby West, who'd worked himself into a heart attack victim while building an industrial empire. Jack had witnessed people working themselves to death in his consulting travels through corporations, and the thing they were after often seemed pointless when they were dead.

Stella said Classy Electronics, better known as CE, imported electronic goods and sold them to retailers. He was now familiar with the two-slice toaster. Martin had bought software to improve the operations in the warehouse. The implementation had been longer than planned. It had run over budget, and now it was operational, the situation in the warehouse was worse than before they installed the software. Martin had heard what had happened at the Link Industries factory in Plymouth, and he'd phoned Stella asking for a recommendation. Stella had sent Jack's email address to Martin.

The assignment did not sound complicated, and Jack was familiar with the warehouse management software.

"There is one thing we can't put our finger on," said Martin. "We have always had a fairly consistent shrinkage problem in the warehouse."

"By shrinkage, he means theft," said Peter.

Jack was aware of shrinkage being the corporate euphemism for theft but nodded toward Peter in acknowledgment.

"Quite so," said Martin. "When the system first went in, it improved for a month, but the warehouse has become chaotic, and the shrinkage figures are back to where they were before."

"I'll see what I can find."

"Can you start today, Jack?" said Martin.

It was odd starting work on a Friday. It lacked continuity.

"I can start on Monday. There's a ranch I have to babysit, and I can get myself settled there this weekend."

"Stella said you lived in San Francisco," said Martin.

"I do. Diamond Heights. The ranch belongs to my uncle. I'm just staying there until he can find a manager."

"Will you have to travel far to come here?" said Martin.

"It's an hour away at Mt. Diablo on Marsh Creek Road."

"I know that road," said Peter. "I have friends living there. It's a beautiful area."

Martin clapped his hands together and wriggled them. "Now that's settled, I stopped off at Uncle Benny's Donut and Bagel on the way here."

Martin opened a door through which Jack could see a kitchen and Martin collecting a tray laden with bagels and three coffees in eco-friendly takeout containers. Definitely not the healthy eating Kenny would recommend, but he didn't need to know. No one can ignore the sweet, freshly baked smell of bagels mixed with the acidic aroma of black coffee.

Jack did not mention the driverless forklift, the falling toaster, or the warehouse's four attackers. There'd been no attempts to kill him. More like someone wanted to discourage him. Jack asked about the dog.

"From what the staff say," said Peter, "it arrived about a month ago and took up residence behind the warehouse. No one can get near it. Some people who work in the warehouse leave their leftover lunches. On the weekend, it must exist on rats."

Jack had to get to the ranch. He was feeling guilty about the dog and knew the feeling of having no one to look after you. When the drunk driver went through a red light and killed his parents, him strapped in the back seat of the car, five years old. He still recalled the feeling of loss. His parents didn't answer his cries, and the anger that someone had made this happen consumed him. The PTSD had started at that point. The dog's injury was not his problem. It was an offshoot of people trying to make a not-so-subtle attempt at discouragement with a runaway forklift. Not too dissimilar to what happened to his parents.

Jack went to his Yukon. No one was in sight. He pulled on a pair of leather work gloves, went to the jumble of pallets, and pulled them away until he came to the cardboard box with the snarling dog. A cut from shoulder to hip needed stitches to Jack's eyes. It was a Staffie. Skinny. Not the American, AmStaff. The English one. Smaller than the AmStaff. The dog needed a vet. He went to the truck and fully opened the rear doors. Jack returned to the blood-streaked snarling dog, talking gently and closing the box's flaps with his hands. The package was two feet square and three feet long. Guessing the dog's weight at twenty-five pounds, Jack squatted, sliding one arm under and the other around the box. He stood, walked with his bulky package to the truck, and put it inside. There was no movement inside the box. Jack closed the doors.

He did not have time for this, and the amount of guilt that consumed him puzzled him.

As he drove away, Peter Wassermann was at the warehouse door, watching.

CHAPTER TWO

It had been a one-hour drive from San Francisco to the ranch in a north-easterly direction. He could have stopped at Walnut Creek for groceries, but he liked to support local businesses wherever he lived, so he carried on to Clayton. Population about eleven thousand. From there, it was a short drive to the ranch on Marsh Creek Road.

On the Internet, he'd found there was a vet on Clayton's city limits, conveniently on Marsh Creek Road. Paddocks of different sizes contained a sprinkling of horses and cows. There was a tall woman on a quarter horse in an exercise yard. She was running the horse through its paces around three yellow barrels. The rider and the horse were as one, leaning in at forty-five degrees, making the turns. Glued to the saddle. After the run, the horse came back to a walk. Jack guessed it had taken twenty seconds. She patted the horse's neck and walked it through the gate towards a big brown brick barn. Jack parked the Yukon. The glass door leading into reception had the name of Dr. B. Ross and Dr. H. Ross. As the door closed, electronic bells tinkled.

A tall, slim, red-haired woman in her fifties, wearing dark blue scrubs and holding a stethoscope in her hand, was standing behind a white counter, looking at a computer screen. Her eyes moved to Jack, and a smile appeared like a rabbit leaping out of its burrow.

"What have you got for us today, a horse or a cow?"

She came around the desk. Their eyes were level as Jack explained about the dog and what he was doing at the ranch. She introduced herself as Dr. Beth Ross and gave him a playful punch on the shoulder.

"You're just a big old softie."

Jack felt the heat of embarrassment creeping into his face.

"My daughter, Hailey, will attend to you. I just do large animals. She graduated as a vet three years ago and worked at a small animal practice in San Francisco. She moved here a month ago. You might have seen her in the exercise yard with her new horse."

"I did see someone. Practicing barrel racing."

"That was her. She'll be here soon. In the meantime, why don't you bring the patient in?"

Jack went to the Yukon and collected the box with the dog. Beth led him into the back, where two rows of cages lay. One row of five on the floor and another on top. Cubes of three feet, and Beth opened one at the end at ground level.

"Put the box down, Jack, tip it over and pick up the back of the box. Our patient should slide out."

Jack did it. It worked. They closed the cage door and bent down to survey the Staffie. A female. The blood from the cut had dried, blending in with the other scars on her brindle-colored body. She lay on her stomach, head on the rubber mat, still as a rock. The only parts moving were her eyes.

"What have we got here?"

Jack turned and straightened.

"Hi, I'm Hailey."

Jack shook the outstretched hand. A firm grip not uncommon with horsewomen. An inch shorter and thirty pounds lighter than Jack. An inviting smile made him think of a wood fire on a cold night. However, it was her hair that held his attention. Red like her mother's, but a tangled mass of curls and waves came down to her shoulders like a bramble bush no effort could tame. Her eyes were pale brown, like a lion's. Beth explained the situation with the dog.

Hailey tilted her head as she looked at Jack. "Do you mind if I don't shower? I stink of horse and sweat, but we should stitch her up as soon as possible."

"That's fine with me."

Hailey washed her hands in the sink. "Do you want to stay for the procedure?"

"Yes, I do." Jack was unsure if his intentions were to spend more time with her or see to the dog's welfare.

"Great, I need help sedating her. Take these."

Hailey handed him a pair of gloves that came up to his elbows. He could smell horse coming from her jeans with underlying musky body tones up close.

"They're Kevlar on the outside, padded on the inside."

Jack pulled them on. Hailey opened the cage door, and he reached inside. The dog bared its teeth, trembling. He clamped a hand on each side of her head and pulled her forward. Hailey had a syringe ready and pulled up the skin behind the head, injecting under the skin. The dog didn't flinch.

"You can let her go now. That should take about three minutes."

The dog scuttled like an angry crab to the back of the box. As the tranquilizer kicked in, he watched the dog turn into a blob of jelly and looked next door into a brightly lit operating theater. Hailey unpacked a surgical mat and secured it onto a stainless-steel table. She asked him to pick up the dog and bring it next door.

Her demeanor had changed from friendly vet to captain of the ship, and it was clear the operating room was hers to command. She pointed to the middle of the table.

"Put her down here. You need to wash your hands again." Hailey gave Jack a gown, a mask, and a sealed packet containing surgical gloves. "Now you can just watch, or you can help me by mopping up blood when and where I tell you to."

"I'll mop."

"Great. There're surgical swabs in those sealed bags on the trolley."

Hailey went to work, giving one or two-syllable instructions as she cleaned the wound and stitched it closed.

She was dabbing Gentian Violet antiseptic onto the shaved area with the stitches when she pulled down her mask. "It'll leave a scar. But your dog will be just fine."

Jack's head snapped around to Hailey. "I'll pay for your service, but this is not my dog. She was outside a warehouse. I planned to get her stitched up and take her to that dog rescue place in Bernal Heights."

Hailey squinted at Jack. "You've got to be kidding. No one's going to take this dog home. Look at her."

Jack surveyed the face, limp from the anesthetic, with gray hairs on the lower jaw and the scarred body. Based on her snarling and trembling, emotionally scarred as well. How much? Like people, hard to tell, even if you know their history.

"I'm familiar with the place," said Hailey. "They're good people, but they have limited space. They will probably keep her for six weeks. No one will take her, and then they'll euthanize her. Not to mention the old Chinese proverb."

Jack's eyes went to Hailey. "What proverb?"

Hailey returned to purple dabbing. "The one about if you save someone's life, they become your responsibility. You must have heard it."

Jack's mind reeled back in time to when other people had told him this. "I didn't know it applied to animals."

"Why wouldn't it?" Hailey looked up from her dabbing at Jack.

"It just never occurred to me, I guess."

"Well, now you know." Hailey surveyed her work and looked at Jack. "She's all yours. Some proper food, some love, and she'll be a different dog."

Jack remembered the snarling dog he first encountered. "When must I bring her back to get the stitches taken out?"

"In about ten days should work, and thanks for the help. You did good."

Hailey squeezed Jack's bloodied blue surgical gloved hand. Jack felt a hint of disappointment, like a kid who saw the ice cream truck vanishing around the corner.

CHAPTER THREE

Not everyone liked being on a ranch, but Jack felt those who didn't were missing out.

This ranch was to become Uncle Alan's experiment in sustainable cattle ranching. Three hundred head living on open-range land with no growth hormones, implants, antibiotics, grain, and no going to a feed-lot for further fattening.

The family trust had owned the farm for two years. Uncle Alan had relocated the manager to the farm in Texas. He'd asked Jack to babysit the ranch until he employed another manager. Jack was to be a caretaker, a house sitter, and a ranch sitter. Just him. The idea of solitude appeals to those who know the difference between being alone and being lonely.

Uncle Alan had spoken at length about being a good steward of the land and the herd. He believed ranchers and conservationists were natural allies, not enemies. As the ranch on Marsh Creek Road ran to the boundary of Mt. Diablo State Park, it was to put those beliefs into practice. For him, improving the land and habitat management practices was an ongoing endeavor of learning and practice. At times, he sounded like Kenny talking about martial arts training.

Uncle Alan had become quite emotional as he told how five generations had overgrazed the land and squeezed the life out of the soil. He had described the bare patches of stunted grass trees with leaves and bark eaten away by hungry livestock, like people who had borne too much of the bad parts of life. It took time to rest and recover. At the end of one more year, they would reassess. For now, it would stand empty.

At ten o'clock, he drove over the entrance for the first time. A cattle grid that shook, rattled, and clanged with only a ripple felt through the chassis of the first edition Yukon Denali. Jack had done the maintenance like a religion, so it was not as fast as the latest one, but it was reliable. Jack had to admit a particular emotional attachment to this 5.7 liter, 255hp old piece of understated luxury. The sign said Alan's Acres, a short-term measure so people could find it. That would be its name for now, but sometimes you give places and people names, and they stick. The road to the house was two tire tracks, three hundred yards long, worn down, and not recently repaired, leaving a six-inch ridge in the middle. Brown, overgrown grass ran across to the wire fences on either side. Trees as broad as a man were every ten yards, like brown sentries with green hats between the track and the fences on either side. Jack switched the drive from two-wheel-high to four-wheel-low. Maybe unnecessary, but it was good to feel it in action. The original sixteen-inch wheels gave enough clearance.

Freddie and Kenny were coming over for a barbeque. They would stay the night as they would have more than a few beers as they played catch-up. It had been a while.

The farmhouse was a ground-hugging square made of local stone the color of the earth. It had a low roof and deep eaves covering a verandah that went around the building. It sat halfway up a small hill giving views across the ranch. Perhaps the builder had tried to make it vanish into the hillside. Considering it was a cloudless spring day, the builder had done an excellent job.

Jack parked next to the kitchen, turned the engine off, got out, and slid open the side door. Jack retrieved his bag, placed it on the verandah, and picked up the box of groceries. He thought a cloud must have passed over, for he was now in shadow, which was strange as there had been no clouds.

A voice behind him said, "Can I help you with that?"

Jack spun around. At six feet tall, he still had to look up six inches to meet the man's gaze. Jack estimated this guy to be over three hundred pounds, heading towards double his own one-eighty pounds. His eyes were black in a face, dark, like mahogany with undertones of red. Everything about him was in proportion, like a Greek sculpture, but darker. They'd dressed the same. Workingman's jeans, boots, and shirts the color of a dusty road. The big man stood with his arms hanging by his sides, with hands that would fill a dinner plate. Jack sensed no threat, even though he was within striking range of this monolith and holding a box of groceries.

"Who are you?"

The big man spoke like he couldn't remember his name or had difficulty saying it.

"Aaron Brown."

It came out so low that Jack had to lean forward to hear him. His name was unfamiliar. The man studied Jack like he expected to see a name tag.

"Who might you be?"

"I'm Jack Rhodes. My uncle owns this place, and I'm here to look after it for a while. What are you doing here?"

"Your uncle, Mr. Alan Rhodes, said I could stay here. I sleep in the bunkhouse. He gave me a key. Can I help you with your things?"

Jack put the box of groceries on the verandah. "Sure." Sometimes, it's best to go with the flow until you know what's going on. "Thank you, Aaron. There's something in the back I have to deal with first."

***

Jack reversed across the one hundred and fifty feet of grass-free, hard ground and through the open doors of the unpainted wooden barn. There were stables for four horses on the left. One door had fallen off, and one was drooping, only held up by the top hinge. The other two looked in working order. Beyond the stables was an open section the size of two stables with assorted equestrian equipment. On the right, Jack saw a dusty collection of farm tools, fence posts, rolls of fence wire, and a waist-high object covered with a tarp. Jack opened the truck's rear, pulled the box onto the tailgate, and peeled back the top of the box as Aaron appeared next to him like a giant ninja. Jack had not heard or seen him approach.

"How can I help you, Jack?"

"I've got this injured dog."

Jack explained about the dog as Aaron looked inside the box. The dog bared its teeth, showing its gums, but did not growl.

Aaron's face and voice softened like melting ice cream. "The dog's scared."

"I agree. I was thinking of putting her in one of the stables for now. That way, we can keep an eye on her. And she can stay there when I go to work. When she gets better, we can figure out what to do with her."

Aaron was still looking inside the box, his breathing slow and deep. "I'll look after her."

Jack was about to ask if he was sure about this when Aaron picked up the box and took it into a stable. He placed it on the floor's stall matting like it was a crystal vase and eased the box over so the dog could get out. Aaron backed out and closed the stable door. There was no sign of the dog.

"I got dog food at the vet's and a new water bowl." Jack held up two small see-through packets with labels on them. "One of these is antibiotics, and they only gave me a few as they'd run out. I'll see if they've had a delivery when I next go past. The other is painkillers. They'll both have to be crushed up and sprinkled on her food."

Aaron stepped over to the truck, lifted the forty-pound bag with one hand, and took the water bowl in the other. "I'll give her some food and water. There're some old horse blankets in the back of the barn. Can I fold those up to make her a bed?"

"Good idea. I'll leave you to it then. Just be careful. She's suffered abuse, that's clear, and she might mistake your good intentions."

Aaron nodded slowly, like his head was submitting to gravity, his eyes welling up as he looked at Jack. "You're right. That can happen." Aaron walked off to the back of the barn, wiping his eyes with his wrists. Jack left the truck in the barn and walked to the house, processing what he'd witnessed.

***

The ranch's kitchen was an exercise in white. It ran along two walls, enfolding a dining table to seat ten. The third wall was a floor-to-ceiling pantry with white cupboards and white metal racks looming over six leather armchairs from separate sources. In the center of this pantry was a door, and shelves made an archway. Jack knew this led to a passageway with three bedrooms sharing one bathroom. The front wall was all windows looking down the driveway. There was no front door, just a dwelling where you ate, did your ablutions, showered, slept, got up, and went back outside to work the ranch.

Aaron carried in the box of groceries like a child's lunch box containing one peanut butter and jelly sandwich. "I'll put these away."

"Thanks. I've got no preconceived idea where things should go."

Jack left him to it, as he had some questions for Uncle Alan.

Standing on the verandah, Jack phoned, wanting to be far enough away so Aaron could not overhear. The barn, with the past noon sun drifting across it, looked tired and worn out, like a plow horse that should already be out to pasture. He walked towards it, the phone ringing as he continued into the barn. No answer. In the corner was the lumpy, three-foot-high object with a tarp over it he had seen earlier, and Uncle Alan had told him what it was. He pulled off the tarp to reveal a two-seater electric quad bike with a box tray for transporting work tools or the ingredients for a picnic.

The barn had a mezzanine floor. Jack walked up the wooden stairs to a hayloft with bales of assorted grasses scattered like thrown pebbles. An untidy collection of tools for handling bales and loose grass were on the floor like someone had left them halfway through their working day. There was a long, loud hissing noise up in the rafters. Jack knew what it was and looked up to see the white faces of two barn owls huddled together, peering down. One of them hissed again. Probably the male, Uncle Alan once told him, as the hissing is the noise they make to intimidate predators. Jack went down the stairs, stopping at the quad bike to see if it started. Nothing. A cable was on the handlebars, and some thinking person had left it next to a plug point. Jack plugged it in and returned to the kitchen to find Aaron wiping down the countertops.

"Aaron, can you show me where you're sleeping?"

They walked in silence across the dirt to the bunkhouse, a rectangular structure with six rooms and a communal kitchen, all looking onto a fifteen-foot-wide verandah. Aaron opened the door to his room, and Jack saw the neatly made standard-size single bed.

"You must sleep with your feet hanging over the end."

Aaron smiled. "Most beds, I sleep like that."

"Can I see the kitchen?"

"Sure. I'll show you. It's the room at the end."

Aaron walked down the verandah, his boots making a soft sound like an elephant in the forest. The kitchen had a double-size fridge and a wooden table big enough to seat eight people. On reflex, Jack opened the fridge, which was on, looked recently cleaned and empty.

"Aaron, are you hungry?"

"I am indeed."

"Let's go back to the house."

As they walked, Jack realized he had not seen another vehicle at the ranch.

"Aaron, how did you get here?"

"I walked."

"From where?"

Aaron considered the question, his brow wrinkling, then he smiled. "I don't remember."

Somehow, this lack of memory was not a concern to Aaron. "When did you last eat?"

"I don't remember that either, but judging by how I feel, maybe two days ago."

Jack looked at Aaron, knowing this colossal machine needed to be fed often and in large quantities.

In the kitchen, Jack opened the fridge and pulled out a four-pound cooked pork loin, a whole lettuce, and a tub of butter. He had planned to eat this over the next few days.

"Aaron, can you find a plate, a cutting board, the bread, and take a seat?"

Jack had seen a collection of knives clinging to a magnetic strip above the kitchen workspace. Aaron took a chef's knife and placed it and the pork loin on the cutting board. A three-hundred-pound, six-foot-six-inch guy with a chef's knife, who you don't know. Jack was naturally wary, like a wild animal, but he still didn't sense a threat. "Make yourself some sandwiches. As many as you want. I'm going outside to my truck to get the rest of my stuff."

Aaron was out of his chair and standing. "I'll come help."

Jack smiled. "It's a laptop bag. You stay and eat."

"Thank you."

Jack walked, pulled out his phone, and texted Freddie. *Please bring more steaks, potatoes, salad, and beer.*

Jack collected his laptop bag from the floor of the front passenger seat.

Freddie texted back. *Why?*

Jack responded. *You'll see when you get here.*

Jack carried his bag into the kitchen, placed it on the table, put on the kettle, made two mugs of black coffee, and put one in front of Aaron, who was eating a two-inch-thick sandwich. The lettuce crunched as he bit into it. Jack reminded Aaron he could have as much as he liked, which caused Aaron to swallow what was in his mouth in a gulp to say, "Thank you," and take a sip of coffee and another bite of his sandwich. Jack went onto the verandah. What was he supposed to do with Aaron? The view of low hills with wrinkles draining rainwater down into the river at the bottom was mesmerizing. But it provided no answers. He phoned his uncle again. No answer. Freddie would be here with Kenny in a few hours. Maybe he had answers.

Jack went back inside. Aaron had packed up what he'd not eaten, put it in the fridge, and was at the sink washing the plate, cutlery, and cutting board. He dried his hands on a tea towel and turned to Jack.

"Thank you for the food, Jack."

"You're welcome."

"The barn is a mess," said Aaron, like he was reading one of the Ten Commandments. "I would like to clean it up."

"That'd be great. Thank you, Aaron."

Jack watched Aaron leave the house, but there was a moment, a millisecond, when Aaron's frame filled the whole doorway.

CHAPTER FOUR

Jack heard Kenny's silver F150 arrive and stop at the kitchen door. He walked out onto the verandah and saw Aaron come out of the barn walking in their direction.

Kenny got out of the truck, all six-foot-three, two hundred and ten pounds of him with flaming red hair cut to the high and tight military style. Freddie got out the other side. He was the same weight as Jack and one inch taller.

Freddie and Kenny gave Jack bear hugs and back pounding. They had their backs to the barn as Aaron walked toward them.

"I have a guest," said Jack. "Over there at the barn. I'll introduce you."

Freddie and Kenny turned and looked at Aaron.

"It can't be," said Kenny, squinting his eyes as Aaron got closer. "Is that Aaron Brown?"

Jack's face registered surprise, like the deer suddenly seeing the hunter. "You know him?"

"What do you mean, do I know him? Everyone knows Aaron Brown. What's he doing here?"

Freddie was looking from Kenny to Aaron to Jack, trying to make sense of this.

Aaron came over and put out his hand. "Hi, I'm Aaron Brown. Can I help you guys unpack the truck?"

Kenny's face wore a smile. A rare sight. He shook Aaron's hand.

"Kenny Braithwaite. I'm a huge fan, Aaron. Great to meet you. I think I watched all your games and the replays."

Aaron's smile cut his face in half, showing all his teeth.

"Thank you. A pleasure to meet you, Kenny."

Kenny looked at Jack and Freddie. "Aaron is one of the top three linebackers in the NFL, ever." Kenny turned back to Aaron. "What are you doing here?"

"Well, if you followed my career, you'll know I got my fair share of concussions. In fact, I got a few too many before they stopped me from playing. Then no one was interested in me. I don't know what happened to my money, house, or cars. I was living on the street. Some people found me, and Mr. Alan Rhodes left me a message saying I was welcome to stay at this ranch he owned and he'd find work for me. So, I headed out here. But I get forgetful, and then I don't remember where I was supposed to be going. I don't know how long it took me to get here."

"Alan Rhodes is my father," said Freddie, "and Jack's uncle. Kenny's a good friend. My father mentioned this, although it was some time ago."

"Anyway," said Aaron, "Nice to meet you. I gotta get back to cleaning the barn."

The three of them watched Aaron leave.

"What a tragedy," said Kenny. "And walking along Marsh Creek Road by himself. The guys from The Farm would have stopped anyone walking by themselves."

"What's The Farm?"

"It's a minimum-security facility about ten miles down the road from here," said Kenny. "People who the courts have sentenced for what we call 'lesser crimes'. I've been there to interview prisoners about cases I'm working on. It's known locally as The Farm, being out here in the country. Last count, about seventy inmates. That right, Freddie?"

Freddie didn't answer. His face was thoughtful, like he was trying to remember and recite a Shakespearean sonnet. "I recall my dad talking one day about a film he'd watched. It was about NFL players. Guys who'd had too many concussions and wound up on the street. Cheated out of their money by their managers. True stories. He was shocked and told me he'd start a charity to assist these people. I wondered where he would get the time to do this, as he was already on the board of many charities and ran the family business. That was a while ago. He never mentioned Aaron in particular."

Kenny and Freddie took their bags inside. Jack sat on the veranda and looked at the barn as it cast longer and longer shadows. His phone rang. He looked at the caller's name. Uncle Alan. Jack told him about Aaron.

"Wow. Well, I'm relieved to know that he's there. Are you ok with looking after him?"

Jack thought back to when Uncle Alan and Auntie Louise had arrived at the scene of the accident and taken him to their home, away from the crashed car containing his dead parents. They raised him the same as they raised Freddie. He was five years old. Not knowing about PTSD, he did not understand the feelings of isolation and detachment that were now his companions. These morphed into an aggression that went to live in his limbic system, and only when he met Kenny, who introduced him to martial arts, did this get kept in its cave, only coming out if necessary. Deciding when to let the aggression out was now like flicking a switch.

"No problem, Uncle Alan. Glad to be able to help."

"He's supposed to be on the Mediterranean Diet. Light farm work is sufficient exercise for him and good for his sense of self-worth."

Jack promised he'd see to it. Uncle Alan rang off, and Jack went inside the house to tell the others what he'd said.

***

There was a gas barbecue on the verandah, close to the kitchen door. Jack flipped steaks. While they sizzled, he took his beer and sank into a lounge chair, looking out across the ranch.

Kenny had earlier checked on Jack to see if he was keeping up his training regime but was now sitting with Aaron further down the verandah. They were into a serious discussion about NFL, and Kenny was moving his hands like throwing a ball, catching a ball, arms out to make a tackle. Whatever Kenny was saying made Aaron laugh. A sound like thunder coming out of a beer barrel. Jack and Freddie smiled for no reason other than the sound of Aaron's laughter and Kenny's antics.

Jack turned to Freddie. "Could Kenny stay here for a few days? I've got some work I need to do in San Francisco, and I don't know what this Aaron Brown is like."

"How long do you need him for?"

"Till Monday afternoon."

Freddie got up and walked over to Kenny and Aaron. They stopped talking and listened to Freddie. Jack could not hear the conversation except at the end when Kenny said, "Absolutely."

Jack was always interested to hear what Freddie had been doing since their last time together. Freddie had graduated as a lawyer and now headed up a specialized unit within the San Francisco Police Department, SFPD. Kenny was also in the team with the rank of Sergeant. Jack's computer and forensics skills made him a comfortable living consulting for companies. He met with Freddie's team when he had something to say. If he was not in San Francisco, it was a video call. In these sessions, he updated them on new thinking in his domain. He still didn't know what they did nor the extent of their powers. They just ingested what he said. They never told Jack if they used it, but sometimes, the questions gave him a hint of what they were doing.

"I've got one case that's not getting solved," said Freddie. "It's a serial killer, and the victims have been in other states so far, but it seems like he's moving towards California."

"Have you got a profile?"

Freddie went to his room, came back with a buff-colored folder, and handed it to Jack. "I thought your skills might help here, so I printed out what we know."

"Why have you identified this person as a serial killer?"

"It's a broad definition. For us, it's anyone who commits three or more separate murders, over more than thirty days, with a significant period between them, with an excessively violent and, or sexual component. This person fits."

Jack took the folder, reading it, and saying pieces out loud. "Eight murders, all women, beginning in Amarillo, Texas, and the most recent one in Flagstaff, Arizona." Jack turned to Freddie. Jack could see all the places on a map in his head. "This looks like he's taking a drive down Route Forty. We use that highway when we drive back from the ranch in Texas."

Freddie nodded. "There's more. On the way here, we got notified about another one. Barstow. Here in California. Where Route Forty stops at Route Fifteen. We don't know where he plans to go next. Southeast to Los Angeles, northwest to Las Vegas, or northeast towards San Francisco." Freddie paused like he was considering other possibilities. "So, Jack, did you get to read the MO and the targets?"

"Yes, I did. There are some oddities. The attacker somehow got into the victim's car, made them drive to a national park, and made them strip everything, including their shoes. Then he chased them. The forensic evidence showed that when he caught them, he beat them and then let them start running again. He just kept repeating this process. Their feet were bleeding from running on rough ground, and the forensics report said the only blood was that of the victim. The forensic people found patches of blood on the rocks, footprints."

Jack looked at the photos. "It's odd that the faces were unmarked. The blunt force trauma injuries on the torso, arms, and legs were complicated like someone had gone to great trouble to ensure there was bruising all over the body." Jack had his eyes on the bruising. "It looks like the bruising you see in an MMA fight from an ambidextrous fighter."

Freddie nodded. "Kenny said the same thing. And the bruising pattern's the same on all the victims. Like he's practicing his moves. The coroner's report showed they died through asphyxiation. Seems he struck them in the throat just enough to partially crush the trachea. In this way, the victim would have slowly died through lack of oxygen."

Jack kept reading the profiler's report. The killer, he surmised, had stood and watched them while they suffocated to death at his feet. Male, under forty years of age, very fit and has issues with women in positions of power. These issues were long-standing. He had probably killed before this list of victims. It was just with this list there was a discernable pattern. Maybe all the victims were businesswomen running their own companies. Jack thought of Stella West, the widow, the owner, and CEO of Link Industries, with the Head Office in San Francisco. She fit the profile of the previous victims.

"I don't want to start a panic," said Freddie, "but we will quietly visit all the potential victims. Explain the situation, that this is serious, and they need to be more vigilant than normal and beef up their security. I was going to leave Mrs. West to you as you two seem to have, what's it called, a special relationship."

Jack did not respond to the implied accusation. "Thanks, Freddie. I'll talk to her."

"We have Mrs. West as one of the top three potential victims."

"Could you make her know things are urgent without saying the word out loud?

"I'll talk to her tomorrow."

***

By six am the following day, Jack was driving his Yukon across the Golden Gate Bridge and into San Francisco. Twenty minutes later, he was on Vallejo Street, Pacific Heights. Cars that had no garage lined the street. They looked homeless. He stopped at a beige-colored three-story edifice and used a remote to open the garage door. He parked next to a silver-gray S-Class Mercedes, not the latest model, but an earlier model with the classic lines and the six-liter V-12 motor. It was the car version of Beauty and the Beast. He took his bag from the truck and went through the garage side door, announcing his arrival as he closed it.

"Stella. Hello." His voice did not echo as it hit the carpets.

"I'm in the kitchen."

Jack walked there, dropping his bag, when he saw her pixie-shaped face, not quite heart-shaped, with an elfin hairstyle, the color of midnight when there's no moon or stars. She rarely smiled with her mouth, her amber eyes doing all the work. A neck-to-ankle, white dressing gown, fluffy like a lamb, draped her. She was reaching for a coffee pot from a cupboard above the countertop. She had not tied the gown, and a gap revealed a white negligee stretching down to her knees. It was see-through, thin, like the work of a spider.

Jack put his hands inside the gown and pulled her close. She pulled his head to her so she could kiss him like she was telling him something, then pulled away until their lips barely touched. He put his head down and kissed her neck and throat. Jack could not smell her perfume. A bottle of Christian Dior, Forever and Ever, was always in the bathroom. Today there was just her unique smell. She responded with a sigh. Jack pulled up the back of the nightgown so he could feel her skin. She quivered under his touch.

Stella's job had its frustrations. At ten years older than Jack's thirty years, her gym-trained five-foot-five, one-twenty-pound body would strain against Jack's martial arts-trained physique. As the owner and CEO of Link Industries, she took out her frustrations of the job in the gym, on the shooting range with her Glock 42, and in the bedroom. He had only recently returned from an assignment for her in Plymouth, Michigan. Stella and Jack had tried to make plans to spend time together in Michigan, in some secluded place. It did not happen.

Stella put her mouth to his ear. Her voice had become smooth and thick like melting chocolate. "I was getting things ready to make breakfast for us."

Jack ran his hands down to her bare hips and kissed her just below her ear.

"But it can wait."

***

For breakfast, they made savory oatmeal with cheddar and an egg. Jack sliced Chinese sausage into small nuggets. He mixed these into the water-cooked oatmeal he had cooking next to him, listening to the plop, plop noises as it bubbled like a metronome set to one beat per second. Stella fried eggs and chopped bell peppers. Two big bowls. Sausage-laden oatmeal on one side, bell peppers on the other, and eggs on top of the oatmeal. Jack put the bowls on a tray with the black coffee pot, a white porcelain cup, and a white mug. Thus laden, he carried it to the coffee table in the lounge room with the view across The Bay. The window was floor-to-ceiling and filled the wall. It was a postcard day. The Golden Gate Bridge on the left and Alcatraz on the right.

Jack waited until they had finished breakfast and sipping their coffee before telling Stella about the serial killer. He put down his coffee mug, placed his left hand's fingers under her chin, and turned her head towards him to see her eyes. "I'm not trying to scare you, but you must be more alert until they catch this guy."

"I will be. Crazy people, I treat with respect and keep my distance."

"Sounds like a good idea."

"Do you have plans for the weekend?"

"I had planned to be at the ranch, but I've got Aaron and Kenny staying there, so it's in safe hands." Jack paused, looked at The Bridge, and back at Stella. "I haven't told you about Aaron, have I?"

"No. When you mean Kenny, you mean Kenny from SFPD?"

"Yes. Let me tell you about Aaron."

When Jack had finished explaining, Stella was quiet for six seconds. "I was on a plane when I watched that same movie about NFL players and concussions. It was an eye-opener. Your uncle is quite the guy when it comes to stepping up and starting charities. Maybe Link should make a contribution? Give me his details, and let's see what I can do."

"Kenny and Aaron will spend all weekend throwing the ball around and talking NFL with breaks for Aaron to look after the dog."

Stella frowned. "What dog? I thought the ranch was uninhabited by man and beast, including dogs and cats."

Jack drew a breath and told her about the dog.

At the end, Stella punched him in the shoulder. "You're just a big old softie."

Twice in the last twenty-four hours. Jack had a flashback to the vet's office, the mother and daughter.

"Back to your question. I have no plans for the weekend."

"When do you start at CE?"

"Monday."

"Great, let's lock the doors and keep the world out until Monday."

CHAPTER FIVE

On Monday, 7 am, Jack was at the CE warehouse and looked at the system's screens until noon. He walked around the warehouse, watching the goods come in, packed on the shelves, watching them get picked and packed on trucks for customers, the people following a process. A helicopter view was all he hoped to achieve in the morning. Mentally, it was all noted. Martin had introduced Jack as a software guy who would look at how the software was performing in an operational environment. The staff smiled at him like he was an auditor. The thugs who attacked him were standing at the back of the crowd.

Ian Dickson oversaw the warehouse and was a director on the board. He was a large man of some fifty-plus years with a florid complexion. Jack watched him manage the operation. It was clear through practice he'd turned sloth into an art form. This did not mean he was physically inactive. It was a slothfulness of the mind. He was always striding, not walking, with a single piece of paper in his hand. Uncle Alan had warned him about this tactic. The paper was a deflection that made people draw the wrong conclusion. If we see someone walking fast with a piece of paper in their hand, they must be going to an important meeting. Jack had noted this running around, shouting at staff, and the contradiction of instructions. What Jack couldn't figure out was what triggered these outbursts of Ian Dickson. The panic and tension in the warehouse were tangible, like a heavy mist you wanted to dissolve so you could see better, but it stayed. Jack saw nothing wrong with the software. It was the management of the warehouse that was the problem.

At lunchtime, Jack went to the canteen. Everybody had brought something from home. There was no kitchen serving food. It was just an urn on a counter with a can of instant coffee and milk in a fridge that tilted as two of its feet were missing. A pale shade of yellow, it had gone out of style so long ago it was probably about to come back in. The tables were steel tops with trestle legs that could accommodate six thin people. One table in the middle of the room was unoccupied. It only had four chairs. Jack had brought no food, but breakfast with Stella had been good. Black coffee for lunch would have to do. He made some and found it had the same taste as every factory run-down canteen where he'd had the pleasure to dine. It wasn't bad, just that it gave a new level of excellence to the word, bland.

The big guy and his three accomplices, who'd tried to stop his entry on his first visit, walked in and sat at the center table. In the harsh canteen lights, the muscles, the puffy faces, and the acne, all courtesy of junkie steroid abuse, were on show. To Jack, they had no names, and he cataloged them as Big Guy and Junky 1, 2, and 3. J1, J2, and J3. Big Guy spotted him and spoke to the others, who all looked at Jack. Together they got up and took the long way around to the urn so they would walk well within Jack's personal space without touching him. The big guy came last, giving Jack his version of an intimidating stare.

Kenny advised not to fight unless you have to or it's justified. Jack poured his coffee down the sink and washed out the cup. As he walked away, he could hear the sniggering sounds of what they believed to be a victory.

In the two hours after lunch, Jack witnessed what he'd seen in the morning. He went to Martin's office and explained there was nothing to solve or fix with the software. It was the people part that needed attention.

Martin called Peter and Ian to his office and asked Jack to reiterate what he'd told Martin. He told them. This announcement caused Ian's bulbous vein-riddled nose to twitch as he rose from his chair. His fingers were like sausages, which he rolled into fists and placed his knuckles on the table. He glared down the table at Jack with muscles coiled like a lion preparing to pounce on a gazelle with the confidence and arrogance of belief in his ability to execute the move.

"If you're so smart, you run the warehouse."

"Well, Mr. Jack Rhodes," said Martin, his face alight like a kid await-ing the fight in the schoolyard. "You've made statements, and Ian has thrown down the gauntlet."

Peter's eyebrows hooded over his eyes like a lizard as he studied Jack, who looked from Martin to Ian to Martin. Jack paused for four seconds as the implications and outcomes trickled through his consciousness like a mountain creek. This was not what he'd signed up for, but like in a fight, things change. "I'll run the warehouse. But with two provisos."

Ian's face showed surprise. He went to speak, possibly to revoke his statement when Martin put a hand out to silence him.

"Like what?" said Peter.

"No interference from Ian. He totally withdraws from any involve-ment in the warehouse."

"Sure," said Martin as he motioned with his hand for Ian to sit down.

"And the other proviso?" said Peter.

"It is not my intention to stay here forever and run the warehouse.

So, once I've shown that it's running successfully, I've completed my assignment."

Martin looked at Peter. Peter shrugged and nodded his head once, like an owl with only a few gray feathers on its head.

"Agreed then," said Martin. "You start tomorrow. First thing tomorrow, I'll be in the warehouse and let everyone hear it from me about the change in management."

Ian's face was red as he shot up from his chair, sending it backward, his hands now fists, as he glared at Jack.

"Ian," said Martin with a voice from a military parade ground. "Stand down."

Ian looked at Martin and strode out of the room.

Martin looked at Jack and chuckled like a cheeky chipmunk. "Well, Jack, I don't think you'll be getting a Christmas card from Ian this year."

***

Jack drove the one hour back to the ranch. Stella had invited him to stay at her place. A tempting offer. Looking after the ranch was an obligation. Compounded by Aaron and the dog.

He stopped at Clayton Valley Shopping Center to stock up on food for him and Aaron. He put together an array of vitamins at the pharmacy and a medical kit for people and dogs. Aaron had arrived at the ranch with only the clothes he was wearing. He piled workwear into the Walmart's trolley in the Big Men's section.

Driving out of town as the sun was setting, he saw the lights were on at the vet. Might as well take a chance and see if he could collect the dog's medicine. The doorbell tinkled as Jack opened the door and walked into the empty room. Hailey came through in a rush with a smile that made him smile back, her blue scrubs again highlighting her wild mane of red hair.

"Just been finishing up a horse in the barn. Normally I'd be gone by now. My mother's already gone."

"I saw the light and took a chance to pick up the rest of the dog's medicine."

"We got a delivery this morning. Let me put it together for you."

From under the counter, Hailey pulled out a packet that looked like it held hundreds of tablets and started counting white pills onto the counter. "Have you given the dog a name?"

Jack had no plan for the dog, so he'd not given the matter any thought. "Not as yet."

"Are you working at the moment or just babysitting the ranch?"

"I have a software project in San Francisco at a warehouse belonging to a friend of a friend."

"Sounds mysterious."

Jack laughed. "I can assure you it's not."

"So, you're driving an hour each way every day?"

Sometimes too many actual details, especially about Stella, can make the situation awkward. "Yes," said Jack.

"Who looks after the dog while you're at work?"

"I have a guy staying on the ranch. His name's Aaron Brown, and he's decided to look after her."

Hailey stopped her pill counting to look at Jack. "You're not talking about Aaron Brown, the NFL player, are you?"

A few days ago, Jack would not have been able to answer the question. "I am."

"You have to be kidding me. Aaron Brown. You've got Aaron Brown staying at your place? Wow. I'd love to meet him sometime. I'm a big fan."

Seems she's in the same fanbase as Kenny. Jack was thinking he should get onto the Internet and see what he could find out about Aaron's playing career, but Kenny would probably tell him, anyway.

Hailey looked down at the pills. "I've lost count. You gave me such a surprise." She smiled with all her teeth, her eyes laughing, making Jack smile back.

"I'm not in a hurry. Take as long as you need."

Hailey went back to counting pills, half-talking to herself. "Imagine. Aaron Brown, way out here on Marsh Creek Road."

"I'll tell you what, when I bring the dog back to take out the stitches, I'll bring him along."

"I've got a better idea. Can you ride?"

Jack thought back to the time he'd spent on Uncle Alan's ranch in Texas. He would send Freddie and him out to round up cattle and bring them back to the stockyards. "I can, but probably not as good as you. You being a barrel racer."

Hailey's eyes went big as she looked at Jack. "How'd you know that?"

"When I drove in here yesterday, I saw you practicing."

"Oh. That was a new horse I'm schooling."

"It looked pretty good to me."

"Thank you." Hailey was registering impatience as she moved her weight from foot to foot. "But back to my idea. On Sunday, I'll bring two horses to your ranch. I'd like to see it. And what better way than from the back of a horse? While I'm there, I can get to meet Aaron Brown."

Hailey looked with anticipation, like a child waiting to open their Christmas presents. Jack liked the idea and found he enjoyed Hailey's enthusiasm. "Sounds great to me. I haven't had a chance to explore the ranch. Be good to get on a horse again."

"Thank you." Hailey took hold of Jack's left upper arm in her right hand and squeezed it. "I'll be looking forward to that."

Hailey put the pills in a clear, sealed bag the size of her hand. As she passed the packet to Jack, she looked at him like she was seeing him for the first time. "You've got yourself quite an odd couple of strays."

***

Jack reflected on what Hailey had said as he drove from Clayton until there were no more suburbs or streetlights. He continued along Marsh Creek Road until he got to the ranch. Her words did not align with his plan for solitude on the ranch. There was no light in the house nor the bunkhouse, but a dull yellow light was on in the barn.

He parked next to the kitchen, half expecting Aaron to pop out of the dark. Jack walked to the barn, the clear night sky showing the stars like sparkling diamonds. If you looked long enough, they seemed to get closer. Aunt Louise had taken Freddie and Jack to art galleries as part of their education. Looking at the sky, he could see why Van Gogh had chosen that particular blue for his sky in The Starry Night.

Jack walked into the barn looking around for Aaron. No sign of him. The barn looked a lot tidier. He'd raked the floor clean. He'd also nailed loose timbers in some stables back in place. Aaron had been busy. Jack walked to the stable where they'd put the dog. There was Aaron, sitting on the floor of the stable, back against the wall, fast asleep. The dog was lying in the middle on a six-inch layer of old horse blankets, felt side up. She was fast asleep, resting her head on her paws, facing Aaron. The water bowl was brimming, and she'd left some pellets in the feed bowl.

Jack backed away, went to the kitchen, and put on the lights. Outside, he slid open the sliding door on the side of the truck, collected his purchases, and brought them inside. He didn't close the sliding door as it would likely wake Aaron.

Jack had all his purchases unpacked and on the table. He was catering for Aaron and needed to leave him food for tomorrow. Jack had this idea of making a cowboy meal of onions, ground beef, pinto beans, corn, and chili to give it a Tex-Mex flavor. He made enough for four people.

The black cast-iron pot was bubbling like a hot tub when a knock at the open door made him turn.

"Come in, Aaron."

"Hello, Jack. Can I help?"

"You sure can." Jack explained what he was making. "There're some tomatoes and lettuce in the fridge. You can slice some to go with what I'm making."

Aaron got to work. "I didn't hear you come in."

"I went to the barn when I got here. You and the dog were sleeping, so I left."

"Kenny left about an hour before sunset. I was keeping the dog company and must have dozed off."

"How's our patient doing?"

"Fine. She eats and sleeps a lot. I can't get close to her, but from what I can see, her wound looks ok."

"And you, Aaron? How are you?"

"The headaches have stopped. I still get dizzy, and when I get dizzy, I get scared."

Jack couldn't imagine this colossus feared anything, but there it was.

"Of what?"

"I dunno. Just scared. If I knew what I was scared of, maybe I could do something about it."

"When did you get dizzy today?"

"In the barn when I was working."

"Good job on what you've done in the barn. But you must take a break if you get dizzy."

"I do. It's what the doctors told me to do. I sit with the dog. She's also scared."

Jack looked at Aaron but could not see his face as he bent over the chopping board. He saw him wipe his eyes with the back of his wrist.

Jack said nothing as he felt Aaron had more to unload. "Flashbacks are more often, and then I get angry. At what, I don't know. So, I sit with the dog."

Jack knew the feeling from his own experience and the feeling that no one understood.

"Aaron. I still get flashbacks."

Aaron's face was one of puzzlement, like a child having geometry explained, as he stopped chopping to look at Jack. "Why?"

Jack related his history and how Kenny made sure he kept up his martial arts training to deal with his PTSD.

Aaron chuckled, which was not the reaction Jack was expecting. "Who'd have thought we had something in common?" Aaron held his hand up in a fist. Jack fist-bumped Aaron's granite-looking fist. "Maybe I should roll up some of those horse blankets in the back of the barn, tie it with rope, and make a punching bag."

"That's a great idea," said Jack.

"It won't be pretty, but it should do the job."

"That's all that matters, I guess."

This statement seemed to bring Aaron a stillness, like he was watching something inside his brain. Then he nodded his head and went back to chopping.

"How many horse blankets are there?"

"I used six for the dog. Four I'll use for a punching bag. Probably still be ten left."

Jack finished stirring the pot. "Grab a bowl, Aaron, and help yourself."

They sat at the table. In between mouthfuls, Aaron explained what he wanted to do in the barn to fix it up. And the quad bike he'd check out, too. They all seemed like good ideas to Jack, so he kept saying Aaron must go ahead but not overtire himself. Aaron was finishing up his second bowl of food when Jack thought of Hailey's question. "Have you thought of a name for the dog?"

Aaron didn't hesitate. "Not my dog. So I shouldn't be coming up with a name."

"Well, you did say you'd look after her. So I think that gives you the right."

Aaron looked at Jack. "Thanks for the food. I'll come in and do the dishes in the morning. I'm off to bed."

"Goodnight, Aaron," Jack remembered his other purchases. "I got you some clothes today. They're over there in that bag, and the small plastic packet next to it is the dog's medicine."

"Thank you, Jack."

Aaron picked up the bag and the packet and left. Jack followed him to stand on the verandah and look at the stars. Aaron was walking into the barn.

CHAPTER SIX

At 7 am, in the warehouse, Martin announced the change. Ian had declared himself ill that day and stayed at home. Peter stood with Martin, not speaking. His presence, Jack noted, added a gravitas to the occasion. The staff did not look like the believers one sees in Pentecostal churches, and Jack understood their uncertainty. Maybe this new guy would make things worse.

The warehouse manager, Dan Venter, a chunk of a man with broad shoulders and no neck, said nothing but kept pushing his glasses back onto his nose, although neither his glasses nor his nose had moved.

Martin and Peter left. Jack told the staff he would meet Dan and then return to the team. They dispersed and went back into the racks of shelves. Jack looked at Dan. "Let's take a walk."

Together they walked through the aisles laden with electronic products.

"Ever been in the military, Dan?"

"I'm still in the National Guard."

"Rank?"

"Sergeant."

"Great, then you'll understand what I'm about to say."

Jack explained the chain of command. The processes to be followed were to be as documented. Anyone with an issue with that must revert to Jack. He explained what degrees of freedom Dan would have in exercising the processes down through his troops.

"How does that sound to you, Dan?"

"Sound great, Sir. Thank you, Sir," said Dan, smiling and saluting. "We can now win this battle. But there's one guy we need to keep an eye on."

"Who's that?"

"Remember that big guy we passed as we went through the aisles? Bigger than the rest, and he tried to give you a shoulder bump as you passed him."

Jack remembered him from when he'd arrived for his first meeting with Martin and Peter and then in the canteen with his accomplices. In this latest incident, the guy was pushing a trolley laden with products down an aisle. When about six feet away, he'd looked back like he was checking something, then looked forward, swinging his shoulder as he did. Jack had already spotted the move and had stepped away before he turned. The big guy stumbled as he connected with nothing. The action would have looked accidental. "Who is he?"

"Lyle Dickson. Ian Dickson's nephew. Lazy, a bit crazy, but loyal to Ian. He's been Ian's unofficial enforcer with his three sidekicks."

"The rules and processes are crystal clear. Anyone who breaks them or doesn't follow the process gets reported and leaves the warehouse until the next day. Three strikes, and you're out. Anyway, we got bigger fish to fry than his silly school-boy antics."

"I agree."

"Also, ask the staff what color they'd like for the canteen."

***

By Thursday, Jack's troops in the warehouse believed in his message on operating the warehouse, passed down from his sergeant to his corporals to the soldiers. Over one hundred sets of boots on the ground. Jack did not have an office. He had a table with a chair in the warehouse. His laptop perched on top of the table connected to a seventy-inch screen showing the warehouse's fill rate and backlog. Plain for all to see. Every two hours, Jack would take a tour through the warehouse, from receiving to dispatch, observe the process in action, talk to the people on the ground, and listen to what they had to say. Like all people working in a warehouse, this was not their dream job. This was a job they could get, something they could do. It paid the bills. Jack empathized with them and listened as they told him about themselves as he made his walks through the warehouse. Everybody had their assigned roles and places of operation. Lyle Dickson and his henchman ran dispatch, and they would glare at Jack and come close with their trolleys as they loaded the trucks.

Each day he drove the one hour from the ranch and the one hour back. Upon arriving back at the ranch, he would find Aaron sitting in the stable with the dog. They were sitting closer each day. While making food, Jack would ask him if he had a name for the dog. Each night he would say he was still thinking about it. After eating, Aaron would head back to the barn.

Stella was away visiting the factory in Plymouth, Michigan, where she appeared in a San Francisco paper as a candidate for Business Woman of The Year. Freddie phoned him to express his concern as he felt this was painting a target on her back for the serial killer. Jack agreed with Freddie and said he would speak to her about it. There wasn't much Stella could do as she did not do the nomination, and the reporter had mentioned the other four candidates. Freddie said he had given his message to the other four as well.

At mid-morning and mid-afternoon, Peter would come shuffling across the warehouse, stand and look at the screen and the activity in the warehouse. The big-screen figures had improved since Jack took over and showed everything was operating at the requisite level. What was available on the screen was on Peter's laptop in his office. Yet, he seemed to like watching the warehouse's activity. His hands clasped behind his back, glasses halfway down his nose, hunched forward like a bird in a tree. His work attire never altered from when they first met. Black pants, black leather shoes, a white shirt, no tie, and an unbuttoned pale gray cardigan that seemed oversized and flapped as he moved. After fifteen minutes, he would compress his lips together, nodding at Jack, then shuffle off, his cardigan flapping like a broken wing.

***

Mid-morning, Jack went on his walk around the warehouse, this time starting at dispatch. His mind was on Stella, so he was loitering. The racks were getting low with inventory, and Jack could see through them into the dispatch area. Lyle Dickson had what Jack assumed to be the picking list in his hand, which got folded and then put in his back pocket. He looked around but did not notice Jack and gestured to two of his henchmen, who went into the racks and returned with a flat-screen TV box. From where Jack stood, he could read the box. A 65-inch model. Lyle watched the TV get loaded into the truck. Jack stepped backward until he was out of sight and went to his desk, where he called up the picking lists and found the one which was at dispatch. There was no TV on the picking list.

Jack couldn't see Dan Venter, so he phoned him. "Dan, there's a truck that Lyle and his team have just loaded. Don't let it or the driver leave the premises. Get your team at receiving to count the stock on that truck and bring the count sheet to me."

At Stella's factory in Plymouth, Michigan, he had uncovered theft. It had been a sophisticated operation, and this seemed a lot simpler and opportunistic, like kids stealing from the school canteen when no one was looking. Why hadn't he picked up on this earlier? He ran through the usual possibilities, as this may not happen on every delivery. A particular driver was in collusion? They only loaded when they had an order from someone where they would offload it for cash? They had their own stolen goods warehouse?

Peter arriving, interrupted Jack's thoughts. He dragged along a two-wheeled hand trolley. On it lay a two-foot-long cylinder labeled Oxygen, and tubes ran from this to his nose, held in place by an elastic around his head.

"What's all this, Peter? What's wrong?"

Peter dismissed the questions with a wave of his hand.

"I would like to talk to you, Jack. In private."

"Sure. I'll come up to your office."

"No. Not here. Can you come to my home?"

Jack's curiosity woke up at this unexpected invite.

"Sure. When?"

"Do you like cricket?"

Jack had a fascination with cricket. Not so much the game, but why people enjoyed it so much. He had worked in England, colleagues had taken him to matches, and he'd taken the time to learn the game's rules. Bottom line, it just didn't do it for him. Maybe not the answer Peter would like. Jack said, "Yes."

"Wonderful, can you come to my place this Saturday at 3 pm?"

"Sure."

"We can watch a game while we talk."

Jack looked at the oxygen cylinder.

"Can I bring some beers?"

"Excellent idea. Nothing above three percent alcohol, though. My wife will prepare some snacks. Here's my address."

Peter reached with his claw-like hand into the pocket of his cardigan, pulled out a two-inch square of folded paper, and passed it to Jack. Jack watched Peter walk away. Peter walked behind Dan Venter, who was in conversation with Lyle Dickson and his friends. It was a loud conversation.

On Tuesday, Dan had sent Lyle and his friends from the warehouse for not following the process. Today would be about counting the stock on the truck. Lyle pushed Dan in the chest with both hands. Dan staggered back until his feet stopped at Peter's trolley with the oxygen bottle. He went over backward. The trolley twisted in Peter's hands, taking him to the ground, his arms outstretched. His head hit the concrete floor, forcing a groan as he rolled onto his side. The bottle came off the trolley. Lyle advanced on Dan, kicking the bottle out of his way. It bounced away, taking the tube with it. Jack could see Peter trying to suck in air like a stranded fish. This was wrong, and the dark gray thing that lived within his limbic system shot through his system without being invited.

Jack never knew how he did it. Because it was a blur. He got to the bottle, dragged it to Peter, hauled him to a sitting position against the wall, inserted the nose probes into Peter's nose, and turned up the oxygen.

Lyle was now kicking Dan, who was trying to protect himself by rolling into a fetal position and wrapping his arms around his head, which saved his face and frontal area, but not his back. Lyle stabbed a kick into Dan's kidney. Dan straightened out and emitted a shriek of pain. As the dark thing slipped from its cave and rushed up Jack's spine, he knew Peter would quickly need more attention, but he had to stop the attack.

Jack came up behind Lyle, grabbed a handful of hair, and shoved the side of his foot into the back of Lyle's knee, pulling him backward and over onto the ground. Jack ensured Lyle's head produced a solid cracking noise, like a dropped coconut, as he hit the concrete. Lyle should have stayed down, but he chose to continue with his left hand pushing him off the floor, his right hand reaching behind him. Jack saw the knife's handle and didn't wait to see the steel. He stepped forward, bent his knees, and delivered a left roundhouse punch into Lyle's temple. This made him stagger, but he was still ready for a fight. Jack brought him to a standstill with a right roundhouse punch to the temple. Lyle spun with the force of the blow and collapsed face down on the floor. A knife with an eight-inch blade fell from his hand and clattered toward Jack, who kicked it toward Dan.

Jack heard loud voices and swearing. Lyle's three steroidal associates, J1, J2, and J3, were advancing on him in a frontal attack, each carrying a three-foot black soundbar over their shoulder like a baseball bat. Jack slipped to his left so they were now behind each other. Jack was now fighting them one at a time.

J1 swung the soundbar like a batter at Jack's head, twisting his hips to deliver maximum force. Jack leaned back, the soundbar missing his face by two inches. The momentum and weight of the soundbar carried J1 around. Jack jabbed a right punch into J1's right kidney, making him arch forward with a groan and his knees jellify. The soundbar came loose from his hands, spinning into the face of J2, causing an explosion of blood from the nose.

Kenny's advice was never to leave an opponent where he might recover and make a comeback.

Jack threw a roundhouse kick to the temple of J1, putting his foot down to continue into a reverse kick to the crotch of J2. It was a stretch to get there, but his heel connected, making J2 drop the soundbar and fall to his knees, protecting his prized possessions with both hands. Jack kicked backward again, catching J2 in the throat on his way down. J2 was confused about what to hold on to as he landed at the feet of J3, who was coming in with a yell and a downward swing of his soundbar.

Jack twisted away, so it landed on J2's stomach. In one movement, Jack reached for a soundbar on the floor and swung it into the side of J3's knee, who screamed as his knee made a crunching noise upon impact. The sound bar bent and shattered into shards of black plastic, exposing the internal electronics. Using the force of his legs, Jack stood and hit J3 with an uppercut to the jaw, which snapped J3's head back as it turned out his lights.

Jack went and kneeled next to Peter, who had an abrasion leaking blood on the left side of his forehead, breathing normally, surveying the scene like he had a front-row seat at a movie with a grin bordering on a laugh.

"Why are you grinning?" said Jack.

Peter patted Jack's hand. It felt soft, like old crepe paper. "It's the most excitement I've had in some time. Nice moves, by the way. I liked the two roundhouse punches in quick succession. Very good. I used to box at college."

"By the way, Peter, I think we've solved your shrinkage problem."

"Wonderful. An excellent way to end the week."

Dan was back on his feet. Jack stood and pointed at the four bodies. "I want them secured with cable ties. I want an ambulance, and I want the police."

Dan held up his phone, saluted, and smiled. "Ambulance and police already on their way."

"Thank you, Sergeant."

CHAPTER SEVEN

Peter's house was in a retirement village. Jack had looked it up on the Internet. It was one of those places where as your age increased and your health declined, you moved from one section to another. Here, the lie of the land was such that each move was physically downhill. A sign of what was to come.

At 3 pm, Jack pressed the buzzer and waited, a six-pack of light alcohol beers in his hand. A woman in her early seventies answered the door and looked him up and down.

"You must be Jack. I'm Hannah, Peter's wife. Come in."

Jack stepped through the door and took the offered hand, which was as soft as a rose petal but firm.

"Nice to meet you, Hannah."

"Before I take you to Peter, I want to thank you for looking after him. Peter glossed over the details, but I get the impression that if you weren't there, this could have turned out far worse."

Jack felt he should say something, but the details would only upset her and not make her feel better about what happened.

"I just happened to be the closest, that's all."

Hannah smiled like a fox. "Why did I think you'd say something like that? Let me take you to Peter."

They walked down a passageway with a serviceable mid-gray carpet to a room of some thirty feet by thirty feet. Concrete-colored wooden strips covered the floor. Two oversized, black leather chairs faced a fifty-inch screen. Peter was in one, attached by a tube in his nose to the oxygen cylinder on the trolley. He glanced at Jack, revealing the purple bruise on his forehead, indicated the seat, and nodded at his wife, who left with the beers.

"How's the head, Peter?"

Peter raised his arm, flicked his wrist backward, dismissing the question, and pointed at the screen. "There are three more balls until the end of the over."

Which Jack knew meant the over was halfway through. He must sit and not talk, and he could see England was playing against Australia.

There was a two-foot by one-foot table in front of the chairs. A one-foot diameter silver tray held an array of snacks, none of which he recognized.

In under ten minutes, they'd completed the over, and all the players left the field. As the sky was overcast, and Jack did not know where the game was being played, he did not know if this was a tea break or the lunch break. Peter swiveled his body in the chair, juggling the plastic tube as he moved.

"Thanks for indulging me and coming here. And welcome."

"Thank you, Peter."

Hannah arrived with two jugs of beer, placed them on the table, and put her hand on Peter's shoulder. "Do you need anything else, dear?"

Peter took hold of her hand and kissed it. "I've got a great cricket match, a friend to watch it with me, beer, wonderful snacks, and, I've got you." Peter kissed her hand again. "What else do I need?"

Hannah hugged Peter and left the room, dabbing at her eyes with a tissue as she went.

On the screen, the players had not returned. Jack was curious about the reason for the meeting. He waited. Sometimes it is best to let things unfold of their own accord.

Peter waved his hand at the oxygen bottle like royalty acknowledging its subjects. "To cut to the chase, as they say, I am dying, as we all are, but usually we don't know when. In my case, the doctors have predicted more accurately when this life of mine will all be over. But for now, let's eat, drink, and watch the game. Then I'll explain why I invited you."

***

"The Dubinski family came from Lithuania," said Peter. "More like they fled from one of the pogroms that had taken place. The father was a cobbler, a maker of shoes. By all accounts, he was a master of his craft. Yet, they were poor. You don't make a lot of money making one pair of shoes at a time and shoe repairs, no matter how good the quality of the work."

Jack was thinking of the footwear factories in Asia, where he had done consulting work. The size of the operations and the automated technology in place were impressive to watch. What was not impressive were the low labor rates. Yet, people queued at the front door looking for work to feed their families. They came from the poor parts of the cities and the outlying farms where there were too many mouths to feed. On the surface, it looked like these massive factories preyed on these people. Yet Jack knew the low wages and the long hours were a step up for the average employee. Bleeding heart journalists had written about it, deploring the situation. The US factories moved their production to Asia putting people in the US footwear industry out of work and on welfare. Faced with the labor situation in Asia, the loss of jobs in the US, and profit. The companies chose profit. Jack didn't moralize over this. It was what it was.

"They encountered anti-Semitism when they arrived. The father had their name Anglicized and registered them as Dubin. This sounded like the leather conditioner called Dubbin, with two b's, so knowledge of their Jewish ancestry fell away. They settled in Walnut Creek. The father grew the business. They had one child, Barney, who wanted to join the business from a young age and worked there from the age of twelve. The father insisted Barney get a degree after high school. He got good marks and applied to the University of California, Berkeley. Got accepted into the Business School. Berkley was a twenty-minute drive from their home in Walnut Creek. So, he lived at home, drove in and out each day, studied hard, and did not get up to the time-wasting activities available to a student. Graduated cum laude. Barney's mother and father were very proud of him as he was the first one in the family to get a university degree."

Peter wheezed, adjusted the nasal prongs, and turned up the flow rate on the oxygen cylinder. He held up his hand to Jack, indicating he needed a moment before he could continue his story. "I was also at the Berkeley school. It's where I met Barney. Through chance, we worked on projects together." Peter snapped his fingers. "We just hit it off." Peter picked up a snack. "Have something to eat before I continue. My wife will be offended if we don't finish everything on the plate."

They finished the snacks and half of their beer tumblers. Meantime Jack had been thinking. "Peter, that must have been fascinating. An old-world craftsman and a university student who was working his way through a business degree."

"You would think that Barney, with all the vim and vigor of youth, would be thrusting the ideas he had learned down his father's throat. But it was not like that. As he had worked in the business, he was very aware of his father's skill and knew he did not come close to his father in that regard. But he did know what troubled his father in the business."

Peter looked at Jack like a teacher expecting his pupil to answer the question.

Jack had done consulting in men's footwear factories. The cost breakdown was labor, overhead, and material, the same as any factory. If you had good designers, good craftsmen, and a good reputation, you could get a premium for your product.

"Prices of the shoe are normally agreed upfront before manufacturing begins. Labor costs you control by where you decide to make the product. The same with overhead costs. It's the cost of the leather that can make or break you." Jack recalled being in the leather room at shoe factories, watching the quality inspectors examine the hides. The enthusiasm, the shock, the delight, the anger.

Peter nodded and continued. "Barney was a good negotiator of the finished product, but his real talent was Trading. Buying leather at a below-average price for his father's business which had already employed fifty people and was selling to high fashion retail outlets."

"While we were still at university together, Barney got requests from other footwear factories to buy leather for them. Back then, he did all this on a calculator and a telephone on the campus grounds. His database of deals was in a notebook he carried with his textbooks. He made a lot of money. So much that he was able to buy a ranch in the foothills of Mt. Diablo. This he did for his father. Coming from Lithuania, the thought of having such a big piece of land was beyond belief. He was able to get his father to retire to the ranch where he could grow tomatoes. I stayed in touch with Barney. Helped him with some financial restructuring from time to time. But I never got involved in the day-to-day operations. He recently contacted me asking for advice, and that's where you come in."

Jack sat and waited.

"His father passed on over ten years ago. Barney has run the business for over twenty years as his father gradually gave him the reins, but Barney's health has been declining for two years now, which has affected the business. He and his wife Sarah have two children, Ralph and Stewart. Spoiled rotten by their mother while Barney was busy growing and running the business. Ralph went to university. Computer Science. He was programming even before going to university. Has never expressed an interest in the business until recently, when he has descended like an avenging angel, convinced he knows what to do."

Peter paused, gasped, and continued speaking.

"His knowledge of business, per se, is based on glossy articles in business magazines. He's taken Barney's knowledge and contacts and put it onto an online commodity trading platform he's developed with some seed money from Barney to get him started. Stewart graduated in Business Administration. He's lazy but good at selling, as he's hard to dislike and is now the sales arm of this trading platform. They now have an investor as well. This investor has hides and leather to sell but no tanneries. That's all I know, but I plan to find out more."

"Can't Ralph provide all the information about this investor? That's a standard process before letting anyone invest in your business."

"Ralph told Barney he's done all the due diligence, and Barney must stop interfering and let him run the business as he sees fit. As I mentioned, Barney and Sarah are indulgent parents, so they did not press him on the matter."

Peter had worked himself up progressively, sitting further forward until he was now on the edge of his chair. His voice had become louder and louder, and his breathing more labored.

"I have a bad feeling about this, but I can't put my finger on what's bugging me. My concern is that everything Barney built is in the hands of these two, and I fear they'll cost Barney a lot of money with their spoiled, entitled view of the world."

Hannah came into the room, concern tightening her face. "What are you talking about, Peter?"

"I'm telling Jack about Barney."

"You know that upsets you. But I also know it's why you wanted to speak to this young man. Now, you stop talking, sit back, and breathe."

Hannah patted Peter on the shoulder until he sat back in his chair. This had the look of a well-practiced routine. Hannah turned her attention to Jack. There was an earnestness about her gaze that Jack liked. "Peter has expressed his concerns to Barney in many conversations. But they didn't know what to do until now. He's told Barney about your work at CE. Peter wants to know if you will investigate and possibly rescue Barney's business from the stupidity of his two dreadful, spoiled children. You would be doing Peter a tremendous personal favor, and of course, Barney will pay you most handsomely." Hannah paused to look at Peter, then back to Jack. "Barney has early-stage Parkinsons. The stress of this will most likely worsen the condition."

Jack looked at Peter, whose eyes had welled up.

"Where is this business, Hannah?"

"They run it from the ranch. Near Clayton, it's on Marsh Creek Road in the Mt. Diablo foothills."

Peter's breathing was slowing down to a sound like a whisper. Hannah kept her hand on Peter's shoulder like she would start patting him again if he moved or spoke. "Peter has been telling me about you. He said you're babysitting a ranch which is also on Marsh Creek Road."

Jack was thinking of his workload at CE, and he did not have another assignment on the horizon other than that. It was good to see someone trying to help a friend.

"I'll do it," said Jack.

"Wonderful," said Hannah. "I'll tell Barney. Now you two can go back to watching cricket, and more snacks and beer will be on their way."

She left with a triple pat on Peter's shoulder and a smile for Jack.

CHAPTER EIGHT

Sunday, 8 am, Jack was standing on the verandah watching Hailey's F250 with a horse trailer roll into the yard and stop next to the barn. The vet practice's logo was on the side of the truck and the trailer. As Jack stepped down to the ground, Aaron appeared from the barn. Hailey sprung out of the truck and went around to Aaron with her hand outstretched. Jack couldn't hear what she was saying, but she was talking fast, like a machine gun on full auto. Aaron smiled and nodded when she stopped talking to take a breath.

When Jack got to the trailer, Hailey and Aaron were already pulling down the rear ramp. Hailey was still talking, and Aaron smiling as they backed the horses out of the trailer and tied them to a rail on the side of the trailer.

"Morning Hailey, I see you've met Aaron."

"Sure have."

Hailey switched her attention to Jack. "Are you ready to ride?"

"Sure am."

"But first, I'd like to check the patient. Where is she?"

"Over here," said Aaron, his hand swinging towards the barn door as he turned and walked.

Jack and Hailey followed him until all three were looking at the dog in the stable. The dog went into a crouch from where she had been lying on the horse blankets.

"I guess you'll want to see her up close?" said Aaron, not taking his eyes off the dog.

"That'd be better," said Hailey.

Aaron nodded, opened the stable door, went inside, sat on the floor, and patted his leg. "Come here, Princess." The dog moved like it was walking on eggshells. Each step ready to retreat, keeping its eyes on Hailey and Jack until it got to Aaron, where it curled up on his lap, and he put his hand on her.

"Wow," said Hailey. "That's impressive. You stay right there."

Hailey snapped on her blue surgical gloves. Jack opened the stable door for her, and she moved sideways so as not to appear threatening. She dropped to her knees, her hands twelve inches away from the dog. The dog moved up against Aaron's belly and looked at Hailey like a lion watching a buffalo. Fight, flight, or freeze flickering across her senses.

"Aaron, can you move your hand a bit so I can see the whole cut?"

Aaron was murmuring as he moved his hand, exposing the cut. Jack and Hailey could not hear the words, but the dog seemed to register with them. Hailey leaned forward, looked at the wound, sat back on her haunches, and looked at Aaron and Jack. "Which one of you has done all the nursing?"

"Me," said Aaron, his brow furrowing with concern. "Why? Is there something wrong?"

Hailey wiggled her blue hands and smiled that big smile of hers. "No, no. Quite the contrary. You've done a great job. It's an ugly wound. You must have been treating it day and night."

"I did."

"Good job. You can come work for us anytime."

Jack wasn't sure if it was a throwaway comment, being kind, or if she was serious.

"I'd like that," said Aaron flicking a look at Jack.

"Let me talk to my mom and to Jack. But in the meantime, I think she can come out of the stable. Where will she sleep?"

Aaron looked at Jack. "She can sleep in my room. That ok, Jack?"

"Fine with me, Aaron."

Aaron hugged the dog to his face. "Thank you, Jack."

"I heard you call her Princess," said Hailey. "Is that her name?"

"It is. Is that ok, Jack?"

"Seems she's your dog. So you get to name her."

"With all the scars," said Hailey, "she's more like a warrior queen. I mean, she's underfed but get some bulk back on her, and you'll see she's a magnificent specimen."

Aaron looked at the dog, who was licking his neck. "She's a princess to me."

Jack reached down, offered his hand to Hailey, and helped her to her feet. Her eyes were brimming, and she was wiping them with the back of her wrists as she looked at Jack.

In a voice as soft as cashmere, she said, "At moments like this, I'm reminded why I do this job." Hailey pulled off her gloves, blinking her composure to return. "Well, Jack, are we gonna ride or what?"

***

Hailey and Jack cantered together to the top of a low hill in the center of the ranch, then brought the horses back to a walk. He recognized their mounts as quarter horses with their big behinds and chunky stature. Jack could see from her poise in the saddle she was the better rider. By comparison, he sat hunkered down in the saddle. The way you spend all day rounding up cows.

"Do you only have quarter horses?"

"That's right. Fifteen hands high." Hailey patted her horse on the neck. "And geldings."

"Is that your preference over stallions and mares?"

Hailey laughed. Her teeth were bright like a toothpaste advertisement, and her red curls rippled. "Ask any two-barrel racers that question, and you'll get three answers. But for me, I like their gentle, laid-back nature, having lost their stallion qualities and not coming into heat as mares do."

"And color?"

"Mostly their brown-red sorrels like these two. I buy based on ability, not color." Hailey pointed. "Look."

A dozen black-tailed deer, consisting of females with offspring, were grazing two hundred yards away. They lifted their heads and stopped feeding to stare at the approaching riders.

"Well spotted," said Jack

"Practice from riding in the country."

"I didn't see them until you'd pointed them out."

"Only the bucks have horns," said Hailey standing in her stirrups and doing a full sweep of the landscape as the horses kept walking. "None of them are there."

"Let's walk on. Maybe we'll see some."

The range was paddocked-off squares, rectangles, and triangles of varying shades of brown. Traces of green as a scattering of trees clung to the edge of creeks like patients plugged into a lifeline, too scared to move as they knew they would die of thirst like everything else.

"It reminds me of a brown patchwork quilt I had as a child," said Hailey. "See, Jack, the fences look like stitches."

Jack smiled at her imagination and said he could see it. He was more concerned for the browning trees, not next to the creek. They seemed to be wishing they were green and verdant.

In the first generations, man's desire to farm had, through ignorance, destroyed the land. A river ran through sandy stretches, the color of popcorn, into lakes, the color of the water from the washing machine. It was now a tough forbidding place where it looked like the land would squeeze and suck the life out of you, leaving you like the dead trees covering the ground.

It was hard to see any beauty in what remained. Yet, one could not help but feel sorry for the land, like watching someone who had battled on stoically. The days becoming years until they realized the futility of it all, and they either died on the land or sold it and found somewhere else to live. Then they would slowly die, clinging to the memories of what they hoped for and did.

A verse from the Bible slipped into Jack's mind.

Father, forgive them, for they know not what they do.

Five generations had held the farm, the first would not have known the impact of their actions. The most recent, the ones who'd sold the farm to Uncle Alan, had inherited a mess. They'd just wanted to get rid of the problem. It would take time, love, and money to get this place back on its feet. They got to the back of the ranch, where an overgrown path headed toward Mt. Olympia. Hailey pointed at the shale spilling out from the track and under the fence.

"That will take you all the way up to Mt. Olympia. This first part goes up to a small plateau, but the going's slippery as it's shale all the way to the plateau. From there, the going is easy."

Hailey reined her horse back one step, peered down at the ground, got off, and picked up a piece of flat gray shale the size of her hand. "That's blood."

Jack got off his horse. The drops looked like wet paint. Hailey dropped the slate and walked forward, leading her horse and pointing at the ground. "Those are buck footprints. A big one. See the blood trail. There're boot prints over the buck prints. Two sets. See the different sizes. Look at the print. Hiking boots. When I first saw the blood, I thought it had to be an injured animal. Maybe two bucks were fighting. Now I don't know what's going on. Maybe someone's injured, and the buck prints are coincidental."

Hailey was back in the saddle before Jack, moving in a slow trot, leaning to the side of her horse's neck following the blood trail, coming back to a walk when the blood drops thinned. Jack kept pace behind her deferring to her tracking skills. After two hundred yards, Jack could see the prints were still traveling together. They rounded a clump of oak trees fifty yards further on.

The black-tailed buck was on the ground, its antlers making its head look up at the sky, which it would never see again. Jack could see two people in camo gear. Two compound bows with arrows were leaning against a tree. Three arrows were sticking out of the buck, and the people were cutting off the buck's head. One of them looked like he was cutting between the vertebrae at the base of the skull. The other grabbed the antlers, twisting, and pulling, the head turning around like an owl. Both were so absorbed in their task that they did not hear the walking horses.

"You're on private property," said Jack as he surveyed the two men. They were in their mid-twenties, shoulder height to Jack, ten pounds heavier, and looked alike.

They stopped like startled rabbits and looked up at Jack and Hailey as they reined their horses to a stop ten feet away. Jack could see that all three arrows were in the abdomen, meaning they were poor shots or had taken the easy way out by gut-shooting the buck and following it, the arrowhead slicing back and forth through the internal organs as it ran.

The pain the buck had experienced made the dark thing at the base of Jack's spine tremble and move.

"Says who?" said the one who'd been twisting the antlers. The one with the knife kept cutting at the tendons in the buck's neck.

"Says me. My uncle owns this property, and hunting's not allowed. Do you two even have hunting licenses and deer tags? You know you only get two tags per license per season."

"Why did you gut-shoot the buck?" said Hailey in a voice like ice, her face flushed. "I don't like bow hunters on a good day, but at least make a clean kill."

The antler-turner walked over to stand in front of Jack. "I don't have to answer to you, and how do I know this is your uncle's property? You could be lying." Then he turned to Hailey. "So, you don't like bow hunters. Let me tell you, I kill bucks in the most effective way possible. And that's gut-shooting. Big soft target, then I follow them until they drop."

Hailey backed her horse up one step, making it coil like a spring, then jumped forward. Hailey swung her right foot forward at the antler-twister. His hands went up to protect his face, the toe of her boot slipping through his hands, catching him under the chin. His hands clawed at her, grabbing her leg, his legs jellifying as he reached up and grabbed her arm as she backed up her horse. He fell to the ground, pulling Hailey off her horse, his head landing in the puddle of blood next to the buck's head. The killer and the killed together. Hailey landed on top of him as he clung like a monkey onto her leg and arm.

Jack had swung off his horse as Hailey was in mid-flight. The antler-twister let go of Hailey's leg and reached for his knife, the blade becoming visible as Jack kicked him in the temple knocking him out. Jack took the knife from his hand and helped Hailey to her feet. "Run." Hailey took off towards the horses, quietly grazing a hundred feet away. A tranquil, rural scene.

The knifeman stood, the hunting knife in his right hand, looking at the man on the ground as one would a creature that wasn't supposed to be there. Blood was on his hands, the knife, and the cuffs of his camo shirt. He looked at Jack. "I'm gonna cut you for what you've done to my brother. You should have minded your own business and not bothered us."

Jack had seen demonstrations of these hunting knives, and a strike across his stomach would open him up. The knifeman came in, doing short jabs with the blade to the stomach. Jack sliced at the knifeman's face, making him stop, then start again with the jabbing. Jack kept backing away until he came to the tree where the bows were leaning. He reached for one, took it by the end, and swung it at the knifeman's blade, knocking it to the side. Jack kicked long and hard with his back leg connecting with the knifeman's groin, sending him to the ground. He dropped the knife as he held and protected his jewels. Jack picked up the knife and went to the two backpacks, shaking out the contents. The second bag had what he thought they had. Cable ties to strap the head and antlers to the backpack to carry it out.

Jack secured the knifeman first, as he was still conscious. Ankles strapped together and wrists strapped together. Hailey walked in, leading both horses.

Jack looked up at her. "You hurt?"

"Just my pride that I got pulled from my horse. I should have ridden over him."

"Next time, maybe."

Jack walked over to the unconscious man, who was now moving.

"Where'd you learn to fight like that?"

Not a conversation he wanted to get into. "I just grabbed what I could, and I guess I got lucky."

"Yeah, right."

The unconscious man was regaining consciousness. Jack secured his legs before he could become a problem, then his wrists, and returned to the contents of the backpacks scattered on the ground. "There's no hunting license or deer tags."

"I'm phoning the Park Rangers at Mt. Diablo. They'll know what to do with these two."

Hailey flipped through her phone and dialed. The person on the other end was female and excited to hear from Hailey until she explained the situation with two illegal hunters. Her tone turned cold. Jack heard Hailey explain where they were and hung up.

"She said they'd be here in fifteen minutes. You'd better tell Aaron to let them in."

Jack phoned Aaron and told him as they walked one hundred and fifty feet away from the two bound bodies and sat on a fallen log, the horses grazing next to them.

"Do you have the Park Rangers on speed dial?"

"Remember, I grew up here, and I'm a vet. They call me out sometimes, and I know most of them. That woman I spoke to, we went to school together. It's a big territory but still a small town."

"So tell me, what was it like growing up here?"

Hailey's face lit up like a blooming pink rose as she described it. Her hands were also telling the stories, and her red mane flowed from side to side as she stood and moved around to explain it better. As she told the story, she became more animated, and disappointment arrived with the Ranger's truck stopping the storytelling.

CHAPTER NINE

The ranger's name was Sandra. Jack was watching her reverse her truck up to the two bow hunters when he saw Aaron arrive on the electric quad bike. He looked like a bear on a bicycle. Princess sat between his legs, surveying the scene. He parked next to the truck and looked at Jack.

"It just needed to be charged. I thought I'd follow the ranger and see if I could help."

"Thanks, Aaron," said Jack. "Glad to see the bike working."

Princess jumped off the bike to sniff at the carcass. Sandra, the ranger, stared at Aaron as he walked over to the dead buck and looked at the bow hunters on the ground, his face changing to an anger like a tornado rising inside him. Jack was sure this was not helping Aaron's PTSD as Aaron spoke with a voice that came from a throat choked with emotion.

"Did these two do this?"

This situation would get ugly unless Jack kept a lid on Aaron.

"Yes, Aaron, they did. Our job now is to load them into the truck's tray, and the ranger will deal with them."

"I'll do it," said Aaron as he reached down, grabbed the knifeman by the shirt, and lifted him until he looked in Aaron's face for two seconds. "Never come here again. Don't speak. Just nod if you understand me." Knifeman nodded three times. "And maybe you two should stop bow hunting, or else this could happen to you. An accident." Aaron flung him like a pillow through the air, where he did not land as softly as a pillow, his head crashing into the side of the tray as he spun onto his back. Jack didn't consider intervening but went around picking up bows, knives, and backpacks. He threw them onto the bow hunter, groaning on the tray as the second one spun through the air to land on top of his brother.

Aaron slid his arms under the buck, picked it up like a patient, its half-severed head hanging like a grotesque parody of a patient that Hailey could heal, and placed it on top of the two bow hunters. Sandra was still staring as she climbed into her truck and drove away.

Jack went to Aaron, who was looking at the blood on the ground, holding Princess, so she couldn't sniff and lick the blood.

"It's wrong, Jack."

The instructions from Uncle Alan on how to support Aaron with his concussion and PTSD ran through Jack's head. Having Aaron involved in this incident was definitely not in the things to do. Telling Uncle Alan would not help anyone. Jack reached up to put his hand on Aaron's shoulder.

"I know, Aaron. But it's done. Why don't you take the bike and Princess and ride along the boundary and see if there are any breaks in the fence and when you get back could you rig up some of those old horse blankets as a punching bag?"

"Good idea." Aaron squeezed out a smile. "Two good ideas."

Jack watched Aaron get on the bike with Princess. "Take your time, Aaron. There's no rush to get back."

***

Jack and Hailey walked their horses through grassland, moving uphill to the top of a ridge. Hailey pointed. "See where the grass and trees are thick and green, running in a line? There could be water there."

They walked their horses downhill into a tangle of trees, following a deer track that led them to a circle of blue water one hundred feet in diameter. On the opposite side, a twenty-foot-high cliff had a thin trickle of water falling into the green and blue below.

"The color is too beautiful," said Hailey. "You just wanna dive right in."

"Can you see the shades of black mixed with the blue and the green? The Chinese say it's nature's color, and their name for it is Qing."

Hailey frowned as she looked at Jack. "How would you even know that?"

Looking at the Qing-colored lake had brought back memories, but he was not going there. "I can't recall. Somewhere in my travels, someone must have told me." Sometimes deflection is a good strategy. "Should I get the water tested?"

"You should get all the water points tested. California's had its fair share of water problems with the introduction of mega-farming. But the black-tailed deer must be drinking water somewhere, and chances are there are more places like this."

"Would you like to come out again, and we can do some exploring? Next time with a map and some small bottles to collect water."

"I'd like to go exploring with you."

Jack was reading something into that. He looked at her face for more, but she had turned away to look at the trickling waterfall, only her profile and a mass of red curls to help him.

Hailey looked at her watch. "We should start heading back. I have some patients at our ranch that need my attention."

They walked the horses in companionable silence for about ten minutes when Hailey snapped her head around to look at Jack.

"I never thought to ask. What do you do, Jack? I mean for a job."

"I do forensic work on a company's computer systems. Sometimes it gets a bit more involved." There was no reason for her to know how involved and messy it could get and what he'd done. "But that's the gist of it."

"Oh. I figured you to be doing something exciting."

"No, no. All pretty dull stuff. I have one right here on Marsh Road I need to do. Maybe you know them."

"Who?"

"The Dubin's family business. I'll be working for Barney Dubin."

Hailey screwed her face up, which on anyone would have made them look ugly, but on her, he wanted to kiss her.

"Now that family's a mixed bag."

"What can you tell me?"

"Well, if you're working for Barney, that's ok. He's a gentleman from the old school, always dapper and always polite. His word is his bond. His wife, Sarah, is a breath of fresh air in the environmental community. A proper whirlwind. This has been her life since the boys, Stewart and Ralph, left her loving shackles. Until then, you would have thought spoiling her children was a career, and you would have been right. But she's lovely, and I enjoy her company. We're on some Mt. Diablo environmental committees together."

A ground squirrel ran in front of the horses, clattering through dry leaves, stopping at the base of a tree, grabbing something in its mouth, and climbing it. The horses were unmoved by this and kept plodding along. Jack also wanted to keep plodding along with Hailey, and ideas floated like mist in the back of his mind as he imagined when they could next do this. Sometimes, it is better to enjoy the moment, shut down any planning and let the future ferment of its own accord.

Jack remembered Peter's wife, Hannah's view about the two children. "How did the boys turn out with this spoiling?"

"Well, let me start with Stewart. He's the elder by two years. A lovely guy, full of fun, jokes, and happiness." Jack watched her smile at some remembrance. "Not a care in the world, even if he does have problems. And totally useless. He is excellent in the sales side of the business when he chooses to be. But it's sporadic."

Hailey stopped smiling and frowned like an unhappy child. "Then there's Ralph. He's like Stewart's evil twin. Everything Stewart is, Ralph is not. But it would be best if you watched out for both of them. Stewart will put you in harm's way due to incompetence. With Ralph, it will be deliberate."

Jack took this in. *Forewarned is forearmed.* Like in the MMA days, with Kenny pointing out the moves of an upcoming opponent. Then into business, Strengths, Weaknesses, Opportunities, and Threats. SWOT analysis. The learning pattern was the same.

"When do you meet Barney?"

"Tomorrow. 9 am."

As the horses walked side by side, sometimes Hailey's knee would bump into Jack's. To Jack, it was as if her knee was reaching for his. Anything was possible.

Jack waited until his thoughts about knee bumping subsided. "You seem to know a lot about the Dubin family."

"Can't help it. My mum's ranch is next door to theirs. I went to school with Stewart and Ralph. I was in the same class as Ralph. I got to see or hear about every nasty little thing he got up to." Hailey looked at Jack. "Clayton's a small town. In some ways, I was glad to get out of it when I went to college and then to vet school at U. Cal, Davis. But after working in San Francisco on small animals for a few years, I thought of returning and working with my mom and dad. My dad was also a vet. Together they ran the practice. Wonderful man and a great vet. He died doing what he loved. Dad was in the stable checking out his favorite horse, which was recovering from colic. He had a heart attack and dropped dead on the floor beside his horse. When they found him, his horse was nudging him with her nose to help him get up." That's where my mom found him. Hailey dabbed at her eyes with the cuffs of her shirt and sniffed. "So, I packed up my life in San Francisco and moved back."

"U. Cal, Davis? They have that great logo with the Mustang." Jack looked at the sky like he was looking for an answer. "I can't recall the name."

Hailey smiled. "Gunrock. Why would you even know that?"

"I went to U. Cal. I checked out all the U. Cal. campuses before deciding on Berkeley."

"What did you do there?"

"Computer Science." Jack left out his Master's degree, teaching at Berkeley, and how this was the basis of his work. Likewise, how he helped Freddie's team at SFPD without knowing what they did.

Hailey leaned forward and squinted her eyes as she looked at Jack like she was trying to focus, her calf pressing against Jack's calf. "You don't look like a computer nerd. I didn't think nerds even rode horses."

Jack chuckled. "You found me out. A nerd disguised as a cowboy."

They rode comfortably along with Hailey pointing out trees and grasses and their effect on rejuvenating the land. As they got within sight of the ranch, they saw Aaron emerge from the bunkhouse with Princess behind him. He walked at the pace of the limping dog, stopped, picked her up, and went to the barn.

"Were you serious about Aaron coming to help you at your practice?"

"Of course I was."

"You saw how he behaved with those bow hunters."

"If I were as big as Aaron, I would have done the same. Probably more. And yes, I would like him to help at the practice. That's not something I'd say as a throwaway comment. Aaron has a nursing talent, and currently, we don't have anyone. My mom and I are doing it, which takes up our time when we should be consulting. Your place is on my way in, so I can pick him up. What do you say?"

"I think it's a good idea. But I think Aaron and Princess will come as a package."

"I'd already guessed that. It's ok."

They watched as Aaron came out of the barn carrying Princess and a bag of dog food. He reached the bunkhouse verandah, lowering Princess to the floor at the door and tickling her under the chin. Princess raised her head to get the tickles and watch Aaron. He carried the dog food bag into the kitchen, and Princess followed him.

At the horse trailer, they off-saddled, hosed down the horses' legs, and put them in stables in the barn with some hay. Aaron had made a punching bag from horse blankets and hung it at the back of the barn. It had been tied at four places making the top piece look like a drooping head. It would do the job. After Hailey had gone, he would get to work on the bag with Aaron, helping both of them to work through their PTSD. Not looking for a magic cure. But more stability would be good. They had no gloves. The rough weave of the horse blankets would soon shred the skin off their knuckles. Electrical tape. Freddie had used it on him before, getting Jack accustomed to hitting a heavy bag without gloves.

Jack and Hailey walked over to the bunkhouse kitchen, where they told Aaron about working for Hailey. A smile like sunshine appeared on his face as he picked up Princess and hugged her as she licked his chin.

"Hailey, I'll leave you to work out the details with Aaron. I'll get some coffee going."

Jack put his phone on the kitchen table and noticed a missed call from Freddie. Must have come through while dealing with the bow hunters. Jack tapped the phone with his index finger. Freddie answered after three rings with no preamble to the conversation.

"We've got another murder. I'll need your help."

"I can be there by two tomorrow."

"That works. See you then." Freddie hung up.

Clearly, there was a lot going on.

CHAPTER TEN

The Dubin residence was more palatial estate than ranch. Dogwood trees lined the 200-yard driveway. At 9 am, the sun showed their pink flowers coming into full bloom to their best advantage. He wondered who would pick them up in the fall. Then he saw two gardeners who answered that question, one with a wheelbarrow and the other trimming a hedge that already looked picture-perfect. Still, the gardener seemed not satisfied as he made adjustments with his shears.

Jack had been up at 6 am with Aaron to work on their makeshift punching bag. Kenny had taught that a street fight rarely goes past one minute. So, for one minute, Jack went at the bag with fists, feet, elbows, and knees, working to control his breathing and mood. Then it was Aaron's turn for a minute, Jack talking to him about keeping his mood and breathing under control as he pounded at the bag. Jack could see Aaron had some boxing training by his stance and how he held his fists and used them on the bag. The result was the bag reacted to Aaron's punches like a wrecking ball was hitting it. They kept at this for forty minutes. Jack could feel his PTSD coming under control as the dark thing at the base of his spine went to sleep in its cave. Aaron's shoulders, which he'd bunched up, relaxed, and dropped as the exercise progressed. Each to his own in dealing with PTSD. Kenny had pointed Jack in this direction, which worked for Jack, and maybe it would work for Aaron. For breakfast, Jack cooked three eggs for himself and six for Aaron, with black coffee for them both. A shave and a shower, then time to go to work.

The front door opened as Jack walked up the three, ten-foot-wide sandstone steps to the rough-timbered door. Jack had not noticed a security camera, but then again, he had not been on high alert and looking.

A woman with shoulder-length, well-groomed gray hair stepped through with her hand extended. She said his name like it was a question, with a smile she probably bestowed on her grandchildren. "Sarah Dubin. Welcome. Barney is on the phone in the Gathering Room." Jack shook a firm hand with skin as smooth as rose petals. Her face, which had seen about seventy summers but was not sun-damaged, had an unlined forehead. She had not dressed for ranch work. A waist-length mauve chiffon kimono overlay a red shirt and the top of a black skirt with sensible black shoes that could only have come from Italy. A light touch of makeup and what looked like one-carat diamond earrings completed her ensemble. Side by side, Sarah Dubin and Hannah Wasserman could be sisters with the same taste in hairstyle, dress, and looking after themselves.

Halfway down the fifty-foot hallway was a high wooden skinny table with a vase of roses. Behind it was a three-foot circular mirror reflecting the roses. It looked good. Jack would mention this to Aunt Louise. The Gathering Room was the size of a six-car garage with one floor-to-ceiling glass wall. Brown leather chairs, sofas, and glass-topped tables with tortured, unpainted steel legs surrounded a fireplace that supported a four-foot by three-foot painting of a blue cottage with a red roof.

A man of some three more years than Sarah, of modest build, put down his notepad and pen when he saw Jack and pushed himself out of the chair with a grunt

"Nice to meet you, Jack," said Barney as he took Jack's hand in a two-handed grip. Jack would not have noticed the slight tremor in Barney's left-hand unless Peter had mentioned it.

They exchanged pleasantries, drank coffee, then got down to business. Barney explained what Peter had told him verbatim but not as disparaging about his children, except when he pointed to the painting.

"That's a painting of where my father came from in Lithuania. We had no photos, so he described it from memory to the artist I employed. It hangs there to remind us of where we came from and not take what we now have for granted." Barney looked at the painting with a sigh like a whisper and spoke as if a thought had become audible. "But that message does not reach everyone."

Sarah patted Barney's arm like she was consoling a child while looking at Jack. "You come highly recommended by Peter. We would like you to investigate our business and determine what's wrong so that we can get it back onto a more profitable footing."

Before Jack could answer, a voice announced someone's arrival. "But you'll have to be strong to do this. Are you strong? It's Jack, isn't it?" A bald, chunky, short man with a Cheshire Cat smile bounced into the room like a chubby cherub and stuck out his hand, which Jack stood to shake. "I'm Stewart. But back to my question. Do you think you're strong enough?"

"I think I am."

Stewart's smile spread wider when his gaze clamped onto Jack's face. "But are you really, really sure?" Each syllable spread out as he leaned forward. "How do we know?"

Caught somewhere between irritation and amusement, the theatrics made Jack lean towards amusement, so he went with the flow. "Do you want to arm-wrestle, Stewart?"

A laugh like a happy child came from Stewart. "What a great answer." He turned to his parents. "I like this guy. You should hire him. Anyway, got to go. Have things to do." He kissed his mother on the cheek, shook his father's hand, and bubbled down the hallway with a "Ciao for now."

Jack could see why Hailey had said he was hard to dislike. He smiled as he turned to Barney and Sarah and agreed to their request.

"When can you start, Jack?" said Barney.

"Now is good."

"Thank you, Jack," said Barney. "I appreciate it. I could tell you more about the business, but I prefer you to see it with fresh eyes."

Barney looked at Sarah. "My love, will you please take Jack to meet Ralph? I'm going take a stroll and see what the gardeners are up to."

Barney's left hand had the slightest of tremors as he picked up a mahogany-colored wooden cane with a leather handle and struggled to his feet. Sarah didn't help him, but concern caused her eyebrows to droop. When he was gone from sight, Sarah turned to Jack.

"When Barney started the business, there were no computers. We recorded everything in hand-written ledgers. Barney's brain did the constant juggling of the trades. Leather trading is a very volatile business as it depends on one hand, the production of the cattle industry in each state of the nation. And on the other, the economy, dictating what leather products people can afford and how many."

Jack had done some homework and was surprised to see the degree of volatility, but the laws of supply and demand in the whole supply chain gave him the explanation. He didn't comment but let Sarah continue.

"In some ways, it's like being a bookmaker at the races. But the significant edge we had, in addition to Barney's brain, was his personal relationships with people in agriculture, the tanneries, and retail. The phone never stopped ringing, with people wanting to talk to Barney. The old expression, *his word is his bond*. Barney did that from the very beginning. It's in his genes. He was particularly sympathetic towards ranchers, especially the small ones, as it's a tough life. He would loan them money. Interest-free. They always paid him back. With money and, more importantly, with loyalty."

Sarah stood, walked to the window, watched Barney talking to the two gardeners, and spoke. "Do you see these two men Barney is talking to?"

Jack got up to stand next to Sarah. "Yes, I saw them as I walked to the door."

"They're from the Marsh Road Detention Center, which is just down the road. It's locally known as The Farm."

"What are they doing here?"

"The Farm is a minimum-security facility. The prisoners are in there for two years or less. These two have almost served their sentence. It's difficult to get a job once you have the stigma of a jail sentence. That's where Barney comes in. He gets them a job through one of his many friends."

"What did these two do?"

"Caught shoplifting at Walmart. They were homeless, and not the first time they'd been caught. Very sad, and they used to have big jobs. These two came as a couple. Both stockbrokers. They were legally married before going to prison."

Jack could appreciate the altruism involved, but there had to be more. "Why does Barney do it?"

Sarah turned her head to look at Jack. "When he started doing this, I asked him that same question, and his answer was, 'There but for the grace of God go I.'" She turned back to watch the trio. "I never asked again."

CHAPTER ELEVEN

Sarah and Jack got into a golf cart outside the kitchen at the back of the house. They'd walked from the Gathering Room into the dining room with its dark solid wood table, which comfortably accommodated the ten high-backed leather chairs, into the kitchen, which was restaurant-grade except instead of the aluminum look found in restaurants, this was white marble countertops with matching cabinets and four leather-topped high-stools. These sat on beige tiles, none of which were the same size or shape, making them look like a collection of remnants.

Sarah drove them along a dappled brown brick driveway through a maze of gardens and trees for over a hundred yards to a square building snug up against the foothills of Mt. Diablo. From the outside, a miniature version of the main house, but not that small, was some thirty yards long on each wall.

"Your property's beautiful, Sarah. Very different from where I am down the road, and I don't see any boundary fences?"

Sarah chuckled. "Thank you, Jack. In the design, we hid the fences behind trees and bushes. We didn't want to see them. The property itself is small, just six acres."

Jack opened the door for Sarah. They walked inside to what was more nightclub than office. Black concrete floor, black walls, purple lighting on the ceiling, and footlights along the base of each wall. All it seemed to lack was a stage with a pole. Two thin as sticks, blonde, twenty-something women in black yoga pants and halter tops sat on the sofa. They could be twins.

Three sixty-inch, flat screens adorned one wall. Two chairs used by video gamers faced the screens, far enough away so they could see them all. There were numbers, graphs, and photos of hides appearing on the screens. Fusion architecture. NASA meets strip club.

"Mummy. How wonderful of you to join us."

Sarah leaned towards the voice. "Ralph, come out from the dark so I can see you."

A shadow peeled off the wall, walked to Sarah, and kissed her cheek. Black seemed to be the theme. Black jeans, black combat boots, and a skin-tight black T-shirt. Whereas Stewart was all baby-fat, Ralph had minimal fat over muscles with a 'steroids-fading' puffy look. Jack placed him at twenty pounds heavier, their eyes on the same level. He had a high forehead with black hair combed back, which under the lights, had a sheen like gloss paint.

"Ralph, may I introduce Jack Rhodes? Your father and I explained what Jack is going to be doing."

Jack put out his hand. "Nice to meet you, Ralph."

Ralph surveyed the hand like he was weighing up whether to shake or whether he was unfamiliar with this traditional meeting process. Then he took the hand in a grip like a vice, applied pressure, and kept unblinking eye contact. Like being back in the schoolyard, but some men still did it. But better than the dead fish handshake. Kenny had taught Jack where to place his hand when dealing with the macho grip. It was declared a draw as Sarah spoke. "Ralph, turn up these lights so I can see."

Ralph clapped his hands, and the number of lumens increased.

"More," said Sarah.

Ralph clapped twice in quick succession, and the room became visible. The occupants shaded their eyes and groaned like they were waking up.

"Mummy, I told you and Daddy that I don't need help. I know what I'm doing."

Ralph had his hands by his side in fists and his shoulders hunched like a petulant child. Jack waited for him to stamp his foot.

"It's your father's decision, and there will be no more discussion about this. Now I have things to do. You take Jack and show him what you're doing. And behave yourself. I don't want to hear you withheld information or access to anything."

There was silence between Sarah and Ralph as she held his gaze. Everyone in the room watched the interplay between mother and son. Sometimes withheld information has the most information. "Oh. Alright, Mummy. I'll play nicely with my new friend."

He showed his teeth to Jack which was not the same as smiling.

Sarah patted him on the cheek with a smile like she regretted something, then walked across the room and through the door. Ralph clapped his hands twice as the door closed. The room reverted to its earlier ambiance as he turned to Jack. "Where do you want to start?"

"Take me through the software, then walk me through how you're using it."

Ralph looked at the two women on the sofa. "Eeny, Meeny, Miney Mo. Wow, Jenny, you win. Please take my new friend through the software. His name's Jack."

One lookalike stood, her thin frame exaggerated by her height. Six foot, he estimated. Blue eyes. High cheekbones cast a shadow below them. Black hair pulled back into a ponytail that went down between her shoulder blades. Face, devoid of makeup, which hadn't seen the sun for a while or used a lot of sunblock.

"Follow me, Jack."

Jack trailed behind Jenny to a desk with a keyboard and a twenty-inch screen. "Pull up a chair."

Jack took a chair from a desk and sat down.

"Sit closer so I can show you. I won't bite." She cocked one eyebrow.

How do people do that?

"Unless you want me to."

Jack shuffled his chair close enough to smell her familiar perfume, but he could not put a name to it. Her fingers tapped at the keyboard while she talked. "What do you know about trading platforms?" A webpage appeared. HTT. Hide Trade & Track.

"I had a client who traded oil. Brent crude. On the NYMEX. I got to watch how they traded and the business operated."

"The good old New York Mercantile Exchange. I did my time developing trading platforms around NYMEX."

"So, you're a software developer?"

Jenny looked at Jack and drew her head back in an attitude of disbelief.

"Yes. What did you think I was? Ralph's girlfriend?"

Sometimes you can't help but judge a book by its cover. How to get out of this one without causing an upset?

"I had no idea what you did."

She nodded and seemed satisfied with his response. "The NYMEX, as you may know, is regulated by the CFTC, the Commodity Futures Trading Commission. So, all the software has to conform to its rules and regulations. This, on the other hand, is like the Wild Wild West. You can build a platform and simply put it out there. Let me show you."

Jenny took fifteen minutes to demonstrate how she would set up

Buyers and Sellers on the system and how they could be brought together for a trade. The products were hides, skins, and leather, and there were photos, videos, statistics on the products, and the state of the offers.

"It's more like an online auction than a trading platform."

Jenny looked at Jack like her star pupil was performing above expectation. "Exactly."

"I didn't see futures trading. Does the software handle that?"

"We stayed away from that. It's another level of complexity to develop, particularly on the financial side."

"So, how do you handle the money part of the transaction?"

"My sister, Janey, over there on the sofa, is really clever using blockchain technology. Between us, we built our own blockchain-based payment platform."

"Can I use crypto-currency?"

"You sure can. Or from your bank account."

"These crypto transactions require a lot of electricity to process, and I've read that it uses more than a hundred and fifty dollars of electricity for each transaction."

"Very good. You've been reading." Jenny nodded her head. "This building has its own power line, and Ralph has included the cost of the electricity into the subscription fee. But he has plans to build a solar farm with battery storage."

There was a missing piece of the puzzle. "How do the goods get from the seller to the buyer? Or do they have to organize that themselves?"

"We take care of that. We have a whole supply chain module."

Jack watched as she showed how this worked. The transporters, the paperwork, the tracking, and the transaction settlement via blockchain. "The system is hosted in the cloud, and people all over the globe can trade twenty-four-seven. It caters from the abattoir to the tanner to the finished retail product."

"Where did you get the knowledge about leather trading?"

"My sister and I worked at what is now a competitor. Ralph found us and offered us more money to build a better platform. What we built is not just better but bigger, faster, more user-friendly, and more secure." Jenny smiled as if she was to be the class valedictorian.

"So, you're pleased with what you've developed."

"Sure am." Her smile widened.

"Do you do any trading yourself?"

"No. I don't have the nerve for it. Janey doesn't either. Ralph does, but sporadically."

In Jack's experience, traders had to trade. It was a variant of gambling addiction. Jack looked across to where Ralph sat behind his desk, his thumb scrolling through his phone. No compulsion there to do trade.

"Why are you still here, Jenny?"

"Software support, bug fixes, and integration to third-party products."

Ralph's phone went ping, which stopped Ralph's finger scrolling. He looked at the message, put the phone on the desk, turned to his screen, and started typing. Every five to ten seconds, he would look at the phone, then back at the screen and continue typing. He was too far away and at the wrong angle for Jack to see if he was making a trade or emailing.

Janey got up from the sofa, walked over, and stood behind Jack, placing her hands on his shoulders and looking over his head at the screen. "Tell me, Sis, has this handsome man learned enough about what clever us has developed?"

Jenny looked up at her sister. "I think so. He seems pretty sharp."

"Good. Because I need a break from here. Can we go back to the hotel? If Ralph wants us, he can call us."

"Where are you staying?" said Jack.

Janey rolled her eyes. "Ralph, the big spender, put us in a

bed-and-breakfast in Clayton, and the building must be forty years old."

"Let's go," said Jenny. "We can do some practice in the pool."

"Are you swimmers?"

"No, freedivers."

Jack looked back and forth at the twins.

"Not what you were expecting, Jack?" said Janey.

"No. You did surprise me. I do scuba dive when I get a chance, and it never crossed my mind to do freediving. However, I've read a bit about it. What's it like?"

They looked at each other, getting a lot more animated than when talking about software like they were deciding who would go first.

Jenny started. "Look at us." She did a pirouette, and Janey did the same as Jenny was halfway around. "We're not great hulking physical specimens. There is an element of physicality, but it's mainly mental. That's what is incredible about freediving. It's not about your physical ability, but about your mental skills and mental training."

Janey jumped into the conversation. "You need to let go of everything you know and everything that makes you feel good or bad. So, it's a very liberating process."

Jenny dived back in. "But having stressed the mental side, you still need to stay completely aware of your body and where you are."

"That's right," said Janey. "Be entirely in the moment. That's the best part."

"How deep can you go?"

"We're relative beginners, but we can go down to fifty feet," said Janey. "Ralph has become interested as well, and we've done some practice sessions with him in the pool at the main house."

"Before you go. Can I have the access codes to a demo environment where I can play with the software and the development environment where I can see how you built it and the production environment?"

"No problem," said Jenny. "Mrs. Dubin's word is the law around here." She leaned forward like a conspirator. "Despite what Ralph thinks and says. Now show me the Notes section on your phone."

Jack typed on his phone and passed it to Jenny, who typed away with two furious thumbs and gave it to Jack. "That's everything you'll need."

The twins picked up their phones and purses, slung the two-foot-long thin straps over their bare shoulders in unison, waved to Ralph, who didn't notice as his focus was on the screen, and left the building.

Jack stood in front of the big screens watching the auctions and trades taking place. The screen was as busy as the Arrivals/Departure Board at San Francisco Airport. Out of the corner of his eye, he could watch Ralph toiling away at the screen while referring to his phone. Jack thought about the development cost of the software and the operational running costs. His phone pinged with a message from Freddie.

When can you come help us?

I can be there by 2. That Ok?

That works. See you then.

Jack watched Ralph, who seemed to be finished with his toiling and was hammering his phone with his thumbs as he typed. When he finished, he fell back into his chair, looking at the ceiling and breathing like he was meditating. Once he was composed, he noticed Jack standing unattended and hurried over, looking left and right.

"Where are the twins?"

"They left. Said they were bored."

Ralph's brow furrowed as he rubbed his chin. "Really? They have so much to do."

"Yeah, they mentioned the future development you wanted done."

Ralph's face went from hunter to hunted like a fox chasing a rabbit, then hearing the baying of the hounds. "What did they tell you?" Ralph did a quick intake of breath and held it.

"Not much, except it involved the integration from your system to a third-party product."

"Did they mention the name of the product?"

"No."

"So," Ralph did a slow release of the air in his lungs. "I guess you're done for the day unless you have any questions for me?"

"Just one for now. Where'd the money come from to fund all this? Your mother told me they gave you five hundred thousand to fund this. But I've been in enough software development projects and taken them operational to know that what you have spent here is far more than that."

Ralph waited five seconds as if he was weighing up which response to use. "Isn't that outside what you were asked to do?"

"Not at all. Your parents asked me to look at what you were doing in its entirety. There were to be no boundaries or topics that were off-limits."

Ralph managed to combine agitation and acceptance into his demeanor. "There is an investor."

"Are they based in San Francisco? I know a lot of the local guys."

"They prefer to stay anonymous."

Jack nodded. He'd get a copy of the financials from Mrs. Dubin. Any investment of funds had to show up on the balance sheet.

"Before I go, just one thing."

Ralph looked nervous and aggressive, like a rodeo steer, and he had the muscles. "What?"

Jack put the same request to Ralph as he had to the twins. *Just how cooperative was Ralph?*

"Can I have the access codes to a demo environment where I can play with the software and the development environment where I can see how you built it and the production environment, so I can understand things better?"

Ralph surveyed Jack like a cop with a felon. "I'll give you access to the training environment, and that's all."

Jack nodded. *Well, that settled that. Not very cooperative. The twins'll be a better source of information.*

Ralph rattled off a username and password, which Jack typed into his phone. "If you go to the website, you'll see the training environment." Ralph opened his mouth to speak, stopped like he was working out the order of the words he wanted to use, and enunciated each word like he was in an elocution lesson. "Make sure you stay within the boundaries of what you've been asked to do."

"I always do. But in this case, I've been instructed that there are none."

Before Ralph could reply, Jack said goodbye and left. The heat of Ralph's gaze bore twin holes in his back.

CHAPTER TWELVE

Jack stopped halfway back to the house to feel the sun on his face as he looked up at Mt. Olympia. He concentrated on Ralph. Not the first time he'd met someone behaving like Ralph. The thoughts came without being asked.

Was Ralph hiding something? Was he just naturally difficult? Or was this Ralph protecting his turf?

Things to keep on the edge of the mind while doing the work the Dubins were paying him to do.

Jack spared a thought for Stella as he returned to the main house and into the Gathering Room where Sarah Dubin was sitting.

"Sarah, could I have a set of the financials emailed to me?"

Sarah smiled like she was a fortune teller. "I was expecting that request and have already sent them to you."

"Great. Thank you. I'm going to be working from the ranch tomorrow if that's fine with you."

"That's totally up to you. We won't be dictating how, when, and where you choose to work."

"Thank you, Sarah. I need to get going. Where's Barney?"

"He's still outside with the gardeners."

Jack walked out into the garden where Barney Dubin was talking to the gardeners, the ex-stockbrokers. They were standing near his truck.

Was there such a thing as an ex-stockbroker if it's in your DNA?

Both were early forties, with intelligent eyes, mousy hair with flecks of gray, cut short and neat. The effects of living on the street ingrained in the lines on their faces.

"Jack, may I introduce Bryce Woods and Aidan Hart?"

Everyone had a firm handshake. They looked about one hundred and sixty pounds each. Bryce was the same height as Jack, so he looked skinnier than Aidan, two inches shorter.

"I hear you guys were stockbrokers before you switched careers to gardening." This brought laughter all around. "Any chance you might go back to share trading?"

"Well, we didn't get disbarred for wrongdoing," said Aidan. "We stole because we were hungry."

"We crashed and burned," said Bryce. "So, we could, but we'd have to regain our confidence."

Jack looked at Barney. Sometimes an idea pops up like a virus and gets its own momentum. "Barney, could Bryce and Aidan help me with what you've asked me to do?"

It was a pleasure to see Barney's face; he looked as happy as a kid at Christmas. "What a fantastic idea, Jack. What do you say? Bryce? Aidan?"

"What would you want us to do?" said Aidan.

Jack explained about the trading platform. "One of you could be the seller, the other the buyer, and run scenarios. You could also try making trades as well. The more scenarios you run, the better for me."

"You could do this," said Barney. "I'll put computers in your room."

Bryce and Aidan looked at each other and seemed to be

telepathically communicating. Jacked waited until they turned back to look at him.

"Yes, Jack," said Aidan, like he'd accepted a job offer. Which they were.

"When do we start?" said Bryce.

"Forget the gardening," said Barney. "You can start now."

Jack gave them the usernames and passwords and restated the web address.

As he drove onto Marsh Creek Road, he had a good feeling about getting Aidan and Bryce involved. In more ways than one. He passed the entrance to Alan's Acres and settled down for the one-hour drive to San Francisco.

***

Freddie's office was inside the San Francisco Police Department Training Academy on Amber Drive. The unit Freddie commanded was amongst what looked like junior school buildings from a bygone era. Not surprising as this was the purpose of the original facility. A sign said Room 51. There were no rooms beyond Room 26. One of Freddie's fifty-strong team was a joker, referencing the secret facility in Nevada called Area 51. Despite government announcements, the public did not know what really went on at Area 51. Freddie's unit was less known, and the extent of their authority and powers were not visible to Jack, even when he assisted them.

The staff greeted Jack like a long-lost relative as he wound his way through the randomly laid-out desks to Freddie's glass cube of an office. A fifty-inch screen on a stand with wheels was in a corner. Freddie was on the phone, leaning forward, his left hand holding the phone while he wrote on a yellow pad with the other. He stopped writing, looked up, saw Jack, waved him to come in, and pointed at a chair. Jack didn't get to sit. His phone rang. Stella. Jack stepped outside Freddie's glass cube.

"Hi Jack, when are you next in San Francisco?"

"I'm in Freddie's office."

"Could you visit me after that? I could do with some help."

"Sure. When are you home?"

"I'm here now."

"I'll text you when I'm on my way."

Jack phoned Aaron, knowing he was at the vet practice with Hailey and Princess was with him. He took the time to listen to Aaron recount his nursing of each dog and how he had treated wounds and administered medication. It wasn't just that Aaron enjoyed the work. There was a happiness Jack had not heard in the brief time he'd known him. Hailey would drop him back at the ranch at about six.

Through the glass, Jack saw Freddie end his call and go back into his office, where Freddie exhaled like he was in a Tai Chi class.

"Thanks for coming, Jack. I could use someone to look at this serial killer case from a different perspective."

"Glad to help. What have you got that you haven't shown me already?"

Freddie pointed at the big screen, typed on his keyboard, and the screen blinked to life.

"We've gathered more information about each victim."

Jack turned his chair around to get a better view as Freddie took him through the nine victims. There was a summary at the end. Women in their early forties, CEO, and owner of the company, either built the company from the ground up or inherited it. All entrepreneurs. The companies and the victims were as diverse as the United Nations.

"Jack, we're looking for a pattern to help us find this guy. We can't find one. That's where I need your help."

"In the profile, it said it was a guy. Why are you sure it's a male and not a female?"

Jack had seen female MMA fighters in action. One underestimated them at your peril.

"That's just a statistic. More than ninety percent of serial killers are male. The profiler just put that in the report as the most probable. But yes, it could be a female, and if it is a female, it could explain one thing."

"What's that."

"Why the victims let the killer into their car? Maybe they were comfortable with a female."

"Maybe they got them at gunpoint somewhere and forced them into the car?" said Jack.

"Could be, but that would be a lot of exposure for the killer in getting the victim to the car. These are high-profile people going from meeting to meeting. There is usually someone with them."

Jack thought of Stella's business life. Freddie had summed it up correctly.

"And that's another thing. Most serial killers are opportunistic. For example, truck drivers pick up sex workers at truck stops. All they need to find out from the victim is if anyone would be likely to report them missing if they vanished. So why kill high-profile people? There are easier targets."

"Maybe this killer likes a challenge?"

"We've thought of that, and the profile is pretty clear the killer has issues with women. Serious issues. Obsessive. Exhibited by the elaborate lengths to chase them naked through a forest and then beat them to death." Freddie shook his head. "The profiler says this is not just a killing. It's punishment."

"What does the profiler say about them being naked?"

"He said that's all about humiliation due to our culture and norms. Suddenly being naked in that situation can be disorientating as well."

"What does the profiler say about the time difference between the killings?"

"It's about four months. Psychologists say there is a cooling-off period after a killing, as the urge has been satisfied and builds up over time until they kill again. But the profiler put forward this may not be so much a cooling-off period but preparation time, due to the nature of the victims."

"Show me the victims again in date sequence," said Jack.

Freddie typed, and the data appeared on the screen. It was like clockwork. Every four months. Jack did the math in his head from the last killing until today.

"Three months and three weeks since the last killing."

"Exactly, and we got nothing."

CHAPTER THIRTEEN

At 4 pm, Jack was seated in Stella's lounge room, looking across The Bay, listening to her explain the problem.

"At Link Industries, I'm getting a cybersecurity system installed. A standard product, but best of class. I've requested a few extra dashboards, which I've sketched out."

"Knowing you, I thought you would have had something installed long ago. And why now, have there been attacks?"

"No attacks. There is software installed, but it's outdated. I've been monitoring the system myself and picked up nothing." Stella's eyes smiled like a fox. "Maybe the hackers think we've nothing worth hacking."

Jack knew Stella was probably the best hacker he had ever encountered. There was no hacker name associated with her. She had a progressive random algorithm that arrived at a unique number each time she appeared on the web. In the folklore of hackers, they called her *Numbers*. Freddie and his team had been looking for her. But as she only operated when she needed to, then vanished, like a cyber will-of-the-wisp, they had been unsuccessful. Freddie had asked Jack to help, but he'd told them only what they knew already.

"Why then?"

"Audit report. We have a younger lead auditor this time, and it came up in our audit report that we didn't have a system in place. I don't mind. I should have done it already. The company has contracted with external consultants who install this product for a living. Their skills are good. They're just slow," she said.

"You know more about cybersecurity than I do. Why not handle this yourself?"

"First, I can't let on how much I know about cybersecurity. Second, I'm busy running Link Industries, and speaking of which, there's a company in Detroit I'm looking to buy. I need someone who knows enough about cybersecurity, can get a software implementation back on track, and someone I can trust. You. If you would be so kind." A cheeky grin and a curtsy were all it took for Jack to agree.

Stella crept onto Jack's lap like a cat stalking its prey. "And what can I do for you in return?"

Stella kissed Jack hard and leaned her body into his. They did not make it to the bedroom but romped on the sofa with the floor-to-ceiling glass presenting a picture of the sun descending on San Francisco Bay. They didn't notice the view.

By 5 pm, their heart rates had returned to normal, and they lay languid as a drooping flag.

"Remember, I told you I was at Freddie's office earlier?"

"Yes."

"He's asked me to help with that serial killer case. The one where you fit the profile of the victims, and I asked you to be more alert."

"I did listen. I have been more watchful about my surroundings and people near me."

Jack told Stella all they knew about the victims, the profiler's report on the killer, and Freddie wanted Jack to find a pattern. Time was running out, and the only pattern they had was the frequency of the killings.

"Can I help?"

"Well, I did have the beginning of an idea, but not sure where it would lead me."

"What? No suspense, please."

"Would you be able to get me a data dump of the victims, their companies, their staff, their software, the data on their servers, everything they have?"

"You know we're talking millions of rows of data."

"I know. But if I have it all, I can start looking for patterns."

"How do you plan to do this?"

"Well, as you know from your hacking, search engines use various algorithms to deliver data back to you. My process is pretty much the same. You input data, there is a sensing phase where it extracts the data features, classifies them, and then the processing begins."

"And my job is to get you the data?"

"Yes, please, and by data, I mean everything. Cause I don't know what I'm looking for."

"I'll put the data in the cloud and send you the secure link so you can start doing your magic. You have a week to find this person from what you're saying."

"That's what the profile says," said Jack, inclining his head. "Also, send me all the data from your company. I'll use that first as a baseline."

"Speaking of my company, I need to get to the airport. I have an early morning meeting with the owners of that company in Detroit I'm interested in."

"You be vigilant."

Stella put her hand on Jack's cheek. "I'll be fine, and there are far more successful women than me for your killer to go after."

Jack frowned as he held Stella by her shoulders. "You can be quite exasperating, you know. Yes, the victims have been successful women, but the profiler has not determined the other criteria the killer uses to select a victim."

"Noted, as my lawyers say. And I do like having you concerned about me. But I will be vigilant."

***

It was 7 pm when Jack crossed the rattling cattle grid to Alan's Acres. He drove along the dirt road to where he could see the outline of the barn, the bunkhouse, and the main house. Everything was in darkness. He parked outside the kitchen and walked onto the porch. Lights flickered from where he had just come. Another vehicle. He stood and waited in the dark. The vehicle drove to the barn, and he recognized Hailey's truck. He went into the house, put on the kitchen lights, and went outside to stand on the porch. Aaron waved to Jack as he went to the bunkhouse with Princess trotting at his feet. Hailey was walking to the kitchen as Jack waved back at Aaron. Hailey stepped up onto the porch.

"Sorry we're late. An emergency case just as we were closing."

"I beat you here by two minutes."

Hailey stood close to him. Well inside the normal boundaries of physical proximity. One's personal space. There was a womanly physicality and aroma about her, like an Amazon. "You also had an emergency?"

"Something like that." Jack retrieved his manners. "Can I offer you something to drink? You must have had a long day. Not much on offer, beer or wine?"

"A beer sounds good."

Jack took two Bud Lights from the fridge, popped the lids, and held one up. "Do you want it in a glass?"

"It's already in glass."

Hailey smiled, that smile that made Jack feel like the sun had warmed him. The room felt smaller, and Hailey seemed closer.

"Why don't we sit outside?" said Jack, passing a bottle to Hailey.

They sat on a brown three-seater leather sofa, cracked with wrinkles and smelling of leather conditioner. A three-foot by two-foot table made of a split log was in front of the couch. Now there were choices of where to sit. Jack took the lead and sat at one end, and Hailey could now choose the middle or the end. She chose the middle and slumped down on the sofa.

"You can put your feet on the table if you like. It looks like you had a big day."

Hailey put her sneaker-enclosed feet on the table. "Thanks, it has been a long day. Aaron has been a great help, though."

"Yes, I wanted to ask. How's he doing?"

"He has a natural gift for dealing with animals. It's pretty rare." She took another mouthful of beer.

"So, do you want to keep picking him up in the morning and dropping him off in the evening?"

"Of course. At work, Aaron's a gentle giant. The way animals respond to him is, well, I don't really have words. My dad had it. It's rare."

"That's really good to hear. My uncle will be pleased."

"We talk about football, driving there and back. It's great. You should have seen him in his heyday. He was ferocious. And fast. For such a big guy over a short distance, no one was even close to his speed. Also, he had some sixth sense of where the players would move. It was uncanny. Let me tell you one instance."

Jack watched the vibrancy of this woman, her curls moving, her mouth wide and open as she used her hands to explain a particular legend played by Aaron. She got up, beer bottle in hand, moving around the porch to explain the move. She finished the move, downed the remainder of her beer, clumped it onto the table, threw her hands in the air, and shouted, "Touchdown."

Jack smiled as he stood with his empty bottle in hand. "Can I get you another beer?"

"I'd love to, but Mum and I take turns with the cooking. Tonight is my night, and I'm already late."

She stepped forward and gave Jack a brief hug, which caught Jack by surprise. He wished it was longer. The unexpected things that happen in a single second grab your attention, like water on your face from a mountain stream. Jack watched the rear lights of her truck turn into twinkling stars as it went down the road. He stood there a moment longer. This was one of those times when the mind was thinking but not sure what it was thinking.

CHAPTER FOURTEEN

Jack knocked on the door of the Dubin's ranch house at 8 am. He had not seen Bryce and Aidan doing gardening duties, and there were two more cars than last time. A red Mustang Shelby GT500 and a white Toyota Camry.

Sarah opened the door, and they chatted about what a pleasant spring they were enjoying as they went to the Gathering Room. Peter Wasserman and his wife Hannah were seated there with Barney. They greeted Jack like the return of the prodigal son. Peter had his oxygen bottle on a trolley. Jack had coffee with them but said no to the chocolate babka. Sarah insisted he take a slice as Hannah had made it, which was one of her specialties. Jack looked at Peter, who shrugged his shoulders halfway to his ears as if to say, "What can you do?" Jack ate the babka and murmured enough to show he thought it was excellent, which it was.

Sarah wanted to know how he had progressed with Ralph. "You can speak openly in front of Peter and Hannah. They are family."

Jack gave them an overview.

"Ralph came to me yesterday," said Barney. "He's furious that Bryce and Aidan are also testing the software and that you gave them the user-name and password?"

When someone tries to block you from seeing something you thought was ordinary, you want to see it because it can't be ordinary.

"Did Ralph say why he had a problem with that?"

"He was going on about you can't go around handing out usernames and passwords without clearing it with him."

"But I've got carte blanche, haven't I?"

"Absolutely," said Sarah. "I was here when he was going on about it, and I reiterated this to him. He left in a real huff."

"As far as helping Bryce and Aidan," said Barney, "I told him that is also important. For their self-esteem. He told me he wasn't interested in their self-esteem, and I gave him a lecture after that."

"Which," said Sarah, "fell on deaf ears."

"Anyway," said Barney, with a dismissal wave of the hand, "Bryce and Aidan have been hard at work on their computers since you left them yesterday. They have set themselves up in their kitchen. It's a common area for the cottages."

"I'll check on them before I leave," said Jack. "Anything else before I go?"

"Sarah told me you wanted a copy of the accounts," said Peter as he patted a buff-colored folder on a side table. "I've completed them, and this copy's for you. It has the Income Statement and Balance Sheet."

"Thank you. Can you send me all the transactions that make up those documents or give me access to the financial system, and I'll get them myself?"

Peter smiled and looked at Barney, "I told you he'd ask for that." He pulled a scrunched pink piece of paper from his cardigan pocket and held it out for Jack, who took it from the claw-like arthritic hand. "Jack, there are some anomalies in the accounts, and I have put in comments where I've noticed them."

"Great," said Jack. "Well, let me get to work. Thank you for the coffee and wonderful cake."

"By the way, Ralph has visitors up there today," said Barney. "They came in that fancy red sports car outside."

Ralph was sitting at his desk with two men seated opposite. Same dress code. A dark blue suit, white shirt, no tie. One was more significant than the other by a good six inches in height, and shoulder width with a bald head, like an enormous potato stuck directly onto his shoulders as he had no neck. The other had slicked-back black hair with designer stubble. Baldy and Slick.

Ralph saw Jack and waved him over. Jack walked past the twins, who were sitting at a computer screen. They looked over the top of the screen at Jack but did not acknowledge him. One of them had the fingers on her left hand wiggling. The signal for a 'Problem' used by scuba divers, or was she indicating uncertainty to her twin regarding a software issue?

Today, Ralph was not for morning pleasantries like Jack's recent coffee and cake experience in the main house. "How dare you get those two gay, ex-stockbroker criminals involved in what you're doing? And you got those stupid developers of mine," Ralph pointed at the twins, and his voice rose in strength and decibels, "to give you access to the development environment."

Ralph's face had gone darker in the dim light. Sometimes it was better to keep someone angry and see where it went.

Jack smiled his best smile. The one where he didn't have a care in the world. "Good morning to you too, Ralph." And waited. Jack counted seconds in his head. He got to six when Ralph stood and moved towards Jack, his hands coming up when an arm as languid as a cat stretching reached out from Slick and put it in front of Ralph. "Sit down, Ralph, and let's discuss this with Jack." Slick looked at Jack. "You don't mind if I call you Jack?"

Up close, Slick had androgynous features, with a heart-shaped face, high cheekbones, long thick eyelashes, and the designer stubble, a declaration of masculinity. Baldy still looked like Mr. Potato Head.

"That depends on who I'm talking to."

"My name is not important. What is important is that we are friends of Ralph."

"Great. Good to know Ralph has friends."

"We want you to stop snooping into Ralph's business. It's upsetting him."

Jack looked at Ralph. "You did tell your friends who's paying me and what the job is?"

"Jack, Jack," said Slick with a smile that beckoned someone, anyone, to slap it. "We know all that. I was hoping you could just quietly stand down and stop bothering Ralph."

Slick paused like he was waiting for a reaction from Jack. There was none.

"To show I'm trying to help, I've taken the trouble of writing your report for you. Here."

Slick handed Jack a blue plastic folder. Jack took the folder and looked at it as if it was an archeological relic he was battling to understand. "If you agree to this arrangement, I will give you a very healthy bonus for a job well done. Providing, of course, as I said, you don't bother Ralph anymore."

"Well, I'll tell you what I'll do. I won't be here to bother Ralph. I'll work from home. I can do everything I need to do from there. I have all the access I need, and my Internet connection's superb."

Baldy looked like he had been processing a thought as he stood. "Maybe you need me to explain this a bit better."

"No need," said Jack. "I've finished talking."

Jack turned his back on them and walked away. As he passed the twins' desks, one of them gave the Problem signal again, or maybe it was her way of waving. He waited in the sun for four minutes to see if one or both twins wanted to talk to him. No one came, so he went to where Aidan and Bryce were working.

He put his head through their kitchen door, and they greeted him.

"You guys want to work at my place?"

It sounded like an invitation to a toddler's play date.

***

After returning to the ranch, Jack tidied up the kitchen and put on the drip coffee machine that made twelve cups. Aunt Louise had made sure proper coffee would be there for guests. This model had an automatic bean grinder on top, all loaded with beans, and one only had to press the start button.

Jack put his laptop on the table in front of the furthest chair on the right-hand side so he could see the door. Bryce and Aidan set themselves up opposite and got working. Jack had placed the mugs of coffee in front of Bryce and Aidan and was picking up his mug when he heard the rumble of a big motor. He walked out, mug in hand, onto the verandah and looked down the road leading to the gate. A red Mustang Shelby GT500 was creeping along, wiggling from side to side, so the low-slung undercarriage didn't scrape on the ground.

He recognized the car. The occupants were as expected. Ralph's friends. They got out of the car and headed towards the verandah. Slick had a dark wooden walking stick with a knob on the end that his hand could not encompass. There was no limp when Slick walked. The walking stick looked like a shillelagh, and Jack knew their original purpose was as a fighting stick when the Irish were forbidden to have weapons.

So, was this a fighting stick or a decoration? Jack held up his left hand like a traffic cop indicating stop. "You do realize you're on private property, and I definitely didn't invite you."

Slick held his hands up to his shoulders like he'd been arrested, and it seemed a gesture he'd performed before. His blue jacket lifted up and back so Jack could see the pistol on the hip in the speed holster. Not close enough to make out the brand or model. Right now, any firearm would do damage, and they were close enough that it would be difficult to miss.

"It seems I didn't really make myself clear enough in Ralph's software center. I'm now telling you to stay away from Ralph. No further involvement with Ralph or his business. Nothing."

Jack went to take a sip of his coffee, but it was too hot. "And if I don't?"

"Then my large associate next to me will beat you unconscious. I will take you to an alley in the back of a strip club in Clayton, stab you in the carotid artery and let you bleed out. Your wallet I will take and destroy. It will look like you were at the club, left to go home, and a mugging took place but went wrong."

"Sound like you've done this before," said Jack.

Slick smiled like a smug adolescent. "Maybe."

"We both heard what you said." Jack recognized Aidan's voice but didn't turn around, keeping his eyes on his unwelcome visitors. "You have made a death threat, and the last time I checked, that gets you seven years in this state."

"I'm also a witness," said Bryce. "So maybe it's best you leave before this goes any further."

Jack wished Aidan and Bryce hadn't decided to get involved when Slick drew the pistol and moved it side to side, scanning them. It looked like a Glock 19, and Slick had not racked the slide to load a round. There would be a round in the chamber, as that's what you do when you put a magazine in a Glock. Insert magazine and rack it. Or Slick had forgotten. Not enough time to do anything.

"Oh dear," said Slick, "now you've complicated things."

Slick shot Aidan in the thigh, making him grunt, grab his leg, drop the fish knife he'd been carrying, and tumble off the verandah at the feet of Slick. Bryce looked at his partner falling to the ground, and a trip switch must have gone off as he took two steps and launched himself through the air at Slick with a scream like a leopard, a chef's knife held ready to stab downwards. In mid-flight, Baldy threw a roundhouse punch into the side of Bryce's head. He was unconscious before landing at the feet of Slick, who shot Bryce in the back of his right thigh and smiled like a kid at a birthday party.

To Jack, the noise from the pistol was softer than he remembered from a Glock 19 with its nine-millimeter ammunition. The noise and the bodies piling up at Slick's feet were enough of a distraction for Jack to flick the hot coffee into Slick's eyes and step to the side as Slick screamed with his left hand on his eyes, banging his head with the knob of the shillelagh and firing four shots where Jack had been standing. That was six shots. Jack heard the hammer click as Slick tried to squeeze one more out of the barrel. Baldy moved towards Jack, picking up the fish knife next to Aidan's limp body in his left hand, the chef's knife next to Bryce's, an equally inert form in his right hand. He moved towards Jack, but Slick was in his way. Jack kept it that way, circling, keeping the whimpering Slick tottering around with his shillelagh and pistol.

Jack stepped in and wrenched the shillelagh from Slick's grasp. It was heavier than he had anticipated as he stabbed Slick in the temple with the knob end, causing him to fall in a heap between Aidan and Bryce. Jack had a nanosecond to reflect on the irony of the three on the ground before giving Baldy his undivided attention, which seemed like a good idea. Baldy thrust with the fish knife. Jack stepped back, and Baldy swung the chef's knife like a saber. He stepped back again, leaving Baldy quarter turned. Jack whacked the back of Baldy's elbow with the shillelagh. He grunted like a weightlifter as he dropped the chef's knife and did a quick shuffle to regain his balance as he opened and closed his right hand. Jack must have hit Baldy's funny bone, the ulnar nerve, which would take a minute for the hand and forearm to regain their function.

Kenny's drilling was roaring through Jack's head as he bent his legs low and spun in the opposite direction, winding the speed of the shillelagh up like an Olympic hammer-thrower, bringing it around and down to strike the middle of the right shin. There was a sound midway between a snap and a grinding pepper shaker. One of Kenny's mantras, *no legs, no fighter,* went through Jack's head as he watched Baldy fall like a dead tree, grasping at his shin.

Jack took the Glock with two fingers from Slick's grasp in case he came to and had a spare magazine squirreled away. He raced into the kitchen and came back with cable ties. He used them as tourniquets for the legs of Bryce and Aidan and hogtied the hands and feet of Baldy and Slick, ignoring the whimpering of Slick and the low moaning and deep rapid breathing of Baldy.

Jack returned to the kitchen to get his phone and looked at the Glock to read the model number. It was a Glock 44, the same size as the Glock 19, but it only fired twenty-two caliber rounds. Only. Jack realized he was making this sound like a good thing, which it was, in a way. Less damage. But a bullet in the leg is still a bullet in the leg.

Jack took photos of Baldy and Slick with the shillelagh on his chest and sent them to Freddie. Then he phoned Freddie. His first words were, "I need ambulances at the ranch for two males, both early forties, gunshot wounds to the leg in each case. These are not the two in the photo. Phone me back when done."

Jack rarely spoke to Freddie like he was giving an order, but it was expedient in this case, and Freddie would not take offense. He knew Jack would only do this if there was a real need. The phone rang in under five minutes. Freddie.

"Two ambulances, a doctor, and police officers are coming from The Farm. They're already rolling. Should be there in a few minutes. What's going on there?"

As Jack filled Freddie in on what had led up to this and what had happened, Jack could hear sirens getting closer.

"And those two photos you sent through," said Freddie. "We know them. Chat later."

CHAPTER FIFTEEN

By 1 pm, the people from The Farm had collected Bryce, Aidan, Slick, Baldy, the Glock, and the Mustang and taken them back to The Farm. Alan's Acres was as peaceful as a sleeping child. The people from The Farm had taken their photos and what blood samples they could get. The blood of Bryce and Aidan was a shrinking stain on the dirt as Jack sprinkled it with dirt. It helped fill in the time as he waited for Freddie to phone back. Jack had questions.

Twenty-seven minutes later, Freddie called. "Your friends and the two bad guys are in the medical wing at The Farm, and the only difference is the bad guys are fitted with handcuffs and ankle cuffs and manacled to the bed."

"Who are the bad guys?"

"They're from the Doyle crime family. The one you photographed with the shillelagh is Liam, the only son of the head of the family. The big guy is muscle, but he's just one of many they use for their activities. Drugs, prostitution, protection, loan sharking, money laundering."

"A diverse enterprise." Jack frowned and paused for four seconds. "But why would they be interested in a software company?"

"Good question. But our intel has picked up that a year back, they started buying tanneries. Not big ones, small ones."

"That's about when Ralph first had the idea of a leather trading platform."

"Can you join the dots on what's the connection?"

"Not at the moment."

"If you can get Ralph's financial records, that could help. I don't have probable cause to get them." Freddie huffed.

Jack looked at the kitchen table, where the buff-colored folder Peter had given him lay unopened. "I'll see what I can do."

"Speaking of joining the dots, do you have any update for me on the serial killer?"

Jack cringed inwardly like a kid caught not doing his homework. He hadn't checked what data Stella had put in the Cloud for him. And speaking of Stella, there was a need to check she wasn't putting herself at risk anywhere. As for her software project, he hadn't looked into that either.

"Not just yet, still collecting data."

"I'm going to send someone as security to the ranch until further notice. The head of the Doyle family won't be happy with what you've done."

"What's his name?"

Freddie laughed. "A bit sexist there, Jack? It's a her, not a him. Her name's Clodagh. Clodagh Doyle. She looks and speaks like she could be one of Mom's friends."

"Is there a Mr. Doyle?"

"Nope. Never married. Doyle's her family name. Let me tell you what we know. The business started with her grandfather, who owned one saloon. Her father expanded it into the criminal activities I just mentioned. She was an only child but got pregnant when she was eighteen.

The rest is rumor and gossip. It's unclear whether the pregnancy was due to consensual sex or rape. The children's father started beating her up one day while she was pregnant. The story goes that she was in the kitchen when this happened, grabbed a steak knife that was on the countertop, and repeatedly stabbed him until he was dead. Even after he was dead, she kept stabbing him. Her father got rid of the body. What we do know is that we don't know who he was. Nobody ever came and filed a missing person's report. She took over the business after her father died peacefully in his sleep, which is unusual for a gangster."

The sounds of keyboard keys clicking echoed down the line, then Freddie spoke.

"Her gang is all family members and people she has taken under her wing. She pays for their kids' schooling and medical expenses, ensures they all get three meals a day, have decent accommodation, and gives them loans as deposits for a house or a car. They all live within a few blocks from the bar she operates out of in the Tenderloin. It's the kingdom of Clodagh Doyle. The gang members are fiercely loyal to her and carry at least one weapon. She has a reputation for vengeance if slighted, and retribution is violent."

The word retribution made Jack think of Ralph while trying to keep the dark thing at the base of his spine in its cave.

Freddie inhaled and exhaled like a diver surfacing. "She'll come after you."

***

Jack's anger had turned into wrath, one of the seven deadly sins, as he drove to the Dubin ranch. It was like a heartbeat felt throughout his body. He did his breathing exercises to gain control, and the fury turned into an ice-like calm as he parked his truck in front of Ralph's office. He went through the door and towards Ralph's desk, where he sat at his screen. The twins saw him and wiggled their fingers like sea anemones with the Problem signal. As Jack approached, Ralph stood and came around the desk with a smirk that was drifting towards a sneer, holding out a collection of papers. "I trust now that my friends have chatted with you, you will submit this report to my parents and then vanish?"

At two steps away, Jack pointed at the ceiling and looked up. Ralph's gaze followed like a puppet on a string. Jack closed the gap and hit Ralph with a right uppercut to the stomach, hips twisting to add force to the punch, driving up into Ralph's solar plexus, which stopped sending nerve impulses to the diaphragm. There would be no cuts, abrasions, or bruises.

Ralph dropped to the floor in the fetal position, trying to suck in air, but failing. When he could gasp great lungfuls of air, Jack offered his left hand and helped him to his feet where he stood, hands-on-hips, breathing so hard he couldn't speak. Jack punched him again in the stomach, driving up into his solar plexus, and down he went. Second verse same as the first.

Jack waited and offered his left hand to help him up. Ralph was not interested and waved it away.

Jack took a step back. Ralph crawled across the floor to his chair, clawed his way up, and flopped into it like a sack of potatoes, his eyes on Jack, who took a step towards Ralph. "Start the App that runs the CCTV footage and show me the last ten minutes."

Ralph hesitated. Jack grabbed Ralph's ear, twisted it, and took a step back, pulling Ralph's ear towards his hip. Ralph's head followed his ear until his chair skidded out from under him and fell to the floor with Jack still holding his twisted ear.

"Let's try that again, Ralph. Get up on your chair and show me the last ten minutes of CCTV footage."

Ralph was compliant and showed Jack. "Now, Ralph, delete everything for today."

Ralph complied but had a smirk on his face. "Next step, show me the backup."

Ralph's smirk shrunk away. "There is no backup."

Jack pulled Ralph off his chair by his ear and then assisted him back to the chair the same way.

"The backup, Ralph."

Ralph typed away to reveal the backup for the day. "Delete it, Ralph."

Ralph did it. Jack let go of Ralph's ear and let him flop back into his chair, holding onto his ear, frowning, and grimacing, his eyes shut in hopes of making the pain disappear. Which doesn't work.

"Look at me."

Ralph's eyes opened as slits. Wary, like a fox, keeping vigilant for what may cause pain or worse.

"Let me give you an update since we last met. Jenny, Janey, come over here. You need to hear this as well."

The twins scampered over and sat on the chairs opposite Ralph's desk. Jack stood at the end of the desk to see all three and gave them the short version. As the tale unfolded, Ralph looked Jack up and down like he was seeing him for the first time. The twins each had a hand to their mouth as if this would keep out what they were hearing.

"What are you doing with the Doyle family?"

Ralph's eyes went from slit to round. "How do you know who they are?"

"Doesn't matter. I know. Now answer me."

"They're investors. That's all."

"You mean in the same way they invest in drugs and prostitution?"

Ralph swallowed and nibbled on a fingernail, blinking two beats per second while watching Jack. "I'm dating the daughter."

It came out in a rush. Then he sat still as if he'd confessed to a priest and was now free of sin.

Jack waited for five seconds as the implications of this ran scenarios through his head.

"Is that who she is?" said Jenny.

"She's lovely, as well as beautiful," said Janey.

"Shut up, you two," said Ralph.

Jack spun on Ralph. "No. You shut up until I ask you a question."

Jack turned his attention to the twins. "Where did you meet her?"

"She's been here sometimes when we get to work," said Janey.

Jack turned to Ralph. "You're sleeping with the daughter of a known gangster?"

"I didn't know who her mother was. I'd had a meeting in a club with people in the leather industry, and I'd noticed her in the crowd when I arrived. It was a successful meeting. You don't need to hear the details."

"It's a great story," said Janey. "Sinead told us."

"That's her name," said Jenny. "Sinead."

More information is always better than less information. Never know when it could be helpful. "I'd like to hear the story."

The twins looked at each other. "You tell the story," said Jenny.

"Ralph is quite the smooth operator when it comes to the ladies. He sometimes takes us to the clubs where we have to pretend we're his sisters so the ladies don't feel threatened. I mean, think about it. He must be a decent guy if he takes his sisters to a club. Right? And he has lots of great lines. So, with Sinead, he sent her over a drink. She brought it back to the table, thanked him very politely, and told him she had a boyfriend. He says, 'that's fine, but can I ask a question?' She says, 'Sure.' He's not pushy. He asks her what she had for dinner last night. She is surprised at the question but answers, 'Pasta.' And the night before? She answers, 'Pasta.' Ralph then hands her his card and says, 'When you get sick of pasta, send me a message.' And then he exits the club leaving her standing there."

Jenny leaped into the conversation. "Three days later, at lunchtime, she texted him and said she was tired of pasta. Ralph told us we would be going home early. But the next morning, she was here. We had coffee with her while Ralph made phone calls and handled emails at this desk. She's very nice and quite beautiful, even without makeup."

Jack nodded at the end of the story and looked at Ralph. "So, how did her brother get interested in your business?"

"Sinead wanted me to meet her mother as '*all this sneaking around had to stop*'. I met her at this bar she owns, and she asked me what I did for a living. She was interested and asked lots of good questions, especially about the state of my business. She's a bright lady."

"And where does the brother fit in?"

"He was there when I met the mother. It seemed I needed his approval as well. About a week later, Liam invited me back to the bar." Ralph breathed in. "He knew what was required to get a software business up and going beyond the application programming, server setup, and management. He asked me what I was doing about branding, marketing, customer support, and the one everyone overlooks, operations. Mine was becoming a money pit."

"What about the funds your parents gave you?"

"I'd burned through that already. I needed cash to keep going. I couldn't let my parents down. Liam said they wanted to invest, and nobody else was interested, so I agreed."

"This was about the same time as they started buying tanneries."

Ralph's face was like a stunned fish. "How would you know that?"

"Doesn't matter. I do. So, tell me about the tanneries."

"Nothing sinister about it. Liam explained to his mother that tanneries, small ones, those in financial trouble, would be a good investment."

Maybe a good place to launder money from the other Doyle enterprises. Just need to sell the finished product.

"Liam trades their hides on my platform. Again, nothing sinister."

"If, as you say, there's nothing sinister, why would he threaten me and shoot Bryce and Aidan?"

Ralph shrugged as if he did not know the answer but then made an attempt. "Anyone in the family is very protective of the family, and they see me as part of that. It seems, to me, it just got out of hand."

"Out of hand?"

"That's what I'm thinking. As I wasn't there. Being overly protective."

"Do your parents know about any of this?"

"Are you kidding? Of course not."

"Then how do I explain why Bryce and Aidan got shot?"

"I have no idea. That's your problem."

"Think again, Ralph. If you're genuinely in love with Sinead."

Ralph interjected like a member of Congress. "Which I am."

"Let me finish. Do you plan to marry?"

"We haven't discussed it, but yes."

"Your parents are lovely people. How do you plan to break the news to them that you're planning on marrying the daughter of a known criminal?"

"I don't have a plan. For the moment, I just live one day at a time."

Jack's phone rang. Freddie. He walked to the door and answered as he stepped outside.

"The Farm had to release Liam Doyle and the muscle from custody," said Freddie. "Their lawyer said that Bryce and Aidan had knives, and his clients felt their lives were in danger." Jack started to speak, but Freddie cut him off. "It's ridiculous, I know. Their lawyer's top drawer. So, for now, we roll with the punch."

Jack had to agree with Freddie as he continued.

"Their lawyer was making noises about laying a charge on you. Grievous bodily harm. But they got talked out of that idea." Freddie could change direction like a quarter horse in a barrel race. "Any luck with finding the serial killer?"

"I'll work on it when I get back to the ranch." Stella had not returned his call. Probably in a meeting, but anxiety has a habit of behaving like tiny bubbles when water first shows signs of boiling. The word, expedite, blinked like hazard lights.

"Freddie, is it within the extent of your powers to get Bryce and Aidan released to me?"

"On what grounds?"

"The Dubins are elderly, and it is unfair to burden them with the responsibility of looking after them. How does that sound?"

"It could be enough. Why do you really want them?"

"They got shot while they were with me. I feel guilty and haven't told the Dubins that they're in a prison hospital with gunshot wounds. I'm hoping The Farm could release them to me, and they could convalesce at the Ranch."

Freddie went quiet, which Jack knew was Freddie processing his options, so he threw something into the mix he'd been thinking about and knew would get Freddie's attention.

"I want them to work on the serial killer case with me as well as Ralph's software company."

"I'll see what I can do."

CHAPTER SIXTEEN

Jack returned to the studio, where Ralph sat at his desk, mumbling into his phone. As Jack got to the desk, he ended the call, leaned back in his chair, and looked at Jack.

"That was Clodagh Doyle. Very unhappy. Clodagh wants me in San Francisco for a meeting." Ralph had a grin on his face like a rat who'd just stolen all the cheese. "I'd grow eyes in the back of my head if I was you."

Jack watched as Ralph left the studio, leaving him and the twins looking at each other.

"You've been flashing the 'Problem' signal at me, or do you have a funny way of waving?"

"We need to talk to you," said Janey.

"Even before you arrived on the scene, we've been thinking about leaving," said Jenny. "But now you are here, we want to get out of here, and maybe you can help us."

"Why? I was under the impression you enjoyed the work. The working conditions seem good. What is it? Ralph doesn't pay you enough?"

"We get paid more than double the going rate, even for a top-notch developer," said Janey. "We're in way over our heads. We're pretty sure Ralph and Liam are doing something illegal with the platform, but we don't know what."

"Why not?" said Jack. "You wrote the software."

"The system is developed as many components."

"That's standard practice. How else would you manage the complexity unless you break it down into manageable parts?"

"Yes, we know that, but we don't know how these software components are integrated. What I can tell you, though, is that the architecture we built has a two-level structure. So, you can place the components at the end-user level, that is, what the customer would see, or at a deeper level like a system administrator would use."

"Again, standard practice." Jack shrugged.

"Agreed, but some of the components we built enable the manipulation of the data, and this definitely would not be at the end-user level."

"I would pick this up when I looked at the components, wouldn't I?"

"Not unless you went through every line of code. Each component's identity is a number. There is no description."

"So, who knows what each component does?"

"We do, Ralph does," said Janey, who picked up a pink cardboard folder and passed it to Jack. "And now you."

Jack opened the folder and flipped through the first few pages. One column with a number, next to it a description. "Who controls what components go where?"

"Ralph does. He built his own module to do this. Nothing to do with us."

"How do I get access to that?"

"We don't know. The only way would be if someone could hack into the system."

Jack pulled out his phone to see if Stella had phoned. Nothing.

"Why are you telling me this now?"

"Because if it comes out that Ralph is doing something illegal, then we would be accessories to whatever crime he's committing."

"Why are you so sure there is a crime?"

"Two things."

Jack's phone rang. Kenny. Jack stepped away from the twins. There were no preliminaries to the conversation, Kenny's way of saying it was urgent. "Those two guys, Bryce and Aidan, Freddie's made arrangements. The Farm will deliver them to you, and you will be their new guardian."

"Great. I'm at the Dubin's place. I'll collect their things and bring them with me."

"And if you can stand my company for a few days, I'd like to come and visit you."

Jack went quiet as he realized Kenny was to be his babysitter.

"The Doyles are bad, Jack."

"You're always welcome, Kenny. When will I see you?"

"Before sunset." Kenny rang off.

Jack turned to the twins. "Now, about those two things."

Jenny started in like there had not been an interruption.

"There are only a few components we have written at the user level. The others, the ones where you can manipulate data, must be residing in the administrator level."

"So, if, as you say, Ralph is manipulating the data, when is he doing this, and why is he doing it?"

"Don't know and don't know."

"What's the other thing?"

"Ralph's company pays us a small sum each month," said Jenny.

"But you just said you are well paid."

"The rest, we get in cash."

"How do you get it?"

"One of Ralph's people, mostly a different one each time, brings it to us at the hotel in a pizza box, but there's no pizza. Just two Ziplock bags with cash."

"So long as you declare the cash, there's nothing wrong with that."

"There's the problem. We haven't. The first few payments we spent on clothes, shoes, and freediving equipment. But now we're sitting on, which for us, is a lot of cash. So, you see, this has become like a perfect storm. All we want to do now is pack up and go to Laguna Beach. There's a great place there for free diving. But we want someone to know we're not involved in any illegal activities of Ralph's. And you came along, so it's you."

"Thanks, guys."

"You're most welcome," said Janey.

"When do you plan to leave?"

"Well, now that you know, we can leave anytime. Just got to pack our bags, sell this car, get an SUV, load our dive kit and drive."

"Sounds simple enough."

"We want to simply vanish for now. This is probably the last time we'll see you."

With that, they got in their car and drove away. Jack watched the car's rear as he thought someone had to tell the Dubins what had happened. Or a version of what happened. As Jack walked to the main house, he ran plausible scenarios through his head.

***

In the Gathering Room, Barney and Sarah were having coffee. They invited Jack to sit on the sofa, which was difficult to leave. Barney poured Jack coffee while Sarah glided like a swan to the kitchen to get Jack a slice of what they were having. Coffee cake. Sarah returned with the brown portion on a porcelain plate with a fork. Sarah said he must try it before he spoke. Jack knew the recipe as Aunt Louise made it sometimes. Kenny would approve of the walnuts, pecans, cinnamon, and eggs, but the brown sugar, flour, and chocolate chips would ensure the cake did not get onto Kenny's table.

"This is very good, Sarah. My Aunt Louise makes this, but there's something in it which she does not use."

Sarah smiled. Her face seemed to take on a warm glow from the simple pleasure of doing good. "Raisins. I use raisins as well."

"That's it. That's the taste. May I share your secret with my aunt?"

"Of course. I'd be delighted. Now, what did you want to see us about?"

"Nothing major. Bryce and Aidan have asked if they can stay at Alan's Acres. I'm happy with that, as it means we'll have more time together to check out Ralph's software. If you're happy with that, I'll contact The Farm and make the arrangements."

The Dubins looked at each other without any change of expression. It was Barney who replied. "That's fine. Whatever is good for them."

Jack thought getting shot in the leg was not good for them.

How long before they'd walk normally again?

"I'll pack their things, and you can take them with you," said Sarah.

Somehow, knowing these people had the Doyles almost on their doorstep, thanks to Ralph, left him with a sense of unease.

Was leaving them in ignorance better than ruining their day?

How many times had he seen people not clean up their mess but close their minds until it all came undone, and you watched where the pieces fall on the guilty and the innocent?

***

At the kitchen table, Jack read the financial statements Peter had given him and the notes written in a copperplate style. He must have used a fountain pen. Twice he'd phoned Stella. She was most probably in a meeting. Jack was making notes on Peter's notes, thinking he needed to call him to discuss. But knowing what he now knew about Ralph's operation and involvement with the Doyles, these notes weren't a surprise.

The weapons cabinet was open, displaying the Remington 700 rifle chambered to 223 and the Remington 870 shotgun loaded with 12-gauge shells. Both had internally loaded magazines with five cartridges, and the safeties were off. These were hunting equipment, not military-grade weapons.

His phone rang. Stella. He inhaled and let it escape like he was meditating. "I got so many missed calls from you. I'm assuming you missed me. Will I see you tonight?"

He heard the rumble of vehicles and stood, looking through the kitchen door. A cavalcade of three had just come through the gate. "I just wanted to check you were safe." It was too far to recognize the vehicles.

"Of course, I'm safe. You must come over and see how safe I am."

"That's tempting, but something's come up." Jack pulled the shotgun barrel free of its clamps, letting the butt rest on the cabinet's floor. "Can I call you back? There's something I need to attend to."

Jack watched as Hailey's truck came into view, with Aaron in the passenger seat. Kenny's truck was behind it. The third vehicle was long and low. It had revolving flashing lights on the roof with a sign saying, Ambulance. Jack pushed the shotgun barrel back into its clamps and closed the steel cabinet and cupboard door. Just your average kitchen.

Outside, Kenny and Aaron were greeting each other like long-lost pals. The ambulance guy got out, looked across at Kenny and Aaron, and said, without looking at Jack. "Is that Aaron Brown?"

"It sure is."

The ambulance driver took off and had his hand out thirty feet before getting to Aaron. Hailey appeared next to Jack and rubbed his upper arm, which felt better from her touch. "Busy here today? What's with the ambulance?"

Jack talked as he walked to the back of the ambulance. "I've got two more visitors."

Jack opened the door, and Bryce and Aidan were lying on benches holding forearm crutches. They struggled up to a seating position. "Hi guys, you're looking much better than the last time I saw you."

They laughed. Hailey looked from one to the other.

"Definitely," said Aidan.

Jack looked at them. They looked like they were going on holiday except for the prison clothes. "Just stay here for a minute, guys, while I sort out a few things."

"Will do," said Bryce. "We're not in a hurry."

Jack needed to talk to Aaron. He turned and bumped into Hailey, almost falling, grabbing her, and stumbling around as he regained footing.

"Is that your idea of dancing, Jack?"

"Come with me. I need to explain a few things."

Jack left Kenny with the ambulance driver and took Aaron and Hailey towards the barn, out of earshot of Aidan and Bryce, and gave them an update on what had happened, leaving nothing out.

"Hailey, if you don't want to come here anymore," said Jack, "that's fine. I understand. Aaron, the same goes for you. I can speak to Uncle Alan and arrange for you to stay someplace else and get you there."

Aaron picked up Princess and held her in his arms. "Princess and I are not planning on going anywhere."

"For me," said Hailey, "it'll be business as usual."

"Alright," said Jack. "Now, about Aidan and Bryc." San Franciso was probably the gay capital of the world, and diversity was part of its culture. Still, Jack did not know if Hailey and Aaron held these views, so better to put it out there that this is the way it is. "They're gay and legally married."

Hailey shrugged. "Other people's personal choices are of no consequence in my life. But nice to hear they got married."

"There are gay players in the NFL," said Aaron. "They're quite open. What Hailey said is correct. In the NFL, we all just went out onto the field and got the job done."

"Ok," said Jack. "Let's get these guys out of the ambulance and settled in their room."

The ambulance guy raised the tail-lift so Bryce and Aidan could shuffle onto the platform. He lowered it, and the two patients walked off the platform like stick insects and towards the kitchen. Hailey walked behind them, inspecting their gait like they were horses. "Jack, these guys shouldn't be walking. Aaron, can you please put them in the kitchen? I want to see their dressings."

Aaron nodded, scooped up Aidan as he was the closest, one arm under his legs and the other under his back, carried him like a baby to the kitchen, and did the same with Bryce. She had them drop their trousers and inspected the dressings. There was leakage seeping through the gauze. Hailey went to her truck and returned with antiseptic, cotton wool, bandages, and an ointment that had a picture of a horse on it. After re-bandaging, Aaron carried them to the room Jack indicated. There was the thumping sound of footsteps on the roof. Jack went outside. He had to step well away from the house to see Kenny up on the top with a knapsack.

Stella. Jack had to phone her back. It took three rings for her to answer. "You seem awfully busy, Jack. I thought you would be relaxing there on the ranch."

Jack looked at the rear of the ambulance as it drove away. "Not quite.

I need to update you." Being this was Stella, Jack held nothing back in telling the events to date.

"Wow, Jack, my software issues are insignificant compared to this."

"I'll attend to those as well."

"I'd already told the development team that you were coming. That seemed to put the spurs into them. They're performing a lot better. It's looking good from the feedback sessions I've had and what they've shown me."

"If it's going better now, do I still need to come there and have a look?"

"Oh, definitely. I want this software in production."

Jack was thinking about tomorrow, looking at Kenny on the roof. Marvelous how thoughts trickled like water down a mountainside, then two came together to form a bigger trickle. Jack needed to talk to Kenny.

"If I get to your office about 3 pm, would that be ok?"

"That'd be perfect. I'll tell them you're coming. Will you come to my place after that?"

"Only if I'm invited."

Stella laughed. A throaty sound that belonged in a bedroom.

"You, good sir, are officially invited."

CHAPTER SEVENTEEN

Kenny had put his knapsack on the kitchen table and gone back out to his truck. He returned carrying a rifle case in his left hand and three tubular, eighteen-inch-long by six-inch diameter soft bags. He had his police-issue Sig Sauer 40 in its holster, the gun belt on his shoulder.

The rifle case he put on the floor. The soft tubular cases he placed on the table. He hung the gun belt over a chair. From the knapsack, Kenny pulled out a laptop and fired it up. Two images in shades of gray, black, and white were moving across the screen.

"That," said Kenny, "is Aaron. And that moving on the ground next to him would be Princess. What you're looking at is military-grade infra-red thermal sensing equipment. It's good for two miles. You'll even see the cars driving past the entrance. I mean, you'll see the hot parts, the engine, the tires, the brakes. The glass in the windows reflects infrared, and the steel body will allow a weaker picture to come through. Any combatants you'll see once they get out of the vehicle."

"Combatants?" said Hailey. "What if it's just me to pick up Aaron?"

"Good question, Hailey," said Kenny. "How to tell friend from foe?"

Kenny went out to his truck, was gone for five minutes, and came back with a twelve-inch square box, three inches deep, put it on the table, and retrieved an item from inside it. It was a one-inch camo-green plastic semi-sphere with a surrounding sucker attachment. "Back to your question Hailey." Kenny pointed at the screen. "Look at my truck."

Above where Kenny's head would be, were three dots in a straight line about one inch apart. Kenny opened his hand like a magician. "This is a military-grade infrared emitting device. I want three in your truck, where I put mine, and Jack, the same with you."

Kenny gave Hailey and Jack three each. They went outside, fitted them, and returned to the screen. It was clear. Three dots above head height in each truck.

"Thanks, Kenny," said Hailey. "I need to get going."

"I'll walk you to your truck," said Jack.

Twilight was gone as they walked to Hailey's truck. The atmosphere was balmy, like being wrapped in a light blanket.

At the truck, Jack reached for the door handle to open it for her but didn't. "Listen, Hailey. You don't need to put yourself at risk here. This is my problem. Maybe best if you didn't fetch Aaron for a few days until I sort this out."

Hailey seemed to become closer to Jack without moving her feet. At the same height, her face was now six inches away. There was an electricity as intangible as the air in the space between them.

"With all the tech-wizardry and the firepower, I'm sure we'll be safe. Besides, I need Aaron at the practice. And I like coming here." Hailey leaned forward and kissed Jack on the mouth for six seconds, spun around, got in her truck, and drove off, wheels spinning. Jack sidestepped to avoid the dust. Sometimes things came from nowhere, like shooting stars and unexpected gifts at Christmas.

Jack walked back into the kitchen.

"Hailey really shouldn't be here," said Kenny.

"I know. I just spoke to her about it."

"And?"

Jack rubbed his lips with his fingers. "She was adamant she wants to keep coming to fetch Aaron."

"Ok then. At least we have a good defensive perimeter." Kenny pointed at the screen.

"Defensive. Can we talk about that?"

"Sure."

"Remember, in our training. You always preached that a good defense is a good offense."

Kenny smiled. "Preached is a bit strong, but yes, I did say that. Why?"

"I want to meet with Clodagh Doyle."

Kenny's face was like the sphinx as he processed what Jack had proposed. "Take the fight to the enemy. Not a bad plan. There's a risk, of course, but you know that. You could be handing yourself over to her on a platter."

Jack started to speak. Kenny's raised hand stopped him. "It's a good plan. Let's do it."

"There was no us in my plan."

"I'll come along for the ride. Gives me a chance to meet Clodagh Doyle without a warrant."

***

The pub was green and glass, not dark green, the lighter shade, the color on the Irish flag. Inside the bar was dark wood, and Irish memorabilia covered the walls. The lunchtime crowd with jobs had left, and the remaining few seemed to have nowhere else to go. Kenny was sitting in a booth facing the door, sipping on something. Jack knew it would be non-alcoholic and non-sugar, which would have narrowed the choices for this bar. The barman took the glasses out of the dishwasher and put them on a rack to dry and cool. He had black pants, a white shirt, and a green waistcoat, the color of the green on the Irish flag.

Out of the corner of his mouth came an Irish accent. "What can I get for you?"

"Nothing. Is Clodagh Doyle in?"

"What do you want with Clodagh?"

"I'm here to return her son's walking stick." Jack raised the stick to show he had it.

The barman stopped and looked at the walking stick like it was the Holy Grail. "Wait here. Jimmy, keep an eye on the bar for me. I'm going to see Clodagh."

"Awright," said a man, pushing his way out of another booth where there were cards. It looked like Solitaire. Clearly a slow day at the office. He had the same uniform as the barman, but this was custom-made to accommodate a body two inches taller than Aaron and fifty pounds heavier. His night-black hair was a two-inch tall brush cut, and he was clean-shaven. He walked behind the bar, stood, seemed to realize he should do something, reached under the counter, found a damp cloth, and started wiping down the bar.

Kenny moved out from the booth and over to stand next to Jack. The barman returned, giving Kenny a confused look, like he was working on a crossword.

"A friend," said Jack.

"Ok, follow me."

They walked behind the bar through an industrial stainless-steel kitchen to a door of the same material. They walked into an office that would have suited the CEO of a large corporation. The smell of sandalwood came from an incense burner on the five-foot-long mahogany desk that faced the door. A laptop was peeping out from behind a vase of pink carnations. To the left of the desk was a standup piano with ornate woodwork, and next to it was a wooden rocking chair with cushions covered in material the color of mud. It had a hundred years of chips and scratches, but the fabric looked new. A two feet wide and three feet tall picture of two people hung on the wall above the chair. Jack recognized Liam. The woman standing next to him wasn't just beautiful. She had classic looks like a movie star from the golden years of Hollywood. To the right of the picture was a floor-to-ceiling bookshelf with some books, but mainly bric-a-brac, which had the look of mementos. More to do with memories than beauty.

On the right was a staircase against the wall. They followed the barman up the stairs to a door leading to another door six feet away, which led into a conservatory some twenty-five feet by forty feet on the roof. The sun came through the glass ceiling, making patterns on the mist, migrating like clouds. They followed the barman to a woman in workman's jeans, boots, orange rubber gloves, and a plaid shirt, trimming with gardening scissors the red flowers of a plant. A man with the physique of a gorilla, dressed the same as the woman, was holding a bag with his fingertips. On the side, it said, 'Compost, fifty pounds'. He did not watch them approach. His attention was on the woman like he was waiting for an instruction, which maybe he was.

"Clodagh," said the barman, "sorry to disturb you. This is the fellow with Liam's walking stick, and this is his friend."

The woman stopped trimming, stood, and turned to look at Jack. It was clear she was the mother of the woman in the picture. Jack guessed her to be five foot two inches tall, one hundred and twenty pounds, north of fifty years and south of sixty, somewhere in the middle. Her blond hair would fall to her shoulders when it was out of the ponytail. She took in Jack like she was drinking water. When it seemed she'd had her fill, she laughed. It was a raucous sound like a crow. She clapped, the dirt flicking off her gloves as she kept clapping.

"So, you're the guy who cracked Fergal's shin and took Liam's walking stick. Liam had a gun. How'd you do that? Liam and Fergal are too embarrassed to tell me the details. What's your name?"

"I'm Jack, and this is Kenny." There was no offering of hands. "This is a beautiful garden you have here, Clodagh."

"First, thank you. Have you ever been to Singapore's Changi Airport? The gardens there gave me the idea."

"I have, and yes, I have seen the gardens. Spectacular."

"But challenging to raise a garden to that standard. I now have this app on my phone that tells me how much water each plant needs each day."

"Nothing like a little technology to help, Clodagh."

"Second, it's Miss Doyle to you."

"My apologies."

Clodagh pointed her left hand at Kenny. "You look familiar."

"I've got a common enough face. I get that a lot."

"A comedian. Don't worry. It'll come to me."

Clodagh held out her gloved hands to the barman, who grabbed them by the fingertips and slipped them off. Jack held out the walking stick, and Clodagh took it. "You're either brave or stupid in coming here."

"I came here to talk to you before things got out of hand."

"Well, now, a talker as well as a fighter. But as you've returned with my son's walking stick, I'll listen before I decide what to do with you. Let me shower and change. You can wait in my office. Can I organize something to drink, just to show I'm not inhospitable? Coffee, tea, beer, Irish Whiskey?"

"We're fine," said Kenny.

"Ah, so the big fellow speaks." Clodagh stared at Kenny for two seconds, then shook her head. "It'll come to me where I know you from."

***

134

Jack and Kenny sat in the visitors' chairs for ten minutes under the gaze of the big, tall man who was still behind the bar from when they followed the barman to Clodagh. Up close, he had a face that could have gotten him a job as the leading man in a movie, except it was super-sized, like a hamburger. He was immobile and expressionless. An obelisk dressed in black pants, a white shirt, and a green waistcoat.

Clodagh arrived in black pants, a white blouse with ruffles, and black shoes, which did not increase her height. She wore pink lipstick the same color as the carnations and shook a transparent, plastic hand-held mixer. The yellow of a raw egg yolk moved like a balloon amongst a viscous green fluid, like pond scum, until it faded, making the green turn into chartreuse.

She sat behind her desk, pulled a coaster out of a drawer, stood the mixer on top, leaned back in the leather chair which matched the desk, and noticed they were watching her mixer.

"Kale and a raw egg. I'm a runner. Ok, Jack. You came here to talk. Talk."

"Your guys came looking for a fight."

Clodagh didn't change her posture, but her blue eyes took on a shade you only find in polar regions. "From what I heard, they came to tell you to mind your own business and stay away from Ralph and his business. Which, if the message didn't get through that time, then I'm telling you now."

Jack held her gaze and composure and slowed down his speaking voice. "I'm afraid, Clodagh, I've got a job to do. So I can't do that."

"That's too bad. Because you will stop snooping into Ralph's business, I'll see to that."

"That sounds like a threat," said Kenny.

Clodagh studied Kenny's face. "It's bothering me where I've seen you before. No, it's not a threat. Think of me as someone with mystical powers who can see the future."

"That's quite a gift," said Kenny. "But tell me, why are you so keen to stop us from looking into Ralph's business? It can't be just because he's going out with your daughter."

"My reasons are my reasons."

"Your daughter is a beautiful young woman, and Liam's a good-looking guy," said Kenny as he pointed at the painting. "Plain to see where they got their looks from."

Clodagh turned to the painting, her face a mixture of rapture and sadness, like she was staring at Jesus on the Cross in a cathedral. Kenny had interrogated many people and could change his tone and voice to suit the moment. His voice softened, and he spoke like he was the shoulder on which you could rest your head, and all the bad stuff would disappear. "We just wanted to agree that there will be no retaliation, so no one gets hurt on either side."

Jack was unsure if Clodagh was listening as she stared at the painting. Kenny signaled to Jack to wait by slightly raising his right hand. One of Kenny's mantras. Waiting can be a strategy. Clodagh looked at the picture for another minute, then shook her head and rolled her shoulders like a boxer. She blinked a few times like specks of dust had found their way into her eyes, took a sip of her shake, and looked at Jimmy.

"Jimmy, can you show these two what we do with people who interfere in our business?"

Jimmy stood, looking to Clodagh for direction. She pointed at Jack and Kenny. "These two, Jimmy."

Kenny held up his hand to Jimmy like a traffic cop. "Hold on there, Jimmy. I just got to show Miss Doyle something."

Jimmy was hearing conflicting messages and stopped, not knowing what to do. Kenny reached into his hip pocket, pulled out his wallet, flipped it open, and leaned over the desk so Clodagh could see his SFPD badge. Clodagh didn't lean forward, read the badge from where she sat and laughed.

"Kenny Brathwaite. Now I know where I know you from. A few years back, you used to be an MMA fighter. A good one. Heavyweight division. So, did you go soft and join the SFPD? Jimmy, sit down."

Kenny did not reply. Jimmy sat down.

"I came here," said Jack, "to return Liam's walking stick and see if we can agree that there will be no retaliation. Or else we'll have to defend ourselves."

Clodagh locked eyes with Jack. "Go. Just go." She signaled to Jimmy to follow them out.

Jack and Kenny walked out of the office, through the bar, and into the afternoon sunlight. Jimmy stopped at the doorway as they continued down the street. Kenny never walked fast or slow. A pace designed to fit in with the flow of the crowd. Helpful in following someone, but Kenny had disadvantages with his size and hair. He could wear a cap for the red hair, but the bulk would still be there.

"What do you think, Kenny?"

Kenny turned his head to Jack. "She's coming after you. But it won't be today."

CHAPTER EIGHTEEN

After 5 pm, Jack put his truck next to Stella's Mercedes. He closed the garage door, walked into the kitchen, and heard Stella talking in the living room with its views across The Bay. She was pacing, bare-footed, wearing her diaphanous robe, the afternoon sun highlighting her naked body underneath, talking on her mobile, glass of red wine in the other hand, fresh from the shower, her hair wet, the smell of Victoria's Secret So Sexy hair shampoo easing up his nostrils. There was always a bottle of it in the shower. He inhaled through his nose, like a bloodhound, to feel the full effect. She smiled with her eyes and pointed to a glass of red wine on the coffee table. He gave her the thumbs up, sat on the lounge, took a sip of the wine, and savored the taste, the view of The Bay, and the view of Stella.

Kenny had gone back to the ranch. Jack had told Kenny he had some more work to do with the software people at Stella's office and would stay at his apartment in Diamond Heights, returning to the ranch in the morning. Guilt was with him for not being back at the ranch with Kenny, but the data Stella had pulled on the murder victims may be the telling of how the serial killer abducted his victims. He also wanted to give her feedback about her development team. Somehow, his mind kept all these thoughts moving in the ether like a juggler. A thought would come down, no solution, then back up it would go. Sometimes it was better to leave them in the catacombs of his mind until a solution presented itself.

Jack's phone rang. Freddie. There was no preamble from Freddie.

"Jack, are you crazy, going to visit Clodagh Doyle? Kenny gave me a full update. What would Mom and Dad say if they knew? They would ask me why I didn't stop you."

Having grown up with Freddie, Jack knew the anger was from caring, so he waited six seconds. "Maybe that's why I didn't tell you beforehand."

"She's a career criminal and a very dangerous individual. I have eight cases where she's the main suspect."

"Fools rush in where angels fear to tread."

"Exactly. Alexander Pope. His poem, An Essay on Criticism, 1709. Mom used to read it to us. Remember?"

It was possible for Aunt Louise to make her reading of a poem into a Life Lesson. The ranch in Texas. A cold winter. An open-hearth fireplace. Flames reaching up the chimney. She would read the poem, then, line by line, delve into the meaning, then end the evening by reading it one last time. As they grew older, they had to recite and explain the poem.

"Of course. I can still recite the poem. Do you want to hear it?"

"Not necessary. I know you can."

When had Freddie assumed the older brother role? How many years now?

"Ok, Jack, keep me updated with what's happening. Everything."

Jack considered the data he had asked Stella to pull. *Maybe not everything.* "Sure, Freddie."

"By the way, this Ralph Dubin guy, has he told his folks he's dating the daughter of one of the worst criminals in San Francisco?"

"Nope. He hasn't gotten around to that. Probably say Doyle is a bar owner and leave it at that."

"If you do stumble over any information on Doyle's criminal activities where I could lay charges…" Freddie let the sentence hang.

"Will do, Freddie."

"By the way, my guys reported to me that the hacker guy, Numbers, remember him, has been active again. Usual MO, appears and disappears, and now has vanished again, and my guys couldn't trace him."

There are conversations where being drawn in could lead you to a place you did not want to be. "Interesting, Freddie."

Stella finished the call, put her glass and phone on the coffee table, took Jack's glass, placed it next to hers, straddled him, and kissed him like it was the first time. She pulled away.

"Listen, Freddie. I got to go. There's something I need to attend to."

Jack flipped his phone onto the lounge and put his hands on Stella's thighs.

"SFPD believe you're a man."

Stella smiled without showing her teeth, eyes glistening. The cobra and the mongoose. Jack wasn't sure who was which.

"Really."

***

"What do you make of my development team?" said Stella as they sat under the neck-high bubbles of Stella's bathtub. Their activities had moved from the couch to the floor, which was too hard, to her bed, which was too soft. Jack felt like Goldilocks as they climbed into the tub, which was just right. The floor was a hazard, slippery with soap suds, daring for someone to walk on it so it could bring you slipping, sliding, and crashing to the floor.

"I haven't done much. Just went into the system and poked around a bit. From what I saw, the team seems more than competent enough to do the job. Some of the work is quite exceptional. Especially the front-end work, the user interface."

"That would be Mary Berry. Her brother Jamie does the back-end work."

"Is that the team?

"Just the two of them."

"Well, again, from what I've seen, the work is well done."

"If they're so competent, why are they taking so long?"

"I'm guessing they didn't break the work into small packages. They just tackled this one big chunk of work. I don't understand why they didn't do this. It's normal practice. I'm sitting with them tomorrow morning to break it down to see how much work is needed to get this into production. I can monitor and test from the ranch and have a daily video call. It'll come right, don't worry. I've seen worse developments that got turned around. I've even given thought to them helping on this other job with the Dubin family. Their two developers have resigned rather suddenly."

"Well, check with them. I'm not sure what work they have after this. And the ranch? Are you going back after meeting with them tomorrow?"

"Yes, I need to. Kenny and I had a meeting with Clodagh Doyle a few hours ago. It didn't end as I'd hoped."

Stella's eyebrows rose in question. Jack gave her the details of the meeting.

"She threatened you. Can't Kenny arrest her?"

"She'd walk in an hour. I know Kenny wants her to do something that'll stick."

"Sound like a dangerous plan to me."

"Don't worry. Kenny can call up the cavalry if necessary. Anyway, let's talk about something else, like the data you've been collecting on the murder victims."

Stella stood, her gym-toned body dotted with white bubbles like she'd been caught in a snowstorm. "Let's go to my workroom." Stella sloshed across the floor, trying not to slip. She opened the towel cupboard, threw a five-foot-long Turkish cotton towel to Jack, and wrapped herself in another. She threw a third one at the doorway to stand on before they spread water any further.

They walked down the carpeted passageway to the workspace. There were no esthetics here. The walls were an off-white shade with strip lights, making everything easy to see without glare. A custom-fitted wooden desk ran twenty feet across one side with a large screen connected to a laptop standing in front of it. A printer was at one end of the desk like an orphan child. The walk-in gun safe was still there, with Stella's ammunition reloading equipment on metal tables spread down its wall. A whiteboard, fifteen feet long and four feet wide, was on its own wall.

Stella attached a printed photo of each victim on the whiteboard with a magnet in a timeline, and on the big screen showed their biography, family, friends, enemies, the company, the nature of the business, financial information, and management reports. She had financial accounts on how it had grown, the directors, and any other companies where the directors were on the board or had an interest. She also had information on staff, competitors, business grudges, personal interests, criminal records, and doctor's reports. Numbers was back in action.

"Well, there you have it," said Stella. "A data soup, full of both structured and unstructured data."

"Thank you. And as usual, I am impressed. And I trust Numbers has vanished from the Internet."

"Gone like the wind. But I must confess to having enjoyed being out there again, albeit briefly."

"Safety first, remember."

"I know. I know. I don't need a lecture. What are you going to do now?"

"I'm going to run a clustering algorithm over your data soup. I like that description, by the way, and I'll use a fuzzy clustering algorithm for what you've given me."

"I've read a bit about clustering. What's a fuzzy?"

"Do you really want to know? It's super-geeky stuff."

Stella's eyes widened. "And what Numbers does is not super-geeky?"

"Point taken. Well, it's what's called a soft clustering approach. With this, the algorithm calculates and assigns a probability score to each data point that belongs to a particular cluster. The method works by allocating membership values to each data point correlated to each cluster center based on the distance between the cluster center and the data point. Does that make it clearer?"

Stella chuckled. "It makes it worse."

"As I said, it's super-geeky but essential in the world of machine learning. Let me get to work, and then we can look at the results in the morning. It'll run for hours with the gigabytes of data you've accumulated.

***

At dawn, they were back in the workspace to see the results. The highest correlations were sitting on the screen. They had linked the audit reports to the financial statements. The murders occurred approximately four months after the audit, done by the same firm with the same audit partner in charge. Sam Dodd. The result was a correlation of ninety-three percent.

"I know Sam," said Stella. "He did the audit here at Link Industries."

"How long ago?"

Stella didn't have to think. "It was about four months ago."

"What do you know about him?"

"Nothing much. Good at his job. The results of the audit were a fair assessment. Well-spoken, polite. He came across as a gentle person. Conscious of his health and what he ate in the canteen. He'd go to the gym before coming to work. I never thought of him as a threat in any way."

"Get me everything you can on Sam Dodd. I want to put that in with the data we have already and rerun everything. I'll make breakfast while you do that."

While Jack made avocado on whole-grain toast with a fried egg on top, a dash of sriracha, and fresh coffee, he thought about what to do with Stella. The idea of leaving her alone at her home, even with security, was worrying, and the killer could get close to his victims and abduct them without anyone knowing the victim was missing. She could be in danger at the ranch if Clodagh launched an attack, which seemed likely. The least, worst option it would have to be.

Jack walked into the workspace carrying the tray of food, on which perched a white porcelain cup, a white porcelain mug, and a steaming coffee pot. A man's face was on the screen. He was clean-shaven in his early thirties, with a pleasant look you felt you could trust and a haircut his parents probably approved. Jack put the tray on the counter and poured the coffee.

"Meet Sam Dodd," said Stella as she reached for the porcelain cup. Stella scrolled the screen showing the details.

"He fits the profile," said Jack, "even down to being an active practitioner of Muay Thai. I see he's a resident of Diamond Heights, between my apartment on Red Rock Way and the SFPD Training Academy on Amber Drive.

Jack reread the details, letting it sink in like butter on hot toast. "Stella, I think you should come and stay at the ranch with me for a while."

"What? I've got a business to run. Tomorrow, I fly to Detroit. There's an automotive parts business I'm in negotiation to buy. I don't see a serial killer following me there. And the ranch may not be such a safe place with Miss Doyle looking for revenge."

"I don't have an answer to that. None of the options are perfect."

"If Sam Dodd is the killer, and the police arrest him, he confesses, then no more need to worry. Although, I find it difficult to believe it could be Sam."

"Why? Serial killers don't come with writing on their forehead."

Stella bit into her breakfast, chewed, and swallowed. "I know. I know. Nothing definite, but the name Sam Dodd and the words, serial killer, for me, don't really go together."

"Ok, let's let the data do the talking. I'll add the data you have here on Sam Dodd and the SFPD profile into the mix and see what the algorithm produces."

"How long will this take?"

"The algorithm did the heavy lifting last night. These two new data sets will run against the results from last night. There'll be just enough time for you to finish your breakfast but not your second cup of coffee."

Jack's estimate was a good one. Seven minutes later, Sam Dodd's name came onto the screen with a ninety-five percent correlation.

"I see the data," said Stella, "but Sam Dodd, the serial killer? I dunno."

"Think of Ted Bundy. He was handsome and charismatic, and his victims never saw him as a threat until it was too late for them. Anyway, all I can do now is give Freddie the details on Sam Dodd and the correlation I got."

"Won't he ask about the data you used and where and how you got it?"

"I'll just give him the broad categories, and he'll not want to know how I got it. Once Sam Dodd is officially a suspect, Freddie can show probable cause and get the data himself. He won't need all the data we have. That would raise far too many questions. I'll point him in the right direction regarding the subset of data he needs to get. I'll work with his guys to replicate what we did here, and then if anyone asks, it's SFPD who arrived at a correlation of ninety-five percent for Sam Dodd."

"With no mention of me?"

"Correct. And Numbers must stay offline." Jack took a sip of coffee. "Let's deal with today. After I finish with your developers this morning, I will go to Freddie. Then he can find Dodd, and we can stand back and let justice take its course."

"Ok, but what about Clodagh Doyle?"

"I don't have an answer to that."

CHAPTER NINETEEN

At 8 am, Jack sat with Jamie and Mary in the Link Industries boardroom, his laptop connected to the eighty-five-inch wall screen at the short end of the boardroom table. He had taken a moment to message Freddie saying he needed to see him and would 10 am work for him.

The brother and sister offered no resistance to Jack breaking the work into smaller packages. It was micro-management. Most people would object, and Jack would have to deal with that, but they politely complied. There was not much more to be done.

Freddie messaged back that 10 am would work.

There was a list of twenty-seven work packages on the screen. Jack highlighted three. "If you complete these three, we could upload a Beta version for the users to start testing."

Jamie and Mary frowned at the list, like a Rottweiler deciding friend or foe.

Jack leaned back in his chair. "Think of it as a highway. Complete these three, and you'll have taken care of 80% of the usage." Jack flashed up the specification document on the screen, scrolling down to the usage figures, and pointed with his cursor. "See, there."

Jamie and Mary nodded. "So long as we set the expectation that this version we release is not the final version," said Jamie.

"I'll handle that," said Jack. "I'll explain what is in and out of scope for this release."

Jamie pointed at the screen. "The third one is mine, which should take me a day. Mary, what about you?"

Mary stared at the screen for six seconds. "One day also."

"Excellent," said Jack. "Any questions?"

"None," said Jamie. "What you've suggested makes sense, and I'm happy to go along with it. What do you think, Sis?"

"Me too."

How many years now dealing with some of the ego-fueled developers he'd dealt with in the past? An unexpected, pleasant change is always good. "What do you guys have planned after this?"

"We have some irons in the fire," said Jamie. "But nothing confirmed."

"I've got a project," said Jack, "where the two developers have departed unexpectedly and suddenly."

"What's involved?" said Mary.

"It's a trading platform for leather, and I need the application documented."

"Is there any documentation as a starting point?" said Jamie.

Jack looked at Jamie. "There's a video and an online training manual for the customers. But nothing detailing what's going on in the back end nor the admin functions. You'll have to work through the code line by line and reverse-engineer it into documentation."

Jack turned his attention to Mary. "There's also some development required on the front end."

"What language is it written in?" said Mary.

"Python, same as here."

"And where is this place?" said Mary.

Jack explained where it was.

"That's far," said Mary. "Can we do this remotely?"

"I don't see why not. Where are you staying?"

"There's an old hotel less than ten minutes walk from here that the owner converted into a hostel for backpackers. It's painted green, and the window frames are bright yellow."

"The Green Hostel?" said Jack.

"Yes. That's it. It's nice. Each room has a big built-in desk, free Wi-Fi, and a gym on the top floor. There's a great vibe to the place."

"You guys know enough about cybersecurity. Just need to ensure you have a secure link. What do you say? Interested?"

Mary looked at Jamie. It was like watching two rocks talk. Mary turned to Jack. "We're interested. When can we start?"

"Well, there's one day's work to finish this. Then we can take this live. There'll be some support work and handholding for a while. You'll need to be on-site here for a while. That'll taper off. You should have time on your hands to start this in about a day."

***

At 10 am, Jack was walking towards Freddie's glass-walled office. He could see Freddie was on the phone, pacing up and down. Freddie had seen Jack but did not beckon him. Clearly, that phone call was for a restricted audience. Jack was a helper, a source of knowledge, new ideas to Freddie's team, but that did not make him privy to everything. If he was, he could learn what Freddie's team did and the extent of their powers. It had been an idle thought that popped up from time to time with Freddie and Kenny but remained unanswered. He watched his cousin as the idle thought scampered around when his phone rang with an unknown number.

"Hello. Hello. Is that Jack Rhodes?" There was a note of panic in the question, like an attacker was closing in, yet the voice was not unfamiliar.

"It is. Who is this?" Jack wanted to ask how this person got his number, but the caller cut in before Jack could speak.

"Where's Ralph?"

"Who is this?"

"It's Stewart Dubin. Where's Ralph?"

"How should I know where Ralph is and why the panic?"

"The hotel manager where those two developers, the twins, stayed, he's looking for him. The twins left without settling their account, and he said he'll go to the police unless someone pays up."

Jack had a flashback. He could see Ralph leaving the studio to go to Clodagh and the two developers leaving on the same day. Coincidence. Anything was possible, but likelihood could gnaw at the nerves like white ants at a table leg.

"Sorry, Stewart, I can't help you."

Freddie stopped pacing, put his phone on his desk, and waved Jack to come in. Jack walked through the door as his phone rang. Unknown number. He answered.

"Where's Ralph?" Jack recognized Clodagh's voice.

"And the top of the morning to you, too, Clodagh."

"Don't get smart with me, boyo. I don't know where Sinead is, and she's not answering her phone. Where's Ralph? He's not answering his phone, either. There's a hotel manager after him, and he's talking about going to the police. Ralph must settle this account immediately. I don't want the police looking at any of my businesses. Even the ones I don't fully own."

"The last time I saw Ralph was yesterday. You phoned him and said he must come and meet you. Then he left the studio."

"What are you talking about? I never phoned him."

"Well, I didn't actually hear your dulcet tones. Ralph just said it was you and left in a hurry."

"If anything has happened to Sinead because of you." Clodagh let the sentence hang in the air like a gallows noose.

"I understand your concern as a mother, but I don't know where they are or who phoned Ralph."

Clodagh went quiet like a meditating monk, so Jack left her to her thoughts until Clodagh stopped the call. Jack's phone went as silent as the hush of evening. He sat in the visitor's chair at Freddie's desk, took a sip from the coffee mug Freddie had just filled and looked at Freddie. "Well, that was unexpected."

"What was?"

Jack told Freddie about the two phone calls.

"So," said Freddie. "Do you think your lovebirds have flown the coop?"

"Maybe. Who knows? Anyway, let me show you what I've got so far on your serial killer."

Now that Jack was on a secure network, he fired up his laptop and took Freddie through the data that led him to Sam Dodd.

"I'm not going to ask," said Freddie, "how you got this data. But thanks for the analysis. Sam Dodd is now a Person of Interest. Where are you off to now?"

"To the ranch. But on the way, I'm going to stop in at Ralph's studio."

"Do you have time to chat with two of my guys? They've been trying to track down Numbers since he recently resurfaced, and they're not getting any closer than the last time Numbers appeared."

Some conversations should be avoided despite invitations to join. Jack looked at his watch like he was checking if he had time. "Sorry, Freddie, I need to get going. Maybe another time."

***

Stewart was sitting at his desk in the studio. It was 2 pm, and the studio smelled like banana bread. Stewart did not notice Jack's presence until he was next to his desk. The speared piece of banana bread on its way to Stewart's mouth fell from the fork as Stewart's head snapped around, landing in his lap, disintegrating upon impact. "You mustn't sneak up on me like that. I'm already jittery. I had that hotel manager here this morning asking about the twins and looking for Ralph, and I had to pay him before he'd leave."

Jack watched as Stewart focused on picking pieces of banana bread off his clothes and putting them on the plate next to three brown one-inch cubes awaiting their journey to Stewart's stomach. "Have you heard from Ralph?"

Stewart didn't answer, as he had found more particles in the crevices of his designer jeans.

"I was hoping you'd have some news."

"Nothing. Are any of his clothes gone?"

"I had a look. It looks like it's all there, but I have never been in his closet before. The clothes he most often wears, they're all there. All his toiletries are there. So where do you think he is?"

"I don't have an answer for you, Stewart. But after you called, Clodagh phoned looking for her daughter and Ralph."

Stewart frowned, causing horizontal corrugations like an old dusty road on his forehead.

"Stewart. Ralph got a phone call, and he told me he had to see Clodagh, then left."

"So she must have seen him last."

"She said it wasn't her who phoned."

"What?" Stewart let the word hang in the air like a semi-inflated balloon waiting for the wind to tell it where to go. Stewart's face came alive as he considered a thought. "Maybe it was Sinead."

"She would be my guess, but then why bother to tell me he was going to meet Clodagh."

"Maybe you heard wrong. Maybe, just maybe, Ralph said Clodagh's, meaning the bar."

"No. No mistake. Ralph said Clodagh phoned, and he had to go see her. Tell me about the hotel manager."

"Oh, him. Yes. As the twins worked here, they wanted to meet the CEO, Ralph. But as he wasn't here and I couldn't say where he was, he started interrogating me like I was covering up for Ralph. He showed me an invoice. I didn't know if this was the correct amount, but I paid it. He stood next to me while I paid it online."

"What do your parents know about any of this?"

"They know about the twins, and both are very upset about that as they are fond of them."

"Did you ask your parents if Ralph had phoned them?"

"No, of course not. My parents are sharp, particularly my mother. You must understand, Ralph and I are very close, always have been."

Jack thought about his relationship with Freddie.

"Such a question would invite many questions," said Stewart.

"Do you think Ralph's contacted your parents?"

"Can't say for sure, but if I can't get hold of him, then I doubt he's phoned them."

Stewart picked up his fork, speared a cube, and put it in his mouth, chewed, looked at Jack, and talked around the semi-masticated object in his mouth. "My manners, where are they? Have a piece, Jack. It's delicious. Mother made it. Old family recipe, she says. Personally, I don't care where the recipe came from. It's perfect."

Jack could see Kenny's face if he told him he'd been munching on banana bread. "No, thank you, Stewart, but thanks for offering."

Stewart stabbed one of the remaining cubes and put it in his mouth.

The art of talking around what was in his mouth he had refined into an art form. "And now, with the twins' unexpected departure, we have no software support."

"Leave that to me, Stewart. I'll sort something out."

"Great. Then I'll get back to selling. Customers don't just come walking through the door without a bit of prompting."

Stewart picked up the last cube of banana bread, tipped his head back like a pelican, and dropped it onto his waiting tongue.

**

Jack had spent the last two hours sitting at the table in the bunkhouse kitchen with Bryce and Aidan, listening to their findings. They had compiled a document containing a collection of notes. Not a report. Facts, screen clippings, thoughts, speculations, comparisons to other trading platforms, anomalies. From time to time, they would get up to make coffee. Jack had offered, but they said the doctor had told them they must start moving around but within limits. That limit being, don't let the wound open. What was of most interest were the inventory anomalies that appeared and then disappeared.

Jack's phone rang. Freddie. Jack walked out onto the verandah and down to the end. Freddie came straight to the topic.

"We picked up Sam Dodd and brought him in for questioning. He's looking more and more like our man." Jack didn't speak. Freddie had phoned to give him an information dump as that's what Freddie did. "He still trains at an MMA club. On the weekend, he likes to go hiking. Maybe this was his way of finding a place to take his victims. At the companies where he did the audit, and the CEO is a man, an entrepreneur, there were no issues, but all the places where it was a woman, that's where our serial killer struck."

"What's his family background?"

"Father left when he was eight. Mother, a high school dropout. She bought a pizza place because she could cook pasta and make pizza, and she sold the business and bought a diner. Over the course of her life, she must have bought and sold over twenty companies. All to do with food. She got mugged, beaten up badly, and died in hospital from her injuries. No suspects. Case remains unsolved."

"What does he say about his relationship with his mother?"

"He's got a lawyer now, who interrupts our questioning or tells him not to answer. Back to your question. We don't know. But we have asked for an account of his whereabouts on the day of the murders, with witnesses."

"How did he react to your questioning him about the murders? And that he is a suspect?"

"He appears horrified. But the guilty can make a good effort at looking shocked."

"As do the innocent."

"True. But the pieces of the puzzle are falling into place. If it turns out it's him, there'll be a sigh of relief among the women entrepreneurs."

Jack figured he could stop worrying about Stella.

"Well, good job."

"Thank you for helping. We wouldn't have gotten this far without the info you gave us, and I still don't want to know how you got the data you did."

Jack didn't respond. For this was his way of inviting an answer. They said their goodbyes, and Jack walked back to the kitchen.

"Sorry for the interruption," said Jack. "Back to the stock anomalies."

"Right," said Bryce. "See this stock item on the screen? It's what's called a Texas Heavy Steer Hide. THS. Remember, we are in the production system. I watch this hide because it's heavily traded, and I can see the system in action as the trades occur."

"Got it. So, what's the anomaly?"

"THS trades at about forty dollars per hide. With all the suppliers and tanners on the system, about ten thousand hides are available at any point in time. Sometimes I've been watching the trades, and it suddenly moves up to almost fifty dollars as the availability of hides has dropped by twenty percent. Supply and demand in action. I go to the audit trail to see the transaction that caused this twenty percent reduction, but I don't find anything. I go back to the trading page, and the number of available hides is back at about ten thousand, and the price has dropped back to about forty dollars."

Jack chuckled. "Maybe you imagined it."

"You laugh. At first, I thought I had."

Aidan jumped into the conversation. "I've also seen it. And it's fast. Like, now you see it, now you don't."

"Software glitch?"

"Can't say," said Aidan. "I did a cursory check to see what companies benefited from this, but it looks random. So maybe it's a software glitch that happens with a particular set of circumstances."

Kenny walked in the door with a football in his hand, flipping it from one hand to the other as Jack was thinking he must follow up with Jamie and Mary in the morning to get them onto the project. Kenny was going to speak when there was the rumble of a truck. They both looked outside to see Hailey's truck coming down the driveway. It stopped thirty yards from the bunkhouse, and Aaron got out, carrying Princess across his left arm, and lowered her to the ground. Hailey stayed in the truck, talking on her cell phone.

Kenny shouted to Aaron and threw the ball. Aaron caught it with a smile and returned the throw. Jack heard it hit Kenny's chest with a solid whack, and he returned the throw, stepping further back.

Hailey got out of the truck, walked to Jack, and stood in front of him. "Do you want to go riding again?"

"Sure thing. That'd be great."

"I finish at lunchtime tomorrow," she said. "How about I swing by after that?"

"That works for me."

"I gotta go."

Jack followed Hailey to her truck. He opened the door for her, and she climbed in with practiced ease and started the truck. She turned to Jack, kissed him on the mouth, held it for four seconds, pushed him away, closed the door, and drove off. Jack's last vision was of the red curls in the rear window.

CHAPTER TWENTY

Jack and Kenny were looking at the screen. The App on their phones had woken them both at 3:04 am, alerting them it was picking up thermal images. On earlier nights, they had seen deer crossing the road. This time, four men, two on each side, lit up like yellow glowworms walking from the ranch gate. The image of a large van, the engine block glowing red, was on Marsh Creek Road. They were walking off the road, next to the fence, weaving between the trees, carrying short-barreled weapons pointed down at thirty degrees. There was a well-practiced military look at how they progressed through the trees, covering ground quickly and continually checking their surroundings. They had traveled fifty yards, leaving them two hundred and fifty more to reach the house.

Jack and Kenny pulled the rifles from the open gun safe. Jack sat on a chair in front of the computer screen, his rifle leaning against his leg as he texted Aaron, Bryce, and Aidan to stay in their rooms. Kenny called The Farm and asked them to send a team. Nine minutes was their estimate.

Kenny stood in the dark, inside the open kitchen doorway, pointing his rifle at the intruders and looking through the thermal scope at them and their weapons. "They look like HK MP5s. They can take a thirty-round magazine, effective range of about two hundred yards and accurate up to one hundred yards. So, if we keep them back one hundred yards or more, we should be safe until the cavalry get here. We take turns in shooting. I'll take the ones on the right. You take the left. No kill shots. Just put it in a tree next to each one in turn. I'm going out the back door and across to the barn. Count to five, then open the gate. That'll make them look back."

Jack had his rifle on the windowsill, looking through the scope as he counted to five, then pressed the button on the gate remote. He watched the four images turn and crouch at the sound of the gate creaking open, their weapons sweeping back and forth. They stayed like that for seven seconds, then moved towards the house in a slow, crouching jog.

When the four were two hundred yards from the house, a 308 bullet from Kenny's rifle hit the tree next to the first man on the right. Kenny must have been far enough back in the barn they couldn't see a muzzle flash. The four found cover on the ground or behind a tree. They did not move for fourteen seconds, probably trying to figure out the shooter's location. Jack checked his watch. Three minutes had passed since Kenny phoned The Farm. The four started moving. Jack put a bullet into the tree next to the first man on the left. The four dropped again. The difference in noise between Kenny's 308 and Jack's 223 would clarify they were up against two shooters and would have seen the muzzle flash from Jack's rifle. A burst of five rounds came from the first guy on the left. He was lying on the ground behind a small bush. Jack heard one shot hit the house. His location they now knew. The end of the barrel glowed red. Kenny fired. There was a puff of dust in front of the glowing barrel end. The guy on the ground leopard crawled until he got to a tree and stood behind it. They would now know Kenny's location.

The lead shooters on the left and the right let go a burst at the barn and the house. The other two used this to move forward, leapfrogging to another tree. Kenny shot four times, hitting trees next to the attacker. Jack had been counting shots, and Kenny had fired six times. The magazine would be empty, and there had been one in the barrel, and Kenny needed time to pull out the magazine and install a full one. Jack checked his watch. Five minutes had passed.

The front two shooters kneeled with their barrels pointing at the barn. Jack put a bullet two feet above each of their heads, hoping to get them back behind the tree. They got off a burst of five shots each before retreating behind the tree. The shooters stopped for a minute, and Jack could see the thermal images of their heads turning. Now they knew where the shots were coming from, they were having a driveway meeting to consider their options. As Jack and Kenny had each only fired single shots, the attackers would be considering the risks in assuming they did not have automatic weapons. They would have also realized from the sound of the rifles that Kenny had a heavier caliber.

Jack could not see an image of the attacker on the front right. The others were watching him. Parts of their glowing heads peeped around the side of the tree. He was the leader. Kenny must have come to the same conclusion as he fired, and Jack saw a piece of the edge of the tree next to the leader get torn off by the bullet. Jack followed, tearing off a much smaller portion. Jack checked his watch. Seven minutes.

The first two on the left and right fired a burst of five at Kenny and Jack. Jack heard one hit the house. When he looked up, the next two went past the first two firing a burst of five each. Then the last two ran to the front and fired a burst of five. They were leapfrogging and had gained thirty yards. Jack picked up the shotgun and sighted through the thermal scope. The shotgun had an effective range of one hundred yards. At this distance, it would be spray and pray.

The pair at the front had come to a kneeling position, with their barrels and half their heads visible at the side of the tree. Jack let loose with the one in the chamber and then fired off the five-shot magazine. The muzzle flash through the thermal scope was a thing of technicolor beauty. Jack heard three shouts of pain, ejected the magazine, slammed in a full one, put one into the barrel, and sighted through the scope at the attackers. Three rolled in the grass, not bothering to hide behind a tree. Jack could not make out which one of them was the leader. Jack checked his watch. Nine minutes.

Kenny fired five times into the trees, and Jack followed, giving Kenny time to reload. Jack ejected the magazine, put in a new one, and loaded one into the barrel. He picked up the shotgun and looked through the scope, tracking left, right, and left again like he was crossing the road. There was no movement.

When one showed their face, Kenny placed a shot into that tree. Kenny fired five shots. The last one blew off a piece of tree. There was a scream, and the one on the left fell to his knees, holding his face. That was his last magazine in the rifle. Kenny fired two from his Sig. Two misses, but the muzzle flash and the noise were impressive, leaving Kenny with ten in the magazine.

Jack was watching for the lights of the cavalry. The last two came out from behind the tree, and Jack fired all five rounds from the shotgun. That sent them back behind the tree. If they could just keep them there a while longer.

They both appeared, running at the house, one shooting sideways at the barn, the other shooting at the house. The Sig sound was distinctive, shot after shot. The rear man, the one shooting at the barn, screamed and fell. Still firing bursts at the house, the other kept coming, and it was impossible to keep count of how many he'd fired.

Jack moved to the edge of the fireplace, picked up the poker, and melded into the shadows. The attacker came through the door and fired on full auto until there was a click. Empty magazine. He dropped the weapon, letting it hang from its shoulder sling, and reached for his sidearm. Jack threw the poker horizontally. It spun. The attacker saw it and put his hands up to stop or catch it. It slipped through his hands and fingers, hitting him across the eyes, and clattered to the floor. Jack did not want the sidearm out of its holster. So he dived, beating the attacker to the pistol with his left hand and bringing them both to the floor. The attacker's right hand was on Jack's left hand as he didn't want Jack with a pistol. It was a wrestling standoff. Jack pushed his right forearm into the attacker's throat, who tried to pull it away. They were evenly matched and seemed stuck in this embrace, neither one getting an advantage.

The light came on, and Jack saw Kenny bend over and point his Sig into the face of the attacker. "Let go and stand up slowly."

The attacker hesitated as he blinked at the light. Even in training, Kenny did not like hesitaters, and he always had something to shorten the hesitation. "Do you think I won't shoot you in the face?"

The attacker went limp. Jack pulled the pistol from the holster and used his forearm choke to push himself off the ground. There were lights in the yard, vehicles stopping, and ten men with weapons at their shoulders jumping out. Kenny put the Sig in the back of his jeans, dragged the attacker to his feet, and walked outside. Five automatic rifles pointed at him as he pushed the attacker to his knees and projected his voice as he did on the parade ground. "I'm Sergeant Kenny Braithwaite from the SFPD. I'm the one who called. My badge is in my pocket, and my weapon is in the back of my jeans."

The leader jerked his head at two of his men. One pulled the Sig from Kenny's jeans, and the other pulled his badge and handed it to the leader, who looked at it in the headlights. "He's good. Give him back his weapon."

"There's another guy inside. He's with me. Jack's looking after the ranch. He's got this guy's pistol." Kenny pointed at the kneeling attacker. "Come on out, Jack."

Jack walked out, holding his hands in the air and the pistol with his fingertips. One of the team trotted over, took the gun, and Jack put his hands down. "There are four combatants. Two in the driveway, one over near the barn, and this one here. I think he's the leader."

The guy in charge, who looked like he did a lot of running, sent six of his men in the van back down the driveway. Two others walked over and secured the one near the barn with cable ties, then the same to the one on his knees.

Another van came through the gate. This one looked like a school bus with bars on the windows. The van and the bus met where the wounded lay. The men from the van removed all weapons, secured the injured, and loaded them on the bus.

As they drove to pick up the other two, Jack texted the group that it was safe to come out of their rooms. Aaron, Bryce, and Aidan arrived as the bus returned with two wounded occupants.

The captain looked at the three. "I heard that Bryce and Aidan had been moved here." He paused as he surveyed Aaron. "Is that Aaron Brown?"

Jack smiled without showing his teeth and nodded. "It sure is."

The captain turned to his team. "Hey guys, Aaron Brown's over here." There was a clamor of incredulous voices like children seeing their Christmas presents for the first time. Even the bus driver jumped out, locked the bus, and hurried to Aaron.

The guys from The Farm spent the next twenty minutes taking selfies with Aaron fielding three to five questions simultaneously. Kenny was on the phone with Freddie giving him an update.

Bryce and Aidan were chatting with some guys from The Farm like they were long-lost relatives. There was a carnival-like atmosphere except on the bus, where the four attackers sat looking out the window or at the floor.

What would it be like knowing the wheels of justice would turn, and starting tonight, they would be sitting in jail?

***

"What do you mean they walked?"

Jack had stepped outside the bunkhouse kitchen where he'd been working with Bryce and Aidan. Hailey had collected Aaron and Princess two hours earlier at 6:30 am. Jack waited for a response from Freddie.

"Their lawyer said they were hunters and were lost. They were walking up to the house when you fired upon them, and they retaliated."

"What kind of hunter uses an MP5?"

"Jack, we both know the answer to that. The kind that hunts people. Anyway, the lawyer's pivotal argument was that you fired first, and Kenny confirmed that. I thought they would be a recognizable part of Doyle's crew. But they're not. They're ex-military. Mercenaries. We checked their backgrounds. Guns for hire. They live in Mexico. After they were released, they said they were going back over the border via Tijuana. We'll be watching for them to drive through customs. It's a nine-hour drive. We'll pick up their location if they break the speed limit."

Not for the first time was the extent of necessary surveillance versus personal freedom a fleeting topic, skipping around in the back of his mind. The technologies were there. It was the pervasive access once they were all brought together. But then again, Numbers did it, but that was deemed illegal. What a citizen could do versus what a government body could do. He was glad there were eyes on the bad guys.

"So, no link to Clodagh?"

"The only common thread is the lawyer. The same one got her son and the muscle off the hook."

A sense of being cheated filled Jack, but what to do about it?

CHAPTER TWENTY-ONE

Jack was not getting the answers he wanted. Bryce and Aidan were doing an excellent job of testing the system, documenting each time the stock changed without a transaction. But they weren't getting to the how or why this was happening. He knew his next steps. Jack phoned Mary. He saw an unknown call coming in while waiting for Mary to answer.

"Hello, this is Mary."

Her phone voice sounded much younger than when Jack had first met her.

"Hi Mary, It's Jack."

"Oh, Jack. How are you?"

"I'm good. How are you and Jamie?"

"Also good, and you'll be pleased to hear we've made good progress in the work for Link Industries. We reckon we can put it into production by the end of today, and then we want to monitor it for two weeks to see if the users have any issues. So, from tomorrow, we can start documenting the system you spoke about."

"Good going. I'll send you the code, and we can chat later tomorrow."

"Just one thing. We said we would work from our hotel, but we would prefer to be on-site during the first two weeks of operation, and we can work on your project from here."

"I don't see a problem with that. It will actually work out well for both projects. I'll bring Stella up to speed as to where things are."

"Bye-bye, Jack. Chat tomorrow."

Mary rang off.

He had to phone Stella, there was the unknown caller, and he was not making progress with HTT. So, he went to what he knew. Get the data. He asked Bryce and Aidan to take a break while he downloaded all the data since the system went into production. It would take a while.

Jack went out to the verandah, sat in a chair, and looked across at the barn. It was changing to a lighter red as the noon-day sun bore down upon it. Stella answered in nine rings.

"Jack, what a lovely surprise. I've just stepped out of a meeting. Still in negotiations here in Detroit."

Jack was weighing up risks. Freddie had Sam Dodd in for questioning, and it looked like he was the killer. Stella was in meetings, on planes, surrounded by people, and on the move.

"I didn't mean to interrupt your meeting. Just wanted to give you an update."

"I'm glad you called. I needed an excuse to step out of the room. The other party is being difficult. Let them sit by themselves for a while, then maybe they'll come to their senses. So, what's the update?"

Jack told her.

"Thank you, Jack, and I'm happy if Mary and Jamie work on your project while they do support work at Link. And how is your project going?"

Jack watched the barn. It was like a red canvas on which he could see his thoughts as he explained them to Stella.

"Can I help?"

"Appreciate the offer, but no. If I need your help, I'll talk about it face to face." Jack had a lack of faith in the security of the telephone systems. He'd explained the technologies to Freddie and his team, but they had not grasped it. Some of them were dismissive with their wry smiles until he had eight of them perform a simple test. They each had to phone him and say they wanted to send their beagle to Brazil and didn't know how to do it. The next day, they all got advertisements via social media on beagles, Brazil, travel companies, and transport companies on their search engines. Freddie had nodded in the follow-up meeting, then told his team to put more effort into what Jack had told them. Their wry smiles vanished, and they did.

"Understood. I'm not sure when I'll be back home. The negotiation around this acquisition is dragging on, actually becoming quite tedious. But I'll have to stick it out. I want this company."

Jack chuckled. "Do they know how determined you can get?"

"Of course not. If they knew, they'd be putting the price up. I'm pretending I'm vaguely interested, and I want them selling it to me, not me buying it from them."

"Well, happy hunting."

Jack rang off and realized he still hadn't returned the call from the unknown caller. The data extract would still be running, and he was still musing on the barn wall when he phoned the anonymous caller to hear Clodagh answer.

"Jack. Thank you for phoning back." There was concern in her voice, like a parishioner seeking answers from their priest. "Have you heard from Sinead or Ralph?"

This did not sound like the dispatcher of hardened mercenaries, more like a concerned parent. Jack was deciding if he should mention last night's attack and decided against it, which would keep her guessing.

One of Kenny's teachings. We all do the same drills, and the opponent knows what to expect. Need to do something different.

"Jack. Are you still there?"

"I'm still here."

"Well, have you heard from them?"

Jack listened to her tone heighten with worry. "I've heard nothing, Clodagh."

"You must tell me if you heard anything, Jack. I'm used to getting straight answers. So let me know if you hear anything. Good or bad. That clear?"

"Noted." This comment he'd heard from a lawyer. It meant, 'I've listened and heard what you said, but I will ignore it.' Clodagh must have heard it also, as the frustration in her voice was palpable like a beating heart.

"Are you a parent, Jack?"

"Not that I know."

"Well, let me tell you, as a parent, finding Sinead overrides everything I'm doing right now."

Jack could almost hear Clodagh's mind whirring as she went quiet for six seconds.

"Look, Jack, I think we got off on the wrong foot."

Sending four mercenaries in the middle of the night could also ruin the start of a friendship.

"We should get together face to face and talk."

Keeping your friends close and your enemies closer seemed a good idea.

"Sure, where and when?"

"I'll come to you this time."

"Do you know where I live?" Jack was sure Clodagh knew but wanted to see what she said.

"No."

Cucumbers wished they could be this cool. He gave her the address. "I'll be there at five."

***

Forewarned is forearmed. After hearing Clodagh would be coming, Jack went to the kitchen and started cleaning his rifle and shotgun. They got stripped down, cleaned with solvent, and placed on old newspapers on the kitchen table. He put gun oil on a microfiber cloth and was rubbing down each part when he saw Hailey's truck on the big screen, coming up the driveway. In the passenger seat was the bulk of Aaron. Princess would be in the back seat, her collar on a short leash, and buckled in.

His hands were too oily to shake her hand as she came into the kitchen, but she wasn't interested in shaking hands. She grabbed the front of his shirt with two hands, pulling him to her. Jack kept his hands out wide so as not to get oil on her clothes. She kissed him for nine seconds, which seemed like a long time, and his body was reacting. Hailey must have felt it, for her hips pushed into his. She broke the clinch, wiped her mouth with her sleeve, like wiping off beer foam, and surveyed the array of parts on the table.

"Good to see a man who looks after his equipment." Hailey winked at Jack and bent down to look closer at the rifle parts. "Remington 700. I got one. Chambered to 308. What's this one?"

"223."

"I hear you had visitors last night. You all right?"

"I'm fine."

"I meant in your head. Hard not to get some PTSD issues after such an event."

Jack didn't want to discuss the PTSD he had already or how it manifested itself when he was five. It was bothersome to talk about, had achieved nothing with psychologists, and he had it under control, mostly.

170

"I feel healthy enough mentally and physically."

"If you were a horse, I'd have you resting in a paddock for two weeks."

Jack smiled. "I might take you up on that."

"Do you want coffee?"

"Yes, please."

"Cups or mugs?"

"Mugs, please. Black, no sugar."

"Same as me."

Jack pointed with his oily, rag-holding right hand to where he kept everything, and Hailey went about making the coffee. A domestic atmosphere was creeping in like a warm fog as he watched her figure from behind and wiped the oil on the pieces. His phone rang on the table, and he leaned over to see who it was. Stewart Dubin. Jack wiped his left hand with a clean cloth, picked up the phone, and stepped out on the verandah.

"Hello Jack. I got a call from Ralph, and he and Sinead are alive and well."

"Where are they?"

"He wouldn't say. He used one of those throwaway phones, and his phone is switched off."

"Did you ask why he and Sinead have run away, and are they coming back?"

"I did. He just said it's complicated, and they need some time."

"Have you told your parents?"

"Yes. An edited version. I told them Ralph and Sinead have taken a holiday, and their place has no cell phone reception." Stewart giggled. "My parents didn't know Ralph had a girlfriend, and my mother hit me with a barrage of questions. All of which I ducked. Ralph can answer her questions when he surfaces."

"Thanks for telling me, Stewart."

"Back to business. Have you made progress on the software support?"

"I have, but not finalized."

Stewart grunted like a pig hunting truffles, said his goodbyes, and hung up. Jack phoned the anonymous caller number he called Clodagh on last time, and she answered in four rings.

"Yes, Jack."

"I just received a call that Sinead and Ralph are alive and well but won't reveal their whereabouts."

"Who told you this?"

"It doesn't matter."

Clodagh went quiet. Jack guessed she was weighing up the merit in pursuing who was the source. "Thank you, Jack. You can contact me any time of the day if you hear anything."

"I will."

Jack ended the call and walked back into the kitchen, where Hailey had the mugs of coffee on the table. Jack wiped the parts with a clean cloth, assembled the rifle and shotgun, and placed them into the gun safe, leaving the door open and two full magazines, one for each, on the kitchen table.

"You look like you're preparing for another attack."

"They had to be cleaned as they got used last night."

Hailey put her coffee down, picked up one of the thermal scopes, and looked through it out the kitchen door and then back at Jack, scoping him up and down. "Nice."

Jack did not know what she found to be nice.

"What do you think of the scope?"

"I've got the same brand but not as powerful as this."

"Why do you need it?"

"Wild boar sometimes come off the mountain, and they eat almost anything, roots, tubers, fruit, frogs, salamanders, eggs, fledgling birds, rabbits, newborn animals, and carrion. They're survivors. But they present a risk to our young livestock, cause chaos if they get into the stable, and the horses react badly. Our property is an extension of the vet practice, or the vet practice is an extension of our property. Hard to say some days. It depends on where we've had to house the sick animals."

Jack sipped his coffee, looking over the top at Hailey. "Hungry? I can make us some lunch. Nothing too grand."

"Can I take you up on that offer after the ride?"

"Sure thing. Where would you like to ride?"

"How about that pretty lake you showed me?"

***

The day had heated up when they got to the lake. Ripples from the waterfall spread out in concentric circles. They dismounted, let the horses drink, and walked them back under the trees.

"It's beautiful," said Hailey. "I can't resist it. I'm going for a swim."

"You said I should test the water."

Hailey stood on one leg and pulled off a boot as she looked at Jack. "I'm not waiting for that. Are you joining me?" Hailey pulled off her other boot and started unbuckling her jeans. "What's the matter, Jack? Have you forgotten how to go skinny-dipping?"

Jack was unsure if this would be totally naked skinny-dipping or partially clothed skinny-dipping. When Hailey went past Jack as he was dropping his jeans, her nakedness swaying as she tiptoed over the grass and sticks, he had his answer. Her skin was a porcelain shade of white in contrast to the red hair, which went from a wild bush to a frame around her face as she came up from under the water.

"Come on, slowpoke. I'm swimming to the other side."

Hailey set off in a graceful breaststroke, gliding through the water with the ease of a well-practiced swimmer, each stroke executed with the precision and timing of a lazy metronome.

Jack was glad she was swimming away as he waded into the water, for the sight of her was having a visible effect on his nether regions. He swam to the middle of the lake where Hailey was treading water with a face as cheerful as a chipmunk.

"This is great." Hailey spun around and struck out for the rock ledge on the other side. Her shape reminded him of ivory as her skin glowed in the Qing-shaded water.

At the rock ledge, the water was five feet deep, and Hailey was sitting on an underwater shelf with just her head sticking out. Jack went underwater, his vision now dulled, and swam. Her shape was a luminescence against the Qing. As he surfaced and took a breath, she put her hands behind his head, pulled him to her, and kissed him, sliding off the ledge and holding herself against him.

There was only one way this would end, and it would not involve conversation.

CHAPTER TWENTY-TWO

At 4:30 pm, Jack and Hailey walked their horses up to the horse trailer. They had pulled their clothes onto their wet bodies, and damp patches still showed. Jack's hair was almost dry, but Hailey's curly mass glistened with the retained moisture. Together they off-saddled, hosed the horses down, and put them in the stable with some grass hay to fill their bellies and keep them occupied. With their shoulders almost touching, they walked into the kitchen, and Jack put the kettle on.

Kenny was watching the screen, and Hailey joined him.

Hailey leaned closer to the screen. "Is that Aaron and Princess I see?"

Kenny's eyes flicked over Hailey's damp clothes and wet hair, then he caught Jack's eye and raised his eyebrows. Jack turned his attention to the screen.

"That's them," said Kenny. "Aaron told me he's teaching Princess where she lives. Each day he walks in a different direction and back again, then feeds her."

"Excellent. That's what I told him to do." Hailey's brow furrowed as she squinted at the screen. "Isn't there someone at the gate?"

Kenny displayed the gate camera to see a gold Bentley.

"Must be Clodagh," said Jack. "She's a bit early, but let her in."

The gate swung open, and the car worked its way over a road it had not expected to meet. Kenny and Freddie slammed the magazines into the rifle and the shotgun and placed one round in each chamber. They leaned them next to the door where Jack could snatch one up, walking out or in. Kenny strapped on his Sig. The car halted outside the kitchen door as Jack stepped down from the verandah.

The driver was the same one Jack had slammed with Liam's shillelagh. Jimmy was next to the driver. He stepped out, dressed again in the only clothes he seemed to own or fit him, and opened the door for Clodagh. She was wearing gardening clothes like the first time Jack met her. The driver got out, limped a few steps, and leaned against the car.

Aaron walked past Jimmy without acknowledging his presence or his size. He greeted Kenny, who had stepped out onto the verandah, and looked back for Princess, busy inspecting something in a small bush. She then realized she was separated from Aaron and charged toward him with a smile stretched across her face. Her trajectory took her toward Clodagh and Jimmy, where Clodagh was looking at the house, the barn, and the assortment of trucks parked near the kitchen, taking it all in like one does when visiting the zoo. Jimmy had his eyes on Princess, who was about to gallop past him.

"I hate dogs," said Jimmy, who swung his right foot at Princess, the toe of his shoe going under her chest and belly, sending her two feet into the air and landing ten feet away. She rolled, stood, smiled, and looked for Aaron, who emitted a roar like a primeval carnivore. He charged Jimmy, who saw Aaron coming, and readied himself for the impact. Aaron launched him off his feet. Jimmy landed with a sound like a dropped bag of cement, his head hitting the ground simultaneously with Aaron's first punch colliding with the side of Jimmy's head. The roaring and the blows, left, right, left, right, continued. Jimmy stopped moving, and Aaron kept punching.

"Stop now, Aaron," Kenny said in his best and loudest coach's voice.

Kenny and Jack grabbed Aaron by an arm each and pulled him to his feet. Aaron was shaking like an unbalanced washing machine from the adrenaline rushing through his bloodstream.

Aaron looked at Kenny like he was watching from some faraway place. "It's all fine now, Aaron. Take some deep breaths."

Hailey appeared in front of Aaron with Princess in her arms. Princess was trying to wriggle out of Hailey's grasp to get to Aaron. "She's fine, Aaron. Dusty, but fine."

Kenny and Jack let Aaron go so he could take Princess in his arms. Kenny patted Aaron on the shoulder. "It's all over now. Go grab a shower. We'll talk later."

Aaron nodded and held Princess close to his chest as he went to the bunkhouse. The limping driver was beside Jimmy, grunting as he got down on one knee. Jimmy had his eyes open but was not moving, and Aaron's fists had not improved his looks.

"I should lay a charge," said Clodagh looking at Jack.

Kenny walked over to Clodagh and looked down at her. "Go ahead. I saw it all. It was self-defense. Jimmy kicked the dog. Then he kicked Aaron, and Aaron defended himself. End of story."

Clodagh was holding Kenny's gaze like she had practiced doing it. "We are getting off-topic here, my tall, red-haired friend." Clodagh turned to Jack. "Is there somewhere we can talk?"

"The barn's good."

They walked, Clodagh looking toward Mt. Diablo. "I've lost my bearings. That peak in the distance is Mt. Diablo, right?"

"That's it. It's southeast from here if that helps."

"It does. The peak in front of it would be Mt. Olympia, and the one between them and a bit to the west would be North Peak."

"Very good. I see you know your mountains."

Jack was expecting a comment about how she knew the mountain. Instead, he got another question.

"Have you ever hiked from here?"

Jack wondered if she was figuring out how to gain access from the rear of the property, but anyone with a contour map would see the thin trail from the ranch to Mt. Olympia. To gain access, you would have to first get to the top of Mt. Olympia and then find the correct route down to the ranch. Jack was not about to tell her what he already knew. "No. I don't even know if there's a trail from here."

They walked into the barn, past the horses who were busy eating, but stopped to look in their direction, snorted, and flicked their tails. Happy horses. Jack stood next to his truck and waited for Clodagh to speak.

"I want my daughter back. It's quite simple. I can be your friend to do it, or I can be your enemy."

Keep your friends close and your enemies closer, and here comes Clodagh with it all wrapped up in the one package, almost with a bow on it, like a present. "And how would we be friends, Clodagh?"

"Friends help each other. Maybe there's something I can do for you that you can't do for yourself. Like your big red-headed cop friend. He can do things I can't do, and I can do things he can't do."

"You mean illegal things?"

"I'm explaining a concept here. Friendship, and how we can help each other. I am doing this so I can get my daughter back. It's not complicated."

"So, if I get your daughter back, you'll help me with whatever I ask?"

"Within reasonable limits, of course."

"Would you get Liam to stop his illegal activities?"

"What illegal activities? As a mother, I bought three tanneries for him to run. He must be doing something right. They make good money."

"Have you asked him if he's doing anything illegal?"

"Of course. The tanneries process the skins, and Liam sells them on the trading platform he invested in with Ralph. Liam has shown good trading skills."

"What came first, the investment in Ralph's software or buying the tanneries?"

"It happened at the same time as Liam said we needed to be involved in the whole supply chain."

"You could have just traded the skins on an existing platform."

"True, but Liam said our business should be more diversified, and software was an excellent way to do this. It was also his academic background, so as a mother, I was glad to see my son evolving into a successful businessman."

"And as a mother, you probably helped your son with some cash for the businesses, which neither of you felt the need to declare."

"That would be money laundering, which is wild speculation on your part."

"It would be if you hadn't declared the cash in your books."

Clodagh smiled like she was dealing with an indulgent child. "You're quite right, Jack, but my books come up squeaky clean at every audit."

"I will uncover what he's doing and how he's doing it. And when I do find out, he will go to jail."

"If you find out what he is doing, please bring it to me, and I will tell him to stop."

"Just like that?"

"Just like that."

"But if he has committed a crime, the law should take its course with him."

"But if I get him to stop and no one has died, we can just carry on, and whatever you find never happened. Understand I don't want my son to go to jail. Then I will have lost both of my children."

Clodagh's shoulders slumped like a defeated boxer as this possibility went through her mind like a worm through a peach. Jack gave Clodagh time to ponder what her life would be like as she watched the horses eating the hay. Jack knew what it was like to lose parents. Was losing a child worse? *Maybe there is merit in this arrangement.*

"Clodagh." She exhaled herself out of her reverie like breathing away a bad dream as she looked from the horses to Jack and waited. "Let's give this a tentative try and see how it works out. I'll go first as a sign of good faith."

There was a glimmer of a smile from Clodagh. "All right."

"I have information about Sinead and Ralph."

Clodagh's face brightened like there was a light behind her features.

"They are alive and well, staying in a nice place and getting three meals a day."

"Where are they?"

"That I don't know."

Clodagh's gaze scoped Jack's face like a lie detector. She seemed satisfied as she nodded.

"What do you want from me?"

I want everything you know about someone who frequents your bar."

"Who?"

"Name is Sam Dodd."

"Means nothing to me. I'll ask Jimmy. He pretty well knows everybody. It's his job as a bouncer, and it's what he does without even trying."

Clodagh walked out of the barn, followed by Jack, and over to where Jimmy was sitting on the top of the steps. Hailey was attending to the damage caused by Aaron. Clodagh looked at Hailey. "I've seen a lot of boxers patched up. Good job here. Are you a nurse?"

Hailey didn't take her eyes off the stitches she was putting into Jimmy's left eyebrow. "A vet."

Jimmy wasn't pretty, to begin with, but Hailey's remedial work made him look like the younger brother of Frankenstein's monster. Clodagh's reaction to Jimmy's face was like it was just another day at the office. "Well, Jimmy's as big as a horse, so I guess that makes sense." Clodagh chuckled at her joke, and Jimmy didn't laugh. "Jimmy, I gotta ask you about someone."

"Who?"

Aaron appeared and stood in front of Jimmy, who tensed. "I'm here to say I'm sorry I hurt you, but you kicked my dog."

Jimmy's brow furrowed as he looked at Aaron and considered what Aaron had said. "I'm sorry I kicked your dog. I'm scared of dogs. Got bitten bad by one as a kid. Had to see a psychologist, and all that happened was that they said I have a phobia and told me its name. I didn't get a cure."

"What's it called?"

"Cynophobia."

"Never heard of it." Aaron put out his hand to Jimmy. "So, are we good?"

Everybody watched as Jimmy considered the extended hand, reached, and shook it, looking closely at Aaron. "Haven't I seen you in an NFL team?"

"You have. I'm Aaron Brown."

"Really? Can I come and hang out with you sometime?"

Aaron looked at Jack. Jack nodded, and Aaron turned back to Jimmy. "Anytime."

"Well," said Clodagh, "this is all very heartwarming, but now that we've all kissed and made up can we get back to my question? Jimmy, do you know a customer by the name of Sam Dodd?"

Jimmy was as quick as blinking. "Yes."

"Wonderful. Now tell me what you know about him."

181

"He does MMA but has never caused any trouble. Pleasant to talk to. Has an office job. Likes to go hiking. Always takes a friend."

"Who is this friend?"

"Friends. Men. He's gay. But he's one of those who, what's it called, hasn't come out of the cupboard."

"Closet."

"Cupboard, closet, whatever. Sam doesn't want anyone to know."

"Why would he tell you all this?"

"Clodagh, you'd be surprised how many lonely drunks spill their guts to the dumb bouncer. Either they forget the conversation or think I've forgotten. But I don't."

Clodagh looked at Jack. "Jimmy remembers everything. He's on the autistic spectrum and can't do some things, but he's off the charts when it comes to remembering."

Jimmy smiled behind pressed lips and nodded as if he'd just won a prize. "Sam's at our place about once a week because we're close to where he lives, but mostly he's at one of the gay places."

"Jimmy," said Jack, "from what Sam told you, are you sure he always went hiking with a man friend."

"Definitely. He told me he wouldn't bother going hiking otherwise."

"And the MMA. What was that all about?"

"It was the best way he knew to keep in shape. He just did the training, but he never competed. Never had a fight. He told me he couldn't bear to hurt anyone." Jimmy shrugged. "Not a great attitude for a fighter."

"Thank you, Jimmy," said Jack. He turned to Kenny, who was already getting his phone from his pocket to update Freddie that their number one suspect may have alibis. "Kenny, can you get a picture of Sam Dodd sent to us?" Kenny nodded and walked away, looking like a gunslinger with his Sig low on his hip.

"Jack," said Hailey, "I need some more stuff from my truck. Can you help me?"

"Sure."

At the truck, Hailey said to Jack, "I don't know whether you noticed, but I've been stitching up this Jimmy guy without any local anesthetic. I came here with my mind set on other things." There was a grin that was not asking for forgiveness. "And didn't restock my medicine chest. Do you have a medical kit?"

"I have one in the truck."

"What's in it?"

Jack told her.

Hailey looked at her medicine chest and pulled out two trays. "I'll bring these two. You get your medical kit, and I'll try to put Humpty Dumpty back together."

As Jack got the medical kit out of the truck, Clodagh walked into the barn and waited for Jack to join her. "So now you've helped me, and I've helped you. I want my daughter back. Will you help find her?"

"Why do you think I can find her?"

"Well, I'm thinking your big red-haired friend is probably not the only friend you have in the police force. And from what I've seen and heard, you seem to be quite resourceful. Someone I'd rather have as a friend than an enemy."

Jack knew this was a subtle reference to the police from The Farm who'd taken away her mercenaries.

"Have you registered her with the police as a missing person?"

"Not yet. I was hoping she'd come home or just phone."

"Here's what we do. You register her with the police as a missing person. You give me a recent photo, her credit card details, and I'll see what I can do. Is there any place you think she might go? Does she do a particular sport?"

"She went to the gym. Right now, she is doing whatever Ralph wants to do. She's besotted with him."

"Did she work?"

"She worked for me. Looking after our finances. She has an accounting degree. She's not just beautiful, she's smart as well."

Jack was almost tempted to say, 'like her mother,' but that would have felt weird, and they weren't really friends. More like untrusting, new acquaintances with possible benefits if such a thing existed.

"Would she be using her credit cards or using cash?"

"Probably cash."

The police would need a search warrant to look at the bank details, but the beauty of cash was it was difficult to trace, in most cases, impossible.

"Does she have a lot of cash of her own?"

Clodagh didn't answer immediately, looking into Jack's eyes as if she could decide about trust by seeing something there. Jack held her gaze and waited.

Clodagh sighed. "She does."

"As I said, I'll see what I can do. Meantime Hailey's waiting on this medical kit."

They walked back, with the medical kit separating them.

"Jack, what do you plan to do about HTT with Ralph missing and the two developers who up and left?"

"Ralph's brother Stewart is still active, and I have two developers from another project I plan to use as an interim measure. Their background is in cybersecurity, but they should be good enough for what we need."

"Cybersecurity?" Jack noticed an increase in interest from Clodagh. But then it was a topic that got a lot of attention, where geek meets cool. "Are they good at it?"

"From what I've seen so far, yes, they are. Why?"

"Can you get them to contact me? I need to put cybersecurity in place."

Jack felt a smile sneak onto his face as he turned. "Is this so nobody knows what you're up to?"

Clodagh smiled, showing all her teeth like a wolf. "It's just good business practice, Jack. That's all and nothing more."

Kenny came out of the house with a single piece of paper and gave it to Jack. When Stella had put it on the screen, he'd seen his face but didn't comment. Instead, he gave the medical kit to the driver to hold and showed the page to Jimmy.

"That's him," said Jimmy. "That's Sam Dodd."

"Thanks, Jimmy."

Jack walked over to Bryce and Aidan and handed Bryce the photo as he was the closest. Bryce held it in his hand with his arm extended so that Aidan could see.

They looked at the photo, their expressions changing from interested to quizzical, then Bryce wiggled the paper at Jack. "Why do you have a photo of Sam Dodd?"

Kenny jumped into the conversation. "He's a person of interest in a case we're working on. Where do you know him from?"

"He's a regular at the gay bars in San Francisco," said Aidan. "We knew him back when we were living life in the fast lane. What's he done or supposed to have done?"

Jack looked at Freddie. Freddie nodded, and Jack looked back at Bryce and Aidan. "He's the main suspect in a serial killer case."

There was a joint air explosion from the mouths of Bryce and Aidan as they said, "What? You have to be kidding me."

Jack told them about the circumstantial evidence against Sam Dodd and his reluctance to give an alibi. Aidan shook his head and looked at

Bryce. "Sam, really, he needs to come out and declare himself. He should have done it a long time ago." Aidan turned to Jack and Kenny. "Sam never went hiking alone. He once told us that he felt his privacy was secure and his secret was safe in the forest."

"The dates," said Bryce. "Can you give me the dates when he says he was hiking? We'll make some phone calls and see what we can find out."

"I'll get you the list," said Kenny. "If you find anything, please write down a name and a contact number next to the date. That would be helpful. But I must say it feels strange that we're collecting alibis for Sam."

Jack and Kenny walked back. Kenny smiled and pointed at Aaron and Jimmy sitting side by side on the verandah, chatting away like old friends. Princess sitting next to Aaron on the opposite side to Jimmy. "That was Aaron's trademark," said Kenny. "Off the field, he was known as a true gentleman, like the word says, a gentle and well-mannered man. But on the field, he was ferocious and fast. Did you see how quickly he got to Jimmy and got the first punch in simultaneously with Jimmy hitting the ground? A remarkable athlete and person."

"My instructions from Uncle Alan were for Aaron to do light duties around the ranch."

Kenny chuckled. "I'm going to print out that list for Bryce and Aidan and phone Freddie."

Jack was looking at Hailey packing up her medical kit as he reminded himself to phone Stella and tell her the killer was still out there. And he would need some help from Numbers.

CHAPTER TWENTY-THREE

Jack sat at the kitchen table in the bunkhouse with Bryce and Aidan, listening to them explain their latest round of testing on HTT. It had revealed nothing new. Stella had not answered her phone, and Jack was hopeful she was still in negotiations in Detroit, surrounded by people from both parties. Safety in numbers. He needed a break from HTT, walked to the barn, and looked at his truck parked in the back. It was a quiet place, unintentionally meditative. He phoned Mary and looked at the rafters to see if the barn owls were watching him. She answered after three rings.

"Hello Jack."

"Hi, Mary. Just phoning to see how you and Jamie are doing. You've got quite a few things on the go at the moment."

Mary laughed. A happy sound, like a champagne cork popping. "We'll cope. Don't worry. I guess you want an update?"

"Yes, please."

"We've gone live with the software at Link Industries. It's now in support mode, and we'll be monitoring it closely for the next two weeks. We're sitting at Link at the moment."

"Good work. Stella will be pleased."

"Next is HTT. We haven't made much progress as we've been busy with the Link project, but give us two days, and I think we'll have finished the documentation and then be in a position to provide software support."

"That's quick. You two must be working long hours."

That laugh again. "We have been, but we're getting on top of it."

"Well, take care of yourselves. You don't want to burn out."

"Thanks for your concern, Jack. We'll take your advice."

"Oh, one more thing. Almost forgot. I've got a possible new customer for you. Doyle Enterprises."

Mary took three seconds to reply. "Can't say I've heard of them."

"Family business. Do you know a pub called Doyle's?"

"I think Jamie and I have driven past it. It's in the Tenderloin, isn't it?"

"That's it. The head office is in the back of the pub, and they have other businesses besides the pub. But I rather you speak to the owner and decide if you want the work."

"What's his name?"

Jack chuckled. "It's a her, not a him. Clodagh Doyle's the owner."

Mary made a noise that could have been a combination of coughing and giggling. "My error. I made an assumption."

"She's interested in installing cybersecurity at her businesses. I suggest you phone the pub and ask to speak to her."

"Thanks, I will." Mary sounded as excited as a squirrel with a new source of nuts. "And thanks for the lead. Anyway, I must get back to work. Bye, Jack."

Jack stared at the truck without seeing it. There was an idea swirling around in his mind, like looking across a mist-laden lake, unable to see the other side, waiting for a breeze to clear the mist. Jack returned to the bunkhouse and turned his attention to Bryce and Aidan. "Can I borrow one of your laptops? I want to try something."

Aidan passed his to Jack. "Use mine. For the testing we need to do, I can share with Bryce."

Jack typed away as he spoke. "Have you heard of Deep Learning?"

There was a shrugging of shoulders and shaking of heads.

"Deep learning is a subset of machine learning which is within artificial intelligence, and artificial neural networks are the basis of all this.."

"I've read about neural networks," said Aidan. "They're used to mimic the functionality of the brain."

Bryce frowned and looked at Aidan like he saw him in a new light.

"Yes. It learns by creating a neural network model that acts similar to humans. It allows computers to analyze data by creating patterns as it explores the data. From this, we effectively generate the neural network, and then it trains itself with the available data to generate a model. That's the weakness in what I'm about to try. I'm not sure if we have enough data to create a model. Data is the fuel or food for neural network models."

"I'm keen to see the results," said Aidan.

"Give me about an hour," said Jack.

Jack went into mental isolation as he typed on the keyboard. Bryce and Aidan left him and went for a walk. After seventy minutes, he stood, went out onto the verandah, and called out to Bryce and Aidan. They limped out of the barn and returned to the kitchen, and Jack passed back Aidan's laptop. "It'll probably run for twelve hours or more. Let's see what we have in the morning."

***

The kettle had finished whistling when Jack phoned Stella. "You'll be pleased to hear that we now know Sam Dodd is no longer a suspect."

"That makes me feel better about my judgment of human character."

"It does mean that the whole time the police have been focusing on Sam Dodd, the real killer has been out there, somewhere. And I'm feeling guilty as I provided the correlation which led the police to him."

"You used the data you had, Jack. And as you taught me, if you can get enough data, you can find the truth. Maybe you didn't have the right data?"

"That's been going around in my head since it was looking like Sam Dodd had an alibi. But it had to be someone associated with him, as the correlation I was coming up with was very high. I'm going to stick it in the back of my mind for now and let it bubble along all by itself." Jack looked at the monitor on the counter as he saw movement. Hailey arriving to drop off Aaron and Princess. "Do I need to remind you to be vigilant?"

"I was waiting for that. No, you don't. I'll be careful."

"How much longer will you be in Detroit?"

"I'm getting close to closing this deal. Tomorrow should do it. It'll make a big difference to Link if I pull this off. Just between us, I'll be pleased with myself. This company's a boys' club. They're not used to negotiating with a woman. When I arrived, they were surprised they had to deal with me."

"Good for you," said Jack. "But back to more mundane matters. Your cybersecurity system is now up and running and in support mode for the next few days. I'll monitor it and see if there are any glitches."

"Great, we can talk about it when I get back."

Which to Jack meant there were other things she wanted to do with cybersecurity but wouldn't talk about it over a mobile network. He was in the same boat, but he could mention a topic.

"I had a visit from Clodagh Doyle."

"Really. How'd that go?"

"Interesting. Lots to tell you."

"Looking forward to it. If I wrap this up tomorrow, I'll let you know when I'll be flying back. But now I have to shower and change. They are taking me to dinner, and I'm wondering if they will keep business off the table or ply me with wine, hoping I'll agree to their current proposal."

"Maybe you can ply them with bourbon and see if they agree to your proposal."

Stella laughed and said goodbye.

Jack walked outside to see Kenny and Aaron throwing a football back and forth. Princess was moving wherever Aaron went. Hailey had a horse trailer hitched to her truck and was sitting behind the wheel. Jack went over to her. The sounds of stomping and scraping of hooves were coming from the trailer.

"I've got two horses in the trailer that need rest for a few days. These two don't travel well, so I need to get them home as quickly as I can." Hailey's eyes sparkled as she grinned. "Otherwise, we could have gone for a swim." The stomping of hooves got louder. "Seems like my passengers are getting irritable. I'll see you later."

Jack watched Hailey drive away. Behind him, he could hear Aaron saying he had to feed Princess. He turned to see Aaron walking to the bunkhouse, Princess trotting next to him, tail wagging, and Kenny standing with the football in his hand. "I don't think you need to babysit me anymore. Clodagh's not going to do anything now that she wants me to find her daughter."

"I was thinking the same thing. Also, Freddie wants me back in the office to work on the serial killer case. He feels we have a ticking time bomb out there." Kenny flipped the football from one hand to the other without taking his eyes off Jack.

"If you could also give some attention to the disappearance of Sinead Doyle."

"I will, but there is not much I can do except circulate the info with all the other missing persons. There's a lot, and the attention goes toward children, older adults, and people with mental conditions. Also, if someone is over eighteen, they don't have to return home. It's only a police matter if it can be shown the disappearance was involuntary, as in, say, a kidnapping, which in this case, it looks more like an elopement."

All of this was leading Jack to talk to Numbers. Not Stella. Numbers.

"I'll head back to San Francisco early tomorrow," said Kenny. "What about you?"

"I've got some data analysis running, which I need to look at in the morning."

And depending on if Stella returns tomorrow.

***

At 6 am, Jack poured coffee into a mug and looked on the monitor to see Kenny's F150 leaving. The kitchen door was open, but Bryce and Aidan knocked before entering. Being well-mannered, they usually would have said, 'Good Morning,' but not today. Their faces were alive with excitement, making them look years younger.

"Your program's finished running," said Aidan.

"And we've been looking at the results on the screen. We believe we know what Liam's doing. But we want you to see before we say anything," said Bryce. "Don't want to lead the witness, so to speak."

"Great, let's go."

Mug in hand, Jack walked across to the bunkhouse kitchen. The day was starting out with clear skies and a slight chill in the air, which would soon disappear. Jack sat and looked at the results on the screen. He could see why they were excited, but he wanted to hear from them.

Jack took a sip of his coffee before speaking. "What's your conclusion?"

Aidan and Bryce looked at each other. "You tell him, Aidan," said Bryce, "as you were the one who figured it out."

"I've been watching the trading of Texas Steer Hides as they are an unofficial benchmark in the industry. See THS on the screen. That's them. Now, just before one of Liam's tanneries places THS on the portal, the inventory of THS for about eighty percent of the other tanneries vanishes. Many buy instructions are automated, so the law of supply and demand kicks in, and Liam gets a good price for his hides. Then the inventory that vanished reappears. If Liam's trade happens quickly and you weren't watching the portal, you wouldn't have noticed the inventory vanishing and reappearing."

"That's very clever."

"That's not the really clever part," said Bryce. "Think about it for a moment. As stockbrokers or ex-stockbrokers, we've seen markets manipulated. If Liam had removed all the other inventory and his was the only one on the portal, then, in all likelihood, it would get noticed. But he doesn't. Some tanneries' inventory stays unchanged, and his inventory effectively blends in with the other tanneries. And as he has three tanneries, they never appear at the same time on the portal. It's a clever scheme."

"Well done," said Jack as he looked from Aidan to Bryce with a frown like there was a missing piece of a puzzle. "How come you spotted it so quickly? Seems like you took one look at the results this morning, joined the dots, and came looking for me."

"This is what we were doing," said Bryce. "It's called Pump and Dump. Between Aidan and I, we would target a stock with a low trading volume so that we could control the market with our share trades. Then we would create artificial buying pressure with a lot of hype. The price goes up, then we sell. It is difficult for regulators to catch you doing this if you don't do it too often and mix it in with your other trades."

"We were good at it," said Aidan. "It's stressful, though, as you're trying to manage the trades and not get caught. One of the reasons we crashed."

"Liam, so far," said Bruce, "is playing it as we did. But as I said, it's illegal. If the police got hold of this, Liam would go to jail."

To get a bad outcome, there is nothing like combining two deadly sins, in this case, pride and greed. Uncle Alan would enjoy adding this story to his collection about the seven deadly sins. He had told them to him and Freddie from when they could understand the meaning behind the story. Uncle Alan never moralized. He just told a story and left it at that.

Jack was looking at the numbers on the screen and thinking if he had enough to take to Clodagh. Answer. No. "I'd have to show how he's manipulating the market, wouldn't I?"

"That's right," said Bryce. "But that's your department, isn't it?"

"Partly. I've got some people documenting the system at the moment. Once I have it, I'll give it to you guys, and if you could compare the documentation to your testing, we'll see if there's a mismatch anywhere."

"This Deep Learning algorithm you used," said Aidan, "it really worked well, didn't it? It seems like you did have enough data for it to do its magic." Aidan waved his arms and opened his hands like a magician releasing a white dove from a handkerchief.

Jack remembered what Stella had said. *Get enough data, and you will find the truth.* That thing at the back of his mind started to peep out. How did the data lead him down the path and conclude that Sam Dodd was the serial killer? Jack put it back in the back of his mind. "How are you guys coming along with alibies for Sam Dodd?"

"Just one definite so far," said Bryce. "We'll make more phone calls today."

The sunlight stopped coming through the door. "Good morning," said Aaron. "Hailey's here. I'll see you all tonight.

Jack followed Aaron to Hailey's truck, which had a horse trailer attached.

"Good morning," said Jack. "Have you got more patients in the back?" Jack pointed with his head at the trailer.

"Morning, Jack. No. One of my barrel racers has been resting at home. Taking him back to the vet practice. There're better facilities there to train, and I can get in some training when there's a gap between patients."

"When…" said Hailey, who didn't get to finish what she was going to say as Aaron got in the truck with Princess in his arms.

"Morning, Hailey," said Aaron.

Hailey looked at Aaron. "Morning, Aaron." Then back at Jack for two seconds like she was thinking about finishing what she was going to say. "We better get going, Jack. See you later."

Jack stood and watched them leave until the truck and trailer were out of sight.

CHAPTER TWENTY-FOUR

"They signed," said Stella, her voice breathless with excitement. "I don't know who else to share this with. I wasn't sure if I could pull it off. But now it's done and dusted. They've signed, and Link has already made part payment as per the contract."

Jack had lost track of time as he trawled through the data that had led him to Sam Dodd. He'd seen the time when he'd answered his mobile phone. 10:09 am. "Well done to you, Stella. I'm proud of you. You have every right to be pleased with yourself."

"Thank you, Jack. I feel like doing something terribly indulgent to celebrate."

"What do you have in mind?"

"Haven't decided yet. But it doesn't have to be today. I'm flying back tonight. Where are you? On the ranch?"

"Yep. On the ranch."

"How's it going there? I've been so wrapped up in my own little world I haven't bothered to ask."

"That's alright. You needed to focus on getting this deal done. Again, well done."

"Thank you. Thank you. Listen, I'd better get back into the board-room. Put on my calm and collected face like I do this every day. I'm taking them to lunch and then going to the airport. Be home by six o'clock. Are you going to come visit me?"

A warmth crept up Jack's body, making him smile. "Well, someone has to keep you safe as the serial killer is still out there and, according to the data, should already have a plan for his next victim."

"I'm sure there are many more suitable candidates than me, but I will accept your chivalrous offer, good sir."

Jack's phone vibrated. He glanced at it to see an incoming call. Freddie.

"Freddie's phoning. I better take it."

"And I'm back to the boardroom."

Jack ended his call with Stella and accepted Freddie's.

"Jack? Have you seen the morning paper?"

"And Good Morning to you, Freddie."

"Sorry Jack. Good morning. Stella West is on the front page of the business section of all the local papers. All about this acquisition she's just done of a company in Detroit. They're touting her as the number one candidate for Business Person of the Year. She already had a target on her back, but this has made her a more attractive one."

"I'll speak to her about beefing up her security. The killer has to show his hand in the next day or two. What have you done about the other possible targets?"

"Same thing as what you're doing. Beef up their security. Have you had any more insights from the data?"

"Nothing. But we have an alibi for one of the dates when Sam Dodd said he was hiking. I'll send it through to you. It's just a name and a phone number."

"It may be enough. I'll get Kenny to check it out," said Freddie.

"Does Sam Dodd know we're looking for alibis for him?"

"Not yet, but if this checks out, I'm going to get Kenny to present it to him, then hopefully, he'll give us the rest of the names."

"That'd be good, as I've got other things I want Aidan and Bryce to do."

"Understood. Kenny or I'll get back to you once we know more. Chat later. Bye."

Jack wandered around aimlessly, thinking about Sam Dodd and how the data analysis got it wrong, until he reached inside the barn. He looked up. The two barn owls were watching him.

"Well, what are your thoughts?"

The barn owls moved their feet like they were getting a better grip or preparing to fly and made no sound.

"I agree. I don't know either."

A movement next to the front left wheel of his truck caught his attention. It was half the size of his fist, gray, blending with the gray-black of the tires. It moved, and a tail flicked into view. A mouse. It flicked its tail again and was gone, just the end of a tail disappearing behind an old bale of hay as a barn owl landed on soundless wings where the tail had been.

Jack's phone rang, and the owl flew from its standing position back to the rafters. Mary. Cheerful Mary.

"Hello Jack. I'm not disturbing you, am I?"

"No, Mary, it's a good time to chat."

The owls shuffled up next to each other like they were looking for reassurance.

"We've completed the documentation on HTT. Can I email it to you?"

"Do you guys ever sleep? I didn't expect it so soon. I'll text you an email address."

Mary laughed what Jack called the 'Mary Laugh'. One always pleasant to hear and makes one smile.

"We're contractors, so if there's work to do, we do it. Make hay while the sun shines, kind of thinking."

"I get it. I'm in the same boat. Speaking of which, how's the cyber-security going at Link? Any problems so far?"

"Nothing technical. We've had to do some retraining, but otherwise, all good."

"Good job. Stella will be pleased with what you guys have achieved."

"Speaking of Stella, I see she's all over the newspaper this morning. Number one candidate for Business Person of the Year."

"Yes, it seems she pulled off quite a coup."

"Do you want to meet face to face so we can show you where we are?"

"I think we should," said Jack. "Would 4 pm today be a good time?"

"That'll work."

"I'm going to email the document now, and we'll see you at four."

Mary hung up, and Jack looked up at the owls. "Well, at least something's coming right." Jack looked around for the mouse. Not visible. No doubt hiding behind something in the barn.

Smart mouse.

***

In the bunkhouse kitchen, Jack explained to Aidan and Bryce how he wanted them to check Mary's documentation. "I want you to compare this documentation to the scenarios you've created. If the documentation describes functionality for which you do not have a test scenario, come up with one and test it. If you have a test scenario that is not in the documentation, make a note of it, and you can explain it to me when you've finished this exercise. Any questions?"

"So, you want us to cross-check," said Aidan, "from scenarios to documentation and from documentation to scenarios?"

Jack had forgotten how clever these two were. "Yes."

"I was trying to decipher," said Bryce, "where you were going with that long explanation of what you wanted us to do."

Aidan laughed. "Me too. I thought you wanted us to do something complicated."

"Sorry, guys," said Jack. "It's a habit from dealing with people who don't test their software thoroughly enough but instead wait until some poor unsuspecting user trips over the bug. Then they do the job they should have done in the first place."

"Leave it to us. We know what to do," said Aidan.

"You can phone me when you've finished," said Jack. "Anytime."

Jack figured if he was going to San Francisco, meeting with Clodagh while he was there would be a good idea, so he phoned the pub and asked to speak to her. They said she was busy and would phone back. He went to the kitchen and glanced at the monitor. His phone rang, and a number appeared, not a name.

"Have you found Sinead?"

"Not yet, Clodagh."

"Why did you phone?"

"I have to come to San Francisco today. I wanted to take the opportunity to hear from you more about Sinead that might give me a clue as to where she is."

"We can't do this over the phone?"

"Face-to-face seems to jog memories. That's why the police do it that way," said Jack.

"I'm available at one o'clock. That work for you?"

"It does."

"Good, I'll see you then. Goodbye."

"Clodagh. Wait. There is one thing I'd like you to do before I get there."

"What's that?"

"When I travel, what I take with me, falls into three categories. Functional things, like my electric toothbrush and shaving kit. Any clothing I need depends on the climate I'm going to and who I'm meeting, and my writing materials where I take the cheapest, plainest, spiral-bound, letter-sized notebook one can buy and a particular pen. Based on what Sinead has left behind, I'd like you to work out what Sinead has taken with her, and that may give us a clue where she might have gone."

"The first thing I did was check her closet to see if her clothes were still there. They seemed to be there, but I must admit my checking was not thorough. I'll do it again and look for what's missing this time."

"Thank you. I'll see you at one."

Next was Freddie. There was no answer on his phone, and it went to voicemail. Jack thought he should look in on Peter Wasserman while in San Francisco. He took his laptop outside onto the verandah, sat down, and looked at the barn. His phone rang.

"Hi, Freddie. I'm seeing Clodagh Doyle at 1 pm at her office, and I thought I'd come to your office after that."

"That'd be good. We're not making any headway on this serial killer case."

Jack said goodbye to Freddie and phoned Peter. Hannah answered the phone.

"Wonderful to hear from you, Jack."

"How are you and Peter doing?"

"I'm fine." Hannah paused. Jack thought he heard a sigh, but maybe just an electronic noise on the phone. "Peter's resting."

"I have to come to San Francisco today, and I wondered if I could visit you and Peter. It's short notice, I know, so if it is inconvenient, I can come another time."

"Not inconvenient at all. Peter and I would love to see you. What time?"

"Just after four."

"Perfect. I'll tell Peter when he wakes up. Goodbye, Jack."

Jack put his phone down and started reading the HTT documentation. Not exactly an exciting read, but Mary and Jamie had done an excellent job. The professionalism was appealing, even if the content was a possible cure for insomnia, and he hadn't finished by the time he needed to leave to meet Clodagh. So far, there was no mention of any functionality for tampering with the data.

CHAPTER TWENTY-FIVE

Jack left his truck in Stella's garage and caught a cab to Doyle's Pub. The trip from Pacific Heights to the Tenderloin was a journey from where one could live if one had the money to where one had to live when one didn't. The number of homeless living on the sidewalk increased, as did the drug dealers idling away their day on the street corner. On the block where Doyle's pub sat, it was like they'd swept it clean of any human detritus.

Inside, Jimmy was sitting in his usual chair, the ends of the stitches sticking out of his face like old toothbrush bristles.

"Hello, Jimmy. How are you?"

"You're Aaron's friend. How's he doing?"

"Great."

"When can I come visit him?"

"Whenever you want to."

"Thank you. Clodagh's expecting you. She told me to keep an eye out for you. Go on through. You know where the office is."

Jack walked past several patrons and knocked on the door. Waited. No response. Opened the door to an empty office. The entrance to the garden was open, so he went on through. There was Clodagh dressed in her office uniform, black pants, and white shirt, staring at the garden, her left hand rubbing her chin.

"Hello Clodagh."

Clodagh turned, dropping her hand to her side. "What do you know about reticulation?"

"Only the theory. Why?"

"I'm considering, seriously considering, making changes to the garden. If I do, the reticulation would have to change accordingly."

"I understand, but what has this got to do with Sinead?"

"Nothing. But it helps me with my worrying about her."

"Did you check out her stuff?"

"I did. You must understand Sinead is very particular about what she buys for her own use."

Jack chuckled. "Aren't all women?"

"Within their budget, that's true. In the case of Sinead, there were no limits to her budget. From what I see is missing and not missing, she's not flown anywhere, and she's gone to a beach."

"Please explain."

"Sinead has a travel pillow she always takes on a plane, and it's still here. When she met Ralph, she bought a new bikini, which was very revealing but did show off her fantastic figure. Not long after that, she went and bought a sports bikini. All her expensive sunscreens, lip balms, and hair conditioners are missing. But the one thing that makes me believe she is at a beach somewhere is a missing special bottle of Aloe Vera, which she always lathered herself with when she got back from the beach, and it's the only one she uses."

"You think she's on a beach somewhere? That narrows it down. The west coast has thousands of miles of beaches."

"I can narrow it down further. A beach in California."

"Why California?"

"Because the more she's traveled, the less she wanted to leave California." Clodagh smiled. "She's a true Californian. She wouldn't leave the state."

"Does she have any particular places she prefers?"

"I've already sent one of my people to all the places I know she likes. Nothing. Bear in mind, she always travels five-star, and there are a lot of tiny one-star places all along the coast."

"There are. Too many to go door to door. And you can't think of anything else except two new bikinis and a bottle of Aloe Vera."

Anger pulsed like a heartbeat across Clodagh's face, then it was gone. "Listen, Jack, I have thought and thought, and that's all I've got." The anger vanished from her face as quickly as the death of a shooting star. "But she's her mother's child, and if she decided to vanish, she would. I don't understand why she hasn't contacted me to let me know she's safe."

"But Ralph is in contact with Stewart, so we know they're alive and well. Maybe they only want one point of contact via a burner-phone, and they feel safer that way."

"Safe from what?"

"I don't know. Stewart's also in the dark as to why Ralph up and left."

"Well, if I think of anything, I'll let you know."

"I'll do the same."

"Your cybersecurity people, Jamie and Mary, came to visit me. They left about fifteen minutes before you got here. They seem very nice, but that wouldn't help me decide whether to use them, so I had Liam sit in on the meeting as he has more experience with this than I do."

"He sure does."

"Don't get smart. I already told you if you find out Liam's doing anything illegal, bring it to me first."

"That depends on what he's doing."

"Liam doesn't want to use Jamie and Mary. He says he can do it himself."

"If Liam says not to use them, that is a good reason to use them."

"What are you talking about?."

"For the sake of argument, let's suppose Liam is doing something illegal. To let him install cybersecurity is like asking a fox to put a fence around the henhouse. And why hasn't he done it already? Too busy? Maybe. But then, how come he has the time now? And you've got no way of knowing what sort of job he did."

Clodagh smiled like a teacher patiently explaining something to a child. "You must think I'm stupid. I was waiting to see Liam's reaction to Jamie and Mary. I'm contracting with them. They start tomorrow. They said they'll have some time to get the ball rolling."

Jack was processing what Mary and Jamie had to do. Support the new cybersecurity system at Link, and they'd finished the documentation of HTT, and Aidan and Bryce were comparing that to what they had tested. They had to provide support for HTT now. But Jack wasn't sure of the full extent of Clodagh's enterprises and how much work was involved. The wisdom of introducing them to Clodagh in the first place was questionable. Not just because he could be helping Clodagh hide her illegal activities but possibly putting Mary and Jamie in harm's way by associating with Clodagh and her troops. Then again, they must have worked at enough corporates to see illegal activities going on. Just that there they didn't carry guns. Well, not usually.

"Do you want them to install cybersecurity at all your businesses?"

"Yes. Why?"

"What about the ones you don't want the police looking into?"

"Jack, Jack." Clodagh smiled with her eyes, her lips pressed together. "You make out like I'm some criminal mastermind. Whereas I'm just a lady who runs a pub and likes to garden."

"Of course, Clodagh. What was I thinking?"

"But as you put it so nicely earlier, I want them to put fences around the hen houses. They don't need to know what the hens are doing."

***

"We let Sam Dodd go," said Freddie. "His lawyer, as expected, made a real song and dance act that we shouldn't have arrested him in the first place. We pointed out to him that if his client had provided the alibis as we asked, we would not have arrested him, and it's not our job to find them for people. His client was just lucky that someone else provided them. Anyway, forget the lawyer. Bigger things to worry about. Like a serial killer."

Jack sipped from his black coffee mug while waiting for Freddie to finish his tirade. "Have you got any more leads?"

"None. You?"

"None. And I'm still bothered by the fact that my data analysis led me to the wrong person."

"Don't beat yourself up over it. You crunched the data you had and came up with Sam Dodd."

"Just because Sam had audited all the victims. It could be someone connected with Sam. But the data I had didn't indicate anyone. I'm going back to basics, getting more data, and starting again."

Freddie raised an eyebrow. "I don't want to hear how you get data."

"And I'm not telling you. So long as we find the killer, right? Before we have another death."

"In this case, we're running out of time, so in this case, the end justifying the means looks acceptable to me."

"You're speaking as if I should have asked permission in the first place."

"No comment."

Jack went back to sipping his coffee. "Any news on Sinead Doyle as a missing person."

"Nothing. You know how many missing persons we have? Getting someone to find the child of a known criminal is not going to get much priority, particularly as it looks more like an elopement." Freddie sipped his coffee, looked over the top of the mug at Jack, then put it down in its resting place without taking his eyes off him. "You and Clodagh seem to be pretty friendly. What's going on there?"

"Mutual interest, that's all. I need to find Ralph. She needs to find Sinead."

It didn't seem like the right time to talk about the quid pro quo arrangement with the known criminal. Maybe it never would.

***

At ten minutes past four, Jack knocked on the front door of Peter's and Hannah's cottage. Hannah opened the door and greeted Jack with a smile and a hug like he was the returning prodigal son.

"Come in, Jack. Peter is in the TV room, and there's no cricket on, so you will have his full attention."

They went down the passageway to the TV room, where Peter was sitting the way he had the last time. Peter had an oxygen cylinder on a trolley with the prongs of the nasal cannula up his nose, held by elastic around his head. He didn't rise but smiled and held out his right hand, which to Jack looked more claw-like than the last time they met, and it felt like bones wrapped in parchment.

"Jack, wonderful to see you."

Jack sat opposite Peter with the table between them while Hannah glided out of the room.

"Good to see you too, Peter. How are you feeling?"

Peter lifted his left hand six inches off the armrest and lowered it down. "I'm dying. I told you already."

"We all are Peter. We had this discussion. You're probably one of those people who defies all the medical predictions."

"We'll see. We'll see. What have you been up to?"

"Amongst other things, I'm looking for Ralph and his girlfriend, Sinead. I haven't mentioned it to Barney and Sarah at this stage as I don't know if there's a problem or not."Say that again," said Hannah, who had appeared at the door with a tray and a tea towel over her left shoulder. Jack stood, took it from her, and placed it on the table. Two double-size mugs of matzah ball soup. Jack could smell the chicken broth and see the dumplings floating on the surface.

"The two of them up and left without telling anyone why and where they were going."

"Who is this Sinead?" said Hannah, like a protective mother hen.

"She's the daughter of Clodagh Doyle, who owns a pub in the Tenderloin."

"Never heard of her," said Hannah.

"I've met her," said Peter.

Jack was as surprised as a kid seeing Santa Claus with the Easter Bunny. "Where and why would you meet Clodagh Doyle?"

"She wanted to be a customer at CE. One of her people came to the salespeople, who brought their proposal to Martin and me. Martin at first was keen, but I was not keen as the whole deal didn't seem right."

"What did they want you to do?" said Hannah.

"They wanted a discount based on twenty percent of what they paid us would be in cash. It smelled like money laundering from the get-go. Martin was keen on the idea of getting the cash, and I had to sit him down and have a talk with him. I told him that if we didn't declare the cash, we would be guilty of tax evasion and fraud. If we did declare the cash, then what was the point? I told him we would be part of what I felt was a money laundering scheme with either one of these options. I didn't manage to convince Martin totally, but he was now hesitant to proceed with her, so he sent his salespeople to visit the stores where they sold the goods."

"They were like spies?" said Hannah with a smile that seemed to enjoy her husband was part of a spying operation.

As he paused, Peter seemed to relive the events. "Yes, I guess they were. Anyway, they came back with eight stores spread from Sacramento to San Francisco and down to San Jose. They had acquired them when the previous owners got themselves into financial difficulty. Even so, the purchase price was very low. The rumor back from the salespeople was that cash facilitated the transaction. Martin was now convinced and agreed not to proceed with them as customers. That's when I met Clodagh Doyle. She asked for a meeting with me."

"Hold it right there," said Hannah. "I forgot the crackers, and I want to hear the rest of the story." Hannah left with a flip of her tea towel.

Peter leaned forward in his chair with a wheezing sound and a hand beckoning Jack to come closer. "Not for Hannah's ears, but the salespeople told me there were rumors that she was involved in other activities like drugs, gun-running, and prostitution. And that she controls a large portion of the Tenderloin."

"That's not a rumor. That's true."

"How do you know that?"

"My cousin works at SFPD. He's a lawyer and runs a special unit. I sometimes help them within the limits of what I do, yet I don't really know what they do. But Clodagh Doyle is definitely on their radar."

Hannah returned with a plate laden with crackers. "You haven't touched your soup, either of you. Eat before it gets cold. It's good for you. Plenty of time to talk when you've finished." She patted Peter on the shoulder, smiled at Jack like a mother coaxing a reluctant child, and they both dutifully spooned away at the soup and the dumplings until the bowls were empty. Its chicken-flavored saltiness was comforting, as were the dumplings, and Jack told Hannah as much.

"Generations," said Hannah. "It's taken generations of trial and error to get that recipe just right. Now Peter, continue your story."

Peter made small nodding movements with his head. "I met with Clodagh Doyle in the boardroom. She was well-mannered, well-spoken, and expensively dressed. We discussed gardening for a while. Then she wanted to know why I'd blocked her proposal. I told her why. She didn't get offended. Just said she could arrange to make it profitable for me personally. I told her I would find that insulting. She then implied threats to my family and me. Then I had enough. Hannah, please pass me that photo."

Hannah unhooked a photo from the wall and passed it to Peter, who turned it so Jack could see.

"I showed this to her."

Jack leaned forward to see the twelve-inch wide by ten-inch-tall photo frame with the colored photo of two men in the middle. There was surprise in his recognition of everything in the picture.

"I think I've stood in that same spot," said Jack. "Overlooking the ruins at Masada with the Dead Sea in the background." Jack pointed at one man. "There's you." Jack chuckled. "With long hair."

"Do you recognize the man standing next to me?"

Jack leaned closer to the photo, then squinted. "Wow, Peter. This is a younger version of him, like you. I only saw photos of him when he became the director of Mossad. He was the previous director. Interesting photo, Peter." Jack looked at Peter, whose face was as inscrutable as the Mona Lisa. "Did Clodagh recognize him?"

"I wasn't sure if she would, but she did, and that was that. She thanked me for my time, and I never heard from her again." Peter passed the photo back to Hannah, who placed it back on the wall, fiddling with it until it was unquestionably level.

Sometimes events make you look at people through a new set of glasses, and if they have a secret, leave it with them, as we all have secrets that should stay secrets.

"Do you have a photo of Sinead?" said Hannah.

Jack opened his phone, scrolled through it, and passed it to Hannah, who blinked when she looked at it. "She's gorgeous." She gave the phone to Peter, who considered it like he was reviewing a set of accounts and handed it back to Jack.

"Clodagh believes they are on a beach in California, narrowing it down to over eight hundred miles of coastline. And I don't know enough about Ralph to guess where he might be."

"Have you asked Stewart?" said Hannah.

"Stewart asked me if I knew," said Jack.

"They may be spoiled brats, but those two are close. Growing up, they got up to all sorts of shenanigans, and when they got caught, they covered for each other."

"If I may suggest," said Peter, "sit down with Stewart and let him talk. Sometimes people know things without knowing they know things."

CHAPTER TWENTY-SIX

As darkness crept over The Bay, through Stella's lounge room windows, the lights on The Bridge were turning on. Jack and Stella surveyed the business section of the local papers strewn across the coffee table, where two glasses of red wine stood like chubby toy soldiers. Stella was on the front page of every paper. A reporter had accosted her at the airport, and that interview was running on TV.

"I'm glad," said Jack, "you're getting the recognition you deserve."

Stella held up her hand. "But not when there is a serial killer on the loose. That's what you're going to say."

"Yes."

"Well, I have no control over the timing of business opportunities nor on the movements of serial killers."

"Quite so. But this coincidence, in Freddie's eyes and mine, makes you the most probable target."

"I understand, but I can't lock myself away until the police find this killer. I have a business to run, and with this new acquisition, there's lots to do to bring into Link. It's one thing to do a deal like this and another to execute on the acquisition. And I have to be a visible presence.

Tomorrow, I'm in the office at eight, then fly to Detroit at noon. Not sure how long I need to be there."

"Can't you do this by a video call?"

"You're ignoring what I'm telling you. I have to be a visible presence. It's a bit of traveling, but it won't be for long."

"I'll drop you at your office. Then drive back to the ranch." Jack reached for his phone. "Maybe while I'm here, I should have breakfast with Freddie."

"I didn't think he was the type to take time to go out for breakfast."

"He's not. I'll bring takeaways, and we'll sit at his desk." Jack picked up his phone, texted then turned back to Stella.

"Right. So, after I drop you at your office, you'll have to make sure you're only in the company of people you can trust and that you're never alone. I'll collect you from the airport and bring you back here when you return."

Stella jerked her hands up, fingers spread, her exasperation as clear as a crystal glass. "I get it. I get it. Only people I trust. Never alone."

Jack decided this was an excellent time to top up their wine glasses, take a sip and wait. His phone pinged. Freddie was on for breakfast. Stella sipped her wine, watching the lights on The Bridge getting brighter by default as the remnants of the sun sunk below the hills. It took about ninety seconds before she turned to Jack.

"How's my cybersecurity implementation going?"

"It's up and running. Jamie and Mary did a good job. They're monitoring it to see if anything breaks, but so far, so good. Come to think of it. If I'm dropping you off at your office, it won't do any harm to have a face-to-face update with them while I'm there." Jack texted Mary, who replied like she'd been sitting with her phone waiting for Jack to message her. Meeting confirmed.

"I'll test it myself to see how effective it is."

SCAM AT MOUNT DIABLO

"That's not a good idea. You don't want Number's signature appearing on a Link Industries system. Instead, get a third party to do some penetration testing. They'll give you a report which you can hand to the auditors. In this case, Sam Dodd."

"Agreed. You're right. Can you organize that for me? Speak to Sam. He must know some reputable people."

"That'll be embarrassing as I'm the cause of him being arrested."

"He doesn't know that. I'll give you his details and tell him you'll contact him." Stella picked up her phone, and her thumbs jumped across the keyboard.

Jack heard his phone ping as Stella continued to type.

She finished typing, picked up her wine, and sipped while watching the screen. It pinged. "Sam says he will await your call." Stella put her phone on the table. "What else have you got Jamie and Mary doing? Weren't they going to do some documentation for you?"

"Yes. The HTT system. They documented it, and I gave it to Aidan and Bryce to compare to their test scenarios, and there's a perfect match. So, for Ralph to manipulate data, he would have to come in directly to the database."

"Manipulate data? Ralph? What are you talking about?"

"I'm trying to remember where I last updated you with the HTT saga."

"Start from the beginning. Doesn't matter if you're repeating yourself."

It took Jack eight minutes of talking without sipping his wine or staring at The Bridge, his attention on Stella's face. She didn't speak, sat back in the chair, glass in hand, not sipping like she'd forgotten she held it.

"Do you want me to find out how Ralph is doing this?"

"That would be great, but remember, we wanted to keep Numbers off the Internet radar."

"It would be good for me. A break from Link, and I'll hack in with short bursts."

"That reduces the risk, but it's still a risk. Freddie's people are always interested when Numbers pops up on the Internet."

"Let's start now. I could do with an intellectual challenge. But I'll need your help as you understand the application. Can you please bring the wine?"

***

By 8 pm, the wine bottle was empty. Jack had opened another one and carried it through to Stella's workspace. Numbers was off the Internet.

Jack had everything he needed to show Clodagh how Liam was manipulating data. He had the computer's IP address of Liam's computer that was doing the hacking. Numbers had downloaded the applications Liam ran to choreograph the changes in the data, allowing the trade to happen and then reinstate the data. Jack enjoyed understanding what Ralph had dreamed up and implemented. It was like a ballet with the dancers in a landscape that suddenly changed and would affect them positively or not. Then the landscape would revert to normal like it had been a dream sequence without the dancers knowing how it happened.

"Intellectually," said Stella, "it is quite beautiful."

"It is, but it's still fraud."

"Choices. You show Freddie, and Liam goes to jail, or show this to Clodagh, don't tell Freddie, and Clodagh is in your debt. What's it to be?"

"I need Clodagh's help more than I need to see another fraudster in jail. But I won't be telling her that."

"Do you plan to see her tomorrow?"

Jack reached for his phone. "I'm going to phone the pub now and see when she's available."

"Don't you have her mobile number?"

"No. She always phones me from a no-name number."

"But it's late to phone someone."

"She runs a pub. She's a night owl."

Jack phoned the pub. It took about twenty rings before someone answered, the sound of a busy pub in the background. He announced himself and asked if Clodagh could come to the phone. It took three minutes.

"Jack," said Clodagh, "have you got news about Sinead?"

"No. But I have news about how Liam is manipulating the HTT portal. When can I come and see you?"

There was a pause of four seconds as Clodagh absorbed this and worked through the implications. "Now is good, but you're probably on the ranch."

"I'm in San Francisco tonight."

"Can you come now? I'll arrange for Liam to be here. I want this settled."

Stella nodded.

"I can be there in twenty minutes."

"See you then. I'll organize parking for you out the front. Jimmy'll be outside." Clodagh hung up with no farewell salutations.

"Go," said Stella. "I'll be here when you get back."

CHAPTER TWENTY-SEVEN

It was five to 9 pm when Jack approached Doyle's pub in his truck. He could see Jimmy in his uniform standing guard between two yellow cones. As he got closer, he could see Jimmy smile and beckon him. Jack slid the Yukon between the cones, got out, laptop in hand, and went around the truck to Jimmy. Two drunks were being escorted out of the pub by the staff. They were protesting their eviction using four-letter words without repeating themselves, which indicated a breadth of knowledge of choices regarding swearing. Once outside, the drunks staggered around to push their way back in. Jimmy grabbed each one by the back of his collar and pointed them down the street with a shove. They turned around, fists raised, ready to box, until they saw it was Jimmy, turned, and continued in the direction Jimmy had shoved them, muttering to each other.

"Hello Jimmy."

Jimmy took his eyes off the departing drunks and turned to Jack. "You're Aaron's friend. When can I come visit him?"

This would be the opening conversation Jack would always have with Jimmy. He didn't mind.

"Anytime you like, Jimmy."

"I'm still scared of dogs."

"I know, Jimmy. Where's Clodagh?"

"In her office."

Jimmy looked at two guys who appeared to be idling away the evening by leaning against the wall smoking a cigarette. "Watch this truck. Nothing must happen to it." The guys nodded and went back to idling. "Jack. Follow me."

Inside the pub, people occupied the tables, littering them with plates of food and drinks. The bar was two layers deep with drinkers and queuers. People were dancing to an Irish band composed of a violin, a banjo, and a bass. All traditional instruments for an Irish band, except these, were all electric and belting out cover versions of eighties songs. Jimmy walked through the crowd, and Jack followed like a dinghy following a tanker. People saw Jimmy and moved aside, or the people bounced off him.

Clodagh was sitting at her desk. Liam was in a visitor's chair, looking at his phone, his shillelagh resting against his leg. When he saw Jack, his visage became like a vulture, and Jack was just a carcass.

"Take a seat, Jack, and give me the summarized, non-technical version."

"Just one request. No interruptions until I've finished."

"You got it." Clodagh looked at Liam. "No interruptions."

Liam nodded, drew a deep breath, raised his eyebrows, and rolled his eyes upwards. He tilted his head back to look at the roof and exhaled with a long sigh.

"Clodagh, come around this side of the desk so I can show you on my laptop."

She moved Liam across one chair and sat next to Jack while Jack started his laptop and asked for the pub's Wi-Fi password.

"Clodagh, I'm going to give you a demonstration of how the software works. This is how the customers see it, be they, buyers or sellers. It just occurred to me, have you ever seen how the system works?"

"Liam gave me a demonstration when he first got involved with HTT. That was a while ago."

"Think of this as a refresher course."

She watched the screen and listened to Jack as he took her through the functionality for twenty minutes. "Any questions, Clodagh?"

"No. It's how I remembered it. I saw some new features, but maybe I'd forgotten these since Liam showed me."

"I had the whole system documented by Jamie and Mary and tested by two ex-stockbrokers."

"Are they the ex-stockbrokers from The Farm?"

"Yes. How would you know that?"

"One of my employees is a guest of The Farm. Word got back to me. No big deal."

Before refocusing, Jack took a moment to wonder about the extent of Clodagh's network.

"Now, I'll run Liam's programs and show you what he does with them."

Liam jerked forward as if a taser had touched him. "What do you mean, my programs?"

"Liam," said Clodagh, her voice as cold as the North Pole, "I told you to be quiet."

Jack showed Clodagh, step by step, how Liam altered the data, then restored it once his trade had happened. Liam's face changed to disbelief like he'd seen a ghost, not believing this could be happening as Jack peeled away Liam's indiscretions like the layers of an onion.

"Well, Clodagh, that's it. What has taken me fifteen minutes to show you happens in under five seconds during a trading day. People blink. Think? What was that? Some get an unexpected great trade, and they're happy. The others check the system, and the data's fine. They just view these trades as outliers and get back to work. Where Liam has been clever is in not being greedy. Liam's trades are in amongst others. Hiding a tree in the woods. Aidan and Bryce tested the system with a stockbroker's sense of how trading should work. Their discovery was accidental. They simply spotted an anomaly and started digging."

Jack had more to say, but Clodagh stopped him by raising her hand from the chair, palm facing Jack, as she turned to Liam. "Leave us. We'll talk later."

Liam didn't argue but left like a naughty boy sent to his room by his mom. His knuckles were white on the shillelagh as he looked at Jack, who could almost hear the wheels of vengeance whirring in Liam's head. The door was closed with a click. Clearly, Clodagh didn't abide the slamming of doors from naughty children.

Clodagh went back behind her desk. "I interrupted you, Jack. Please carry on."

Jack closed his laptop and leaned forward. "I think you're worried, not because of what Liam's been up to, but that it leaves a trail like breadcrumbs back to other parts of your business."

Clodagh's face was unmoving, but her eyes were on Jack like a cobra on a mongoose. "Go on."

"Let me run a scenario past you, hypothetical, of course."

"Of course."

"Your businesses, like this pub, generate cash. You don't declare the cash but make it vanish into your tanneries in the form of cash payments for repairs and maintenance, for example. You sell the hides legitimately through a portal like HTT, and the money is now squeaky clean. Now, if Liam's escapades become known, what you're doing would unravel as the police worked their way back through the money trail. Additionally, it becomes more interesting to the police if you were involved in other activities like drugs and prostitution."

"This is hypothetical, of course?"

"Of course."

"And there were opportunities to expand this to other businesses. But not everyone was interested. Like Peter Wasserman at CE."

Clodagh's mask slipped like a lizard shedding its skin. "Peter Wasserman. Where do you know him from?"

"That's how I got involved with HTT. I did some CE work, and Peter asked me to meet Barney and Sarah. Ralph's parents. Peter and Barney have been friends for a long time."

Clodagh frowned. "I didn't know that. What do you know about Wasserman?"

Jack didn't know Clodagh's concern, but he fed it. "We watch cricket together. He's told me his life story over soup and crackers." The concern on Clodagh's face was spreading like a bushfire, and Jack thought he would feed the fire some more. "He's had an interesting life. Not your typical accountant." Jack made a note to ask Freddie about Peter.

Clodagh's face was now one of command, like the master of a ship. "I will speak to Liam, and you have my assurance he will stop this foolishness."

"Foolishness. Market manipulation is not foolishness. It's fraud. Plain and simple."

"I said before. We can help each other. If you forget about Liam's, let's call them indiscretions, then I owe you a favor, which I will honor. Also, there is another problem if you take this to the police."

Jack knew the other problem but wanted to see if Clodagh had also seen the future.

"What's that?"

"Confidence in the integrity of the HTT trading portal. Word gets out what Liam has been doing, customers will stop using the portal faster than you can say shillelagh. It's not Liam's money that's invested in HTT. It's mine."

"All right, let's go with you getting Liam to stop and get out of the business, and you owe me a favor."

"Done. Now that's settled, speaking as a shareholder in HTT, how will the business keep running?"

"Well, I've covered the tech support with Jamie and Mary. Stewart will continue making sales. As far as the running of the business, let me get back to you."

Clodagh nodded, looked at the painting of her two children, and her face morphed to one of sadness like the silence at the end of a favorite song. "Are you making any progress in finding Sinead?"

"None. Except for you telling me they're most probably on the California coast somewhere."

"Remember, if you locate Sinead, I'll happily owe you two favors."

"I do." Jack stood. "Once I find anything, I'll call you. Enjoy your evening Clodagh." Jack paused like he'd forgotten something. "I don't suppose you do takeaways, do you?"

"We do. But the only thing on the menu at nighttime is Irish Stew, cooked with the proper ingredients."

"The proper ingredients?"

"Yes. Mutton, not beef, onions, potatoes, and carrots. The peasant farmers of Ireland only had sheep and vegetables that grew in the ground. That's all. I stick with the traditional."

"Next thing, you'll have me drinking Guinness."

"Good idea. Why don't you sit at the bar and have a Guinness while I talk to the kitchen."

"Can I have two takeaways, please?"

Clodagh had a cheeky grin like a chipmunk. "Is one for a friend, or is it for breakfast?"

"I'll be in the bar."

"Then I'll assume a friend."

Jack left the office and had to edge sideways through the patrons. Jimmy was sitting on a stool at the end of the bar and waved for Jack to join him. More edging through the crowd got him to Jimmy, who pushed the stool away and stood to make room for Jack.

"Thanks, Jimmy. Is it always like this?"

"No. Some nights it's busy."

Jack looked up at Jimmy's face, which was immobile as he scanned the crowd, then headed off to the other side of the room.

"Clodagh tells me you're having a Guinness?" said the barman, who appeared behind Jack as he watched Jimmy moving through the crowd. He placed a glass full of dark liquid with white foam on top in front of Jack, then returned to the other customers waving hands. Jack put his laptop on the bar, picked up the glass, and tasted the malty sweetness with the hoppy bitterness. It was an acquired taste, and he wasn't quite there yet, despite the hint of coffee and chocolate.

The band had moved back in time to the seventies as Jack watched Jimmy walking towards the front door. Two men in jeans and black T-shirts were shambling in front of him. One of them turned back to Jimmy and spoke, which Jack could not hear above the crowd and the band. Jimmy did, and he seemed unimpressed with what was said. He pushed the guy sending him ten feet forward, arms flailing, almost falling. This stopped any further conversation. Jimmy ushered them through the door, followed them out, and returned five minutes later to take up his post next to Jack. The barman placed a paper carry bag on the bar in front of Jack.

"Here's your takeaway."

"Thanks. What do I owe you for the food and the Guinness?"

"Nothing. Clodagh says it's on the house."

"Well. Thank her for me. Much appreciated."

Jack finished his Guinness, said goodbye to Jimmy, and went through the front door, laptop in his left hand, takeaway in his right. The knob of the shillelagh was halfway through its horizontal arc like a baseball bat swinging in from his right-hand side. He lifted the paper carrier bag as protection, which exploded upon impact as it saved his ribs from fracture. Meat, potatoes, carrots, and more gravy than he thought would have been in the containers, exploding over his face and chest.

Jack dropped the bag, and his laptop, grabbed the club with both hands below the knob on the end and looked sideways at Liam's face. The man snarled like a rabid dog, spittle accumulating at the sides of his mouth and chin. Seems exposing him in front of his mother had brought out the brat in him. Liam pulled the club with both hands and leaned back to free it from Jack's grasp. Jack went with the move, spun away from the club to his left, still holding on with his right hand, and sent a reverse kick to the groin. Liam bent down into a squat with a groan but held onto the club. Jack delivered a reverse roundhouse kick, his heel connecting with Liam's head, making him go as limp as spaghetti and collapse to the pavement. Jack yanked the club from flaccid fingers.

Using his hands, he wiped the stew from his hair, face, and clothes as best he could, then his sticky hands on a clean part of his T-shirt. He picked up his laptop, which had a corner of the casing missing, the shillelagh, and went back into the pub to Clodagh's office, entering without knocking. Clodagh laughed when she saw Jack.

"Didn't I mention you're supposed to eat it, not wear it?"

"You did forget. By the way." Jack held out the shillelagh. "Can you please lock this away? Every time I see Liam, he takes a swing at me."

Clodagh's face clouded with motherly concern. "Where is he now?"

"Outside, resting on the pavement."

Her eyes scanned the food on Jack's clothes with distaste as though she had sucked on a lemon. "Stand there, don't sit or touch anything. You'll mess up my furniture." Clodagh picked up her phone and gave instructions without raising her voice. Someone was to take Liam to the hospital, and Jack could feel the stew congealing on his face. Jimmy arrived with a paper bag for takeaways, a towel, and a white shirt like the bartender wore, gave them to Jack, and left.

Jack pulled off his T-shirt, dropped it in the takeaway bag, and saw Clodagh's eyes roaming over his torso. He wiped himself and his laptop with the towel and put on the shirt.

"I see there's a piece missing from your laptop. Does it still work? If it got broken in your scuffle with Liam, I'll buy you a new one."

Jack opened it up and balanced it on his left arm as he typed with his right hand. "It works."

Clodagh's phone rang. She answered, listened, and said, 'Thank You.'

"Your takeaways will be waiting for you at the bar." A smile curved the right side of Clodagh's mouth. "And Jack, try and be more careful this time."

Jack gave a thin-lipped smile in return. "I'll try."

"Can I ask another favor?"

"What is it?"

"It's not for me. It's for Jimmy. He keeps asking me when he can visit Aaron."

"I'm driving back to the ranch tomorrow. Jimmy can come with me. I'll collect him at four."

"Wonderful. He'll be thrilled. What will you be driving?"

"That Yukon you saw in the barn."

"Great, he'll fit."

"He can stay a few days if he likes. There're spare rooms in the bunk-house. What does he eat?"

"No special dietary requirements, but I'll send food with him. I try to stop him from getting fat. Healthy eating." Clodagh's face soft-ened, almost sad. "Jimmy has no friends. People are either scared of him because of his size or find his autism off-putting. That's why this visit to Aaron is such a treat for him."

"Where'd you find him?"

"Some years ago, one of my employees told me there was this big kid bullying the other kids in the neighborhood. They thought he was living on the street somewhere, and the kids were saying he was a bit weird. So, I told them to collect him and bring him to me. It took four of my people to shepherd him down the streets to my office. The first thing I did was feed him. I sat with him in the bar and watched him eat two bowls of stew without speaking. He was far younger than his size indicated. He was only sixteen and already six foot five."

She'd looked away when she started talking, and now she met his gaze.

"Bottom line, I gave him a place to stay, three meals a day, a tutor as he'd not had much education and a job. I had doctors assess him. He's autistic. How far up the scale? Well, that's for the academics to ponder. He's functional, and that's all I care about. He started off doing odd jobs for me. Now he helps me with my garden as his memory is off the charts, and as a bouncer. The result of all this is that he's always been an outsider."

Jack was thinking of the dark thing in the cave at the base of his spine, waiting for his PTSD to kick in. It was not ordinarily visible. Not like Jimmy.

"Where were social services in all this?"

"You're kidding. Nice people. Overworked. Underpaid. They have bigger problems than a giant autistic kid."

"How long ago was this?"

"Five years."

"We had his twenty-first birthday party two months ago."

"How do you know his birthdate?"

"I made his birthday the date I found him as he didn't know, and he'd told me he was sixteen."

Jack raised an eyebrow but said nothing. Maybe there wasn't much difference between Clodagh and Aunt Louise. Apart from Clodagh running a criminal organization, that is.

CHAPTER TWENTY-EIGHT

Jack walked from the garage into the kitchen, placing his laptop and the takeaways on the counter. He called out to Stella, who arrived with Jack's glass of wine and a kiss but recoiled.

"Is it you who smells like stew, or is it the takeaways?"

Jack took the glass of offered wine. "Both."

"I'm hungry, but food will have to wait. You're getting in the shower. Go into the laundry and drop all your clothes on the floor. Where did you get that shirt?"

"Clodagh gave it to me."

"I'll be in the bathroom."

The wine tasted good as he walked to the laundry. He returned naked, placed his glass on the counter, and went to the bathroom. Stella was already in the shower. "Jump in. Let's be quick. As I said, I'm hungry."

Jack knew this would not be quick.

***

At 7 am, Jack drove his truck into the underground parking at Link Industries and parked in a visitor's parking space. There was no one around. Stella took the lift to the executive floor, and Jack took the stairs to the second floor and punched the code on the keypad to the IT department. The room was a bunker. It looked like a bigger version of Stella's workroom at her house. Jack greeted two guys seated at consoles monitoring servers and networks. He found a place to sit, opened his chipped laptop, and started checking and testing the cybersecurity implementation. He made notes in his cheap notebook with his cheap pen.

The implementation was doing the job within the software's limits, didn't break, and had no software bugs. The software also ran on a cell phone. Which he knew was the first place Stella would want to get alerts and see dashboards. The problem with a cell phone screen was that it was small. He made notes on how to improve the visualization on the cell phone. It was too busy, and it looked like they'd taken what was on the desktop and deployed it to the cell phone. More notes. Some of the data feeds to the screen were on-demand with a refresh button. Others were pushed to the phone as and when something triggered an alert. More notes.

Software implementors and developers often saw themselves as new-age artists and could become defensive in protecting what they saw as their creation. His initial dealings with Mary and Jamie had gone well, but now he was about to change things. They could behave like Michelangelo would have if you wanted him to amend his paintings on the Sistine Chapel after he'd finished it.

"Good morning Jack," said Mary. Jamie's greeting followed like an echo.

"Morning, Mary. Morning Jamie."

"Been here long," said Jamie.

"Got in about seven. Gave me a chance to spend some quiet time to go through the system."

"What have you got for us?" said Mary.

"Overall, it looks good. I've just got some usability things I'd like to see done and ways to speed up the screen responses."

"Great," said Jamie. "Let's get started."

What had taken Jack an hour to study, he'd condensed to a fourteen-minute delivery.

"These are great ideas, Jack," said Mary, who turned to Jamie. "How long will it take to make these changes? One day?"

"That's quick," said Jack. "Listen, you're not under any deadline here. I just want it done in a reasonable time frame. Also, I've been thinking about another thing I should have done before, but other priories prevailed."

"What's that?" said Jamie.

"I'd like you to come out to the HTT office at Mt. Diablo and see the facility. You're going to be supporting the software, and it might generate some ideas on how to do it better or easier."

"When would you want us there?" said Jamie. "We have this other work we have to do for Clodagh Doyle, and it turns out it's a bigger job than we thought. There are a lot of businesses, each with its own infrastructure. She doesn't want them moved onto the one where we could have ring-fenced just that one. She wants each one separately ring-fenced with its own cybersecurity."

Seems an excellent way to keep people like the police from knowing the full extent of your activities.

"Jamie," said Mary, "If we finish Jack's changes today, we can go to the HTT office tomorrow. Then we can concentrate on the work for Clodagh Doyle."

"You're right," said Jamie. "How far away is it, Jack?"

"One hour, give or take, depending on where you're starting from. Don't you guys have any questions or comments about my suggestions?"

"None from me," said Mary. "Jamie, how about you?"

"None from me. It's clear what we need to do."

"Great," said Jack. "I'm driving back to the ranch later today." Jack scribbled on his notepad, tore out the page, and handed it to Mary as she was closer than Jamie. "This is the address. When you get there, there's a long driveway to the house, then a side road on the left of the place, which will take you to the office at the back. You'll see my Yukon there. What time will you get there?"

Mary looked at Jamie. "What do you think? Noon?"

"That'll work," said Jamie. "But we better get to work."

"Let me get out of the way then," said Jack as he closed his laptop.

***

Jack was a believer that San Francisco continually redefined the breakfast burrito. It did not seem possible that a simple tortilla filled with two eggs, cheese, bacon, shredded lettuce, sour cream, and chili sauce could taste this good.

At just after 10 am, Jack placed two brown bags on Freddie's desk and pushed one across the table to Freddie. Freddie increased the speed of typing an email, hit Send, and spun his chair around to eat. He took a mouthful, got up, went out the door, and returned with black coffee in yellow mugs and serviettes tucked under his arm.

"Any leads on the serial killer?" said Jack.

"None since yesterday. In case we missed anything, I've got two guys dedicated to re-checking all the information we have so far. It's produced nothing new. Did you tell your friend, Mrs. West, to be extra vigilant?"

"I did."

Sometimes, it was challenging to share a concern with anyone. Rather, it sits like a dark mist at the back of the mind and move the conversation somewhere else.

"Have you ever heard of a Peter Wasserman?"

"No. Who is he?"

"He's an elderly man who's the CFO at CE. I briefly did some work there, and I've been to his house twice. He showed me a much younger picture of him and the previous director of the Mossad. I just thought it interesting."

"I take it you've been to all the social media sites?"

"Couldn't resist it. Came up with nothing. Like a ghost."

Freddie spun his chair around, typed, waited, typed more, and read from the screen.

"He has no police record. The only place he appears is a mention in some military records."

"You have access to military records?"

"Intergovernmental cooperation. I am provided with enough information to check if someone of interest is in the military. It is categorized, and people who reside here but have been in another country's military are also provided. There's a file for him. It just says Israel, Mossad. The file is secured. Maybe he was an accountant in Mossad. Everyone needs an accountant. Anyway, thanks for breakfast. I've got to get back to work. Other cases to work on. When are you going back to the ranch?"

"Later today. I'm going to go to the apartment first and pick up some things."

Peter Wasserman. Mossad. Clearly, Clodagh had more information about Peter than Freddie did. Enough to make her nervous.

***

Jack opened all the windows in his apartment in Diamond Heights and walked up the one flight of stairs to the flat roof. The noontime sun exposed the buildings below the six-story apartment to the edge of The Bay, with hardly a shadow between the buildings. The apartment block belonged to the family trust, but Freddie and Jack still paid rent for their apartments on the top floor. There were two apartments per floor. Kenny was on the fifth floor, and cops from the Academy occupied the rest. Freddie changed the codes for the keypad on the roof and the underground parking once a month and when there was a new tenant.

Jack sat at the gray concrete table with the gray concrete bench sheets next to the concrete BBQ, with the smell and memories of previous BBQs still creeping through the air. Jack opened his notepad and wrote Serial Killer at the top of the page. Then all the towns in date sequence where the killer had struck. He pulled the victims' names and their companies via his cell phone from his cloud storage and put them next to the towns. Jack put a rectangle around the name, Sam Dodd. He had nothing else to write.

At the top of the next page, he wrote Ralph and Sinead. On the first line, he wrote Sinead, followed by the words: accountant, unique new bikini, aloe sunscreen, will be carrying cash, will not use credit cards. On the second line, he wrote, Ralph, followed by the words: gym bunny, no other interests, has cash, will not use credit cards.

He wrote HTT at the top of the third page. On the first line, he wrote: Liam. Stopped. On the second line: need new CEO. He put: Meet with Barney and Sarah Dubin on the third line. On the fourth line, he wrote: Deep Learning. At the bottom of the page, he wrote Peter Wasserman, Mossad, and put a rectangle around it.

**

By 2:30 pm, Jack had picked up Stella and was driving south to the airport. In this traffic, he figured he'd be back in good time to pick up Jimmy.

"What did you get up to today?" said Stella.

"My notepad is there in the center console. Have a look at the last three pages."

It took her four minutes to read each page twice.

"You had success with Deep Learning. Why not try that?"

"In catching Liam, I must have had just enough data for Deep Learning to do its magic. I'm nervous to try it on the data for the serial killer and come up with another incident as I did with Sam Dodd."

"Why don't you run it with the data you have? We'll know you need more data if Sam comes up again, and I'll get you more data. You must just point me in the right direction, so I know what to get."

"I take your point about using Deep Learning with my data, but getting Numbers out on the Internet is always a risk."

"If I do it, it will be from my workspace at home. From there, anyone will battle to track me to my IP address. And after this morning's meetings, I'm not sure how long I'll be gone. A day. A week. I know this is a problem. As you told me, this serial killer works according to a schedule. Maybe the phases of the moon. We should have had this conversation last night. Then I could have got the ball rolling."

"If I recall, something about me wearing Irish Stew and a shower."

"Distractions, Jack. Gets us every time." Stella turned the page to Ralph and Sinead. "I find this very odd, you helping Clodagh Doyle."

"Me too."

"I asked some of my colleagues about Irish pubs, and they mentioned her pub in the Tenderloin. When I asked if it was safe to go there, they said it was very safe so long as you abided by her rules. They had heard that she controls many blocks of the Tenderloin, and that's why it was safe."

"The police have the same info."

"It seems you have not progressed anywhere with finding Ralph and Sinead."

"True, and I don't even know what data to use as they have gone off the grid by only using cash."

"Clever of them and lucky them that they have the resources to have that much cash. Maybe you shouldn't be putting all your eggs in one basket. The data basket."

Stella turned to the third page. HTT.

"What's the problem here? You need a CEO. You have those two unemployable ex-stockbrokers living at the ranch. Make them joint CEOs. I mean, HTT is a trading platform."

Jack shot a glance at Stella. *Sometimes you need another set of eyes to look at a problem.* "That's a great idea."

"What is this Peter Wasserman at the bottom of the page?"

"He's the CFO at CE. It's a reminder for me to phone him."

CHAPTER TWENTY-NINE

By 5 pm, Jack and Jimmy were an hour into their trip to the ranch. Jimmy's suitcase, a cooler-box, and overflowing cardboard boxes were in the back of the truck. Jack didn't know the contents, but Clodagh had been out on the street as her staff loaded these into the Yukon. Jimmy had stood there as Clodagh took him to one side and spoke to him like a mother seeing her child off for the first day of school. Jimmy waved out the window at them as Jack pulled away from the curb. For an hour, Jimmy watched the scenery passing by.

"I'm sad that Sinead is missing," said Jimmy. "She's like a sister to me."

"I can understand that, Jimmy. Do you have any idea where she might have gone?"

"She never said anything to me. She just went with her boyfriend, Ralph. Not even a goodbye."

"What about Ralph? Did he ever say anything?"

"He was always coming or going from the gym. Didn't talk to me much. Maybe it was because I told him it was a stupid idea. Maybe I shouldn't have said anything, as he was very excited about it."

"What? Going to the gym?"

"No. Not the gym. He'd got Sinead interested in it, or she just followed him along."

"What were they doing, Jimmy?"

"You go under the water and hold your breath for as long as you can. Some people, they told me, go very deep in the ocean. I told Ralph it was a stupid thing to do. He never talked to me much after that."

Sometimes the mind seems to join the spinning dots like a solar system in the universe of your skull without being asked.

Freediving. The twins. Laguna beach. Was it possible?

Jack was guessing how long to drive there. Maybe eight hours.

"Jimmy, where were they doing this?"

"Sinead told me they were practicing in a swimming pool, but they'd like to try it in the ocean."

"Did she ever mention a place?"

"No. I told her it was a stupid idea. She never spoke about it either after that. I think that sometimes you shouldn't tell people their ideas are stupid, even if they are."

Jimmy slumped down in the seat, stared down the highway, and sighed like a burden was across his shoulders.

It was getting close to 6 pm when Jack arrived at the ranch house. Aaron was walking to the barn when he saw Jack coming but turned back, and a smile split Aaron's face when he saw Jimmy. Jimmy was as happy as a kid getting ice cream at a picnic. Jack explained Jimmy would stay for a few days. Aaron and Jimmy took the contents in the back of the truck to the kitchen.

Jack made a phone call and stared at the barn. He got back in his truck and drove down to Marsh Creek Road.

***

At 6:30 pm, Jack sat in the Gathering Room of the Dubin house with Barney and Sarah.

They had both greeted him at the door. The strain of not knowing the whereabouts of their eldest child had shown in the deepening furrows around their mouths and their sunken cheeks. Jack thought Ralph better have a good reason for putting these two lovely people through this stress.

Barney offered Jack a drink. Jack declined. Barney said he was getting one as he needed one. Barney looked like he needed a drinking companion. Jack changed his mind and accepted the offer of a single malt. Barney asked Sarah if she wanted a drink. "No, thank you. I want to hear what Jack has to say. Come and sit down."

"I know that Stewart told you that Ralph and his girlfriend are missing."

"Yes," said Sarah. "And this girlfriend. Who is this girlfriend?"

"Her name's Sinead Doyle."

Sarah was processing this like an equation in quantum mechanics.

"Sarah, Barney. The reason I'm here. Have you ever been to Laguna Beach?"

"When the boys were younger," said Sarah. "We went there once a year. Why?"

"I have a slim lead and wanted to see if it's worth pursuing."

Barney raised his glass to Jack and took a sip. "To be clear, we went there every year until both boys had turned eighteen. Then I spent my holidays collecting them from bars after the managers phoned me. I said to Sarah, enough is enough."

Sarah looked at Barney, shaking her head. "You're such a grouch, Barney. Jack, they were just young, having fun, and never caused any trouble. It was a phase. Like now. Ralph is in a gym phase."

"Did they have any particular bar they preferred?"

"Stewart told me about one called The Loft," said Sarah. "It seemed this was the place to go if you wanted to be seen by the in-crowd."

"I'm guessing," said Jack, "they won't be going there." Jack had a flash of who might go there. "Any idea where they would go if they wanted to be inconspicuous?"

"None," said Barney. "They only went to places where they could be seen."

If there were places where you could guarantee being seen, you must know places where you would not be seen.

"Are you thinking of going to Laguna Beach?" said Barney. "If you are, I'll cover all expenses."

"I'll keep it in mind, Barney. Thank you."

Barney nodded at Jack and took a sip.

"Can we talk about HTT for a minute?" said Jack. "Remember, that's why I'm here in the first place."

"Of course," said Sarah. "Ralph and Sinead's disappearance is all we have been thinking about."

Jack explained what Liam had been doing, the role of Aidan and Bryce with their testing, and the documentation from Jamie and Mary. Jack left out the illegal acquisition of data, the use of Deep Learning across this data, any fights, and his quid pro quo arrangement with Clodagh.

"So, his mother will make him stop?" said Sarah. "Just like that."

"Yes, she will."

"We need this Liam fellow out of the business. If this gets to the police, it'll have blowback to us as we loaned the money to Ralph, and we'd be under suspicion as co-conspirators."

"I'm working on that. In the meantime, I think Aidan and Bryce should run the business."

Sarah clasped her hands together like a single clap. "What a fantastic idea. How clever of you, Jack."

Mentioning it was Stella's idea would have led to questions he did not want to answer.

"I agree," said Barney. "They can move back here. Then they can walk to work."

Or rather limp to work.

"I'll bring them back tomorrow morning."

"Have you seen my friend Peter of late?"

"I have." Jack did not want to upset them by saying he looked less well than last time. "He's an interesting guy."

"Indeed," said Barney. "I met him after he came here."

"Came from where?"

"Israel. Didn't he tell you?"

"It never came up. Our conversations were about cricket and CE."

And once about a photo of Peter with the ex-director of the Mossad.

"Peter completed his military service in Israel and then came to the US."

"What did he do in the military?"

"He never really got into detail. Just told me it was something to do with accounting?"

"So, he had a quiet time in the military?" said Jack.

"Who knows? It's the Israeli army. What can I say? Remember, he was young, and maybe he did have a humble job as a junior accountant. On the other hand, it could mean he has secrets he has or wants to keep. Either way, I never inquired."

***

At 6 pm the next day, Jack was in the hotel Barney insisted on booking for him. Barney was nostalgic as he said this 1955-constructed hotel was where they always stayed when the boys were younger.

Earlier at 8 am, he'd canceled the meeting he'd previously scheduled with Mary and Jamie. By 10 am, Jack had dropped Aidan and Bryce at the Dubin Ranch and settled down to a seven-hour drive to Laguna Beach. It had pleased Aidan and Bryce to return to a business they loved. Trading. With Aaron and Jimmy on the ranch, Jack wasn't worried about trespassers.

Jack could have flown to John Wayne Airport and rented a car, which would have been quicker, but he needed a road trip by himself. Time to think. There had been no revelations, just what he knew already going around and around in his head. The balcony of his top floor, an ocean-facing room with its wooden table and two wooden chairs invited him to sit down, but standing and sipping water was a better option after the road trip.

The hotel had maintained its original look of leftover art deco. White and pastel baby blue were the colors the painter had used. The exterior was white, and two different shades of pastel baby blue in the bedroom, which didn't seem possible until you saw it. A solitary hotel beach umbrella was on the sand in blue and white segments, like a roulette wheel, monitoring the setting sun as the shadow crept up the beach. Jack looked up and down the beach at the other hotels. The same sunset would differ depending on where you were and who was with you.

What Jack needed now was sleep as he was going out later.

***

At 10 pm, Jack was at The Loft, standing at the back of the room, sipping soda water with lemon. Definitely, the place to be seen. Shorts and designer-label shirts seemed to be the uniform of the day for men and women. The room was a tapestry of colors. People preening like peacocks, watching others, seeing who's watching them. The young and the beautiful were abundant, like rare tropical flowers that only bloomed at nighttime. A guitar player was in the corner doing Neil

Diamond covers. The twins were not there, nor were Ralph and Sinead.

A woman came up and introduced herself to Jack with an outstretched hand bent down at the wrist like Jack was supposed to kiss it. She was wobbling on her high heels, either not used to them or the glass of what looked like white wine. Jack shook her offered hand, which gave his hand intermittent squeezes like a morse code.

"Hello, I'm Holly. Haven't seen you here before."

"No. I'm here for a family reunion. I was to meet them here."

"Maybe I know them. I live in Laguna."

Jack showed Holly a picture of the twins. "These are my sisters." Then scrolled to one of Ralph with Sinead. "This is my cousin and his girlfriend."

Holly looked at Jack. "Good looks run in the family, I see. Your sisters are upstairs. They're often here, stealing the scene from all the wannabe models. Your cousin and his girlfriend, I've only seen here once. They were here with your sisters."

"Great. Also, having a bit of a reunion. I guess."

"Are you going to stay with them?"

Jack kept this persona moving along. "Yes, I am. Why do you ask?"

"I believe they rented a big house on the beach at the edge of Laguna." Holly winked at Jack. "Plenty of room for guests. Listen, I have to go to the ladies' room urgently. I'll be back soon. What's your name?"

Jack had anticipated her question. "Aaron. Aaron Brown."

Holly moved through the crowd, and Jack went up the stairs. There they were, at the center of the bar, with two guys, each with a bottle in hand, drooling like puppies as they spoke to the twins. The twins had matching pale pink shirts and white shorts, showing off their legs. Jack couldn't tell which was Jenny and which was Janey, but at six foot tall, thin, and now with a tan, they had everyone's eyes on them. The guys had fashionable haircuts, short at the sides with a long comb-over to the ear. One was taller by an inch than the twins, the other, two inches taller, their shirts a size too small, showing they spent time in the gym.

The taller one leaned over the twins and said something. The twins looked at each other, picked up their purses from the counter, stood, and slid out between the bar and the two comb-overs. Jack turned away from them as they went down the stairs. The two comb-overs, bottles still in hand, watched them go down the stairs and followed. Jack was behind them all the way to the car park, where the twins got into a Jeep Wrangler. Jack made it to his truck in time to follow them north along North Coast Highway. There was still enough traffic that Jack could keep an elderly Toyota Camry between the Jeep and his truck. One mile along, a car with lights on high beam came up fast behind him and started to overtake. There was an oncoming car. Jack glanced at the overtaking vehicle. It looked like a Porsche. The two comb-overs were inside laughing, bottles still firmly in hand. There was a blaring of horns from the oncoming car, the comb-overs, and Jack as he stomped on the brake to give them space to push in. The sign on the back of the vehicle said 'Carrera S.'

Another time, another place, this sort of behavior killed his parents, and the dark thing at the base of his spine stirred. He concentrated on breathing with his diaphragm as he focused on the task at hand. A sign to Divers Cove came up, and the Jeep took the turnoff, followed by the Porsche. It took the next right into a dead-end street filled with 1930s bungalows built on the beach. The Jeep pulled into one, followed by the Porsche. Jack kept going, turned his engine and lights off, and rolled to a stop. He got out and walked back.

The twins were at the door. Jack could hear raised voices from the twins. The comb-overs leaned onto the twins, who tried to push them away, but all it did was squash their arms to their chest. The comb-overs wanted to kiss them, beer bottles in hand. He heard the twins shout, "No," as the door opened, and Ralph and Sinead appeared. Ralph pushed the shorter one away, and the taller one punched Ralph in the head. He went down in a heap, with Sinead dropping to a knee next to him and screaming. The shorter one threw a slap at one twin, who blocked it with her arms, but the impact was high as she was already against the wall. The dark thing came out of its cave. There was to be no discussion or negotiation. The smaller one was closer. Jack threw a right roundhouse punch to his head, twisting his hips into it, punching right into his head. The man staggered and fell next to Ralph, the beer bottle slipping from his hand.

"Jack?" said the twins in stereo.

The taller comb-over looked at his fallen comrade, turned to Jack, broke his beer bottle on the wall, and stalked toward him.

When you fight with beer bottles, someone will get bloodied.

Jack stepped back into the garden to give himself more room and circled to the right as comb-over held the bottle in his right hand, limiting his stabbing range as he would have to stab across his body to get to Jack.

Jack's foot bumped against the metal watering can. He stooped, picked it up as he kept circling, and held it out at the broken bottle, blocking the short stabbing movements. Jack could see the spade standing in the garden behind Comb-over. Jack circled like a crab to the right, jabbing at the bottle with the watering can, picking up the spade, hefting it like a spear, and throwing it above the watering can. Comb-over saw it too late. The steel blade hit the bridge of his nose, causing a shriek. His left hand went to his eyes, and his right hand with the bottle pulled back. Jack stepped forward and grabbed his hand, twisting it back till he dropped the bottle. Comb-over took a swing at Jack, hitting his shoulder. Jack moved behind him, putting his right arm across Comb-over's throat and his left arm behind, making a chokehold. As Comb-over was two inches taller, Jack had him arched backward as he pulled at Jack's arm across his throat, alternating with elbowing. Jack made him arch more to reduce the effectiveness of the elbow jabs. Jack held the pressure on the neck and waited. Twenty seconds was what Jack was anticipating. Comb-over went limp at fifteen.

Ralph was getting to his feet, and Jack dragged the shorter one to a sitting position and slapped his face. His eyes opened and showed fear when he saw Jack, who slapped him again.

"Are you paying attention?" said Jack, who waited for a response. He raised his hand to slap him again.

"Yes, yes. I'm paying attention."

"Wonderful. You're driving. Get up." Jack grabbed him by the hair and pulled him to his feet. He wobbled along as Jack walked him, bent over to the driver-side door of the Porsche, and opened the door. "Get in."

Jack went to the taller one and nudged him with his foot. There was a stirring. He saw Jack and lashed out with his foot. He stomped on his stomach, his target being the solar plexus. Jack was on target, and the taller one went into a fetal position as he tried to suck air. Jack didn't want him to recover fully.

"Get up."

Jack took a handful of the comb-over and dragged him to his feet, keeping him bent over where he hunched with one arm across his stomach and the other wiping blood away from his eyes. Jack walked him to the Porsche and opened the door for him. "Here, let me help you." Jack put his hand on Comb-over's head and pushed him down and into his seat, as the police do.

"Now, guys, I'm not going to explain what will happen if I see you near these people again. Oh, and don't mention this to the police. If you do, I'll find you, and we can do this all over again. Now go straight home. Get a good night's rest, and you'll feel better in the morning."

Jack closed the door. The Porsche started and drove away like Aunt Louise was driving.

Jack walked back to the front door where the twins and Ralph and Sinead were standing. The latter stared at Jack as if they were meeting him for the first time. Which they were.

"Let's go inside," said Jack. "We need to talk."

CHAPTER THIRTY

The room had one oversized leather U-shaped sofa in front of the sea-facing window.

The twins sat in the center of the U. Ralph and Sinead, huddled together, holding hands, with Jack opposite.

"Thanks for saving us, Jack," said the twin on the left. "Where'd you learn to fight like that?"

Jack would not be answering that as he felt the dark thing retreat into its cave. "Which one are you?"

"I'm Jenny."

"Right. Now I know why you two are here. Freediving." Jack turned to Ralph and Sinead. "But why are you two here? Your parents are worried sick about you. Why would you do that to them?"

"Did my mother hire you to find us?" said Sinead.

"I'm doing a favor for her and for Ralph's parents. So, talk."

Sinead looked at Ralph as if they were seeking the other's approval.

"Listen, Sinead. I know what your mother does. If I call her right now, she'll send as many people as it takes to bring you home. So, at the moment, talking to me's a better option."

Sinead let out a sigh like she was exhaling all her troubles. "It was all becoming too much for us." Sinead spoke faster. "I don't know what you know, but Liam was doing market manipulation on Ralph's trading platform, and I was the accountant for all my mother's businesses. Ralph and I would go to jail if the police ever found out what was happening." Sinead looked at Ralph, then back at Jack. "We talked about it, and we couldn't see any way out of what were criminal activities in which we were implicated by just going to work every day. So we ran. We knew the twins were here, freediving. We'd got into it, so we thought coming here would give us some space to figure out what to do."

"Were you expecting an underwater revelation?"

"Freediving reduces stress," said Janey. "These two are far less stressed than when they arrived."

"I don't know what we were expecting," said Ralph. "It was just becoming overwhelming."

"I get the freediving reduces stress thing, but it does not make the problem disappear. But there have been some changes."

Jack gave them an update.

"My compliments, Jack," said Ralph. "You have really got my computer science mind spinning. But I've got a question. How did you get the data to determine what Liam was doing?"

"It's irrelevant, Ralph. Bottom line, Liam's been uncovered, and Clodagh says she will stop him from any further involvement with HTT."

Ralph looked at Sinead. "Can she do that? Does she have that sort of control over him?"

"She can and will, and yes, she does."

"That's great," said Ralph. "Aidan and Bryce will do better than me as joint CEO. Stewart is a super-salesman, and I can go back to developing without worrying about Liam."

"It would be good if it were that easy," said Jack. "Problem is, Ralph, you were the CEO at the time when market manipulation was going on, and Sinead, you're still the accountant on record of what is a criminal organization and has been for some years."

"Your mother's a gangster?" said Janey. "How exciting."

"More likely, how nerve-wracking," said Sinead. "I know how the money moves in and out of every business, and there are lots of them, not just the pub, the tanneries, and HTT."

"Not to mention the blocks of real estate she owns in the Tenderloin, the drugs, and the prostitution."

"My mother's interest in the Tenderloin is both historical and philanthropic."

"Philanthropic?" said Jack.

"Yes, she took over the business from her father. With that came some Tenderloin real estate. She has a soft spot for the homeless. Well, let me say, a soft spot as long as they live by her rules. She finds them a job, usually working for her. They were mostly unemployable despite some of them having great skills and aptitudes. They'd just fallen on hard times, but it's difficult to shake off the stigma of being homeless. She put a roof over their heads as she had the real estate. They pay rent when they have a job. It became a spiral moving out from the pub. More homeless people meant the need for more real estate."

"And these people became loyal to her?"

"Yes. More than any samurai you've ever read about."

"So long as they obeyed her rules," said Jack. "What about the drugs and prostitution?"

"My mother realized they would always be a part of the Tenderloin, so she took control of these operations rather than having random drug dealers and pimps working within what she considered her territory. It's not perfect, but it's the best she could do. Unless you have a better idea."

"Nothing right now," said Jack. "Let's get back to why you two left."

Sinead looked at Ralph. "Sinead told me that she was sure Liam was up to no good with HTT. His trades were consistently so much better than the norm that it didn't seem possible. I could see his transactions but couldn't figure out how he was doing it. By the way, I'd like to know how you got the data and analyzed it."

Jack ignored the question and looked at Sinead. "Did you tell Clodagh your concerns?"

"I did. She questioned Liam, and he asked why everyone was suspicious of him just because he's good at what he does. Also, he was buying hides. These purchases were questionable. He was buying hides at a twenty percent discount to the average price of what we sold out of our tanneries. It looked like money laundering. I raised the matter, and again he had a story. He said he simply had a good relationship with the suppliers. It was always the same three."

"I hear you. But let's be clear, Clodagh runs a criminal organization. This arrangement should have suited her."

"That's what I tried to explain to her," said Sinead. " I'm one of the few people who have any idea of the size of the enterprise she has created. It's bigger than many well-known corporates in San Francisco. The beauty of what she has done is to keep it all under the radar. To be as low-key as possible. Liam was pushing to get involved in the other parts of the business. Any mistake by Liam could bring us to the attention of the cops. The organization's like a tangled ball of string, but if they got hold of one thread that had become visible, they could untangle the whole thing, and we'd all go to jail."

"So we ran," said Ralph. "It hasn't solved anything, and now we've had a chance to sit back and think about it, we're more concerned than ever. But we're open to suggestions if you have any."

"Clodagh asked me to find you. My mandate didn't include advising a criminal organization."

A hush fell over the room like fog before the mist before the rain. Sinead put her head on Ralph's shoulder. The twins watched and looked at each other with that communication thing they did.

"We'd like to help," said Janey.

Sinead sat up straight. "You're kidding me? Until now, you didn't know what my family did, and I've tried to keep you away from it."

"That's why," said Ralph. "When you left unexpectedly, we were relieved. You've become our friends, and we were glad you were no longer involved."

"But now," said Jack, "I've got two other people involved in supporting HTT and installing cybersecurity for Clodagh's businesses. If Liam is as much of a loose cannon as you say, these two innocents could be viewed by the police as implicated, particularly as they are installing cybersecurity."

Sinead looked at the twins. "Why would you want to be involved?"

"It sounds exciting. Most of our assignments are boring for boring companies."

"You do realize," said Jack, "you'd be working for a criminal organization that's already on the police's radar."

"We're not stupid," said Jenny. "We'd create a company which we would own and offer IT services. We would not be employees of Clodagh. There would be a services contract stating our services, which would make it clear we were not involved in any day-to-day business activities, just boring old IT work. What we really did for you is a different matter. But before we do this, you have to sort out Liam. Remember, he's the reason we left."

Jack was thinking what Freddie would do if he knew Jack was having this conversation. Not to mention Aunt Louise and Uncle Alan.

Ralph looked at Sinead. "It could work."

Sinead frowned as though her head hurt. "The problem is that Liam is a compulsive, narcissistic liar. I'm his twin, and it feels bad to speak about him like this. But it's always been this way. He lied to my mother about what he was doing at HTT, which is inexcusable, but he'll have justified it to himself. He always has. Those three suppliers I spoke about earlier. I looked them up on the Internet. Not one owns a tannery. Yet they are selling hides to Liam. Where do these hides come from, and why sell hides to another tannery when they could just as easily sell them on HTT? I looked further, and the same company owns all three suppliers."

"What's the name of the company?" said Jack.

"Autumn Center."

The twins pulled their phones from their purses and started typing like it was a race.

"There's lots of Autumn Centers," said Janey.

"They're all recreation centers for the elderly or old age homes," said Jenny.

"There's one in Delaware," said Sinead. "Tax haven."

There was a pause of four seconds as the twins scrolled through their phones, Janey talking as they did. "That's what we must do. Set up a Delaware company and live and work from here at Laguna."

"Got it," said Jenny. "Autumn Center Delaware."

"Me too. There's not much on their website to make it clear what they do," said Janey.

"When I asked Liam about it," said Sinead, "he said he didn't know and didn't care. So long as he could buy hides at a good price, he was happy to deal with them."

"I don't believe him. He's lying. The problem with Liam being a narcissistic liar is that he keeps telling a lie for so long he believes it himself in the end. Take the shillelagh he carries around and tells everybody it's a family heirloom. He bought it on eBay, and I know because he paid for it through company funds, so I saw it as I'm the accountant. When I asked my mother about it, she said to let him be. It was no big deal in her eyes. It was a harmless lie. These so-called harmless lies of Liam's, I fear, have grown into a web that permeates the whole business. And we don't know the extent of it."

"Well," said Jack, "you've had time to realize that running away from it won't help. So will you come back to San Francisco with me?"

Sinead looked at Ralph. "We have no choice. Whatever we've got ourselves into, or rather whatever Liam's got us into, we have to work our way out of it."

"I agree," said Ralph, who turned to Jack. "When do you want to leave?"

"We can leave now, share the driving, and be in San Francisco for breakfast."

***

At 9 am, Jack sat with a glass of freshly squeezed orange juice at a table in the bar of Doyle's. The room had the smell of someone breathing Guinness on you while talking around a mouthful of Irish stew overlaid with industrial floor cleaner. It would be good to get back to the ranch.

Ralph had phoned his parents from the car and was in the kitchen with Sinead and Clodagh. Jack phoned Stella. She answered and spoke briefly, saying she was in a meeting and would call back later. Freddie didn't answer his phone, and Jack did not leave a message. Clodagh appeared from the kitchen with a smile and asked him to come to the kitchen. Once there, she handed him a plate, and he helped himself to bacon, scrambled eggs, skipped the pancakes and maple syrup, and poured a cup of black coffee. He took this back to his table, where the orange juice was waiting. His phone rang. Freddie.

"Morning, Jack, I'm about to go into a meeting. What's up?"

"Do you know of a Delaware-based company called Autumn Center?"

"Where are you, Jack?"

"I'm in San Francisco."

There was a pause from Freddie for six seconds. "Can you be at my office at ten?"

"Sure. See you then."

Jack put his phone on the table and started eating. His phone rang again. Barney Dubin.

"Hello Jack. Barney here."

"Hi, Barney. How are you and Sarah?"

"We're fine, Jack. When are you coming back to your ranch?"

"Probably be there about one o'clock."

"Great. You must join us for lunch. We want to thank you in person for finding Ralph and getting him and Sinead to return."

"Glad to have helped. But they'd have come to that realization themselves. Just needed a bit of coaxing. Lunch, though, sounds great."

"Excellent. I'll phone Peter and see if they can join us."

Clodagh sat down at the table with a plate of scrambled eggs and a cup of black coffee, looking at Jack's plate. "Can I heat that up for you? You've spent more time on the phone than eating."

Jack smiled at Clodagh. "Thanks. It's hot enough."

Clodagh nodded and started eating as Jamie and Mary walked through the door. Clodagh looked up from her plate. "You two hungry? Plenty of food, freshly made, in the kitchen."

"We're fine," said Mary.

"Take a seat in my office. I'll be there shortly."

Jack's mouth was full of food. He put down his knife and fork and held up his hands while he finished chewing and swallowing. Mary and Jamie waited until Jack had his last swallow.

"I know it's short notice, but I'll be out at the HTT office on Marsh Creek Road this afternoon. I know we agreed that you would do the work remotely, but I just had a phone call, and I'll have everyone there except for you guys. I thought this would be a great chance for you guys to meet everyone. If you can make it at, say, 3 pm."

"That's a good idea," said Mary. "We'll see you at three."

Jamie and Mary didn't need directions and walked to Clodagh's office.

Clodagh turned to Jack. "I'm taking them through all the companies I want ring-fenced with cybersecurity. They've been pleasant to deal with, and even Liam seems to rate their competence."

"Speaking of which, Clodagh, you have a problem with Liam that you're not facing up to. Sinead and Ralph left because of Liam. They're committed to address the problem as best they can. But you need to acknowledge the problem and figure out what you're going to do. Let me ask you this. What would you have done if this was one of your employees?"

Clodagh looked at Jack, her eyes flinty as a rock. "You know what I'd have done. But Liam's my son."

***

"Autumn Center, Delaware," said Freddie.

Jack had brought Freddie a toasted bacon and egg sandwich from Doyle's kitchen, but Freddie ignored it in his agitated state as he stood and paced around the room.

"Who are you associating with? It can't be Clodagh Doyle. She's a criminal but not a terrorist. At least as far as we know."

"Terrorist?" said Jack, internally reprimanding himself for repeating what someone had said, like a parrot.

"More specifically, it's believed they indulge in criminal activities to fund terrorists. It's not my investigation. It falls under a separate branch of Homeland Security. They just told me what I needed to know and to report back to them if we picked up anything. How would you even know of their existence?"

"It's a long story."

Freddie shook his head. "It always is."

"So, this, Autumn Center, are they anti-US? Planning an attack?"

"They're anti-US, but their primary interest is Israel. Funding terrorist groups that are anti-Israel."

"Where did you hear about them?"

For Jack, lying to Freddie was like taking dreadful-tasting medicine, but like medicine, sometimes it had to be done. "I overheard some guys in a bar talking about nursing homes for their parents. One guy had parents in Delaware and found this place on the Internet called Autumn Center, which he thought was a nursing home, but it turns out it wasn't. He said he didn't know what it was. It sounded odd. That's all."

Freddie looked at Jack and shook his head. "And you expect me to believe that?"

Jack felt uncomfortable, like sleeping on a lumpy bed, tossing and turning in the hope there was a position that wouldn't keep him awake. Instead, he said, "Be great to chat further, but I've got to get going. Have some pressing matters to attend to. Enjoy your sandwich."

CHAPTER THIRTY-ONE

The Dubins had gone all out for the return of the prodigal son, Ralph. They greeted Sinead with hugs and tears. Stewart gave Ralph a back-slapping hug and Sinead a kiss on the cheek. Aidan and Bryce shook hands with Ralph. Peter and Hannah sat in the Gathering Room and waited for Ralph and Sinead to greet them. They all went to the dining room, where the table held a roasted brisket and vegetables. The wine and the conversation flowed with laughter and sometimes tears of joy from Sarah.

After lunch, Ralph, Sinead, and Stewart adjourned to the HTT office with Aidan and Bryce. Each held a glass of wine. Jack said he would join them shortly and offered to help clear the table, but Barney and Sarah were having none of it as they said he'd done enough by getting Ralph to return. Hannah helped them, leaving Jack and Peter in the Gathering Room, each with a cup of black coffee.

"Peter, have you ever heard of a terrorist organization called Autumn Center with its registered office in Delaware?"

Peter's eyes hooded like a hawk as he took a quick breath as though startled and then a low, slow one as his eyes closed and opened. "No.

Does such a place exist?"

"It does."

"I'm not going to ask how you know this, but what's your interest in this place?"

Jack explained Liam's involvement with them.

"Some people, Jack, can be stupid as well as clever. Why are you telling me?"

"I thought your friend in the photo you showed me may be interested. Could solve a common problem."

Peter breathed in what seemed like two lungfuls of air and let it out like a slow leak in a tire. "I'll mention it to him."

Jack sipped his coffee and looked at Peter, who was rubbing his chin with his forefinger.

"And Jack, tell Clodagh from me to keep Liam working in the bar for the next week where there are lots of witnesses to his whereabouts."

"I'll tell her."

***

When Jamie and Mary arrived, Jack took them to the HTT office, where there were introductions all around. Ralph offered them food, wine, and coffee, which they declined. Aidan and Bryce gave them a tour of the facility, with Ralph explaining the technical infrastructure as they went. Stewart explained that none of this would exist without his selling abilities, bringing friendly abuse like warm rain falling on his head. Stewart laughed.

"Any questions? Mary? Jamie?" said Bryce.

"This facility," said Jamie, "is very nice, and the countryside's amazing. We didn't even know Mt. Diablo existed. It's just that."

Mary interjected. "Jamie is trying to say that we don't want to sound rude, but it's far. Well, really far from anywhere. We plan to work remotely, but sometimes we agree it is necessary to go to the office. How often would we have to come here?"

Sinead looked at Ralph, and he chuckled. "Sinead and I have been talking about that. This place started off as my bachelor pad on the ranch, and the business grew up inside of it. It wasn't like I chose this place to start a business. It was just convenient."

"My mother," said Sinead, "would like me living closer to her. There's a disused office two blocks from the pub that we can have rent-free for a year. The rest of the building is apartments; my mother owns the whole building. It's not as slick as this setup, but it has good Internet connectivity. We could be up and running in two, maybe three days."

"That sounds great," said Jamie, "and we've been to the pub in broad daylight, and without sounding rude, isn't the Tenderloin a bit of a dodgy place to live?"

"It does have a bad rap, but my mother will ensure our security, and Jimmy lives on the ground floor."

"Who's Jimmy?" said Mary.

"You'll meet him," said Sinead.

"We have some news," said Bryce, "and, I can speak for both of us." Bryce paused as he got his breathing under control. It looked like he was hyperventilating. "We are so excited about what you're telling us."

Bryce put his arm around Aidan's shoulder. "Our parole hearing's been brought forward." Bryce waited for four seconds, looking each person in the eye, holding his audience like a stand-up comedian until Sinead could not wait. "So, tell us, when is it?"

Aidan threw his arms in the air and jumped forward out of Bryce's arm. "Tomorrow."

"That's great news," said Ralph."

"How did that happen?" said Jack.

"Barney and Sarah," said Bryce, "wrote a letter of recommendation.

I should say, a fantastic letter of recommendation, and that started the ball rolling."

"If all goes well tomorrow," said Aidan, "we want to move back to San Francisco. So, if there's a spare apartment in that building, that would help us get started, and we'd be close to work."

"I'll arrange something," said Sinead. "May not be five stars, though."

"We've been in prison," said Bryce. "Just being free is five-star."

They all laughed and raised their glasses. Ralph put on some music. They wanted a photo that Jack took and looked at the seven of them engaged like chickens in a hen house, all talking at once and moving their feet. Jack left without farewells and walked down the path to the house. Mt. Diablo was behind him. It was growing between one and two inches a year at almost four thousand feet high, sitting on over ninety thousand acres of converging earthquake plates. It was easy to see why it was sacred to many Native American groups around and near the mountain. Jack felt like it was watching him, and he didn't know why.

On the back verandah, Peter was sitting in a cane chair with his constant companion, the oxygen cylinder. A crystal glass was next to him, with half an inch of amber fluid. Jack thought he looked pale, but then he'd never seen Peter in the sunshine. Barney was pouring himself a whiskey from a decanter when he saw Jack and held up the decanter.

"Whiskey, Jack? It's a single malt."

"Yes, please."

Barney poured a generous tot as he judged by eye, the whiskey glugging into the crystal glass, and passed it to Jack. "Here's to you, Jack. Job well done. Everything seems to have come together. All's well that ends well, as they say. Can't recall who said that, do you, Peter?"

There was a prolonged intake of air before Peter replied. "No one said it. It's the name of a play by Shakespeare."

"Quite so," said Barney.

Peter nodded and took a sip of his whiskey. More like he let it wet his lips. His tongue wiped his lips, and he lowered the glass, letting it sit on his leg.

"How are things going up in the HTT office? Everyone getting along?" said Barney.

"They are. They're making plans to move the whole operation to San Francisco. The Tenderloin, to be exact."

"Where do they plan to live?" said Barney.

Jack reiterated the conversation that had just taken place in the HTT office. "They're all very excited at the moment," said Jack. "There's a lot of detail they must deal with to make this happen, but that's for tomorrow."

Barney considered this and turned to Peter. "Well, old chum, we'll probably be moving next door to you. Sarah will want to be close to the children."

Peter shrugged as if this was an inevitability of life. "We can watch cricket together."

Barney grimaced as if he'd sucked on a lemon. "All right, but only if we watch baseball together."

Peter smiled with all the love a brother could have for one who is not a brother but is. "All right, Barney, that sounds fair."

Barney's eyes welled up, and he looked into the ice bucket as a diversion. "No ice. I'll go to the kitchen and get some. Be right back. I'll also tell the ladies the news."

Barney bounded out of the room like a kid with a new toy, but all he had was an ice bucket.

Jack was looking at the mountain across the garden, which had fallen into some disarray since Aidan and Bryce weren't attending to it. He thought he heard his name. The magic of the mountain. There were legends about voices on the mountain.

"Jack." It was Peter, barely audible. Jack turned. Peter had taken on a paler shade.

"You don't look all right," said Jack.

Peter dismissed the inquiry with a flick of his hand and spoke with a voice as soft as fog.

"I spoke to my friend. The one who is in the photo. I told him about that place, the Autumn Center. The one in Delaware. He said he'd look into it." He smiled at Jack. "Could you fetch Hannah for me?"

Jack went to the kitchen and came back with Hannah. Peter was staring at the mountain, slumped in the chair, on the verge of sliding from it, his jaw slack. The whiskey glass had fallen from his grasp and shattered. Hannah dropped to her knees and put her head in his lap. Jack walked towards the mountain, tears running down his face for a man he barely knew. There was no boundary fence. He continued from the man-imposed garden to where the mountain started with a vertical incline. Jack put his left hand on the rock and realized his right hand still held the whiskey glass. He raised the glass to the mountain. The sun hit the glass and flicked into his eyes, making him blink and flush the tears down his cheeks. He lowered the glass and drank the contents in one swallow.

Secrets. Sometimes they reveal themselves. Sometimes, they fade away with the bearer.

CHAPTER THIRTY-TWO

At 6 pm, Jimmy wanted to go back to San Francisco. Jack looked at him and said they could go back tomorrow morning. Jimmy was happy with that, said he'd phone Clodagh, and headed back to Hailey's truck, where she was unloading two horses with Aaron.

There had been lots of tears and grief at the Dubin ranch with the death of Peter. It had taken almost two hours before Jack could slip away and drive the few miles back to Alan's Acres. He was twitchy like a horse with flies on its back. Since getting back, all he'd done was phone Sam Dodd, based on Stella's advice, to talk to him about organizing penetration testing at Link. They had agreed to meet at 10 am at Link's head office.

"Thank you for letting me keep these two beauties here," said Hailey as she walked with Jack to the barn, leading the horse she'd ridden when they'd ridden together. Aaron led the horse Jack had ridden, and Jimmy followed with a hay bale in each hand.

"There's plenty of room in the barn, and we've enough grazing for two horses."

"We've just got too many sick and injured horses at the moment. We're keeping those at the practice and at home where we can attend to them. These two are fine. If it's all right with you, I'll leave Aaron here tomorrow to look after them."

"Fine with me. I have to go into San Francisco tomorrow, and I'll be taking Jimmy with me."

"Hey, Aaron. Do you want to throw the ball?" said Jimmy.

"Sure," said Aaron as he caught the ball Jimmy flicked at him.

Jack and Hailey stood in the barn watching them. Jimmy was clumsy, and Aaron was patient, narrowing the distance between them and softening his delivery so Jimmy could catch every throw.

"Quite a turnaround from when they first met," said Hailey.

"Sure is. Let me help you with the hay nets."

"You all right? You look like a puppy that can't find its food bowl."

"A friend of mine died today." Had he known Peter long enough to call him a friend? But then, how long do you have to know someone before they can be called a friend? Calling Peter an acquaintance felt wrong, so friend it must be.

Hailey put a hand on Jack's forearm. "That's terrible. What happened?"

Jack explained while he filled a hay net and hung it up in the stable, leaving out the parts about Peter's nebulous connection to the Mossad and his effect upon Clodagh.

"Come here," said Hailey, who grabbed Jack in a hug and pulled his head into her neck.

The womanly smell of Hailey, the hay, the horses, the feeling of loss, his senses felt inflamed like a bushfire raging with a strong wind behind it. He wanted to take her there and then on the stable floor.

"Jack, you're squashing me."

Jack had Hailey pushed up against the stable wall, his hands on her hips. He pushed himself off the wall and took a step back, his breathing ragged. "I'm sorry. I don't know where that came from."

"Hey, I'm not complaining. It just seemed you didn't know your own strength." Hailey ruffled her tangle of hair and bit her lip while looking at Jack. "Maybe we can continue this another time and maybe not in a stable. But right now, I have to go. There are sick horses at home needing my attention."

Jack breathed deeply and exhaled slowly as his whirling emotions subsided. "Sure. Sure."

Hailey looked Jack up and down. "I'll tell you what. I'll leave the horses' saddles here. Maybe we could go for a ride again."

Jack carried the saddles into the barn, and after a hug as brief as a butterfly kiss, a plume of dust from behind her truck and trailer hid her from view.

***

There were yellow traffic cones outside Clodagh's pub at 9 am, which Clodagh's people on the sidewalk removed as Jack approached in his truck and parked in the space. Jimmy jumped out and greeted everyone, as pleased to be home as when he left. Clodagh was standing there in her running gear. Compression shorts, the same green as the pub, black running shoes, and a white long-sleeved top. Two twenty-something men built like greyhounds and in the same colors flanked her. Jimmy waved at them and rushed inside.

"How did it go?" said Clodagh.

"It was fine. Jimmy was no trouble."

"I heard from Sinead that they want to move HTT to the Tenderloin. Obviously, I'm thrilled with that. She said that you've created a good team."

"Not so sure it was my creation. It just sort of came together."

"Serendipity, with some knowledge."

"I guess you could say that." Jack inclined his head.

"I don't know all these people. Sinead gave me names and what they would be doing."

Jack reached into his jacket, pulled out his phone, and scrolled until he got to the team photo.

Clodagh leaned towards the photo. "Sinead looks happy. Those two have to be the twins, and there's Jamie and Mary. And those two men must be Aidan and Bryce."

Jack nodded. "That's the team."

Jack's phone rang with an unidentified caller sign.

"Take it," said Clodagh. "I have to do my stretching exercises with my running companions."

Jack walked fifteen feet away as he pressed the answer button.

"Hello Jack. Is this a good time to speak with you?"

Jack did not recognize the voice or the accent. "It depends. Who is this?"

"I am Peter Wasserman's friend. The one in the photo he showed you."

Jack now placed the accent. Israeli. "Excuse me. How do I know you are who you say you are?"

There was the hint of a chuckle and a nasal sound. "It is good to be careful, Jack. You gave Peter some information about a place called the Autumn Center. The one in Delaware. Which he passed on to me."

Jack was thinking who else he had told about that. He had enquired with Freddie, and that was it. "Alright, let's assume you are who you say you are."

"I have heard you were with Peter when he passed."

Besides Peter's immediate family, who else would have known that? Jack frowned as the caller now sounded more authentic. "Yes, I was."

"Could you do me a great personal favor and tell me what happened?"

Jack described the moment and felt a wave of emotion rising like a tide, slow but not stopping.

"Thank you, Jack. He was a dear friend, and he had grown fond of you. Do you like cricket?"

"Not really. Do you?"

That same snorty chuckle. "Not really. Seems we both suffered through that silly game. Anyway, I must go now. But two things. First, thank you for the information about the Autumn Center. We are looking into it. And second, Peter, I know passed the message along to you. Tell Clodagh Doyle to keep that son of hers at her pub with many witnesses for the next few days."

The call ended with no goodbyes.

Clodagh stopped as Jack walked back.

"Peter Wasserman died yesterday at the Dubin Ranch," he said.

"Oh. What happened?"

"He passed away quietly while looking at a mountain."

"Well, I've heard of worse ways."

Jack held up the phone. "This call was from his friend. The one in the photo Peter showed you."

Clodagh became still. "What did he want?"

"Just to remind you to keep Liam in plain view with many witnesses."

"I'm doing that. He's inside the pub."

"He also said he is looking into the Autumn Center in Delaware."

"What does that mean?" she said.

"I don't know. Let's wait and see."

Clodagh relaxed. "I'm going for my run. Takes about forty-five minutes. You be here when I get back?"

"I've got some work to do, and I have a meeting. Have to get over to the Financial District."

Clodagh pointed at one of her staff, leaning against the wall but standing straight when he realized Clodagh was pointing at him. "The Irish breakfast we serve. Please put it in a container for Jack to take with him. The cook has just finished making soda bread. Put some slices of that in as well."

"Thanks, Clodagh."

"It's the least I can do." Clodagh looked at her two running companions, who looked like greyhounds waiting to be let off the leash, then back at Jack. "These two are getting impatient. I better get moving."

Jack watched the three set off. One greyhound in front and one behind. The people she passed greeted her with smiles and a wave of their hands.

***

In the computer department at Link industries, Jack had found a soundproof room containing a three-foot diameter round table and two black office chairs, each with five chrome-coated wheels. By 10 am, he had a secure connection to the site where Stella stored the extra data he'd requested and started the download. While this happened, he took his food container from the pub to the department's kitchen and found a plate, utensils, and the microwave.

After dining alone, he returned to the soundproof room, where he saw the download had finished. He figured this would be far shorter than the original download, as all he asked Stella for was additional data. He started the Deep Learning algorithm, made coffee, and returned to the room. Watching algorithms run is second to watching paint dry, so he was glad when Freddie phoned. He told him what he was doing and would contact him if the analysis revealed anything new. Again, Freddie made it clear he did not want to know where or how Jack had retrieved the data. Jack smiled as Freddie regaled him with the legal implications in a courtroom of information gained by illegally acquiring data. The lecture was a familiar one, but Jack was patient and let it run its course.

"Understood, Freddie."

"Having said all that. We'd be grateful for any help at this stage. This killer, we feel, is already a bit late in taking his next victim. Which means there's still a window of time to prevent it from happening."

"I get it. Once this algorithm has finished, I'll call you."

"Thanks. Chat later."

That was the end of the conversation. Clearly, he had other pressing matters to attend to.

The algorithm was still running. Jack phoned Stella.

Her voice sounded like the purring of a cat as she answered. "I missed you this morning when I woke up. Where are you?"

"In a room in your computer department. Where are you?"

"Upstairs, in my office. Lots to do."

"Will you be there for the day?"

"With the amount of work in front of me. It looks that way. Shall we have dinner at my house and watch the sunset?"

"Sounds good to me. Why don't you phone me when you're done for the day, and I'll go to your place."

"I'll do that. Bye."

Jack went back to watching the algorithm run when he heard a knock on the door. He got up and opened the door to see a man an inch taller than himself and probably five pounds lighter. With blue eyes and his fair hair cut neatly, he was much better dressed than Jack in his designer black jeans and a tailored white shirt.

"Jack Rhodes?"

"Yes. And you're Sam Dodd?"

"That's me." A firm handshake with no smile greeted Jack. "Stella said you had some questions for me."

"Take a seat. Thanks for coming."

"I had some work to do here anyway, so it's not out of my way."

They sat down. Jack turned his laptop so Sam could not see the screen.

The algorithm was throwing out names with a percentage correlation, and the higher the correlation, the more they migrated to the top of the screen. Sam's name was bound to come up again, and he didn't want embarrassing questions from Sam.

"How can I help you, Jack?"

"I'm after some recommendations from you for companies that do penetration testing of networks. I guess you know Stella asked me to get involved with the cybersecurity work Mary and Jamie were doing."

Jack saw Sam's name come up on the screen with a 95% correlation.

"Yes, I hear it's working now. Good job. But why didn't you ask Mary and Jamie? They know the names of those companies, and they've had lots of experience dealing with them. But from my experience, only three do a proper job."

"Sam, let's step back a minute. Why do Mary and Jamie have this experience?"

"Well, when I table my audit report and cybersecurity is required, I have to submit five names. That's the process, and the client must then choose."

"How do Mary and Jamie do in this selection process?"

"They are the best of the bunch and could get all the work. So, they can afford to be choosy about the assignments."

Jack looked at his screen. Mary and Jamie had risen to the top of the screen with a correlation of 97%.

"When do they start their work?"

"Normally, about a month after I table my report, and then they're on-site for four to six months, depending on the size and complexity of the infrastructure."

"Sam, can you give me a moment?"

Jack drilled down into the data, which gave the correlation. There it was. They had worked at all the places the serial killer had struck. In the world of data, they had been hiding behind Sam Dodd. Jack looked up at Sam.

"Let me get Mary and Jamie in here," said Jack. "They were fixing a problem earlier, just outside my door."

"Well, they're gone now."

"Weren't they here when you came in?"

"They were with Stella. Downstairs in the underground parking. They were getting into Stella's car. The big Mercedes."

Jack hit redial for Stella. It rang until it went to voice mail. Jack phoned Freddie, and he needed Sam out of the way. "Thanks, Sam, you've been a great help, but if you'll excuse me, I've got some work to do."

Sam left looking a bit put out, like the headmaster was suddenly dismissing him.

Freddie answered, and Jack explained.

"Jack, I've got you on speaker, and Kenny's here with me. Can you send me the details of Mrs. West's car, and do you have a photo of these two?"

"I don't have a photo," Jack said as he typed the car's details, then remembered. "Hang on, I do have a photo. I'm sending it now."

Jack waited while the selfie he had taken of the HTT traveled over the Internet.

"Got it," said Freddie. "Which ones are they?"

"Second and third from the left, between two women who are obviously twins."

"Let me make it bigger," said Freddie.

Kenny's deep voice boomed out. "I know those two. Jamie and Mary Berry."

"From where?" said Freddie. "Have they got criminal records?"

"No, I know them from MMA."

"Both of them?" said Jack.

"Yes. They both fought, but they got banned. The woman was the first."

"How do you get banned in MMA?" said Freddie.

"Punches to the groin, strikes to the eyes, the throat. They did all this but what got them disqualified is that when they won, and the ref intervened to stop the fight, they would keep pounding away. Most times, the ref had to pull them off the person. But there was another thing. Many times, they could have finished off their opponent, but they didn't. They left them standing so they could keep dishing out more punishment. That's the only way I can describe it. It was like they were dishing out punishment."

"The coroner's report on all victims," said Freddie, "had the same remarks."

Jack's mind was battling with the extra information confirming Mary, and Jamie were more than just people of interest, but he had only one objective. "We have to find Stella. From what we know, they take their victims to a national park. I'm assuming they'll get rid of Stella's Mercedes and use another car."

"While we've been talking," said Freddie, "I've already sent out a broadcast to all police in the Bay area, and I've given it the highest priority."

"Do you have access to CCTV footage at intersections?"

"We do, but it's slow work. The use of number plate recognition software is minimal. We have to look at the footage, and hopefully, the camera has taken a decent photo."

"But we know roughly when she left the building, and she could only have gone left or right. Can you check those intersections as a beginning?"

"Jack, Kenny's already onto that. Once he has something, he'll call you."

Jack rang off and sat, frustration eating at him like a disease. Maybe she went home. There was only one way to find out.

CHAPTER THIRTY-THREE

Jack stopped the Yukon outside Stella's garage and pressed the garage remote. As the door went up a foot, Jack could see the tires of the Mercedes, and as it slid up to the top, it revealed the Mercedes. Jack checked the doors of the car. They were locked as Stella usually left them. A weapon. Jack scanned the garage and picked up a four-foot-long garden fork with five prongs, already calculating he could stab with it or throw it.

He stepped through the door into the kitchen and could hear two voices. One male, one female. He moved along the wall towards the room over The Bay. He peeped around the corner to his left, the fork in his right hand.

A man in brown overalls was standing five feet away with his hands on his hips. No weapons in sight. Jack stepped around the corner, grabbed a handful of hair, jabbed into the back of the knee with his right leg, and pulled. The guy came backward and down to the floor. Jack held the prongs in front of the face. It wasn't Jamie. A woman started screaming. Without moving his body or the fork, he looked back towards the screaming. A woman in brown overalls. It wasn't Mary.

Jack stood and told the woman to stop screaming. The man got to his feet.

"Who are you two?" said Jack.

"We're from the cleaning service," said the man. "Who are you?"

"I'm a friend of Stella's, Mrs. West. I thought you were intruders. Sorry."

Jack moved the fork in his left hand and offered his right hand to help the man to his feet. The man looked at the hand, ignored it, rolled into a sitting position, stood, went to the woman, and put his arm around her. "Let's go."

"But we haven't finished," said the woman.

"Mrs. West can clean her own house. Grab your things. Let's go."

"Look, I know you're upset. I would be too. But I'm looking for Stella. I think she's in danger. Her car's in the garage. Did she come in the house with anyone?"

"She never came into the house," said the woman. "I was working in the kitchen. I heard the garage door, the noise of the car, which stopped, and I heard the garage door again. When she didn't appear, I got curious and opened the door to the garage. There was no one there. Just the car."

The man and the woman went through to the kitchen. The woman picked up her bag from a chair and went out through the garage. Jack turned and looked at The Bay through the window, hoping for answers. His fist still held the fork. He put the fork back in the garage as he phoned Freddie.

"I'm at Stella's house. Her car's here, but no sign of her. There were two cleaning people here, and they heard the garage door open, the car drive in, and the garage door close."

"Are you thinking they used her garage as the best place to dump her car?"

"Yes, and then take her away in another vehicle?"

"Sounds a good plan on their part."

"I'll tell our surveillance guys to stand down and cancel the call to look out for the car. We'll keep monitoring her phone in case it comes back on. What are you gonna do?"

"I don't know."

Freddie said his goodbyes, and Jack looked across The Bay. He went to his truck, collected his laptop, sat down, and started searching back into the data for the type of parks that matched where the killers had used previously. The algorithm ran while Jack paced the floor like an expectant father, knowing that with each second, Jamie and Mary would be taking Stella closer to a park of their choosing. He tried not to look at the algorithm running, but like a moth to the flame, he kept looking at it as he paced.

It had been running for over an hour when he heard the front door close with a soft sound like a bump. He had not heard it open and was now expecting trouble.

"This is a pleasant surprise," said Stella as she swept into the room, sunglasses on her head, placed her handbag and a carry bag on the table, and kissed Jack.

"Where have you been? The whole of SFPD is looking for you."

Jack went to her and held her tight. Stella put her arms around his neck and kissed his throat.

"Well, if this is what happens when I go missing, I'll do it more often."

"This is no joke. Where are Jaime and Mary? They left with you."

"What's going on? I dropped them in the Tenderloin, and I was coming here. They said they were going to the new offices for HTT, so I offered to give them a lift. A small detour for me. No big deal. Again, what's going on?"

Jack dialed Freddie. He started explaining to Stella. Freddie's phone went to voice, and he phoned Kenny, also, straight to voice.

"Where's your phone? It's switched off. No one could trace you."

"That's my fault. I got a call from the owner of that acquisition I spoke about earlier. He wanted to meet at that French restaurant on Fillmore Street. The parking's terrible there, so I left my car here and walked. Gave me time to clear my head before the meeting. It's a lovely day, two blocks across to Fillmore and three blocks down. At the meeting, the owner insisted that we give our full attention to our discussion. We had to turn our phones off. I forgot to turn mine back on. The meeting had gone better than expected, and I decided to reward myself by popping into a shoe shop on the way back. Hence the bag." Stella pointed at the bag on the table.

"Back to Jamie and Mary. You now think they're the killers. Really? Last time it was Sam Dodd."

Jack finished explaining what had led to Jamie and Mary becoming the prime suspects.

"I understand what you're saying your data analysis has revealed, but if that's the case, why didn't they abduct me? You've been saying I was the most likely candidate, and in the time I was driving them to the Tenderloin, they could have pulled a gun on me, dumped my car in a parking garage, and taken me away in another car."

Stella had just echoed his fear.

"I don't know."

"Maybe someone else fitted the profile better."

Jack looked at Stella, staring unblinking, wondering why they wanted to go to the Tenderloin. Was it really to go to the new offices?

Jack phoned Bryce, who answered in four rings.

"Hello Jack. Nice to hear from you. We are busy settling in here at the new offices. They will be great when we've finished."

"That's good to hear, Bryce. Tell me, are Jamie and Mary there with you."

"I haven't seen them today. Shall I get them to call you if they come here?"

"Yes, please."

Jack ended the call and looked at Alcatraz, thinking of the Tenderloin.

He phoned Jimmy, who answered in two rings.

"Hello Jack. When am I coming to stay with Aaron again?"

"Whenever you want to. Can you get Clodagh to come to the phone?"

"Sure, Jack."

Jack could hear voices in the background changing as Jimmy walked through the patrons. Doors opened and closed. He heard Jimmy shout, "Liam, where's your mother?" and Liam reply, "I don't know. I've been busy here."

Jimmy came back on the phone. "Jack, I can't find her, and her car's here."

"Did Jamie and Mary come there today?"

"Yes, I saw them here ninety minutes ago. I saw Jamie leave about thirty minutes after that. I didn't see Mary leave, but I haven't been on the door all the time."

"Jimmy, there are always some of your people out the front. Ask them if they saw Mary leave."

Jack waited as he heard Jimmy talking but couldn't make out the words.

"Jack. No one saw her leave."

"Thank you, Jimmy. Now you said Clodagh's car is there, the Bentley."

"Yes. But her father's truck is gone."

"Her father's truck?"

"Yes."

This conversation was like pulling teeth, but Jack knew it was better to be patient.

"Jimmy, can you describe that truck for me?"

Jimmy described the truck like he was reading from a catalog.

"It's a thirty-year-old Ford F150. Two-tone paint job. Dark blue with a white roof. Fully restored. Sometimes she likes to take it for a spin."

Jack wrote down the registration number Jimmy gave him and rang off after promising him, again, that he could come to the ranch whenever he wanted. Freddie hadn't phoned back. Jack called him, and after twelve rings, he answered.

"Stella's here with me. I think they've taken Clodagh Doyle."

Jack filled Freddie in on what had happened and gave him the description and registration number of Clodagh's F150.

Jack was pacing past his laptop as he spoke. The algorithm for finding the most likely park had finished.

"Freddie, the algorithm has come up with Mt. Diablo."

"Great. Do you know how many entrances there must be? I'll get onto the Park Rangers and get them to look out for the truck."

"There are also places where you can park a car and walk in yourself on unofficial trails."

"They may switch cars. I'll alert the police departments along the way to put out an alert for the truck."

"What about your friends at The Farm, the detention center? They regularly drive up and down Marsh Creek Road to Clayton and back."

"Sounds like you're doing my job."

"Sorry, my mind's just running on adrenaline. What about drones?"

"I'll deploy everything and everyone I can. What are you gonna do?"

"I'm going to the ranch. At least I'll be in the vicinity if you get wind of anything." Jack turned to face Stella. "I'm taking Stella with me, in case I'm wrong about them taking Clodagh, and their target is Stella."

"It's still a huge area to cover, and I won't be able to get enough feet on the ground to comb the area."

Feet on the ground. An Army. The idea hit him like the teacher had explained a complex problem with a simple answer.

"Thanks for what you're doing, Freddie." Jack rang off and started scrolling his phone for a name, his mind an expanding plan like making candy floss from sugar.

Stella tapped him on the arm. "Remember me? Seems you've invited me. I'm going to get ready."

Jack nodded, "Yes, please." He watched Stella walk away as the number he called answered.

"Sinead. This is Jack. Jamie and Mary have kidnapped Clodagh."

"What?"

Sinead went from panic to calm as Jack explained the background, breathed, then gave instructions. "I want every male over eighteen who falls under the protection of Clodagh to drive to Mt. Diablo. The rangers and police will be covering the main entrances and trails. We'll take the small trails. How many people can you muster?"

Sinead went quiet, then spoke. "About a hundred and twenty. There are a lot of women who don't have small children who'll want to help. I've included them."

"Download a map of Mt. Diablo. I'm sending you a location-sharing app that works in real-time. It's from a start-up in San Francisco. They haven't released it yet. Important for us is that you can text within the group. Your people must not speak when they get to Mt. Diablo, only text. We can't take the risk of Mary and Jamie knowing there's a search party looking for them. Understand?"

"Understood."

"Good. You need to add the mobile number of everyone you're sending. We'll deploy people as soon as everyone is loaded. You must tell your people, all they have to do is locate them. No engaging with them. These two are dangerous, and we must assume they're armed. Will your people be armed?"

"Of course. I've been thinking I'm going to get the word out to every hooker and drug dealer in our area. They'll come, and they'll be armed, bringing our numbers to over a hundred and fifty."

"It sounds a lot, but it's a huge area to cover. The ranch will be the command post. Anything else?"

"Yes. Can you take Jimmy? He'll go crazy if he hears what's happened to Clodagh, and we didn't invite him."

"Sure. It's not out of my way." Jack paused. "Tell Jimmy to bring his drone."

"Will do."

"We'll talk on the road. Bye."

Stella walked into the room wearing camo pants, hiking boots, a brown shirt hanging over her Glock 42, and a small leather shoulder bag. She put two spare loaded magazines into their clip-on mag-holder and put them in the bag as she got next to Jack. "If the bad guys have got guns. I want one too. That's what they teach us at the range."

Jack knew of Stella's ability with the little Glock as she'd gotten him out of trouble before using it.

"Do you mind driving my truck? I want to talk to Sinead as she gets Clodagh's troops organized."

"Troops?"

"Clodagh's people. I'm pretty sure they'll behave like the Spartans at Thermopylae, except this time they have to find the enemy, not hold them back."

"It's still going to be like finding a needle in a haystack," said Stella.

"Yes."

CHAPTER THIRTY-FOUR

At five foot five inches tall and one hundred and twenty pounds, Jimmy's stature didn't intimidate Stella. Her hand vanished into Jimmy's paw like she was shaking hands with a bear. Sinead had not told Jimmy why Jack was picking him up.

"Do you know what kidnapped means, Jimmy?"

"Yes. It's when someone takes someone against their will."

"Well, we think Clodagh's been kidnapped."

Jimmy leaned forward in his seat, so his head was close to Jack's ear. "Who did this?"

"We're pretty sure it's Jamie and Mary."

Jimmy laughed as though Jack was playing a practical joke on him. "Never."

"Yes. Jimmy, they've done this before."

"Where have they taken her?"

"Our best guess is Mt. Diablo. Sinead is getting people together to come and search for her, and we're going to the ranch."

Maybe not a good idea to explain further that this translated to over one hundred and fifty armed civilians from the Tenderloin entering and searching a national park.

"I come to Mt. Diablo sometimes with Clodagh."

Jack frowned and turned back to look at Jimmy. "Why?"

"She gets sick of running in the Tenderloin. Sometimes, she comes to Mt. Diablo to run."

Jack had a flashback, like a movie, walking to the barn with Clodagh, her familiarity with the mountain peaks.

"When we drove to the ranch and stayed there, you never mentioned this."

"You didn't ask me, and there was no reason to tell you. I was there to talk with Aaron."

"Does she take you along for you to get some exercise as well?" said Jack.

"I was there to look after the car. She'd take the Bentley and didn't want anyone damaging it."

Jack had a mental image of a gold Bentley with a seven-foot car attendant dressed in black.

"Do you remember where she parked?"

"Yes. And on the way back home, she'd tell me where she ran."

"Stella, can you pull over so I can get in the back with Jimmy?"

It was like a pit stop in a Formula One race. The truck stopped. Jack jumped out of his door, into the truck's back door, and back on the road. Five seconds.

Jack opened his laptop and pointed at the map. "Jimmy, show me where you parked and where Clodagh told you she ran."

Jack marked up the map with the laptop's software pen and sent it to Sinead and Freddie with an explanation. Five seconds later, he was back in the front passenger seat.

"What have you got?" said Stella.

"Clodagh has run every major trail and more than half of the minor ones. She must know her way around the mountain."

"If that's the case, won't she be able to simply run away and hide?"

"All the victims were barefoot and had damage to one of their ankles. It's the same injury you see with a prisoner wearing an ankle bracelet if it's ill-fitting or rough on the inside, so the more you ran, the more they would chaff. In most cases, they had chaffed to the bone. They would have been able to track them, and bare feet on the rough ground would slow their progress."

Jack's hands-free phone rang through the dashboard. Freddie.

"You're on speaker, Freddie, with Stella and Jimmy."

"What I'm about to tell you is in the public domain anyway, if you know where to look."

Jack knew that was the key phrase. If you know where to look.

"What have you got, Freddie?"

"We couldn't find your potential kidnappers in the justice system. Never been charged with anything. But we did pick them up in the Social Services database."

Jack turned up the volume on the phone as Freddie continued. "He's thirty-five, and she's thirty-three. They went into a shelter program in the Mission District when he was ten and she was eight. They were homeless and found on the street and taken to the shelter. They didn't know where they were born but had always been in San Francisco as far as they knew. Adopted in less than a year by a wealthy couple who lived in Pacific Heights. The Northams. Joseph and Penny. Good solid citizens, it seems. The Northams and the children attended the Catholic Church every Sunday, and the parents generously contributed to various church charities. They insisted on the children attending church."

"I heard about them," said Stella. "They lived not far from me. Someone beat her to death, and they found her naked body at the Presidio. The husband was a hedge fund manager and had died of a heart attack. She was raising the children herself and apparently having a difficult time with it as she took over the running of the hedge fund business. I heard she was good at it. A tough cookie, I heard. Rumor was that the children were difficult. No details, just that they were difficult, which could mean a range of things."

"The reports from Social Services said that there had been complaints laid by the children objecting to the rules she imposed, like going to church every Sunday, and the punishments that followed any misdemeanors. The Social Services' report from when they first found them described physical abuse with bruises on their bodies but no marks on their faces. The children claimed that Penny Northam beat them, but Mrs. Northam said the children had taken a very active interest in martial arts, and that's where they were getting the bruises."

"So, it was a stalemate?"

"Not quite. A later report documented them checking at the children's school. Same story. The children claimed the teacher hit them. The Social Services' report said that whatever trauma the children had endured before adoption had resulted in PTSD that manifested as a rejection of authority."

Jack could empathize with this as his own PTSD was hiding in the cave at the base of his spine, only held in check by rigorous training. It just needed a trigger to let it out. Injustice. Because what happened to his parents was unjust. A drunken driver running a red light. The visuals ran through his head. Not for the first time did he wonder, if it wasn't for the love and support of Aunt Louise, Uncle Alan, and Freddie and the training regime of Kenny, what would he be today? Same as Mary and Jamie. Something broken inside, beyond repair, looking for an outlet. Finding it, then repeating the cycle.

"Jack? Jack? Are you listening?"

Jack breathed. "I'm listening, Freddie."

"There was more from the school. Their problem with authority was only with female teachers, and Social Services wrote that the more authoritarian the female teacher, the more complaints. Male teachers, no complaints. The headmistress ran a tight ship and believed the teachers. She told the children if they continued with this behavior, there would be consequences, like raking up leaves in the schoolyard after school. The headmistress said she and the other female teachers were scared of them."

"When Penny Nathan was killed, did they have alibis?"

"Yes. They were at a party in Pacific Heights. The investigating officers said they estimated more than fifty people were at the party. Alcohol and drugs were prevalent, and it went on till 4 am. If they did slip out, killed Penny Nathan, and returned, no one would have noticed, particularly as they estimated the time of death at about 2 to 3 am. They were all wasted by then. The case went cold. That's all I've got. Except for one odd thing."

"What's that?" said Jack.

"It seems the party broke up when Mary and Jamie got into a fight with two guys and beat them up."

"Mary was fighting a guy?"

"I told you before," said Kenny. "They're both talented fighters. Don't underestimate either of them."

"I won't," said Jack. "Freddie, what troubles you about this fight?"

"Two things. One, the guys they fought, who were both bigger, did not know why the fight started. Jamie said they had insulted Mary, and the two guys swore they hadn't even spoken to her. Second, there was lots of blood, like Mary and Jamie had only gone for head punches. Both guys had broken noses, and you know how noses bleed, and hitting all parts of a head would result in skinned knuckles."

"What Freddie's saying," said Kenny, "is that if you beat someone to death with your fists and feet and you wanted to hide the damage to your body, you get into a fight with someone else. Making sure there was lots of blood and damage to your hands and feet."

"What about DNA?"

"They showered that night," said Freddie "Their clothes they put through the washing machine that same night. The next morning those same clothes they took to the dry cleaners, shoes included. All traces of DNA, gone."

"If you wanted to cover your tracks," said Kenny, "that would be how to do it."

"We're just naturally suspicious," said Freddie. "Goes with the job. And we can't arrest someone for being obsessive about cleanliness."

"Could they have been after the inheritance?" said Jack.

"That's another thing," said Freddie. "Penny Nathan left them with academic scholarships and a trust fund that they could only use to support themselves during their education. The rest she left to the Catholic Church, a fact they would have only known after her death. We can only guess how they reacted to that but assume they would have viewed it as a final act of her installing discipline in their lives."

CHAPTER THIRTY-FIVE

At the ranch, Jack loaded the rifle and the shotgun and placed them on the kitchen table with extra loaded magazines.

"Take one of them with you," said Stella, patting her hip. "I've got my Glock."

"I don't have time to argue. If you see them in the distance, use the rifle. The rest of the time, stay inside and carry the shotgun. If they come through that door, fire, and pump."

"I know how to use a shotgun. What if they have weapons?"

"The profiler's report said that's not their style."

"So, you're going without a weapon based on some nerd sitting in an office?"

Jack smiled, put his index finger on his chin, tilted his head to the side, and paused for two seconds like he was seriously considering the question. "Exactly."

Stella shook her head, then hugged him. "Please be careful."

Jack held Stella's face in his hands. "I plan to help locate them. If I find them, I'll phone for the cavalry."

"Jack, come see," said Jimmy.

Jack and Stella went outside, where Jimmy was test-flying his drone above the barn.

"Come look at the screen."

Jimmy lowered his hands to his waist so Jack could see the high-resolution five-inch screen.

"You've got roof tiles that need fixing, Jack."

"Jimmy, remember you told me you knew all the trails Clodagh ran?"

Jimmy did not take his eyes off the screen or his thumbs off the controller. "Yes."

"I want you to fly your drone over these trails and see if you can find Clodagh. If you do, send me a text. No phone calls." Jack turned to Stella. "Same for you, text, no phone calls."

Jack watched the drone go over the ranch and up the mountain as he walked to his truck and drove to the back of the ranch. When he got out, he saw a white helicopter flying laps on the mountain. The trail up the mountain was uneven and overgrown, and his boots made a sliding, crunching sound as he walked on the shale. The ground went from flat to a ten percent incline, and the last fifty feet was ten percent more. His breathing rate stayed the same, but his breaths were getting deeper and longer as he used his diaphragm to maximize oxygen intake. He got to thinking this is what Peter Wasserman must have put up with every day.

At fifty feet from the plateau, his head was still below it. He heard a sound. His boots had been making the same sound on the shale, but he could hear no voices. Jack stepped onto the side of the trail where clumps of grass struggled to keep alive through the shale. Jack stayed on the grass, working his way up, his eyes looking up. As his head came level with the plateau, he could see a circle cleared of trees one hundred feet in diameter with ankle-high grass. Jamie's head was visible twenty feet away from Jack, so he bent over and slipped behind a tree, climbing higher, trying to stay off the shale, his view improving with each step until all three were visible.

Clodagh was naked. Her skin was white like wall paint with mottled bruising except for her face, which was unmarked. Blood covered the back half of her right foot, seeping from an ankle cuff. Her mouth was open, and she was breathing rapidly, her abdomen moving out and back in. Mary wore mid-brown polyester shorts with a matching sports bra and running shoes, and Jamie had the same shade of shorts, running shoes, and a tank top. These two looked more military than civilian in an age where a collection of runners looked like a sprinkling of confetti. Both had their knuckles wrapped with brown electrical tape. Jack had taped his knuckles in the past to prevent splitting the skin when they delivered punches to bony parts of the body, like the head. Kenny's words about Jamie and Mary came back to Jack. They both looked strong, and there was hardly any body fat, their muscles standing out like an anatomical drawing from the recent run up the mountain.

Clodagh was a standing target, like a practice dummy, sagging at the knees, eyes slit, her hands hanging by her side as Mary did a reverse kick to Clodagh's stomach, sending her reeling backward with a grunt. As Mary turned, Jack saw no weapons on her front or back. Jamie moved behind Clodagh and caught her before she fell. He moved sideways, his back to Jack, also showing no weapon, as he poured water from a flask into her mouth. The water splashed and spurted outwards as Clodagh gagged and coughed at the unexpected rush of water, interrupting her panting. It was like waterboarding. He pushed her forward to Mary, who delivered a left roundhouse kick to her upper leg with sufficient force to make Clodagh wobble but not enough to put her down. This was not a fight. This was punishment.

Jack felt guilt rising like a wave as Clodagh had never been on his radar as a target. She wouldn't understand why they were inflicting this upon her, and it would seem unfair, unjust, and unknown to her, like a five-year-old in a car crash with his dead parents. Jack could feel the dark thing at the base of his spine coming out of its cave.

Jamie indicated to Mary to turn Clodagh around. Seems they were taking turns. As Mary turned Clodagh like a lump of dough, Jamie stretched his right arm out with his hand cupped. To Jack, it looked like preparation for a slap to the ear. This would not incapacitate Clodagh, as there were easier ways to do that, but it would cause a lot of pain as it created a vacuum down the auditory canal, with the risk of bursting the eardrum, with even more pain. The dark thing rushed up Jack's spine as he picked up a three-foot-long dead branch and threw it two-handed over his head like he was throwing an ax. Mary was half-hidden behind Jamie. The stick landed on the far side of the circle, tumbling end over end, making them look in that direction. Jack took two steps up to the plateau and started running at them. Jamie looked back from where the stick must have come.

Jack launched a straight left at Jamie's throat, which Jamie blocked by dropping his chin and taking the punch, slapping it away, and settling into a fighter's crouch, his hands held high.

"Well, Jack, fancy bumping into you. Taking a stroll up from the ranch, are you?"

"I've come to get Clodagh."

"She's a bit busy at the moment. Maybe you can come back later," Jamie grinned like a clown. "But hang on, now that you've seen us, there will be no later."

"You talk like this is a game, Jamie," said Jack.

Mary was circling, trying to get behind Jack so he would have an attacker front and back. Jack circled faster, keeping Jamie between him and Mary. Mary pushed Clodagh out of her way as she moved around.

Clodagh's legs buckled, and she flopped to the ground like a steer in an abattoir.

"Horace Walpole said that the world is a comedy to those that think, a tragedy to those that feel. But I believe he is wrong on both counts. Life is just a big silly game with winners and losers. Like today, here, there's about to be winners and losers."

"The police know all about you and your killings. Is that your idea of winners and losers?"

"What killings?"

"I may not remember all the names and not in the right order, but let's see how I go." Jack recited what he could remember. "How did I do?"

"Hmm," said Jamie as he watched Jack like he had just noticed he had a third eye in the middle of his forehead.

"Why do you think we killed those women?" said Mary.

"A bit of data analysis can reveal all sorts of things."

Jamie guffawed, making a noise like his throat had something stuck, and he struggled to dislodge it. "I've only now realized that you were responsible for the police arresting Sam Dodd."

"That was my error."

"I must say, you did give us quite a scare. But tell me, what led you to us?"

"It was the same analysis. I just needed more data. Anyone could have done it."

Jack knew he had to get them angry, as angry fighters are not as effective as calm fighters. A Kenny saying. Jack's anger was a cold, unfeeling rage, which only knew one thing. Justice, in whatever form that took. There was an expression he'd overheard in Doyle's pub from an old-timer that seemed to make the listener boil over.

"Maybe not you two, as you're a couple of taillights."

"What does that even mean?"

"It means you're not bright enough to be a headlight. You two will only ever be a couple of taillights."

Jamie feinted with a left jab and struck out with a roundhouse kick to the head. Jack blocked the kick with his forearm, which felt like a baseball bat had hit him. He thought he felt his forearm bend. Jack stepped inside Jamie's reach and got in a left uppercut and a right round-house punch which rocked him but didn't make him fall. By his stance, he was now taking Jack more seriously. It was a move so he could defend as well as attack.

"So, you have some moves, Jack. Well done. By the way, how did you know we'd be here? More data analysis? You didn't just stumble upon us as you went for a walk."

"You got it. And there are over one hundred and fifty of Clodagh's people on the mountain looking for you two."

"Is that possible, Jamie?" said Mary.

"It doesn't matter. We can hide on the mountain until they get tired of looking for us. There's enough food on the mountain to get by. Did you see the walnuts and blackberries?"

"I did," said Mary.

"Then let's deal with Jack. Who doesn't think we are particularly clever."

Jack realized he had hit a nerve. Pride. "Well, Jamie, let's talk about the profile you like for your victims. Female, wealthy, have their own business, and strongly disciplined. Clodagh fits the profile, but she's not the richest woman with her own business in San Francisco."

"But you don't know how she treats her children."

"I think I do. What have you seen?"

"We saw how she disciplined Liam. That was enough for us, and someone has to punish her."

That was the missing piece. The trigger and data analysis would not pick that up as it would not have that data.

"So, what are you two? Avenging angels? You're pathetic."

They both rushed Jack, who blocked and spun away.

"Pathetic, are we?" said Mary. "Watch this."

Mary slipped next to Jamie, and they both rushed Jack. Mary arrived first with a flying sidekick to Jack's head which caught him in the chest, sending him sliding and slipping on the shale until he fell back onto the ground. Jamie leaped and landed on Jack's chest with both knees, and Jack's ribs took the strain.

Had any broken when the hit forced the air out?

Jamie grabbed him by the throat with both hands. Jack slammed at Jamie's forearms, but he was too strong. He smiled at Jack.

"Mary. I've got him here. Kick him in the head and finish him."

Was this meant to render him unconscious or kill him?

He assumed the latter. On Jack's left, Mary took two steps back. Clearly, she wanted to do a proper job. Jack's phone beeped with a message as he reached out with his right hand, scratching around for a weapon. The thin edges of the broken shale cut into his fingers. Jack's head swelled with blood, and spots appeared in front of his eyes.

There was one spot that was getting closer and larger. Jack's hand closed on a piece of shale, holding it like a slice of pizza. Jack recognized the prominent spot in front of his eyes as a drone a second before it hit Mary in the head. Jaime turned to look as Mary collapsed. His hands loosened slightly. Jack swung the shale at Jamie's temple. Jamie saw the movement and turned his head away and down, the shale missing its mark and the edge running across his throat. Blood flowed as the shale completed its arc. Jack swung back on the same arc, making another slice across his throat. Jamie let go of Jack to jam his fingers to his throat as he fell off Jack.

Jack heard movement on the trail. Something significant in size, slipping on the shale. Hikers had reported seeing mountain lions, but these sightings were unconfirmed. There were no bears. He moved over to Clodagh and picked up a rock the size of his fist. Jack looked at where the noise was coming from, and Jimmy's head appeared, and then the rest of him as he got onto the plateau carrying the controller for his drone. He walked over to Jack but turned away when he saw Clodagh's naked body on the ground.

"Is she dead, Jack?"

"No, Jimmy, she's not dead. Give me your T-shirt."

Jimmy complied, passing it back to Jack, who got Clodagh into a sitting position and pulled the T-shirt over her head. Clodagh groaned with each movement she made. Her eyes opened to slits. She looked at Jack and Jimmy's bare back, the same shade of white as an elephant's tusk.

"You can turn round, Jimmy," said Jack.

Jimmy sat next to Clodagh, arranging the T-shirt on her as though she were a child. Clodagh sat like she never wanted to move ever again.

Jack went over to check on Mary and Jamie. Both dead. Mary had one of the rotor blades from the drone through her skull and into her brain. Jamie had bled out and looked peaceful, his head in Mary's lap. She was a far more horrific picture with a drone sticking out of her head.

Jack knew from Freddie that the burden of proof that their actions were justifiable would fall on him and Jimmy. They would have to show that no other course of action was open to them. A prosecuting attorney would have an easy task of expounding that there had to be easier ways than navigating a drone into someone's head or slicing someone's throat with a piece of shale.

"Jimmy, this is a strange question but do any of Clodagh's people know how to make two dead bodies vanish."

Clodagh opened her eyes and looked across at the bodies. "Both dead?"

"Very much so. We need to get rid of them."

"Jimmy. Get hold of Jebb," said Clodagh. "Tell him what's happened and that I want these bodies to vanish." Clodagh may have been telling Jimmy to fetch pizza.

Jimmy nodded and stepped away to make the call. Clodagh looked at Jack. "It will take Jebb a while to get here. He's in San Francisco."

"He may be closer. Let me bring you up to date."

Jack explained while Jimmy talked on the phone. Clodagh nodded. "All my people?"

"I don't know how many you got, but that's how many are on the mountain."

Clodagh's face was like granite, covered in sweat and dust as she looked at the bodies, her eyes tearing up but not rolling down her cheeks.

Jimmy walked back. "Jebb says he's five minutes away."

"Jimmy, I need you to take Clodagh down to the ranch. You'll have to carry her on your back as it will hurt her less, and you'll be better balanced as you go down the trail."

Jimmy lifted Clodagh to a standing position and went on all fours like he was a pony. With Jack's help, Clodagh maneuvered flat onto Jimmy's back.

"Put your arms around Jimmy's neck and wrap your legs around him."

Jimmy stood without a grunt or an exhalation, hooking his arms under Clodagh's legs.

Jack went with them to where the trail began.

"I'll wait here for Jebb. My truck is at the edge of the ranch. Use it. Jimmy, remember the vet who stitched you up? Ask her to have a look at Clodagh. And Jimmy, don't slip."

"I won't slip, Jack."

Jack watched them descend, wondering how Jimmy seemed more concerned with Clodagh than he had when he guided his drone at maximum speed into someone's head, killing them instantly. Or maybe this level of violence was not new to him. They were almost gone from view when he heard a sound and turned to see seven men in their early forties walking into the clearing dressed in camo pants. Each wore a loose jacket covering a concealed carry pistol, only visible when the jacket flapped with their striding like they were on a route march. They had sensible hiking boots and camo caps overlooking reflecting sunglasses showing a blue sheen. Definitely not your average weekend hikers.

"Jebb?" said Jack, trying to find out who was who.

The man in the front nodded and walked over to the bodies. He pointed at one man, who went over to a tree, cut a branch with a knife that looked like a KA-BAR, and gave it to Jebb. Four men took Jamie, one on each arm and leg. Two men picked up Mary, one had her arms, and the other had her legs.

They all heard the whop, whop, whop, noise of a helicopter getting closer. Jebb looked around the plateau like a cornered rat and pointed to trees with a low overhang. The men scuttled like crabs, half dragging and carrying the bodies under the branches. The helicopter hovered and came lower but not enough to see under the trees rattling the trees' leaves, blowing dust and leaves in all directions, covering any signs of blood with dust, grass, and twigs, more and more the closer it got to the ground. Earlier, Jack would have considered the helicopter to be his friend, but it was now his enemy. Like people. The helicopter stayed in position for twenty seconds, then lifted off. Jebb pointed at the trail from where they'd appeared. The men picked up the bodies and walked off.

The helicopter had done an excellent job of covering the blood. Jebb looked at the ground where the blood was and brushed the spots the helicopter had not covered until no blood was visible. Jack thought there would still be DNA. Jebb unzipped his jeans and urinated where the blood had been visible.

Would this make DNA analysis impossible? Would animals come to mark their territory on top of Jebb's urine?

None of these questions he would ask Freddie for fear of getting even more questions thrown back at him.

Freddie. Jack reached into his hip pocket, pulled out his phone, and switched it off silent mode. It looked a bit bent. As he phoned Freddie, he watched Jebb scattering handfuls of dirt and leaves over the spots of blood and the trail of urine. There was no answer, so he left a message.

"They found Clodagh."

The man raked some more, then walked off in the direction his seven companions had taken, carrying the branch and a damaged drone, leaving Jack alone.

CHAPTER THIRTY-SIX

The trip back to the ranch was so pleasant he felt he should be carrying a picnic basket. A thought that ran counter to what had happened on the plateau.

Jimmy was wearing one of Aaron's football training T-shirts and throwing a ball to Aaron. Princess was lying on the verandah, paws over the edge, her eyes never leaving Aaron. They stopped when they saw Jack.

"Where's Clodagh?"

"Inside with Hailey and Stella," said Aaron.

"And Jimmy," said Jack. "Have you spoken to Sinead?"

"Yes. She's getting everyone off the mountain, then coming here."

Hailey came out of the kitchen door with her box of vet equipment and supplies. Jack stepped up to the verandah. "How's Clodagh?"

"We showered her so that I could see the damage. A lot of bruising but nothing broken. I gave her a painkiller. She's exhausted. She'll sleep for a long while." Hailey laughed as she saw Jack's expression. "Yes, I took a horse painkiller, cut it into four pieces, and gave her one. Don't worry. I've done it before for myself. The dosage is fine."

"Do you know who she is?"

"Yes, Jack, even out here in the country, we keep up to date and hear things. Clodagh Doyle, Queen of the Tenderloin. You sure have some interesting friends."

"I'm not sure friend is the correct word."

"Then what about Stella West, who's in the kitchen making soup for Clodagh? She's the owner of Link Industries, and she's wearing a concealed carry pistol. Are her and Clodagh friends?"

"They've never met until an hour ago."

"Are you and Stella friends?"

Jack was slow to answer. Hailey waited. "Really, Jack, you and Stella. Well, that explains a couple of things."

Jack's phone rang. Freddie. Jack killed the call.

Hailey stepped off the verandah and walked to her truck. "See you tomorrow morning Aaron."

Aaron threw the ball back to Jimmy. "Sure thing, Hailey."

Jack waved as she drove off, but Hailey was looking straight ahead. Jack phoned Freddie.

"Your message said they found Clodagh."

Somehow lying to Freddie didn't sit well, as though he'd eaten too much ice cream. But sometimes, someone has to make the least worst choice. Jack knew what the following questions would be.

"Yes. The search party who found her phoned her daughter, and she phoned me. I wanted to get hold of you so you could get your resources to stand down."

"Thanks. Did they find the suspects?"

Freddie always playing the ball straight and true. Jamie and Marie were suspects until proven otherwise. That was the correct thing to do.

"Not that I heard."

"I'll keep some people there and the helicopter until sunset. If nothing comes up by then, I'll have to assume they got off the mountain and got away somehow."

"I guess so."

"Did they take Clodagh to the hospital or home? We'll need to speak to her."

"Home. Sinead said they'd look after her there. But maybe give it a few days. She must be exhausted."

"Of course. Anything else you can think of that might help us find the suspects?"

"Nothing at the moment."

"All right. I got to go."

Freddie ended the call. Jack looked back up at Mt. Olympia, then walked to the house.

Jack entered the kitchen, where Stella held a tray with a bowl, a spoon, and two slices of toast. "I heated up some chicken soup for Clodagh from tins I found in the cupboard. She's in the spare bedroom in a pair of your pajamas. She's awake. Come with me. I'm sure she'd like to see you."

Jack opened the door to the bedroom. Clodagh was asleep like she was dead. Jack switched off the light and closed the door.

Stella put the tray on the kitchen table and looked Jack up and down. "No one has attended to your injuries, have they? And you look grubby." Stella smiled with her eyes, her lips a thin line. "Grubby. Now there's a word I haven't used for a while. Why don't you get in the shower? Then we can see what's under all that grubbiness."

Jack had felt the adrenaline draining from his body as he'd walked back to the ranch, and the dark thing had shrunk down his spine and into its cave at the base. The adrenaline had burned almost all his blood sugar, leaving him feeling flat and irritable. He needed to eat. But a shower was a good place to start and see if there was damage, like inspecting a car after an accident.

Jack went into the bathroom and started stripping off, and Stella did the same. Seeing Stella naked was always like the first time. Her skin had not seen the sun for a while, contrasting with her elfin cut hair, the color of midnight with no moon or stars. "Think of me," she said with her thin-lipped smile, eyes sparkling, "as your nurse for the night."

Jack turned on the taps, not feeling so irritable anymore, and yes, food could wait. "Well, nurse, I'm pretty sure I've got places that need some nursing."

***

Jack had heard Hailey's truck arrive at six o'clock to collect Aaron and Princess. Jack picked out clothes from his cupboard, dressed in the kitchen, and went outside. Jimmy was standing, looking forlorn like a kid who'd realized he wasn't getting a pony for his birthday, staring up at Mt. Olympia until he heard Jack's boots crunching on the ground. He turned and smiled at Jack. "I want to stay here until I can take Clodagh home. Is that ok, Jack?"

"Sure, Jimmy. What are you going to do today?"

"Last night, I asked them to bring the Bentley. I'll clean it when it gets here. The old Ford truck they've already collected and taken home. Do you have a vacuum cleaner I can use?"

"There's one in the kitchen."

"Would you like me to wash and clean your truck when I finish with the Bentley?"

"That'd be great, Jimmy. Thank you."

Jack returned to the kitchen to find Stella wearing one of his brown ranch shirts and thick socks. As pale as milk, her legs were sticking out below the shirt.

"Aren't your legs cold?"

"A little bit."

She went to the fridge and reached up to get the cream. Jack watched as the shirt hiked up, revealing she was wearing nothing under the shirt.

Stella put the coffee mugs on the table as Clodagh entered the kitchen in Jack's blue and white stripe flannel pajamas with rolled-up legs and sleeves that reached past her fingertips. Her movements were as wobbly as a newborn foal.

"Clodagh," said Jack as he moved to her, putting his hand under her elbow. Stella was a nanosecond behind in grabbing her other arm. "What are you doing up?"

"I'm fine."

Clodagh winced with each step she took with her lacerated feet like she was walking on eggshells as they walked her to the table and sat her down.

"Do you like coffee with cream?" said Jack.

"I do."

Jack pushed his mug in front of Clodagh.

"Thank you, Jack. Actually, I've got a lot to thank you for. When I first suggested an arrangement where we could help each other as friends help each other, I didn't expect it would wind up like this." Clodagh pulled up her sleeve to sip the coffee revealing brown and purple bruising.

Jack smiled. "Neither did I."

"Sorry," said Stella. "What arrangement?"

Jack was about to speak when Clodagh interjected. "Let me explain as it was my idea, and you were rather tentative in the beginning."

Jack got up and made himself coffee while Clodagh explained. When she'd finished, Stella looked at Jack. "You have been busy."

Jack brought his coffee to the table and looked at Clodagh. "You do realize you can't go anywhere with those bruises. It'll raise too many questions. The cops already had Jamie and Mary on their radar, courtesy of me. Now they've gone missing, thanks to Jebb. Word gets out you're now battered and bruised, and one hundred and fifty of your people had suddenly decided to take up hiking on Mt. Diablo, the police will ask questions that will get increasingly difficult to answer."

"May I remind you, I have a business to run?"

"Well, may I remind you that you have a daughter who is running the business right now?"

"Really?"

"Yes. Really. Give her a chance. I think Sinead is more than capable. You need to vanish, so the police can't talk to you, at least until your bruising has gone."

"And," said Stella, "as the person who showered you, dressed you, and put you to bed, I would say that will take three, possibly four weeks."

"Was that you? Thank you. I couldn't open my eyes. The painkiller the vet gave me really knocked me out. By the way, who are you?"

"I'm Stella West. Nice to meet you, Clodagh Doyle."

Clodagh took this information on board as she looked from Stella to Jack and back to Stella. "Stella West, the owner and CEO of Link Industries?"

"That's me."

Clodagh smiled like a knowing owl as she looked at Stella's clothing. "I take it you didn't sleep in the bunkhouse." Jack jumped back into the conversation as he wasn't comfortable where this conversation had drifted. "Clodagh, we need to come up with a story. When was the last time you took a holiday?"

"When the children were still small. Since they were teenagers, they've been taking their own holidays, and the business has grown exponentially, keeping me busy. And where would I go at short notice where I wouldn't be visible?"

Jack stood, his phone in hand, walked to the door, and stared at the barn without seeing it, his gaze a 1000-yard stare. He looked at his phone, scrolled, hit enter, and listened while it rang eight times.

"Hello Jack. Great to hear from you."

"Which one of you two am I speaking to?"

There was a laugh like a happy child. "Jenny, you're talking to Jenny."

"If I don't see you two often enough, I can't tell the difference on the phone."

"Yes, I know. We often get that. To what do we owe the pleasure of this call? Are you coming to visit us?"

"Not me. But there is someone who I'd like to stay with you for three or four weeks."

"Who?"

"Sinead's mother, Clodagh."

"I've never met her, but sure. She's most welcome. But why would she want to stay with us?"

Jack turned to look at Clodagh. "She had an accident on Mt. Diablo when she was running."

"What kind of accident?"

"She fell. Nothing broken but badly bruised. It will take her some time to recover physically and emotionally."

"Glad to help, but remember, we won't be here to look after her as we're out on a boat or at the dock most days."

"Your place has got five bedrooms, if I recall. I want to get her driver to drive her down to Laguna Beach, and could he stay with you as well? The driver, I should add, is more like an adopted son. He'll look after Clodagh, and she'll pay for food, accommodation, and any expenses."

"Sure, having a man at the house will be good. Those creeps you beat up have started stalking us."

"The driver's name's Jimmy. I'll ask him to attend to it."

"Is he big?"

"Bigger than average."

"When does she want to come?"

"Is today too soon? They could be there later this afternoon."

"That's fine. Just make it after four. That's when we get back to the house."

"Will do. Thank you."

Jack rang off and phoned again. This time it rang twice.

"Is my mother ok?"

"She's fine, Sinead. Just weary with lots of bruising. You're up early."

"I've been up for an hour. Now I'm running things, I've got lots to do and learn."

"I've organized for Clodagh to stay with the twins for a few weeks."

"That's a wonderful idea. She'll love it there. I must phone the twins and thank them."

"They'd appreciate that. Has the Bentley left yet?"

There was a pause for two seconds. "Not yet. I'll pack clothes for my mother. What's she wearing at the moment?"

"My pajamas."

"I'm sure they're a fashion item."

"Can you also pack for Jimmy? He's going to stay at the Laguna house with Clodagh and the twins."

"Ok. I'm on it. Let me do that. I need to speak to you separately. But first, let me first get the Bentley on the road."

Sinead rang off, and Jack went back into the kitchen, where the smell and sizzling of bacon made him hungry. Clodagh slumped over her coffee mug, her forearms supporting her. Stella was slicing onions, and tears were starting in her eyes as Jack moved her to one side and took over the onion slicing. Stella broke eggs into a bowl and whisked them.

"Why do I think this is not the first time you two have made breakfast together?"

Jack kept slicing. "Shouldn't you be resting, Clodagh?"

Clodagh chuckled and sipped her coffee.

CHAPTER THIRTY-SEVEN

Two hours later, Jack and Stella stood on the verandah and watched the back of the gold Bentley as Jimmy drove down to the front gate. They'd laid the passenger seat flat for Clodagh, still in Jack's pajamas, resting, surrounded by pillows and blankets.

"What do you think of Clodagh?" said Jack.

"She's a woman running a large enterprise, and I can relate to that. From what you told me, she had to run the business when her father died. My situation was the same, except it was my husband who died. Again, I can relate to that. The difference between us is I don't have an army of killers working for me."

Jack chuckled. "An army of killers?"

"Well, let's say she has more than I have, and I have none. Is she dangerous? Oh yes."

"And you're not?" said Jack. "What about your concealed carry Glock?"

"Let's just say on the dangerous scale, from one to ten. I'm a one. Clodagh's an eleven."

Jack made a single laugh. "Do you trust her?"

"I do, and she owes you a huge debt which I think she'll honor."

The Bentley turned onto Marsh Creek Road and slid from view.

"What have you got planned for today?" said Jack.

Stella undid the top button of Jack's shirt she was wearing. "Well, as there's no more danger to me." Stella undid the next button. "I should be getting back to my office at Link."

Jack's phone rang, and he glanced at it. Sinead. Stella shrugged her left shoulder, then her right, the shirt falling into a puddle around her ankles. The morning light captured her nakedness like a painting. Nude in the Sunlight by Renoir. Aunt Louise had taken Freddie and him to Art Galleries to instill an appreciation of art into them. Jack noted Stella was slimmer than the model in Renoir's painting and her hair was shorter.

**

Jack sat up in bed, reached for his phone, and dialed. Stella stretched an arm across his belly and continued dozing.

"Good morning, Sinead. Sorry I couldn't take your call." Jack looked at Stella's shape under the sheet. "I was in a meeting."

"Liam's missing."

"But he was supposed to stay in the bar where there would be many witnesses to his whereabouts."

"Yes. Yes. Yes. I know about that, but I don't understand why he had to do that. Then yesterday, when we went looking for my mother, he wanted to help. To be part of the search party. It seemed like he was doing something non-selfish for a change. I agreed as Clodagh's his mother too."

"Did you send him with someone?"

"Yes. But when all the people came down from the mountain, he wasn't amongst them. They phoned him. No answer. It went to voice. I sent people to his apartment. Not there. About fifty people went back up the mountain to look for him. They found his phone but not him. They searched through the night. I had a headcount of all the people who went onto the mountain and returned. The only person missing is Liam."

"Clodagh never told you why Liam had to be in the bar."

"No. Everyone just followed her orders."

"Liam was trading skins for a group who are a terrorist organization or a front for a terrorist organization. This group is anti-Israel. I gave their details to Peter Wasserman, whose friend from childhood is an ex-Director of Mossad. This friend of Peter's phoned me to say they would be taking care of this. This guy said to keep Liam around a lot of witnesses. Because if one, or all of them, turn up dead and Liam had no alibi, as he was doing illegal deals with them, he'd be a likely suspect."

"This all sounds made up."

"I know it does. But Clodagh knew or knew of Peter, and when I told her the information came from Peter, she followed the advice. Without hesitation, I might add."

"What's my mother's connection with this Peter Wasserman?"

"I don't know, and Clodagh never said anything, but the sound of his name did make her nervous. Peter died recently of natural causes."

"Strange, I don't recall my mother ever being scared of anyone, and you say this Peter Wasserman died of natural causes."

"Yes. I was there."

"Ok. Understood. But where's Liam?"

"I don't know."

"Will you help me find him?"

"I'll try. Where have you looked so far?"

"I've got someone waiting inside his apartment in case he turns up there. He has no friends that I know of. He's always been a loner, and I don't really know what he likes and doesn't like, which could give me a clue. Correction, he likes money but has always been trying to find easy ways to get it."

"Where are you?"

"I'm sitting at my mother's desk, working."

In his mind, Jack could see her sitting at the command post, stepping into her mother's shoes. "Don't forget to check on the flowers and plants."

Sinead laughed. "I've already had a phone call from my mother."

"How does she sound?"

"Tired."

"Not unexpected. I'll see what I can do about Liam. Although not much to go on."

Jack rang off, showered, and was in the kitchen making coffee when Stella walked through wearing his shirt from yesterday and into his arms.

"That coffee smells great."

They sat on the verandah, watching the day begin in companionable silence until Jack's phone rang. Aidan.

"Good morning, Jack. Is this a good time?"

Jack looked at Stella and shrugged. "It's fine. What's up."

"Liam phoned Ralph earlier about his access to the system. Ralph put him through to me, and I told him your instruction was that we revoked his access until further notice."

"How did he react?"

"Badly. Like a spoiled brat. Shouting, swearing, making threats, all aimed at you, I might add."

"What kind of threat?"

"That you'd be sorry. 'You didn't know who you were dealing with.'" Aidan chuckled. "It was like something from an old gangster or western movie. But do you think we need to be concerned?"

Jack heard the rumble of a big trick and turned to the driveway to see a big gray truck coming in.

"I'm sure it's all just bluster and wind. How long ago was this?"

There was a pause. "About an hour."

"I would have phoned earlier, but things got busy here, what with setting things up, and I didn't want to wake you. Also, I figured you're safe out there on the ranch."

Jack looked at the approaching truck. All he could tell was that it was black and big. "Safe as houses, Aidan. Listen, I have to go. Thanks for the call."

"You're most welcome."

Jack rang off, went inside, opened the gun safe, and pulled out the loaded rifle and shotgun as he spoke to Stella. "Stay inside. I don't know who this is."

The rifle he put next to the door and the shotgun he held behind his leg as he stepped out onto the verandah. He didn't want to frighten a neighbor he hadn't met. The truck was an Escalade with tinted windows, and the dust from the driveway had left a coating like beige talcum powder. It stopped, and a stocky man got out of the rear door with a pistol in his right hand and Liam in his left. His hand enclosed Liam's bicep, and he pulled him to the front of the Escalade, keeping the barrel of his weapon against Liam's temple as the driver got out with a pistol in his right hand. The driver was two inches taller than Jack, thirty pounds heavier, not steroid heavier, just naturally heavier with muscle. He pointed his weapon at Jack's chest. A center-of-mass shot. Both were swarthy with short black hair, full beards, jeans, boots, and brown T-shirts. Jack had the shotgun pointed at their feet, thinking the rifle would have been a better choice as Liam would get taken out with the shotgun's spray and pray effect.

"Jack," said Stocky. "I need you to give Liam back his access to the trading platform, or else he's no use to me, and I'll shoot him, and my partner will shoot you. Now put the shotgun down, slowly."

The command of English was good, but like they had learned it in Louisiana or Kentucky, with undertones from the Middle East. Jack's gaze took in Stocky, Liam, Big, and his ten feet from them. He was out of options and lowered the shotgun down to the deck of the verandah.

"Anyone else here?" said Stocky.

"No."

Stocky looked at Big and nodded towards the house. Big moved past Jack, throwing a punch to his stomach. Jack felt it hit his solar plexus, and his breathing stopped as he gasped like a fish, bending at the waist and moving to the side to see them both. That move was what Kenny would have done. Big bent down and picked up the shotgun with no change in pace. At the doorway, he looked around and picked up the rifle holding it and the shotgun by the barrels in his left hand. He returned six minutes later and shook his head at Stocky.

"Pass me the shotgun. Put the rifle in the Escalade, and let's go inside." Stocky hefted the shotgun, so he held it with his left hand. "I'm ambidextrous, Jack, so I can shoot you with both simultaneously."

"Is that your party trick?"

"Funny guy," said Stocky with a face that did not look like he laughed at what makes ordinary people laugh. "Let's go inside."

Big walked backward into the kitchen. His weapon pointed at Jack as he followed him. Next came Liam and Stocky.

"Liam, sit at the laptop," said Stocky.

Big slapped Jack across the face with a forehand that made his ears ring and backhanded him, making his mouth split along his teeth inside and out. The metal taste of blood filled his mouth.

"Now, Jack," said Stocky. "You're going to phone your office and tell them to reinstate Liam's access."

"Why are you so keen for Liam to get back into trading?"

"Well, Jack, you may feel under pressure right now, but I can assure you mine is greater."

"I've got two pistols and a shotgun pointed at me. That's pretty significant pressure, and you haven't introduced yourself."

"Who I am is of no consequence to you. What I must deal with is a warehouse full of hides that Liam needs to trade as a certain foreign intelligence agency is getting too close for comfort."

"Is this in the interest of the US?"

"Not really, but that shouldn't be your concern."

"I think it is. What if I don't give Liam access?"

"Well, if you don't, Liam is of no use to me, and I will shoot him in the head with this shotgun as he sits in your chair. His brains will be all over your laptop chair, and…" he paused for effect like an actor, "then I'll shoot you. My large colleague will arrange it to look like you shot Liam, and then you shot yourself. We have done this before, so we will not hesitate if you don't comply. By the way, my large colleague wants to beat you to a pulp as he has strong feelings about our cause, and right now, you are an obstacle. He removes obstacles. However, I've run out of time."

Jack had been measuring distances as his phone rang. Stocky and Big knew what they were doing, staying a sufficient distance away so they could eliminate him if he made a move. "Shall I answer that?"

"Just pull it out and throw it on the table."

Looking over Big's shoulder, Jack could see Stella creeping onto the verandah with his rifle pointed at Big's back.

"Maybe it's important." Jack looked at Big. "Maybe it's for you." Jack flipped the phone at Big, who looked at it as it came through the air, as Stella stepped forward, jamming the rifle into the base of Stocky's spine. Stella didn't speak. There was silence in the room like a tomb.

Jack looked from Stocky to Big and back to Stocky. "Lower your weapons, drop them on the floor. Or else you get your spine blown in half. The shot won't kill you immediately, and it's a weird way to die, lying paralyzed on the floor as you bleed out."

Big had his pistol on Jack.

"Seems we have a standoff," said Stocky.

"It does indeed," said Jack. "What do you suggest we do?"

Jack had doubts lurking like clouds that Stella would pull the trigger. It is one thing to practice with targets and another to take a life. In an emergency, he knew she would, but the longer they waited, the less likely she would pull the trigger if Stocky moved. These guys weren't career criminals; they were terrorists fighting for a cause.

"I'm open to suggestions."

"What about getting Liam out of range of any friendly or unfriendly fire? I mean, you do want him alive?"

"That is a good suggestion. Liam, get out of here."

Liam got up and walked past Stocky, grabbed the rifle by the barrel, pulled it up, and punched Stella in the jaw. The rifle fired a round into the ceiling as Stella tried to hang on, but Liam yanked it from her grasp, hit her again, sending her to the floor, and pointed the rifle at Jack.

"What the…" said Jack as the gray thing came out of its cave at the sight of Stella getting hit.

"Surprise, Jack," said Liam.

"What's going on, Liam?" said Jack. The gray thing crept further up his spine.

Liam laughed like a hyena. "I guess you think it's about the money."

"Who's this?" said Stocky, pointing at Stella sitting on the floor with her hand on her face. "And where'd she come from?"

"I don't know where she came from." Liam looked at Big. "I thought you searched the place." Big shrugged. "I recognize her from the media. That's Stella West, the CEO of Link Industries. We must ransom her, but that's for another day."

"Ransom her? Liam, what are you doing? You said this is not about money."

"It's not. But we need money."

"What do you mean, *we*? Are you part of this?" said Jack, waving his finger between Stocky and Big.

"Part of this?" said Stocky. "There wouldn't be a San Francisco unit without Liam."

"When did this start?"

"University. But enough of this," said Liam, pointing at Big. "Take her to stand next to Jack so he can see. You're going to use your knife on her until Jack does what I'm asking."

Big smiled as though he'd just won a raffle, pulled Stella to her feet, holstered his gun, pulled out a box-cutter knife from his jeans, pushed the blade out, and held it next to Stella's throat.

"Jack," said Liam, "you are no doubt familiar with that ancient torture, death by a thousand cuts. Well, the fellow holding Mrs. West is very good at it and can drag it out for days. It's a dreadful business. Horrific to watch, and I have watched." Big held Stella's right wrist with his left hand and lifted her so she was on her toes, the box-cutter ready. Stella's eyes were open to the max, not blinking. She kicked and struck out with her free hand. Big stood sideways, so her kicks bounced off his legs, and her free hand had to stretch across her body to get to Big.

"Let's begin with a single cut, so Jack will know we're serious. Just a tiny scratch into the meat of the forearm, no blood vessels."

"Ok," said Jack. "I'll do it. Let her down. Give me my phone."

Big opened his hand. Stella came off her toes and moved to Jack, who gathered her to him as he phoned. There was a muffled "Hello."

"Hello Ralph, can you do me a favor and reinstate Liam's access?"

The reply sounded like "What?" and was half an octave higher.

"Ralph. I know it sounds crazy, but please do it. I'll explain later, and can you do it now?" Maybe there will be no later. For now, we live minute to minute. "How long do you need?"

Jack listened, then rang off, then turned to Liam. "Five minutes. Ralph says it will take five minutes."

"Sounds about right. Now you and Mrs. West sit at the table while we wait."

Jack and Stella moved to the table. Princess came trotting through the door and over to Stella, looking for a treat. Liam, Big, and Stocky looked at the dog. Jack knew what was coming and pulled Stella tighter to his body. Aaron arrived through the door in a run like a giant eagle with arms outstretched and crashed into all five of them. The rifle, a pistol, and the shotgun fired as they went into, onto, and over the table, landing in a tangle on the floor. Big had seen Aaron just before he smashed into them and grabbed him by his throat before hitting the floor. Aaron was a punching machine ignoring the hands on his throat. Big took his right hand from Aaron's throat to punch him in the head. Princess charged in with a snarl, savaging Big's ear.

Jack grabbed the barrel of Stocky's pistol with his left hand and held it on the ground, pointing at Big's head. The barrel of the shotgun became sandwiched between them. Jack knew Stocky needed to pump another round into the shotgun, so for now, it was just a club, and he twisted it down toward Stocky's leg. Stella landed on top of Liam, the rifle still in his grasp. Stella held the barrel on the ground as she pulled her Glock and stuck it in Liam's face as he squeezed the rifle's trigger.

Stocky had a snarl on his face until the rifle's bullet hit him in the back of the head, and he reflexively squeezed the pistol's trigger, sending the shot into Big's temple. Stella punched Liam in the face, and he lay still. Her punching ability appeared to surprise her until she rolled off Liam and saw blood had drenched her stomach, but she felt no pain.

Then she looked at Liam's abdomen, which the shotgun had shredded into bleeding flesh.

Jack could hear his phone ringing. Stella stood, followed by Aaron, who pried Princess from Big's ear as Jack disentangled himself from Stocky's body.

Their breathing was audible as they stood and surveyed the carnage on the floor. As Jack reached for his phone, he thought he should phone Freddie, but explaining they shot each other would be challenging. The caller was unknown. Jack answered and heard the voice of Peter's friend from Mossad.

"I've been trying to reach you, Jack. We got intelligence that two operatives from the San Francisco chapter of the Autumn Center are on their way to you at the ranch. Liam Doyle will probably be with them as we've learned he is the head of the chapter in San Francisco."

Jack wondered what Peter's friend had done to get this information. "They're here already."

"Are you ok? Where are they?"

"We're fine. They're dead. Here at the ranch."

"Do you need some help cleaning up?"

"I'd appreciate that."

"We'll be there in fifteen minutes."

***

Aaron made coffee in the bunkhouse kitchen for Jack and Stella, who were sitting at the table. The whoosh-whoosh sound of a helicopter snapped them out of their reverie, where each had been processing the events and the three bodies on the kitchen floor in the house.

"You two, please stay here," said Jack. "Let me handle this."

Jack waited for the helicopter to land and the passengers to disembark before approaching. First out were three men dressed like Jack except for the pistol on their hips. A fourth man in pleated gray trousers, black shoes, and a white button-down shirt was the last, and Jack recognized him as Peter's friend.

"Hello, Jack. Nice to meet you face to face, albeit under unfortunate circumstances."

Jack looked at the smile and the brown eyes with a warmth like a summer sun that had seen so much turmoil and chaos in protecting his country.

"A pleasure to meet you, Sir."

"Peter spoke fondly of you."

"I had become quite fond of him as well."

The eyes changed to arctic cold. "Where are the bodies?"

"In the kitchen."

Peter's friend followed Jack into the kitchen, followed by the other three carrying buckets with mops, cleaning fluids, and blue plastic sheeting. He pointed at Liam, Big, and Stocky. "I recognize them from photos. What do you want us to do with Liam Doyle?"

"This may be a bit presumptuous, but you wouldn't be able to drop the body off at a funeral home where they can patch up the body, so it doesn't look like he died of a gunshot wound and can create a death certificate that says he died of a heart attack?"

"That I can do," said Peter's friend, like he was taking Jack's order for Chinese takeout. "Are you the one to break the news to Clodagh Doyle?"

Jack hesitated for four seconds, thinking of Clodagh recovering from her beating. Some things he would only tell face to face.

"Yes. She is one who would want the truth and soon. But I need to tell the daughter first. Liam's twin. So, unless you need me for anything, I'd like to get on the road to San Francisco."

"Nothing else from our side Jack. You know that none of the tellings will be easy." His face took on a sadness like his flesh held a great weight. "It never is."

CHAPTER THIRTY-EIGHT

Jack double-parked outside Doyle's pub, got out, and Stella slid over into the driver's seat. He watched her drive away. Across the road were Jebb and his crew, who nodded in recognition. Sometimes you unintentionally become part of people's landscape. Jack nodded back, turned, and walked into the pub. It was busy but seemed empty without Jimmy.

Clodagh's office was empty. Jack walked through to the garden where Sinead was looking at her phone, her giant gardening assistant waiting for instruction. She smiled when she saw Jack.

"I spoke to mum. She says she's feeling better. I'm thrilled about that, but she's made me download this gardening app, and I have to check each plant and water it accordingly. I've got a business to run and don't really have time for this. Sorry, Jack, I'm being rude. You came to see me?"

"We need to talk."

Sinead looked at her assistant. "Please go help in the bar. I'll call you when I need you."

Jack waited until he had closed the door. This would be like ripping off a band-aid, better done all at once and quickly. "It's about Liam. He was part of a terrorist organization, and there was a gunfight, and he got killed by one of the group."

Sinead's hands flew to her mouth as if this would keep Jack's news from reaching her, but it was too late. "Where is he now?"

"His body is at a funeral home."

"We have to tell my mother."

"I know. That's why I came here. We should get on a plane now and go to Laguna beach."

Sinead walked past Jack, through her office, and into the bar. Jack followed and watched as she gave orders.

***

Jack and Sinead traveled in silence for the fifteen miles in their rented white Toyota Camry from John Wayne Airport to Laguna Beach. Both lost in their thoughts like two different universes, each with its own reality.

Jack drove the vehicle to the beach house and stopped before turning into the driveway. The curtains covered the windows. The same Porsche as before was there, so he continued for another twenty yards and parked.

"Why didn't you drive in?" said Sinead.

"Last time I was here, the two guys in that Porsche were here hassling the twins, and it took some persuading before they left. One twin told me they'd started to hassle them again, and I said Jimmy would take care of it."

"They must be inside the house. What's happened to Jimmy?"

"No more talking."

Jack and Sinead went to the front door, listened, heard nothing, and tried the door. It opened, and they walked into a scene like a courtroom.

The Comb-overs were seated on chairs with Jimmy standing next to them. Opposite them, Clodagh sat on a couch with a twin on either side of her. On the coffee table in front of Clodagh were two wallets, the contents of which were on display, two pistols, and two mobile phones.

The two comb-overs were the accused, Clodagh, the judge, the twins, the jury, and from Jimmy's face, he was ready to be the executioner.

Except for the Comb-overs, everyone smiled when they saw Sinead and Jack.

"What a wonderful surprise," said Clodagh.

Sinead hugged her mother and cried. Jimmy took four of his steps, and the twins scampered over for a group hug with Jack and Sinead.

Clodagh clapped her hands twice and waved Jimmy and the twins back to their seats.

"Let's finish what we started here."

Clodagh pulled her mobile phone from the pocket of her dressing gown, dialed, put the phone on speaker, and placed it on the table. From where Jack stood, he could read the name on the phone. The name was familiar to Jack. Charles Whitlock. It took twelve rings before being answered. The voice that answered was that of someone accustomed to giving orders, but this time there was an overlay of hesitancy.

"Hello Clodagh. An unusual time for you to phone. What can I do for you? Have you got a new project you want me to invest in? We did jolly well on that last one." There was a laugh like a blustery wind.

"Thanks for taking my call, Charles. We have a situation. Your sons Jordan and Brendon are sitting in front of me."

"They're supposed to be in Laguna Beach."

"That's where I am, staying with some friends. Two young ladies who your sons have been bothering."

"Let me talk to them."

"Say hello to your father, boys."

The 'Hellos' were those of sheepish schoolboys.

"They came here once before, Charles, drunk, and bothered these young ladies." Clodagh looked at Jack. "They were stopped and strongly discouraged from coming here. This time I was here, with Jimmy."

"Jimmy?"

"Yes, Jimmy. He dealt with them."

"Are my sons alright?" The panic was tangible in his voice.

"They're fine, Charles. Relax. Jimmy patted them down and brought me their wallets. I recognized the name, asked them if their father was a venture capitalist in San Francisco, and gave them your name."

"I am very sorry about this, Clodagh."

"There's more, Charles. When Jimmy patted them down, he found they each had a pistol. I am looking at them on the table in front of me. Glock 42s. They have normal gun licenses. They arrived here with them in holsters on their hips, with their shirts covering them. That's concealed carry, which, as you know, depending on the judge, could be a misdemeanor or a felony."

Charles sighed until it seemed there was no more air left. "Clodagh, please don't hurt them." Charles paused. "Or worse."

"Charles, to lose a child must be a terrible thing, so I am not going to do that to you. They'll be on the next flight back to San Francisco. The pistols you can collect from me when I'm back in my office. What about the Porsche? Where do you want it delivered?"

"You keep it as a token of my heartfelt thanks. I will transfer it to you for one dollar. Anything else I can do?"

"Nothing for now, Charles. Let's meet and talk when I'm back."

Clodagh hung up and looked at Sinead. "Take the Bentley. The keys are on the dining table. You drive, Jimmy in the passenger seat. These two," Clodagh waved a dismissive hand at the Comb-overs. "They sit in the back so Jimmy can give any correctional slaps if needed. Make sure they get on the plane."

"But Mom, Jack, and I came to talk to you."

"I'm sure Jack can tell me."

Sinead looked at Jack. "It's fine, Sinead," said Jack. "We'll be here when you get back."

Sinead hugged Clodagh and walked out the door to the balcony, followed by the Comb-overs, with Jimmy bringing up the rear.

Jack looked back at Clodagh. "Where can we talk?"

"The balcony."

Clodagh started walking, and her steps were uncertain. Jack took her left elbow and supported her as they walked.

Clodagh smiled. "Would you like a Porsche Jack? Seems I've got one."

"Thanks, but no thanks. I'm happy with my truck." Jack placed Clodagh on the three-seater lounge, sat beside her, and took her hands in his.

"This is not easy, Clodagh, but here goes. Liam's dead. He was a member of a terrorist cell, the leader of the one in San Francisco. There was a gunfight, and he accidentally got shot by one of the terrorists."

Jack was waiting for the crying and the tears to start. Clodagh looked at Jack, her eyes welling up as her lower lip trembled like someone with palsy.

"Thank you for coming to tell me in person and bringing Sinead." Clodagh swallowed. "I knew he was a member of a group with radical views." Clodagh released a hand from Jack's and wiped tears from her cheeks with a flick of her index finger. "I was always afraid it could come to something like this."

"Did Liam tell you?"

Clodagh looked at Jack. "No. It was Peter Wasserman."

"Peter?" said Jack with immediate displeasure with himself for once again repeating what someone had said.

"He'd phoned the pub and asked to speak with me. I took the call, and he explained who he was and what he did at CE. Which he said was merely background and not relevant to why he wanted to meet with me. When I asked what it was about, he said it was an important family matter. He asked for a neutral location where it would look like two people sharing a park bench reading their newspaper or scrolling through their phone."

"Weren't you wondering what the cloak and dagger business was all about?"

"I was, but he was so gracious and unassuming that I agreed. I've had meetings like this before with people who don't want to be seen talking to me. I suggested lunchtime in the park at the Civic Center as I can walk there, and I've used it before. I sent Jebb and his crew thirty minutes ahead just in case things weren't as they should be."

"Seems Jebb is a man for all occasions," said Jack.

Clodagh looked at Jack like she was considering if this was worthy of a response.

"I arrived five minutes early and sat reading my newspaper, and Peter arrived precisely on time. Our newspapers hid out faces as he told me that Liam had become involved in a group with anti-Israel views and that they had been monitoring him for some time. When I asked who was doing this monitoring, he explained and told me about his friend in the Mossad who had suggested this conversation take place."

"Why would they bother to do that?" said Jack.

"Peter was quite blunt about it and said it was a quid pro quo gesture of goodwill. They knew of my pro-Israel and pro-Ireland views and hoped we could be useful to each other."

"Was that it?"

"Yes. Except Peter gave me a lesson in security as I stood to go. Peter spoke into his newspaper. He told me I had five people stationed as security, which was true. He said that if I looked, I would see that another man reading a newspaper was not far from each one of my people. That was also true. Peter chuckled as he asked me, 'Didn't I think that was a lot of people reading newspapers when in this day and age, people mostly read their phones.' He said they had arrived sixty minutes before the meeting time. He then folded his newspaper, got up, and left."

"What happened then?"

"Well, I confronted Liam, and he denied everything."

Jack looked at Sinead. "Did Liam ever say anything to you about his views?"

"Nothing. His views were always about making money, legally or illegally."

"That's when I bought the tanneries," said Clodagh. "My intention was to put his desire for money to good use. When he came to me and said he wanted to invest in HTT, I thought that even if he had lied to me about having anti-Israel and anti-Ireland business views, he was now re-focused on making money for himself. Remember, no matter what he did, he would always be my son. I thought I'd got him back on track."

"Whereas, in fact," said Jack, "he was a sleeper, making money for the group he'd joined."

"It would seem so."

Clodagh vanished into her thoughts for eight seconds. Possibly a place where Liam was a little boy.

"Jack, there's a good bottle of Irish Whiskey in the kitchen. Can you please bring it and two glasses?"

Jack returned with the bottle, and Clodagh poured three fingers of the golden-brown liquid into each glass. She tried to stand, holding the two drinks, but wobbled, not spilling a drop as Jack supported her with a hand under her right elbow. She handed him a glass and held onto the balcony's railing, looking out at the moon, which threw a silver light from the horizon to the beach.

Clodagh's lips were moving, but her voice was as soft and distant as an angel's, as though her thoughts were finding their way to her mouth like a trickle of water journeying to an unknown destination. Jack only heard the last fragment.

"To trust someone and be sure of what is truly in their heart is rare."

She turned to Jack like she hadn't spoken. "Slainte."

Ingram Content Group UK Ltd.
Milton Keynes UK
UKHW042159080523
421401UK00001B/26